On the Island

———

Books by Josephine Jacobsen

Fiction

A Walk with Raschid and Other Stories
Adios, Mr. Moxley: Thirteen Stories
On the Island: New & Selected Stories

Poetry

Let Each Man Remember
For the Unlost
The Human Climate
The Animal Inside
The Shade-Seller: New and Selected Poems
The Chinese Insomniacs: New Poems
The Sisters: New and Selected Poems

Criticism

Genet and Ionesco: Playwrights of Silence
   (with William R. Mueller)
The Testament of Samuel Beckett
   (with William R. Mueller)

On the
ISLAND

New & Selected Stories

JOSEPHINE JACOBSEN

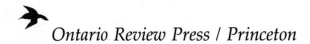 *Ontario Review Press / Princeton*

The following stories—"Nel Bagno," "Late Fall," "Help," "A Walk with Raschid,"
"The Jungle of Lord Lion," "The Glen," "On the Island," and "Jack Frost" were
published in *A Walk with Raschid and Other Stories* by The Jackpine Press, Winston-
Salem, NC, copyright 1978. Reprinted by permission of The Jackpine Press.
"Vocation," "Sound of Shadows," "The Edge of the Sea," "Motion of the Heart,"
"Season's End," and "The Mango Community" were published in *Adios, Mr.
Moxley: Thirteen Stories* by The Jackpine Press/Book Service Associates, Winston-
Salem, NC, copyright 1986. Reprinted by permission of The Jackpine Press/Book
Service Associates. Of the previously uncollected stories, "The Wreath" first
appeared (as "The Christmas Wreath") in *The Commonweal*; "The Night the
Playoffs Were Rained Out," "The Gesture," and "The Friends" in *Prairie Schooner*;
and "The Inner Path" and "The Company" in *Ontario Review*. Reprinted by
permission.

The author wishes to thank The MacDowell Colony and Yaddo, where a number
of these stories were written; and Charlotte Blaylock, whose efficiency went far
beyond secretarial help.

Library of Congress Cataloging-in-Publication Data

Jacobsen, Josephine.
    On the island : new & selected stories / Josephine Jacobsen.
      p.   cm.
    ISBN 0-86538-067-8
    I. Title.
    PS3519.A42405 1989
    813'.52—dc19   88-27128
                                                 CIP

Typesetting by Backes Graphic Productions
Printed by Princeton University Press

ONTARIO REVIEW PRESS
in association with Persea Books

Distributed by George Braziller, Inc.
60 Madison Ave., New York, NY 10010

For Erlend, reader, writer, friend,
with love

CONTENTS

The Mango Community

THE VICE-CONSUL again looked at his shoes. He appeared to be, not critical but, more annoying, embarrassed.

"Mrs. Jane Megan—yes, and Mr. Henry Sewell." He raised very pale blue eyes to Jane's, dropped them to his toecaps. "And Daniel. Daniel Megan. Fifteen? Is that right?"

"That's right," said Jane. She added, "Mr. Adams."

"And your purpose here was a vacation?" This time he got himself together and looked at her quite hard.

"Work," said Jane. "I'm a painter." His eyes flicked to her fingernails. "It's on my passport. Henry is a writer. A novelist."

If she had looked for him to say, "Oh, *that* Henry Sewell," she was wrong.

"Yes, well," said Mr. Adams moodily. "You see my position," he said rapidly but uncertainly. "I can't actually ask you to leave. I mean, there would have to be actual and manifest danger."

She hoped ardently that Harry would not appear, lugging fish and *cristofine*. He and Mr. Adams were temperamentally unsuited to a dialogue. Soothingly she said, "I think you've been very kind to come all the way out here. And I quite see your point. We'll think about it, really we will. But this business has been going on for weeks and weeks, and we leave, anyway, in a few months."

At last Mr. Adams looked cross. "Mrs. Megan, I've tried to explain that if you do insist on staying on under present circumstances," he stopped and repeated more loudly, "present circumstances, the U.S. government simply cannot be responsible for your safety."

"I know that," she said hastily. "That's perfectly reasonable." (All the same, she thought, your problem is that I know, and I know you know, you'd try.) They had reached an impasse. Would it be like suborning a policeman to offer him a drink? "Could I offer you a cup of tea, or a drink, before you leave?" Perhaps the tea decontaminated the invitation.

"You're very kind," he said primly. "I'm going to miss my plane if I'm not careful. Well, the other families, in town, to whom I've spoken have all agreed on the advisability of leaving." He looked at her, and his general disapproval was just diluted by a flash of friendliness. "I do wish you well, Mrs. Megan. You're really very isolated here."

"Oh, there're people next door..." she protested.

He ignored this. "Perhaps you'll pass on to Mr. Sewell what I've said. And there's your son to consider."

The implied reproof made her say jauntily, "I'll keep that in mind." She put out her hand, and the Vice-Consul, unable to do less, shook it and restored it to her. "Good-bye, then," he said, and a minute later the jeep started too fast, kicking up sand.

In an attempt to sort out her mind, she sat down on the eroded planks of the porch steps and stared out over the beach to the mad palette of the Caribbean.

She felt she was muttering, When did it all *begin*? Not irrelevantly she thought that while it had been by laughter that she had first known Michael, it was by a hot and huffy argument, improbably conducted on the fringes of a cocktail party, that the threshold of intimacy had been crossed with Harry. Of *all* things, the Sermon on the Mount. And hadn't that argument, across a sea and in another world, landed her right here between Harry and the Vice-Consul? (Later she had discovered that Harry had much respect for the Bible—its drama, language, characterizations ravished him. Otherwise he found it as terrifying as a juju, drawing from it only one valid instruction.)

Isolated by Harry's intensity, they had found themselves on ancient ground: Overnight, the world could be changed by passive resistance—unflagging, indomitable. To violence, the universal cheek turned, once and for all. In a flash of conviction that evening, Jane had come to believe what she still did, that Harry would let himself, in the proper cause, be martyred without so much as making a fist. After Michael's hair-trigger emotions, which she now saw repeating in Dan, Harry's steady fanaticism of discipline fascinated and baffled her.

"All *right*," she had said, draining the last drops of her martini, "say you're going to be murdered. You're going to be raped . . ." ("Less likely than you, there," he murmured.) "You turn the other cheek; and you *are*. But what do you do when someone else doesn't *want* to be murdered? Turn their cheeks for them? It never tells you about *that*," she said bitterly.

Not then or later had he answered the question to her satisfaction. Was it unanswerable? He never lost that inner assurance that she could see captivating Dan. Undeviating programs are so dear to the young, she thought meanly. But she knew it was more than that.

Quarrel, quarrel, quarrel; in the last months of her marriage with Michael, Dan had been drenched in their bitterness. When the marriage split like an old rowboat—no wonder people said that a marriage was on the rocks—after the divorce Dan seemed scarcely to miss his father, until death closed the case, and Michael, unable to argue or defend, became in Dan's mind somehow a victim, unfinished, unrepresented. It was not in Dan to be chronically hostile, but he closed something; he withdrew; he waited.

It was as though Dan had been waiting for Harry. Disconcertingly, the classic case of preparing an adolescent for a resented stepfather reversed itself. Even early on, Jane became aware of a united front, a sort of silent compact, in which Harry's need to proselytize, and Dan's to be stable, were locked into a kind of dogged intimacy. Why this should frighten her, she had no idea, but it was that image which had set up this tentative ménage.

As she stared morosely ahead, here, loping jerk jerk along the beach, came the three-legged dog. That dog. The most enchanting of the children who burst onto the sand even in this remote section when school was out—a liquid-eyed, gentle-faced charmer with the suavest voice—flung stones at the lame dog. "She ogly! See how she go—so!" and he hobbled, jerking. Entranced, doubled with laughter, the children reached for sand, stones.

Between Jane and the languid sea there was a wink of motion; another tiny beach-colored crab stilting across the heaves of sand into its invisible hole. A faint breeze swung the polished points of the palm fronds. A little way out, a jagged white line marked and remarked the coral reef. In its shallow water flickered a rainbow of fish, a community as discrete and mysterious as the invisible monkeys retreated into the highest hills. Had all the iguanas retreated, too, or like the straggler monkeys, been eaten?

Through the sprays of magenta bougainvillea, the sky of Ste. Cecile appeared as a mosaic—blue, green, lilac—of great depth and serenity.

"Did he come?"

It was Harry who had come, noiseless on the sand.

"What kind of fish is *that*?"

"That is a turbot. Did he come?"

"Yes. He came. And went."

"And said?"

"And said we should leave."

"Had to leave?"

"No. He stopped short of that. If we're stuck and a coup breaks out, he can't promise us help. You know, I think we *should* go," she added, surprising herself. Did she think so? Politically, or personally?

Harry disappeared into the shadowy interior; a moment later he was back. He sat down beside her, plucked off a sneaker, knocking out sand.

"What did you tell him?"

"That we'd think about it. That we really would."

"Very diplomatic. His own game."

He looked perfectly beautiful, sitting there pulling off his other sneaker. The idealized beachcomber, the tropical poster.

"Look, Harry," she said, "I think we're getting in awfully deep."

She could feel the tightening.

"How so?"

"Well, something *is* going to happen. We both know it; its just *when*. We're isolated here. We're strangers—*really* strangers, I mean. It wouldn't be malice, but we'd just be in between."

"*You* look, my dear," he said in his inspirational, persuasive teacher's voice, his hand on her bare shoulder. "We came here for a year. The place is beautiful. The people are marvelous. I'm working, you're painting. Dan's happier than I've ever seen him. This guy is going to be thrown out eventually. In the most civilized way we'll ever encounter. That isn't something to make us run away. That's good."

"He's not going to be thrown out without a lot of people getting hurt."

"Jane, do you know, in a way it's the most impressive thing I've ever seen. They've lost their jobs, shut their shops, been spied on, pushed around, jailed, worse, much worse. Thugs in police uniforms have been sent after them, looting and smashing. The Barracudas are holding a cocked gun to their heads—and they *march*! That's what they do! No guns, no machetes—they just march and chant and pull in their belts."

"Harry, I live here too."

"Well, sure. You know too. But you don't seem to realize how amazing it is. They're forcing the Man out without a shot."

Here came the black-coral boy; heavily lame, he threw out his left leg in an immense arc, lurching. He had fallen from the top of a coconut palm. Jane had a wild vision of the three-legged dog at his heels. The boy had a small waist, broad gleaming shoulders, and an immense smile and lifted hand for them. Now he angled across toward the Montroses' fence, lurching more heavily in the dry sand. Mrs. Montrose appeared at her gate, and they fell quietly into one of those dialogues of which Jane could not understand a word. This, although the Montroses, in their sparse conversations with their American neighbors, spoke an English perfectly intelligible, though more musical and differently emphasized.

The only time Jane had ever seen Mrs. Montrose laugh was when Jane had asked about "mongeese." But when Mrs. Montrose said "four sheeps" and "three mices," it seemed not so much funny as expressive—more mouselike, more sheeplike.

Far out, in the daze of sun, she could see a red object, the Sunfish; and two dots, Alexis and Dan.

Harry got up, sneakers in his hand. "We're not going to settle it this afternoon," he said. She saw that he had already settled it. Well. She could leave and take Dan, but there were too many reasons she would not.

Alone on the porch, she felt a tiny deflection in the heat. The sun had lowered by a fraction; the Sunfish, nearer, was defining itself.

Guns cocked at their heads, said Harry. Barracudas, recruited by the Man from the dregs of this and other island jails. How men loved the sound of a cocked rifle: *Ton-ton Macoute*. Ku Klux Klan. Yet when she and Harry argued, in his domain of words she seemed evasive and cynical. I can't bear the writer in him. In his beginning was the word. Music, even painting, was so much better. Painters, composers constructed a nonverbal problem and resolved it in unobstructed sound and color, while the writer floundered among the shards of the ages' arguments, assembling another articulated fallacy. *For God's sake hold your tongue and let me love . . .*

She found Harry's work disconcertingly superior to her own, but never, never his medium. On this tiny island she remained amazed at the progressive detail of her own sight: new shades of purple and rose appeared in the noon sea. She was stunned by the varieties of green: the serious glossy green of the breadfruit, the translucent green of the fringed plantain blades, the trembling play of the flame trees, the palms' hard glitter. Green, what on earth was it! Behind their stilt-house and its path, behind the road, the hill rose in a Rousseau jungle. On its steep garden patches, in violent blues and reds and yellows, the dark distant figures moved in the dawn light when disoriented roosters and insomniac dogs at last fell silent.

Now here came Mr. Montrose out of the house, a hoe in one hand, machete in the other. In the mornings, astride the burro, his buttocks resting just before its tail, the huge balanced milk cans at his knees, he wore one day a yellow shirt, the next a violet, and a ravelling straw hat. Now he wore only faded khaki shorts that blended with his identically colored skin.

Seeing her head turned toward him, he raised his machete slightly in a courteous but formal gesture. In six months, they had not gotten much further than that. At first the Montroses had seemed friendly, though baffled and a bit nervous. But in exact proportion as Dan and Alexis had plunged into their intimacy, the Montroses had retreated into a pattern formal as armor. Always greetings; now and then a soursop or a sapadillo from their tree, sent via Alexis; once, some cassava cakes made by Mrs. Montrose. Never an acceptance or an invitation.

Twice Jane, meeting Mrs. Montrose coming home from market, or carrying on her head the big wicker basket of clothes to the line stretched across the dusty yard, had rather timidly suggested a cup of tea. Mrs. Montrose had smiled, her teeth strong and white, while she dropped her eyes, saying nothing whatever. Jane instinctively knew this was not rudeness; it was the dilemma of someone unable to accept and not possessing the formulas of refusal. Jane had thorough sympathy for this. Was Mrs. Montrose to say that she had an engagement for tea every day for six months?

Jane did not waste much time speculating as to whether all this was Mr. Montrose. But she knew, infallibly, that it had to do with Dan. She could see that Mr. Montrose, no fanatic, could not well forbid his son to associate with a next-door neighbor of almost the same age; but though he treated Dan with the same grave courtesy, Jane knew that he found Dan an extraordinary phenomenon and feared and disliked the friendship. What was Dan doing here in the first place? Why was he not at school or at work? Why did he call his father Harry? How could his father (did Mr. Montrose think Harry *was* his father?) permit his tone in talking to him? When the Montrose family went to Mass on Sunday—Christabel and Eugenie-Marie in starched dresses and long white socks, Alexis in a crisp short-sleeved shirt, Mrs. Montrose in pond-lilies on red, and Mr. Montrose in dark trousers and a shirt of palmetto palms—their three neighbors could be prone on the beach, practically naked, Dan sulking at Alexis's departure (no cricket); or on the Sunfish; or Jane could have set off with her gear and Harry be rattling on his portable, stopping constantly to curse and bemoan his electric typewriter, useless in its corner.

Jane had had a solitary conversation with Mrs. Montrose. It had left her with a curious sense of warmth and communication, though it had led to nothing whatsoever.

Five or six weeks after the ménage's installation, Jane—possibly propelled by an inability to deal with the evasions of tropic green—had been driven in nostalgic defiance to a canvas of snow crystals. Three lit within the limits of the canvas, one disappeared in midpattern over the edge. On the black background, they looked like stellar intentions.

Coming past in her royal walk, three coconuts in a small basket on her erect head, Mrs. Montrose had unwillingly but helplessly paused.

"What it is?" she said.

"They're snow crystals," said Jane shyly. "Flakes of snow," she added in response to the glance Mrs. Montrose had transferred to her face and back to the canvas.

To this Mrs. Montrose said nothing, and together they stared at the flakes, unmelting in the brutal sun. When Jane thought, we will drown in silence, Mrs. Montrose said, her eyes still on the canvas, "You did see snow?"

"Oh yes. We have it often."

"Is it whiter than sand?"

"Oh, much. When it first falls."

"It does lay on the ground? Right on the ground? You have walked on it? Right on over it?"

"Yes," said Jane. Suddenly envious, she thought, I've never seen snow!

They stood there for a minute, isolated and intimate. Then Mrs. Montrose gave her a small adventurous smile, bent, and cradled the basket in her arms. She raised one hand in the familiar sidelong gesture, and without looking back, went through her wooden gate, across the bare yard, and up the steps into the house.

Jane repeated to herself, I don't think I've ever seen snow, but she felt an exhilaration swell up inside her. She began cleaning her brushes, hissing a little song. Something wonderful had happened. What? Now we can't ever be strangers. She couldn't wait to tell Harry; but she never did. Because peace was his specialty, and she was not sure what kind of peace she had to talk about. Always Harry thought community, but she knew sadly that he hadn't gained an inch on this sandy strip. "The mango community?" she had jeered once.

The Sunfish was right off the beach. It turned over, as usual, and Alexis and Dan, floundering in the water, pushed it in and dragged it up the sand. By now Dan was the same shade as Alexis. Christabel and Eugenie-Marie, like Mrs. Montrose, were mahogany dark.

Jane waved to the boys; they waved hastily back. Already they had the bats and the tennis ball out of the old beached and dissolving rowboat in which they were deposited each morning, shoved down from dogs and other marauders. There had been difficulties over those bats. The boys at first had played, like other children up the beach, with flat pieces of found wood; then one day Harry came back in the minimoke with two cheap cricket bats. At once, Mr. Montrose had jibbed. Finally, it had been diplomatically settled that while both bats were Dan's, Alexis had possession of one.

Now down the hard sand Alexis was running, releasing the straight-arm pitch. At first Jane had imagined that it was because Dan thought baseball as Alexis thought cricket, that Dan could never compare. Then, her trained eye taking in the motions, she saw that it would never change. Alexis ran, and pitched, and batted, as he swam, as he climbed a bare bole, as he dove—with a fluid power. Dan said proudly that Alexis was the best cricketer in his school. "He's going to get a scholarship somewhere— maybe Jamaica, or Trinidad. He's going to be like V. Richards. He's going to be better," said Dan.

Oddly, it was Alexis, daily embroiled in their lives, who stopped Jane. She did, and she did not, know him. Instantly, she had a sense of almost intimacy—a drawing toward. Was it that of a painter? The marvelous texture of the skin, the head's perfection, the movement as worth watching as a secret dance, the quick, deep luminous look? Though he smiled, he never laughed with her, but she could hear him: soft, irresistible convulsions, broken up, falling against the rowboat skeleton, with Dan's staccato yelps.

After a while she began to understand that, the end of a long

year come, she would never know Alexis. Separated, he and
Dan would remember each other as part of the sun and sand
and salt wind, as in patches of light and happiness. She—and
she thought, Harry—would be to Alexis figures come and gone,
strange and not very interesting. She thought of the boys as a
frieze against the sea.

As she went into the house Jane could see through the window
the peaceable kingdom: the water picking up red from the sun's
angle, the red Sunfish on the humped sand; on the gleaming
edge, the boys against the sea.

There was a light steady rattle from behind the door of the
extra bedroom. I couldn't *paint* after that conversation, Jane
thought gloomily. But Harry was so secure; things just reinforced
him. As she stood hesitating, Mr. Montrose called to Alexis to
come now, come; and crossing to the back window she watched
while Alexis rounded the house, crossed the lane and shot up
the hill. She followed his blue trunks through layers of green;
then here he came, the white goat trailing behind on its rope,
stopping to snatch at a frond, and jerked ahead. The green
growth hid, revealed, hid, revealed them. The goat, shoved into
its shed, let out its stammering vibration.

"What did you say to that guy?" Dan had come up behind
her. He was still damp from sweat or seawater, the cricket bat
was over his shoulder. "We saw his jeep when he left. What
did you say to him?"

Conscious of a male alliance, she had begun to feel like a
witness under interrogation. "I told him we'd think about what
he said."

"Which was?" He had picked up Harry's mannerisms, his
inflections.

"Which was that we should get out. Now."

Dan's face darkened, he leaned against the house wall. "Silly
wimp," he said. "Petty official."

Amazed, Jane heard herself shouting on behalf of Mr. Adams.

"Dan! Don't be such an idiot! You know absolutely nothing
about what's going to happen."

"Neither does he."

"Look, there's no use yelling at each other."

"*I* wasn't yelling," said Dan.

"We'll just have to reach some sort of sensible decision. As a family," she piously added.

"Harry says the Man can't take the pressure much longer. He'll have to have elections like he promised. Now the teachers are out, they're going to have the kids march, too."

She looked at him. "Not unless their parents are crazy. People disappear here, Dan. They just *disappear*."

"No kid is going to disappear; he's got to pretend."

"All right, no child is going to disappear. But someone is going to get shot in public, not just in private. And when that starts . . ."

"Suppose Gandhi had said that? Suppose the people who lay down on the tracks . . ."

"Oh go and wash *up!*" she said rudely. "I'm tired of being preached at."

A great beginning, she thought, for the family decision-making process. Why did discussions of peace inevitably produce fury? She put her hand on her fist and stared at the low sun; it was the top half of a blood orange, exactly touching sea level.

The first time she had seen the Man was at close hand. She was walking down the real road, cautiously on the edge of the jagged cavity of its deep stone gutter, when the black big car, flying its small intense flag, had slid past her. Flanked by two burly figures, the face familiar from posters, under the military cap, the eyes invisible behind the ritual dark glasses, had stared straight ahead. A second car followed closely. That was when he was still playing for respectability, still the emerging statesman, the strong but just father of his island, paternal rather than fascist. There was, in the stance of the rigid chauffeur, in the three faces expressionless behind their formality—the middle man's head advanced a little, like a dominant vulture—something that made everything suddenly real. That's what they've all looked like, she thought, chilled.

She went in to the icebox. It was almost empty. Tomorrow, Saturday, was market day. By thinking of how much chance she would have to be alone tomorrow, she discovered the depth of her uncertainty. Was *she* the wimp? When she had arrived in Ste. Cecile, one question had loomed: marriage. It drew and repelled her.

She desired, admired, probably loved Harry; she believed in

his toughness, his kindness, the absolute quality of his integrity. Did it really matter that the expression of his integrity sometimes frightened and infuriated her? He and Dan. She thought meanly, lucky devils! What bliss total commitment must be. How long was she going on this way, perhaps yes, perhaps no, perhaps leaving, perhaps staying? Alone with Harry the choice would be easy. The problem was Dan. But how on earth was Dan going to get hurt? Yet at moments she knew he would. He would throw a stone, he would yell at the Man.

Then all at once, the thread of patience snapped. Tomorrow, away for hours and hours from the pressure of voices, of presences, for worse or better, she would harden her mushy mind. She felt like the heroine of an opera: she even said aloud, "I *am* Dan's mother . . ."

That evening they played Scrabble.

The light from the kerosene lamp enveloped them with mollesse, she thought, a light unknown to the glare of a bulb: cheekbones, eyes, the faded rather dirty shirts took on a luminous look, so that the three sat—man, woman, and boy—untroubled, archetypal, in the light's soft pulse. Outside the sea hissed and hushed, hissed and hushed. A faint indeterminate calypso just touched their ears. The dogs answered each other, near, far up in the hills, bark bark bark. Bark. Bark bark. Already, a manic rooster crowed. This is peace. But she knew it to be armistice.

She was taking the minimoke all the way to Bellemore tomorrow, to paint the new boat; they were building it there. Elevated, the spare ribs were still fresh-cut wood; the shape, bow, prow, already there. It went very slowly. Somehow it was wonderful to see tree turn to skeleton, earth-growth to marine intention; the ancient shape, near any sea, always. She must market first; when she came back, all the best fruit and vegetables would be gone. She was alarmed at how delight rose in her at the thought of being alone.

"Q on a triple," said Dan, and his face lit with just his father's look.

The rough sketch was all right, but the rudimentary painting was a disaster. She stopped, wiping her brushes, going into the bush to pee, sitting on the frame of the inevitable wrecked row-boat, opening her thermos. But even after she decided just what was wrong, the painting balked. The magic of promise in the bare ribs, strong, complex, but still only a shape, was broken. All she had was a mathematical structure. Ah, but she had another structure, complete, in her mind; she knew she could hold to something, once given. She was going to stay.

Everything had been a risk: mixing her life so deeply with Harry's resolute and single mind; pulling up stakes from friends and the full, competitive world of her work; being remote among people of a different race plunged in their own rough struggle. Either it was worth it, or not. The mania that Dan would be shot, would be arrested, would be hurt in some preventable way, left her. Was hero worship so dangerous? In a world of vicious enmities, was it so perilous if Dan saw Harry as pointing the path to light, to which there was one way only?

Her grandmother had used a palm-leaf fan; she hadn't seen one in years, Jane realized. Why had she thought of that pale yellow shine, so remote from its gusty green? Then her grandmother's dictum came, as though the lacquered fan had wafted it: In the inn of decision, the mind sleeps well. Now she entered, tired, rejoicing.

The nets, fishy-smelling, lay on the sand. The haul over, the racks of tiny fish dried in the sun. There was only an old man, grizzled and small, sitting on a log, his pipe out but clenched, his rheumy eyes meeting hers as she gathered up her load. He smiled. His teeth were intermittent, but from leathery lips he said, with the air of a host, "How are you, Mistress?"

At first she had naively winced at the address, then felt a fool for her assumption when she discovered it to be pure Elizabethan courtesy, extended to the washerwoman, the goat tender.

"Well," she said, meaning it. "Thank you, well." She dumped her gear in the minimoke; there was the pile of fruit and vege-tables. Uncertain, embarrassed, she lifted a mango.

"May I offer you this?" she formally asked.

The old man removed his pipe. Screwing up his eyes, he considered. "What it is?" he asked; then, seeing, "Is it ripe?" he asked with interest.

She stepped forward and handed it to him.

He took it in his used-up hands, turning it. "It is ripe," he said. "My wife and I will eat it tonight. I will give it to she." He had not thanked her. It was as though they had collaborated on a logical action.

She climbed into the minimoke and turned the key.

"You are from Cal-i-for-nia?" he called, his pipe in the air. They all asked her that. The movie nearest to him was a tin building at the other end of the island. But he asked the same question.

Cutting the wheel, she called back, "No. I come from Baltimore."

Disappointed by the useless name, he put his pipe back in his mouth and juggled the mango a little in his hands. He had lost interest.

The marketplace, when she turned into it, was empty. Boxes, stands deserted; shards of vegetables, a broken crate. Two Barracudas, lounging over rifles. A hot, sick pang went through her. She tramped on the brakes and leaned out.

"What's happened to the market?" she called to the nearer policeman. He stared at her, less with hostility than contempt. He hefted his rifle. "That does be closed," he called back.

"What's happened? Has something happened?" she shouted at him, but he only gave her a wide cold smile.

She saw now that in all directions the streets were empty. Along the sea wall, two more Barracudas strolled. A very old woman, bent, in bright blue, came out of the Catholic church a steep block uphill.

I mustn't drive too fast, she thought. Small pastel houses, wooden shacks shot by. Here came a whole lorry of Barracudas; forced to the edge of the steep stone gutter, she nearly lost control. Now she began to see a few people, in small groups, on the steps of houses, under the high porches.

They'd never do anything to Dan or Harry. Americans. Not unless there was fighting. And there isn't—look, there's a girl driving a goat home. But all the tension of weeks sang in her nerves. On her right she could see the beach flying past her. At the final turn the minimoke rocked precariously, shot down the lane and fetched up in a shower of sand.

There was Harry, on the porch. He had his arms crossed and he stared at her. She could feel her blood drain.

"Where's Dan?"

"He's in his room."

"Is he all right? What's happened?"

"Of course he's all right," said Harry irascibly.

She had been gripping the wheel so hard she could scarcely straighten her fingers. "What's happened?" she said again. She couldn't decide whether Harry looked angry or exalted; at any rate, strange. At the steps, she cried again, "What's happened?"

"All hell," he said. "His goons broke up a march. A man got shot. Where are you going? Dan's door is locked." He grabbed her wrist. "Jane! Just sit down a minute, will you? Just ease off a little. I'll tell you all about everything. Sit *down* a minute."

But she was already knocking lightly at the door.

At once Dan's voice, keyed high, said, "Not now. Go away. Please, go away."

Harry had followed her. He passed her; at the cupboard he pulled out a bottle of Mount Gay, gathered two glasses.

"Dan's perfectly all right," he said. "Give him a little time. Come on out on the porch."

Like a knot in her gut, Jane could feel the anger swelling. "I take it there was a march." She followed Harry outside.

He poured rum in each glass. "Yes, there was a march," he said.

"You knew about it ahead of time?"

"Not really. Word gets around fast, you know."

"And I take it you marched?"

He held out the glass to her with a small friendly gesture, and she shook her head. "That's right."

"You took Dan?"

"I didn't 'take' Dan. He'd been planning to go."

"I told him he couldn't."

"Jane, a time comes when you can't make that stick."

Angrily she met his eyes; she saw then how badly he was shaken. Suddenly she felt exhausted. Nothing irrevocable had happened. She was undermined by Harry's face.

She took up the rejected glass and leaned against the unsure railing, staring unseeingly at the Montroses' empty yard of dust.

"I can't fight about it now, Harry. But how could you, behind my back? Who was the man? Was he killed?"

"I don't know. Yes. The Barracudas were cracking heads, and he yanked away a police club. It wasn't behind your back. You just weren't here. You couldn't have stopped Dan. He's almost fifteen."

"*You* could!" she said in a flare of bitterness. She saw in Harry's face an odd mingling of the old stubborn glory and a curious timidity.

But he said doggedly, "I wouldn't if I could have. He's old enough to have a conscience and a will, Jane. In three years he could be drafted. He's old enough to know what he believes."

"Was it the shooting?" Jane said uncertainly. "Did he see it?"

Something was unspoken. Harry turned the glass around and around.

"No, actually he didn't."

"Then why . . . ?"

To her amazement she saw Harry's eyes blur with pain.

"It's Alexis."

"*Alexis!*"

He looked at her miserably.

"Alexis got hurt."

"Alexis was marching?"

"He came with Dan."

"They let him?"

"Mr. Montrose was on his route. I think his mother had walked into town. To the market."

"*You* let him?"

"For God's sake, Jane. I've no earthly power over Alexis. He scarcely believes I exist. I didn't want him to come."

"Wasn't he worth proselytizing?"

Harry did not answer.

"What happened to him?"

"A policeman hit him in the head—but it wasn't that. He was knocked flying down into the gutter. You know what those are. He broke something in his back. We didn't even know. It was a madhouse and we were separated."

"How do you know now?"

"Dan and I went to look for him, and we couldn't find him. After we got back, the police came."

"Here?"

"To tell his parents. Montrose had just got back. He went off with the policeman, to the hospital. Dan tried to go, but Mr. Montrose . . . He was so upset he didn't know what he was saying," said Harry bleakly. "When Mrs. Montrose got back, I tried to drive her to the hospital, but—for Christ's sake, Jane, how do you think *I* feel?"

"Well, how *do* you feel?" she said; and then the community of their misery stopped her. "How bad is it?"

"Dan and I went to the hospital. They'd left word we weren't to be allowed to see Alexis. It's pretty bad, I think. Of course, these doctors . . . The back is broken and there are some internal injuries . . . I don't think they're very positive about anything yet. At least, I don't see how they can be." His face looked pared, polished. Round and round he turned his emptied glass. She reached over and touched his shoulder, and in his eyes tears appeared, for whom she was not sure.

They stayed there, silent. The tide was coming in, pushing the curved bubbling fringe up over the high sand. A way down the beach they could just hear faint thin shouts; tiny shapes ran and pitched. Games had resumed.

At that moment, two figures appeared, coming slowly down the path from the road: the Montroses. Ahead walked Mr. Montrose; a few paces behind came his wife. Without hesitation, without a glance, they passed through their gate, across the yard, up the steps to the house.

"I'm going over," said Jane.

"Wait till tomorrow," said Harry quickly. "Don't go right now."

"I *can't* wait," said Jane. "Don't you see? We can't just sit here —us here, them over there. We can't."

"Dan tried to say something to Mr. Montrose. I wish you'd wait."

"I can't." She stood up.

"Look," Harry said in a desperate whisper, "they can't tell

really how bad it is yet. I can't believe it's that bad. But it is bad. Leave them alone."

Jane went down the steps. She thought she had never walked so far as to the Montroses' gate. I won't just keep saying, I'm sorry, I'm sorry. The house was silent. A small lizard darted by her toe. The cricket shouts just reached her ears. She knocked at the door.

As if he had been waiting behind it, Mr. Montrose stood before her. Her instant impression was of distance—the fierce remoteness in his gaze paralyzed her.

She said, "Mr. Montrose, I've just heard about Alexis. How bad is it?" From a million miles, from a million years, the eyes watched her. At last he said, "The back is broke up. The hip, too." Slowly, impersonally he added, "No way they can fix it right."

"They can't say that!" she cried, terrified. "This is just a tiny hospital. In Trinidad—please, *please* let us send him to Trinidad!"

The face changed so that Jane recoiled.

"You go to hell," said Mr. Montrose very slowly. "Where you is come from. Evil, evil, evil. All of you. Go home—if you do have one."

Behind his shoulder appeared Mrs. Montrose's head; her hand covered her mouth.

I can't move, thought Jane. I am here forever.

"You come here," said Mr. Montrose. "Why? Why you come? You are devils. Go where you come from. You are evil." Then he added with formality, "If you do stay here, you will die."

She couldn't tell if it were a threat or a statement. She looked behind him at Mrs. Montrose's face. It had a strange expression as though it were being pulled apart.

"I'm going," she said to the still figure towering over her. "We're going." With a huge effort she moved, turning. Then she stopped.

"Dan and Alexis are friends," she said.

At that suddenly Mr. Montrose let out a kind of howl. "*He* should be there, in that place!" he shouted. "Never he should run again! Bad things will come to him, you have done it. You will see. Bad things."

Mrs. Montrose moved suddenly forward, but his right arm shot out pushing her back.

Halfway across to her steps, Jane heard the door close.

The next morning while there was still dew everywhere and the air was still fresh, Harry drove them to the airport. Dan sat in the back.

He had not spoken since late last night when he had found no shelter.

"I won't go," he had said then.

Jane, beyond tact, beyond persuasion, said, "You have to. I'm taking you home."

"I'm staying here," he said. "I'm staying with Harry."

"No, you're not, Dan," said Harry. They were down to raw statement. "I won't have you. You've got to go with your mother now."

"I won't go. How can you make me? Carry me? Call the Barracudas?"

"You can't stay right now, Dan," said Harry more gently. "How could you? Not here, not next door. Where?"

"I'll stay with the Montroses!" he cried. There was a small silence. Dan began to weep. Jane touched his hand, but as though she had burned it, he flinched. He gazed furiously at Harry. "You quit!" he said thickly. "The very first thing, you quit! You give up! You tell me something, you make a big deal, and then you quit!"

"What's that?" said Jane quickly. "That was a knock."

"It wasn't a knock," said Harry. "It was someone on the porch."

They listened: dogs, dogs; and the sea. Harry got up and walked over to the door. He said over his shoulder, "If someone's here, just give me a chance to talk to them. Right?" At the door he raised his voice: "Yes?"

No voice answered. Harry turned the brown glazed handle and the door opened on the scented night. As it did so, something fell forward onto the floor and lay there shining a little: a cricket bat. They stared at it, its handle oiled with sweat, soaked in sun and salt. Then Dan darted over and snatched it up. He took it and went into his room. The bolt shot in its slot.

A few miles from the airport, dawn arrived. First the outline of tinged clouds, separate in their drift. Then a sort of enormous renovation of the sky—it cleared, produced a faint pure blue, gradually lit all the greens. On the edges of the road children appeared, with cans or bundles. A man overtaken in his loose barefoot stride raised a machete in greeting.

Jane was transfixed by the dailyness to come. Light would come just like this through the Montroses' red curtains; over Alexis, asleep or awake, announcing the day of hours, minutes, seconds. Of the first boats, and the sea's colors, and the sand. And in the afternoons, the rich fall of that blood orange, the yells and shouts and flat hard sound of the plank bats. Alexis would indeed remember his neighbors.

At the airport, the waves ran up almost to the runway. The tiny plane already sat there.

At the head of the narrow steps, the tall brown stewardess obstructed them, her voice bored and musical. Of course the cricket bat would not fit under any seat. Forbidden to frown, the stewardess smiled in annoyance. She took the bat gingerly and, carrying it before her, wedged it upright in the coat section.

Dan would not sit with Jane. But, like a damaging consolation, she knew that already, willing the opposite, he was fleeing—mutinous, looking back—but fleeing something he couldn't bear now or change, ever.

Harry would be confirmed. Or not. How far he went, to them or from them, what happened, what became of everything, was part of the unfinished. Now he still hoped all things, money, doctors, something. The principle was sacrifice; but what of Harry now that Alexis had stolen it, to carry?

They vibrated violently. The tarmac slid toward them. There was the wheels' chock, a wing tilted, and the few dark figures fell away.

They were over the sea, and through the thick glass she saw the green bright land—valleys, dense hills—falling, falling, bright and small and smaller in its particular shape, releasing them to the universal sky.

Sound of Shadows

———

T HE HOUSE IS a little pit, a little valley, between two small but bigger houses. How can that be so, of a row house? But it is. Perhaps, at first, it was a shed? Or a garage?

It is one room wide—a long dark living room, a narrow dark bedroom, a dark narrow kitchen; a long narrow back yard between high, board fences, and on the alley end, a wire fence with a toothed gate.

The front door, that of the living room, is double-bolted; it has not been opened in over a year. Through the wire gate, up the narrow cement across the dusty grass, Mrs. Bart carries the groceries. Now and then bringing circulars or envelopes addressed to *Tenant*, the mailman leaves them at the back door.

There were two friends with whom Mrs. Bart has not feuded: Daisy Bates died thirteen and a half months ago, and The Artheritis nailed Mary Stevens to the phone. She phoned nearly every day, but always inconveniently and always interrupting the enormous activity in the living room; there was less and less chance to talk to her, and finally Mrs. Bart decided the phone was an expensive bother and had it taken out. Since then there have been two visitors. The phone man came from the Chesapeake and Potomac. He was one of the visitors.

From just after dawn (now that it is April) until well after midnight, the living room is crowded. Men and women, children, even animals, come and go. There have, actually, been hippopotami, and sharks; at least twice, gorillas. But it is mostly men and women who go and come, make love, quarrel, eat, even bathe there.

The electricity bill keeps going up and up. Well, Mrs. Bart thinks, if it comes to that, she can always eat rice. She knows the Chinese Communists fought solely on rice. But it has not come to that.

The men and women in the room are, in general, handsome, though there is a tinge of green in their hair or of magenta in their cheeks. Here come crisp afficionados of world events; crippled but courageous children; eminent surgeons, their masks tiredly torn off; women so frightened, their mouths and eyes are perfect O's.

Just after dawn, with the final flutter of the flag, they come flickering, and the living room is alive with their voices: exclamations; comments level, courteous; the squeals of greed satisfied; the haunted query that must wait for tomorrow's answer. There is absolutely no question of desertion—a triumphant table owner (polish held high) may fade, proudly laughing, but a girl and a boy are running through a meadow, hand in hand; even the dog cannot keep up with their slowly flying feet, for all his languorous bounds.

They leave the bedroom alone. No one sleeps there. A year ago, Mrs. Bart moved out. Black and still—after the living room, the shots, the shriek of tires, the final disappearance into a circular hole, a speck of light, a dark—it waited like a cell. She has moved to the daybed in the living room, among her companions. Long, long after midnight, when the knob turns on *the home of the brave* she is half asleep, already en route to well-inhabited dreams. She wakes with a scientist to share her coffee. He is open-minded; UFOs are not necessarily ridiculous.

For several years, Mrs. Bart visited the supermarket almost daily, for the exercise, bringing home four items, sometimes five. Then she found she could go twice a week. Once would be far better, but it is difficult to carry that much. So, twice a week she goes, as she has gone today, in the moist April afternoon. She forgot, in the presence of a home splitting like a vessel at sea, the hour, and she arrived at the worst possible time: five o'clock, with hordes of dreary, cross workers—she assumes they are workers, rushing there at this hour—and they look, if not cross, certainly dreary. It has been a bad experience—in the express-line checkout, the woman two-in-front has forgotten to have her bananas weighed; the line stalls, while the checker runs her pencil butt through her hair and the ten-items-or-less wire baskets gleam in place. To her right, in racks at eye level, a new cancer cure comes in huge letters; also aid for the disliked, the sexually inadequate, the doltish homemaker. Back comes the girl, with the bananas weighed and marked. Now Mrs. Bart sees that the man directly in front has exactly thirteen specific and individual items in his basket. Not even concealed, some below the others. In the Express Lane! She looks behind her; yes, there is appreciation and anger in the faces directly to her rear. Perhaps the girl will eject him—he will have to go to the extreme rear of one of the regular lanes. But no, the sacredness of the queue, fair play mean nothing. The girl rings him right up.

Outside, there are clouds the color of plums, and the sun slants through them on Mrs. Bart's face, a Maryland spring evening.

As she comes up the cement path, the hole in the cellar window stares at her. A stone made the hole last week. It is the landlord who is responsible, not she. But without a phone, the only thing is a letter, and there has not been time for that. His money, for the rent, must go in the money order tomorrow. She will keep back five dollars and demand his attention.

As she fits her key into the back door, groceries in the crook of her arm, she can hear the voices.

"I'm afraid it isn't quite like that, Eloise."

The key turns, and she pulls the door hastily, shouldering it. She sees Eloise, in her mind's eye, one hand at her slender throat, her apprehensive eyes on his face. But he looks away; he will not meet them.

"You can tell me," says Eloise steadily.

Mrs. Bart is in the kitchen; the groceries hit the drainboard.

"You see, perhaps I already know."

There is always a fear until she *sees* Eloise. Eight months ago, a repair man entered Mrs. Bart's house. Squatting on his heels, in the focal corner, he had restored her friends. His last words were, "That should do it," and it has done it. He was the second visitor.

Mrs. Bart eats her supper facing the tension and polished wood of a court of justice. It is windy outside; somewhere, the wind rattles loose tin. Tonight, a flashback: It is a night beach, the breakers thunder in under a gloss of moon, two figures are locked, feet on the gleaming sand. The tin rattles faintly; the surf roars. Another sound is closer.

Mrs. Bart swerves her head like a horse. A girl is standing in the room, by the inner doorway. She is thin, and rather small, her lips are pushed out in a wordless order for silence, and in her right hand she holds capably what Mrs. Bart often sees—a switchblade knife. For a second it is as though she has slipped off the screen, like a trick effect. But she is utterly without color. Her dirty, mouse-colored hair, which does not float or swing, is no duller than her skin; her eyes in the dim light are as pale as her dirty jeans.

"You just shut up . . ." she says, just over the voices, though Mrs. Bart has made no sound. "You just keep your mouth shut." They both stay where they are.

The beach is gone, and the prosecutor's face looms at them.

"Shut that thing off," says the girl, advancing a little. "I can't hear." She cocks her head. Mrs. Bart still does not move, and the girl is instantly across the room, her left hand on the knob. Silence, like a new and terrible sound, fills the room. It is dark; the street lamp is halfway down the block.

"Where's the light?" says the girl. "I can't see a goddam thing." She has found the standing lamp, and the room leaps at them. The tray knocked aside, Mrs. Bart has backed against the wall.

"Now you get out of here," she says, in a faint high voice, into the new silence. "You get right on out. How'd you get in?"

"I'm just going to wait here," says the girl. "A few minutes. Just keep quiet." Her head is still cocked.

"I'll call the police!" says Mrs. Bart, a little louder.

"Before you do that," says the girl, "let's get business over.

Right?" She is still listening. In answer, a whistle shrills faintly, streets away.

"Oh Jesus," says the girl, looking right through Mrs. Bart. "Oh Jesus. I bet that's Tony." She drops on the arm of the stuffed chair, right in front of Mrs. Bart.

"What do you want?" says Mrs. Bart. "How'd you get in here?"

"Oh for Christ's sake, what difference does it make?" says the girl through her little crooked teeth. "You got a hole the size of a house in your cellar window." She adds, standing up, "Where's your money?"

The whole month's rent, and half the grocery money, and some extra bills too, are right under the pincushion on the dresser in the empty bedroom.

"I spent it, for groceries. Today," says Mrs. Bart. In the lamplight the screen is dead. There is no one here but the girl.

"Look," says the girl. She comes right up to Mrs. Bart, and her breath, faintly sour-sweet, is on Mrs. Bart's cheek. "Look. No trouble. Right? Y'know? Just the stuff. As long as I'm here," she says with a quick tiny grin.

Mrs. Bart finds her voice has gone away.

"Look," says the girl, "I might have to split. Y'know? Any time. So come *on*."

Mrs. Bart still stares; the point of the switchblade touches her upturned palm, light as a butterfly, and without pain, a single bright bead appears. "Just the fucking cash," says the girl. "You're not hurt, y'know. Just come *on*."

On her pale blue stained T-shirt, under a transfixed heart, are small red letters: Let's Do It.

Into the bedroom they go, practically in lockstep, behind them the raw brand-new silence.

"Where's the light?" says the girl, but instantly she has found it, and everything is there: the long white bed like a fallen tombstone; the motionless rocker, holding out its arms; Mr. Bart, alert in his frame as on the day he vanished twenty years ago, as soundlessly and miraculously as the girl has appeared. The girl's left hand pounces on the money, right there under the red velvet pincushion. "Where's the rest?" she says, with her tiny grin.

"That's all," says Mrs. Bart truthfully. "It's all there."

"I'll bet," says the girl. But her heart is not in a search. The wind knocks a shutter, and the girl strains. Mrs. Bart can fairly see her listening.

"It's just a shutter," says Mrs. Bart.

After a minute, "Go on back in there," says the girl. She has rammed the bills deep into her jeans pocket. Going back, the toes of her sneakers are right on Mrs. Bart's heels.

In the living room, Mrs. Bart's knees loosen and she drops straight down into the armchair. The girl can kill her if she likes. But she stands biting her thumbnail, her head a little to one side. Drops hit the pane; the rain has come, and the wind is still blowing.

The girl begins to march up and down; Mrs. Bart might not be there. Back and forth she goes, in the short space. Each minute Mrs. Bart thinks, She's going! Instead, suddenly she sits on the edge of the sofa. She puts her hands on the faded knees of her jeans, the knife looks loose and negligent. Mesmerized, Mrs. Bart stares: there is a fine network of grime in the skin of her thin elbows. Her fingers are blunt, and the bitten thumbnail has a tiny trace of dried blood. The silence in the room seems to beat on Mrs. Bart's eardrums.

The girl pats one foot jerkily and doubles her left fist to hit her knee with soft small blows. Suddenly she is up, and Mrs. Bart's heart turns right over because she is at the core of the room; but she only switches the right-hand knob. There is a hum, and a flare and waver of life arrive, but soundlessly. The courtroom is gone forever.

They are at a party, soundless figures move about behind glass folding doors; Mrs. Bart is sure there is music. A tall woman, faintly magenta and green, but clad in clinging gold, opens the doors and sweeps in, closing the glass doors behind her. She buries her face in her hands—is perhaps sobbing?

Astoundingly, Mrs. Bart hears herself say, "The sound's on the left."

The girl's eyes transfix her like needles. "Oh shut up, will you?" she says. "I don't *want* the sound."

Behind the golden woman the glass doors open; a man is standing there. His face is a marvelous mixture of guilt, concern, eagerness. He shuts the doors behind him.

"You got a clock?" says the girl.

"It's broken," says Mrs. Bart. But because the courtroom has gone, she says, "It's after nine."

The girl puts her cheek to her doubled fist and leans against it. Her muscles let go. She might be resting, or asleep.

The man, directly behind the woman, touches, just touches her golden shoulder. She flies around, with a soundless gasp. She retreats.

The girl raises her head, and she and Mrs. Bart stare at the screen. The rain is a dim steady noise now, and they might be hostess and guest.

The lamp makes the screen paler. Slowly, slowly the man comes toward the motionless woman in gold. The focus, changing, brings their faces apart but approaching, right up. Slowly, the mouths wide as fishes', the faces move together, lock, as by suction.

"Oh Jesus..." says the girl. "That crap." And like a snake her arm has shot out and destroyed everything.

The locked forms are gone.

"You *look* at that crap?" says the girl furiously. "Whad'you do? Sit here all night and *look* at that crap?"

At this moment, Mrs. Bart sees the girl and herself as framed by the room. They are something of which she has missed the beginning. It is her turn to answer the girl's crazy question, to say the right, revealing thing. But no words at all come.

The girl is up, looking around her with a quick, complete glance. Contempt radiates from her like a vibration.

"Look," she says to Mrs. Bart. She bends to her, moving the admonitory switchblade back and forth like a teacher's finger. "I'm telling you something. I could have cut you up good," she says without conviction. "Maybe you got a broken clock, but you can figure ten minutes. You better figure it, and some extra. When I go, you sit right there. For ten minutes." A strand of the mouse-colored hair wisps over Mrs. Bart's hand. "I got friends," says the girl. "Y'know? I got friends. And if you start yelling—if you start yelling Police!—well, don't. Just don't."

Once more there is that all-round glance, quick, thorough, as though there might be something she has left. Her eyes stop, listening to the rain coming down hard.

"You got a raincoat?" she asks.

Mrs. Bart can't remember when last she was in the rain, but wordlessly she points to the closet door. But it is grotesque—the sleeves could be rolled, but the hem hangs almost to the sneakers.

The girl says, "Aw shit," mildly, and lets it fall to the floor. She goes to peer down the dark little hall to the back door. She fidgets there on intermediary ground.

It occurs to Mrs. Bart that she is scared, but she looks only disgusted.

"Well," she says finally. "Ten minutes. You better count it out. Here I go..." with her skinny grin. And she *is* gone, fast as a cat; the alley door doesn't make a sound.

The idea of yelling Police! astounds Mrs. Bart. To whom would she yell? The banging shutter, the hard April rain? The girl is as gone as the money.

She stays right where she is, her head cocked like the girl's. But she does not believe in the friends or their retribution. The sofa edge is as vacant as though the girl has switched a knob and vanished. Mrs. Bart looks quickly at the palm of her hand. The dried bead of blood is so small it looks like a speck of rust, not even as large as the blood on a bitten fingernail.

The room seems to move a little, a seasick motion. She has a lurch of confusion, as though the room were boiling with invisible presences—the checkout girl, the man with thirteen items, the girl, whoever she listened for. The raincoat is on the floor and the girl is somewhere dozens of streets away. Mrs. Bart sees her mouse-colored hair, soaking and plastered. She has been sucked into that other world.

The cold remnants of supper are congealed on Mrs. Bart's plate. But the silence has risen, risen, like water in a well, so that she just sits there, feeling it steal up.

There is no frame at all to what has happened. She has missed the beginning, and it is impossible to supply the end. The screen, the knobs are as far away as everything else. She sits by her tray, while the downpour beyond the window turns to a soft April drizzle. She hasn't yet once thought of tomorrow's money order, of the groceries that must, with money, be checked out between the cash register and the cancer cures. As though she were exhausted from running, bolt upright in the armchair she falls asleep.

Instantly she dreams. A tall priest, blond in his black cassock, has the girl by the arm—it is frozen motion. The girl is pulling away, her shining hair swinging out from her head. She is scared, but the priest's kind, knowing gaze is bent on her with infinite intent. Her long oval fingers, pushing at the black sleeve of the cassock, relax their grip; her long lashes lift timidly upward.

Suddenly a totally different girl, the same, flees round the corner of a street—whistles are shrilling, the dream is alive with them, a long black convertible slides to the curb alongside the girl, its door open.

In dives the girl, the driver swings the car right away: "Keep down, keep down..." His teeth flash in a smile. "They'll never even see you." The car rounds a corner so sharp Mrs. Bart's head jerks.

The lamp is on. The rain has stopped. Hastily Mrs. Bart gets up. She steps around the raincoat, and switches the right-hand knob. There is a hum. A pale square lights and wavers, but nothing else. It can't be that late. But it is. There is the tray to take out, the raincoat to pick up, undressing to do, all with nothing, absolutely nothing else, moving.

When she comes back in her nightgown she turns out the lamp, and instantly a thin blade of moonlight is switched onto the floor. Mrs. Bart has her pillow in her arms, and she lays it down on the blade, while she pulls out her bed. Between the moon and the broken clock, she has no idea what time it is, how many hours she must wait.

She gets into bed and crosses her hands. Again for some reason she sees the supermarket aisle: the clerk scratches her head with the pencil butt, waits for the unweighed bananas. Malice, help, in print are close by her eyes. Across the tabloid face red letters run: Let's Do It. Nothing is ordered, nothing is revealed to her. Perhaps the girl was never here at all; perhaps she slipped and fell from the screen and has been rightfully sucked back. No. Like the Chesapeake and Potomac man, like the repair man, she came. The girl got in, she unlatched the broken window, running from something, and got in. The Chesapeake and Potomac man must be asleep. The repair man, too. They get up early. Where can the girl possibly be asleep? Where is everyone?

She does something new. Though there will be no one there at all, not even the flag, flying, following its stripes, she gets up and gently goes over, and turns the right-hand and the left-hand knobs. The square glimmers. Even before Mrs. Bart is back on the couch, a sound—a self-contained low steady hum—enters.

The Glen

———————

O VER THE SOUND of her dishes clacking lightly in the soapy water, she could hear the sound of Harmon's voice. It was his third voice—neither the usual quick tense run of speech, nor even the slower, more accentuated tones in which he spoke to Cora, but his slowest, quietest yet most emphatic speech—as if he put each word, with a soft pause, up for special inspection. Soap bubbles winked and died on the plate which Jessie held still for a minute, listening to that voice wheedle Cora to accept the words. "'You!' said the Caterpillar contemptuously, 'Who are *you*!'"

Futilely and masochistically, as she might have pressed a great dark bruise, she raised her eyes to the little mirror flat on the wall over the kitchen sink, and there she saw them. Cora sat in her small mahogany chair with the cane seat and back. Her red curls shone faintly, under the edge of the firelight's motion; her mouth, slack and open, sagged a little more than usual, in distrait attention; her hands, with their short square fingers whose nails Jessie had cut that morning, lay curled upward, flaccid in her lap. The tomato juice had gone through her bib and there was a great oblong stain over her chest.

"'I don't remember things as I used—and I don't keep the same size for ten minutes together!'"

Suddenly Jessie noticed that Harmon was wearing a sweater, and this instantly brought the autumn to her as had neither the cold steady rain nor the shiver of the dripping asters outside the window. She glanced at the seasonless clock for comfort. Winter seemed at her throat in a leap, and after she had dried the last dish she raised her eyes again to the little mirror—this time to exchange with herself a long, reserved look. The brown eyes, bright and clear as the mercury in which they were reflected, regarded her. She was four years older than Harmon, but she doubted if this knowledge would have affected him had it been his; which it was not. Her fingers reached for the light switch, but lingered a moment, as though she and her reflection had a last important image to communicate.

" 'One side will make you grow taller, and the other will make you grow shorter.' "

It was almost cruel, though of course Harmon's dark, obsessive drive would never see that. The child was not listening, she was unable to listen; but tranced by the familiar voice linking its sounds for her, she gazed with her dull sea-blue eyes into the prancing fire. Jessie could see the skin of her fat little face, that skin which together with her hair was the only gift in all her grossness. Her stepmother was close enough to see its texture. Translucent, fresh as petals, it flushed and paled in delicate shell-tints. In one of her passions, it flamed like a fury. Harmon's voice was reaching some sort of climax:

"Alice remained looking thoughtfully at the mushroom for a minute, trying to make out which were the two sides of it."

Harmon bent over to show Cora the picture, but her face did not change. He said slowly, "She's going to *eat* it and *change!*" With surprise, Jessie saw a shade of expression cross Cora's face; her eyelids squinted.

" 'And now which is which?' she said to herself, and nibbled a little of the right-hand bit . . ."

Cora had begun to breathe quickly; a thin thread of saliva looped to the collar of her yellow dress over the bib. Her eyes turned from the fire to fasten on her father's lips. Harmon glanced at her, and delighted, repeated, ". . . and nibbled a little of the right-hand bit to try the effect."

Cora began to rock lightly in her chair and a sound came from deep in her throat. In the kitchen Jessie switched out the light. Anything to do with eating, she thought with an angry hopeless-ness. She took off her apron, came round and into the room and slipped into the big wicker chair by the lamp.

"She was shrinking rapidly: so she set to work at once to eat some of the other bit . . ."

So there they were, arranged in their places: the fire, the rain, the child, and Harmon's pausing voice.

Long after Cora was in bed, about ten, the rain stopped; suddenly they could hear the rush of the little stream to one side and below them.

Until a few nights ago, since the quarrel, the late evenings had held an awkward quality; it was as though they brought echoes. But the change which had come in Philadelphia and altered Jessie's world again—already too altered in the past year—had freed them both, though Harmon knew nothing of it. For Jessie herself it was undefined. As soon as this change had showed itself in her voice, in her renewed ability to laugh, it had been reflected in their eagerness to touch each other. It was as though it was Harmon who was reprieved.

"It's stopped raining," she said. She went to the door and opened it, and the cold damp rush of the night air chilled her face and her bare arms.

She could feel him behind her, and yes, there came his hand on the back of her neck. At that minute the moon tore loose from its black cloudbank and rode out into bare sky. The smell of dead leaves, of wet earth swirled round them and Jessie thought, exultant, "I'm not afraid of it now. I am stronger. I can wait for whatever I must wait for." And she spun round and pressed her face to Harmon's. He caught her to him so quickly that she gasped. He slammed the door with his left hand, and for the first time in weeks, locked together they moved softly into the room where the moon picked out patches on the counterpane.

The next morning the sun burned off the mists early, and by the time the Buick bounced down the drive ruts and, beyond the white rail fence, towards the city, it was warm. Jessie went to see what Cora was doing before she let herself take a final cup of coffee into the sun on the porch steps.

The little girl was on the floor in her room, squatting in a bar of sunshine, moving about the brown nutshells she had brought into the house yesterday. The smooth arc of her elbow and the red curls on her neck might have belonged to any child, who would now look up from this baby play and smile and greet her stepmother. But it was Cora, and she had no intention, even, of making one of her sounds—she seldom did, except in distress. She was absorbed in moving, very slightly, the shells: first so, and then almost back, and then back. It drove Jessie wild to watch her—the sheer stupid hopelessness of the play, which could not even be called play at all, but was some sort of lost and imbecile task; she could feel the nerves tingle with revulsion all down her spine.

She went out softly, turning the key in the lock behind her. The coffee could wait. Suddenly she must walk somewhere very fast, even if only for a few minutes. In the house, she could never let Cora run loose; she might squat there for hours, altering the position of her nutshells, or she might equally well pull the contents out of Jessie's drawer, or crush a brown raw eggshell in her fingers. Outside she was all right. She never went toward the road, seldom now even to the glen, which she had taken to so in the summer's heat. In August when she had not been lying in the cool dirt under the house, like a small white panting bitch (Jessie had even given up replacing the lattice), she was clumsily and carefully trying out the little glen, cutting her feet on its rocks, staining her shorts with its cresses and weeds, falling flat on her face in the stream's inches of water, from which she came dripping in excitement, making her noises which were more convulsions of muscles than true sounds. Lately Jessie had been cautious in meeting the child's blue, clouded gaze. Once Cora had dropped asleep in her small cane chair, and Jessie, looking at her for some moments, had noticed that the lids were after all parted. Inexplicably, as she watched, Cora began plunging and almost grunting in fright, flinging from her chair and catapulting herself out of the room and all the way into Harmon's closet, where, a minute later, she had faced her stepmother as though Jessie were a stranger, and a bad stranger at that. Jessie was horrified. She spent a quarter of an hour in overtures, and finally Cora, as though Jessie had been one of those night-shapes which terrify, only to resolve themselves into a familiar lamp-shade or table cover, had ended on the floor with her head in Jessie's lap. Cora seemed to forget this; Jessie did not. Sensing a true danger, she redoubled her efforts to please. Her passion for smoothness, for being wonderful, came first; but under it, deeper and wider, was the knowledge that, whichever way the cat jumped, Cora's friendliness or trust was absolutely essential.

Cora had taken to Jessie immediately; her vitality, the sort of animal friendliness produced by health and self-assurance, had drawn the child. Perhaps that was why and when Cora began to get on badly with Sue; perhaps her mind could hold only two affirmative figures. Or perhaps, as she became, irremediably, no baby, but a great girl almost seven, her rages, her balks, her vast stubborn tempers had killed Sue's knack with her. The *coup de grâce* had been Jessie's trip to Philadelphia. When she had come back from those precious days, it had been to disaster. For all the hours of Harmon's daily absence, Cora had been in revolt: she fought and bit when Sue tried to dress her, wept soundlessly for hours, threw things; the last day before Jessie's return, Harmon had to stay home from work. A month earlier, Sue had quit the job, but five years had struck down roots and she had promised even to beg off from her next position to come now and then, or in an emergency. After Jessie's trip, her return was tacitly never mentioned again. Now Egbert, the next-door farmer's son, came, not too unsuccessfully, every other afternoon, and sometimes for the evening.

Jessie went soundlessly through the kitchen, and down the steps onto the sparkling grass. The sumac bushes were a rich angry red, and the invisible stream sounded stronger after the rain. She knew this lovely pause before winter: it was the sort of day in which quail got up, mushrooms popped to the gold light, and squirrels turned nuts in their rapid, clawy paws. She walked, along the lawn to its east edge where the grass degenerated at the lip of the tiny ravine Harmon dignified by the name of glen. She stared down into its dampness with absentminded distaste. In summer it had been ferny, bosky, lush. Now it was moist and dark-brown and full of things rotted by the early frosts; and winter, she knew, it would hold forever, with snow dirtying itself, and a cold mist of superficial melting as its response to the thin sun.

She had seen arbutus there in spring, she remembered, on the first day she had seen the house at all. And she remembered very clearly indeed how in August she had crouched on the rock, close to the tiny stream's line, which was then merely a bright movement over mud, on the morning of her first, her only, savage quarrel with Harmon. The realization that she had lost, that not then or ever would she be able to change Harmon, came back strong and bitter, even in her new confidence. At first she had thought it was because she had broached the thing badly, that Harmon had resented the mingling of love and pressure. She had still been glowing with the forbidden prospect of France, and she had approached her solution eagerly; but in the very midst of passion it had frozen Harmon. Harmon did not freeze like ice, but went soft with the rotten feel of stalks and stems still upright but touched by frost. But it was not until after the quarrel the next morning, until his pale set face in the oven of the Buick had disappeared down the drive, that she had faced things.

She had walked to just where she stood now. In that August haze of heat, cicadas were thick in the trees and three fields away the sound of a dog barking hung in the air. She had sunk down on just this rock. She remembered how her hand, cold with rage and fear, had felt it warm to the touch. The rage and fear had come with the quarrel, but it was only as she sat in the brutal heat, invisibly circling in her trap, that illumination after illumination came upon her in widening waves. At the center was her realization of Harmon's full wickedness, of how he had trapped her, of how both their lives were to be fed, as propitiation, to his insane sense of guilt. Odile's death, and Cora's fate, were somehow upon his head—it was as though that ghost of childbirth were standing at his shoulder, instructing him in his slavery. But widening her rage and despair came the small hard conviction that Harmon's primary reason for marrying her had been Cora; passion had been luck and secondary. And since passion was secondary, there was no way in which it could be utilized to circumvent his obsession.

It was difficult for her to realize this; she had great faith, if not in passion, in its techniques. While she had never seen herself as seeking Cora's head upon a charger, she had truly expected to control the disposition of the child—a kind and sensible disposition. Jessie came of people who were Wonderful; wonderful about circumstances and what circumstances brought to those they observed. If "Business as Usual" was not graved on their escutcheons, "Let us not be morbid" might have been. She admired wholly the women in her family: her aunt who had been wonderful when the fate of mosquito and primate alike had overtaken her young husband, in the form of an automobile crash; her mother, whose wonderfulness had never been better exemplified than when her husband, faced with a long and unpromising illness, had died from an overdose of his carefully regulated medicine. She knew that Harmon had not been wonderful about Odile, any more than he was wonderful about Cora. In this sense, he was wonderful about nothing, evidencing instead a neurotic strength of resistance to the healing powers of change, a subborn fidelity to shades and shadows.

The shade of Odile lay on the bones of Cora's face—the wide forehead, the widely spaced eye sockets, the short nose. There was in her face, Jessie rejoiced to note, no hint of Harmon. The shadow of Odile lurked in Harmon's study—in three bizarre cookbooks, in a book on herbaceous borders, on mushrooms, in a deframed photograph, bent at the corners, thrust into the back of the desk drawer.

That morning it had seemed to Jessie that life was to repeat itself, differently as usual; that she would have to divorce Harmon. It had seemed possible because of the rage, freshened at every turn by the thought of how easily he could *not* ruin everything in the wickedness of his monomania.

It had been coming, of course, to a head—but all within Jessie, who knew how to wait. She saw as her strongest card in a benevolent game, her fortune in winning Cora—insofar as that flickering mind and obscure heart could be won. Time was what she had, and if she had hoped for a solution before winter set in, she could even face the house in the country, the most recent bastion in a steady retreat from life, through the snows and into the resolving spring, if need be.

It had been stupid, perhaps, for Harmon to tell her of the transfer offer; but actually, in the long run, what difference would it have made? He had told her so simply because it had never occurred to him as a possibility.

"But *why*?" she asked. "Actually, why couldn't we?"

He had stared at her as though she were mad. It was late at night, in their bedroom, and with every window open the heat hung on them like a diffused weight.

"But it's in Lyons, in the city. If I couldn't manage Cora in town, can you imagine—in a foreign city—another language—a strange world . . . !"

She began to brush her hair again, and said gently, "But shouldn't we think about it? There are so many inquiries we could make. You speak French so well—perhaps Cora . . ."

He came up behind her and put his hand on her moving arm.

"Jessie, darling," he said. "Make it easy for me. Don't you realize how I'd have loved it—such a change . . . ?"

Her fingers discarded the brush and moved to the lamp. When it went out, they saw the moonlight on the floor. "I want what you want, Harmon," she said, almost inaudibly. "You know that."

"I do," he said, putting his hand on her small shoulders and drawing her back to lean against him. "By God, I do."

An hour later she had spoken again, and the false step had been made.

In the morning she had panicked, utterly panicked. On rising waves of comprehension, her fear, for the first and last time, had shaken her judgment. Harmon, knotting his tie, had turned, transfixed, at the shaking voice: "It's a disease—you're so warped now you can't *think* any more! What about Cora? What's her future? To hide out here with us, lying under the house, throwing her food about, ripping her clothes in her rages?"

He shot her a look, but she couldn't stop. "Don't you realize how life could be, for all of us? I've tried—you know that— you've *seen* it! Cora trusts me—I've never complained in all these five months. But she's *got* to be where they can help her—where they're prepared."

He came toward her slowly, and his voice was unnatural.

"Jessie. You know Cora cannot be 'helped.' We've been through all that. Nothing is going to 'help' her, except maybe somehow, somewhere, love—love from people she belongs to. The kind of place you're talking about costs a fortune—far more than I have yet. And if it were free—do you hear me, Jessie?—if it didn't cost a goddamned cent, do you think—in your *presumption*," he suddenly, bitterly added, "that you can hand my child—Odile's child—over to strangers—snap the one link she's got with human beings—turn her into a cared-for animal? She's not an animal. She's not an idiot. She's a speechless, defective child. My child. And the child of her dead mother."

The perversity of it, the specious plausibility, stung her beyond endurance.

"You fool," she said slowly. "You married me to take care of Cora. You stupid, stupid fool."

He looked at her so long without speaking that she turned and walked dizzily out of the room. As she went past Cora's closed door, she could hear the bed beginning to rock. She heard Harmon slam the screen door, and, an instant later, his steps on the concrete floor of the garage. He'll have a headache, she thought, in a curious detachment, in this heat, with no breakfast. The sound of the car died away. Then, alone, Jessie was gripped by a single, lucid, intense fear: that she had gone too far.

Jessie poured cold milk into a clean solid jelly glass, peeled a banana, put both on a small tray and went to Cora's room. The child's skin, fresh from sleep, was flushed with heat and her hair curled damply. She was pitching from side to side of the bed with a plunging motion, but she sat up as Jessie came in. Close to the bed, Jessie saw her eyes darken and the lids contract—it was her greatest sign of attention. Jessie set the jelly glass of milk on the bedside table—it was almost certain to be spilled in the end, no matter what she did with it. Cora's hand reached out for the banana, the loose lips closed over its end. Jessie looked at the child, chewing. Those lips never kissed, or spoke; they only consumed.

"I have to go out, Cora," she said, gently and distinctly. "Jessie has to go out for a little while. I'll be back soon. I'll be back."

She went to the door. "I'll turn the key," she said smiling. "So you'll be quite safe." Cora might have flung the banana, and the milk, too, on the floor—sometimes she would not be locked in. Then there would be a scene, or Jessie would stay in the house. But now the taste of the banana absorbed Cora. Jessie went out, turning the key quietly behind her. She went through the screen door, and although it was so early, the heat struck her heavily.

She walked over the browning grass into the shade at the lip of the glen. There was a flat-topped rock, poised solidly over that damp and still-green slope. Below, the small stream ran with a cool, busy sound. She sat there quietly, motionless. She rested, and gradually a peace and certitude welled up in her. She could feel power and purpose calming her pulse. She did not examine its sources. She rested in it gratefully. She sat and watched the ferns shiver lightly in a breath of air. A cardinal landed on the mud of the little stream bed and ducked its head delicately into the thread of water. She thought of nothing, but scenes moved slowly across the heat: the out-of-state registry office where she and Harmon had been married at a chilly April ten o'clock; Cora's cereal oozing across the kitchen floor on the night she came into the house from her honeymoon; then she saw the gallant, steady, cool smile in her mother's eyes as they met hers outside the deathroom door. Never had Jessie asked a question.

Florida was too far, and Jessie found she wanted less to talk to her mother than to visualize her. She got Sue to come for four precious days, and she had left Harmon and gone back to Philadelphia. There was no idea, on the part of either her husband or herself, that this absence was the preliminary to a separation; but she knew, infallibly, that it would be a progressive strain for Harmon; as it might, in some degree, have been for her if she had doubted its outcome.

In Philadelphia, she had recreated, as far as possible, the life she and her mother had lived after her father's death and before her first marriage, staying in the same small good hotel, visiting exhibitions and vintage films, calling up a few old friends. She even renewed her faint acquaintance with French irregular verbs,

feeling herself at times under the small steady smile of her
mother's eyes. She would sit, in the sterile, grateful coolness of
her air-conditioned room, the small green book in her lap. Harmon had destroyed his opportunity. But, Jessie said sensibly to
herself, it was in these particular cards that there would be other
chances. "... j'aurai ... nous aurons ..." she said silently, while
the room hummed on one tranquil note.

Soon she felt curiously renewed. When she came back, she
knew exactly what she had to do—but she had not the faintest
idea how she was to do it.

Now in the autumn morning, it struck her ferociously that
she had only circled back, like a desperate animal, to this rock.
Driven by the image of Harmon's sweater, she stared into the
small audible stream, seeing in it the advancing winter, choked
with snow, the rusted ferns broken by ice.

The sumac leaves were almost gone—the polished wood
shone below the peaked, furry, crimson cones. Toadstools had
sprouted overnight—three sprang from a rotted limb by her feet;
one—tall, pale—lifted white gills straight from the ground. A
squirrel sat up suddenly, near her, the bulbous eyes in his triangular head fixed, or not fixed, upon her, his paws shortened
over his heart. As though a lever had been pressed in her head,
what she gazed at was replaced by another scene: the firelight
moving, Harmon's voice, Cora's gaze darkening and contracting.
She sat still. The wet leaves shone around the sumac roots, in
flowing bounds the squirrel leaped away. Though she sat absolutely motionless, inside her a great response had bloomed. It
was as though an organic process had been initiated. She turned
this response over and over in her mind, as the squirrel had
turned its nut: at first she touched it gingerly, then as its strength
and beauty became apparent, with growing confidence. From
each angle it presented a flawless surface. Each flaw, each pitfall
from which its predecessors had suffered, was finally and totally
absent. It had a fatalistic perfection, as though she had been
building it all her life, and as it turned before her eyes, fresh
virtues, fresh inevitabilities were revealed.

She stood up abruptly, and for a moment the world pitched
around her as though all her bearings were strange. She went

over slowly and with her foot knocked off the three fat toadstools sprouting from the log, crushing them under her heel. She looked carefully and quietly at the rock, the rotting log, the tangle down toward the stream, the whole small lucid slope. Then she turned and went straight back to the house.

As though the one condition of her revelation was that she should not temporize, she went rather quickly through the door, through the living room, and into Harmon's study. She moved directly to the bookcase and took down an elaborate book with a slick, heavy jacket, illustrated in tones of ochre and acorn. She carried this to Harmon's desk, and sitting down, leafed through the pages, tentatively; but there was no difficulty. She had been absolutely right. The straight, regal shape rose on the page, pale and tall, single, springing from the earth, carrying its volva. She took Odile's book back to its shelf and began looking rapidly through all the three shelves, but fruitlessly. She looked around her, at the chair, the daybed; but there was no book lying about, and she went back into the living room, still looking rapidly around. Then she saw the red cover; it was on the little table by the fireplace.

She went to the wicker chair, sat down and opened the book, leafing lightly through until the picture arrested her. She looked at it for a moment; then she laid the book open on her lap, and sat there. She could hear the dog barking again, very faintly, and beyond the distant hedge and fence, the tires of a car passing.

Without warning, Cora began to pound on the bedroom door, heavily, as though she were hitting it with a wooden block—the noise was brutal. Jessie got up lightly, eagerly. "I'm coming, Cora!" she called, and she crossed to the door, turned the key and the handle and stepped back. Cora stood in the doorway, turning her head from side to side.

Jessie didn't speak; she walked back and sat down again. She picked up the red book and stared at the picture, which represented a caterpillar, seated on a toadstool, blowing smoke from a large black hookah, while a tiny Alice faced him below the toadstool's rim.

Cora came, with a slight scowl; she had got cross pounding on the door. But the red book seemed to touch a fuzz of recollection. She came up and looked over Jessie's elbow.

"Daddy read you this," said Jessie, staring at the child full on. "Remember, Cora? Last night? About Alice. About *Alice.*"

The sea-blue eyes, set wide, regarded her without a flicker of interest. Their faces were close; it was as though Jessie had never seen Cora so distinctly.

"She *ate* the *mushroom*," said Jessie in a low clear voice. "She *ate* it all up. To get *bigger* and *smaller*. Remember? Remember how she *ate* the mushroom and *grew*? Daddy read you."

This was within Cora's power. Her eyes left Jessie's face and fastened on the confusing picture. The short blunt finger came up hesitantly and touched the glazed image and drew back, dissatisfied, from its texture. She lifted her eyes and fastened them instead on Jessie.

"I saw it!" said Jessie, and she smiled radiantly at the child. "I *saw* the mushroom, the one that made her *bigger* and *smaller*. It's here, it's right *here*. At the top of the glen, near the rock."

There was silence, in which the dog barked again, distantly; he must be chained. Cora still looked at her with a wide absence, but her brows were drawn together. Jessie could hear her own voice, light and sure as a smile, caressing Cora. "The *mushroom* Alice *ate*!" she cried triumphantly. A quick squint contracted Cora's lids, her eyes darkened slightly. She turned them to the book, but then quickly back to Jessie. "It's by the rock, just at the top of the glen. The mushroom Alice ate. And grew smaller. And bigger."

They stared at each other for a minute. Then Cora contracted the muscles of her throat in an almost soundless tiny roar. She swung around, and Jessie, motionless as the transfixed squirrel, watched her to the screen door, which she opened. Then she stopped and turned around, glaring in confusion; but Jessie gave her a clear, secure smile. At that she contracted her lids and suddenly stretched back the corners of her mouth—it was almost a smile. It was, a kind of smile. She stood, big against the light, rocking slightly in a tremendous excitement. Then she stepped carefully down onto the grass and the screen door slammed behind her.

For a minute Jessie did not get up, and by the time she silently shut the wood door and went to the window, Cora was stumping with her ugly rocking walk across the lawn. It would take her minutes to get to the lip of the glen, and it was quite possible she might forget what she had come for.

With the door shut on the morning, the house seemed cold. Harmon had laid logs for tonight and there were paper and twigs below them. Jessie struck a match and stood, a little crouched, before the hearth, and sure enough, there came the stealing orange, flowing upward in a liquid mesh of flame, over the rough brown bark. There was no sound anywhere. But now in the silent room the fire began to pop and crackle faintly.

Nel Bagno

B EFORE MRS. GLESSNER shut her large suitcase, which she had just weighed, she went into the bathroom to get the final articles for her toilet bag. The open door impeding her in the small space, she thrust it to with her heel. The breeze from the open casement caught it at the same moment, and as it slammed shut, the knob fell off on the inside.

It was a glass knob, cut in facets, and it made a hard, thin sound as it hit the tile floor. Now it was possibly chipped, and the tile too, perhaps. Annoyed, Mrs. Glessner snatched it up; neither showed any sign of damage, and she took the knob with its projecting metal tongue and inserted it carefully back in its hole. But it refused to attach itself, and conscious of limited time, she knelt on the tiles with their small blue flowers and put her eye to the hole. She couldn't make out anything, and she again inserted the knob, but it refused to mesh with whatever ratchet caused it to function; released, it would not even balance there.

She glanced furiously at her wrist, but it was bare. The tiny watch was propped a dozen yards away, on her bedroom bureau. How many minutes before the taxi? Fifteen? Ten?

She put the glass knob on top of the yellow wicker laundry hamper, next to the Italian pocket dictionary and the box of Kleenex. It was perfectly quiet in the bathroom, except for the sound of traffic from the parkway, coming faintly but steadily through the casement window, which the breeze, sucking back, had slammed shut. With a sudden uneasy movement she went to open it again. It resisted, and she had to yank hard on the handle; but then it flew open, revealing the small darkened screen, the tops of rusted, rosy maples and, far below, the edge of the little wood at the back of the school.

She was still not in the least alarmed, mostly because of the ludicrousness of the situation. The notion of her missing her taxi, her plane, Italy itself tomorrow, trapped in the most incidental of rooms, was the stuff of drunken parties.

But five minutes had certainly passed, and how, actually, would she get out? She sat on the edge of the tub for a moment, to get things straight.

She had, at most, ten minutes. She leaped up, went rapidly to the medicine cabinet—yes, scissors right where they belonged. Again she knelt before the door, the scissors closed, prying delicately for the hinge that would draw back the tongue. It yielded, slightly, each time, but immediately something arrested it. By the fourth or fifth try, she knew it was no use. She knelt there on the floor, humiliated by the ineffable absurdity of her situation. Could she break down the door? She looked about her. Small toilet articles ranged on three glass shelves; the toilet; a circular, bristly toilet brush; the long narrow tub, with its porcelain soapdish; the wash basin; the medicine cabinet, filled with bottles, tubes, vials; a metal radiator, very shiny; on the wall, a small Haitian painting, next to it a wall clipboard with snapshots and a torn-out newspaper column; on top of the hamper, an Italian pocket dictionary and a tiny transistor radio— these put out conspicuously for her handbag—a blue quilted Kleenex box, and the glass door knob, the sight of which brought her round again to the handleless door.

Her entire distress was concentrated on her plane. Something *must* happen before the taxi came. She took off her right shoe. It was a black leather pump, and looking at its heel, she at once knew better than to try; nevertheless, she swung her arm in a big arc and crashed the heel against the indented panel. The blow sent a violent jolt all the way up to her neck, and made a raw scar in the paint. The wood itself was not even marked.

She put her pump back on, with dignity, conscious of keeping her head. She did not think for an instant of anything subsequent to the taxi's arrival. All right, she would make her clownish predicament public. She would yell for help. It would have to be out of the window; old Mrs. Abernathy, below, was in Wisconsin, and this was the top floor of the small condominium.

She went to the window and was struck by how narrow it was. The screen prevented her leaning out. Genuinely furious, she picked up her scissors and began to hack at the screen, feeling a savage satisfaction as the blades burst through, the screen ripped and curled. It scratched her hand badly, but she yanked a big piece inward and back, and thrust her head cautiously through the opening. For the first time, a curious twinge went down her spine.

The window was too narrow to get her shoulders through, and without leaning out, all she could see were the treetops, the empty cinder path below with the wire fence along its boundary, and far to the right, a tiny segment of sidewalk. The late September air was fresh on her face. She glared out at the empty afternoon; but, at first sheepishly and then louder, she called, "Anyone? Anyone!" She *would not* call, "Help!" It was still too ridiculous. "Anyone?" she yelled. "Anyone there?"

Exactly in answer, a bell rang distantly in the kitchen. It was, by the familiar tone, the downstairs front door. It was, she knew, the taxi.

Mrs. Glessner stayed just where she was at the window, resisting with success an impulse to tears. The taxi would be by the front door, on the other side of the building, parked in front of the red brick steps and small white columns, a scene which she now visualized. She had not heard the taxi pull up nor would she hear its departure. The bell rang again, a long irritated peal. Mrs. Glessner turned toward the door, stood close by it with the wild conviction that an irascible driver would ride the little elevator to the twelfth floor, seeking his delinquent customer. It was very unlikely; but that is what he did.

After a silence of some minutes, during which his customer envisioned the pumpkin-colored rear of the cab receding toward the parkway, there was a short, sharp brring. Now she did yell, quite shamelessly. "Help! Help! I'm in here!" but the bell only rang again, and again, and then stopped.

Mrs. Glessner retreated to the edge of the tub, sat down, folded her hands, took a deep breath. She was, she had always cheered herself by thinking, a tough nut. But in the silence after the bell, the reality of the taxi, the plane, Italy, dropped from her mind. Why shouldn't she die here, slowly? Starve here? Die? Because—people did not starve to death in suburban bathrooms; because—nothing of the sort happened; because people from the outside came—gas men, painters, Barnie the janitor, checking something. Because people phoned repeatedly, and then wondered, and came. Because, from time to time, small boys walked along the cinder path at the back of the school, looking for lost baseballs.

Mrs. Glessner was by profession a writer of what she called non-fiction prose, and now she thought of this. Still torn between a sort of abashed amusement—she would dine out on this yet— and what she was afraid was the onset of fear, she said aloud: "All right, how would I sum it up? My immediate chances?" Gas man? The meter was in the basement. Workmen? She hadn't commissioned any. Barnie, checking? For what? She had already told him goodbye. He had a key, but why should he use it, except perhaps for a brief inspection before she got back at the end of the month? Friends? Oddly, only then did she think, Maury? Maury. But for weeks everyone would think her in Italy.

Still, the improbability of any real disaster under such circumstances encouraged her. Why she? If she were writing this . . . but suddenly she felt a chasm open, widen, between her own reporting and the thing reported. The thought was unpleasant, also irrelevant, and she skipped to the next consideration. Resources, immediate resources.

She looked around the small room, small, she supposed, as a cell. Such amount of wall space as rose to the high, narrow ceiling was papered with a water-resistant surface on which pale blue and lavender fish cruised in and out of deeper purple clusters of marine growth. The shower curtain was a scattering of purple shells on a sand-colored background.

Since there was nothing else she could immediately do, she was above all concerned with keeping cool, as she still phrased it to herself. She totted up her advantages.

She had electric light for when the dark came (if she were still here). She need not soil herself, or her room. She had heat if the night were cold. She had, above all, water. She had a radio. She could, she thought with dour mirth, go on improving her Italian. She could—but as she looked at the medicine cabinet, she got up and, without any clear idea of what she was going to do, opened the cabinet door, took out a round vial of yellow capsules, emptied them in the toilet and pushed the handle. Immediately, she thrust her hand into the coiling water and tried to sieve up the capsules, but they rushed through her fingers, and she retrieved only one.

This totally unexpected performance shocked her literally off her feet; she sat down on the little rug, put her head on the hamper and tried to understand what had just happened to her. The implications of both her first, and then her second, action were insupportable because identical, and because both came straight up from some involuntary self-knowledge that had not filtered through to her consciousness.

She had thrown away a perfectly good vial of sleeping pills in a melodramatic gesture, a committing of herself to the fight under any circumstance—inherited from heaven knew what fictional or cinematic conditioning, she thought scornfully. But then her hand, like the paw of a starving bear after fish, had darted down, in case, in case. Why? She knew exactly why, and knowing, she crossed into a new dimension. She was in here, and it was by no means, by no means whatsoever, certain how or when she was going to get out.

She remained sitting on the floor, her head on her hand, leaning lightly on the hamper. She thought again of Maury. She had not, in the chaos of the last ten minutes, thought of him at all, but now it was of his phone call that she thought, a transatlantic phone call that would save her.

They had agreed that he would not call. She needed her unhampered trips—no mail, no phone calls across all those wastes of ocean, plugging in the always complex past to the sunny, simple present. *She* would call, when and if she felt like it.

But now, in her blue and lavender cell, as the brightness through the small window softened and muted itself, she was convinced that Maury would call. He had called her—last year—in Yugoslavia to repeat to her something a little girl had said behind him on the crosstown Forty-Ninth Street bus. He would call her again, at the Regina this time, and staring over the swollen hydrangeas in the lobby, the desk clerk would say politely but pointedly, no, no, the Signora had not taken up her reservation for the day before yesterday; he would say that, in Maury's terminology, she had not showed. And then (she went step by step) came the phone, pealing in her bedroom, hour after hour, and finally worried Maury turning the key in her front door lock, his shocked gaze taking in her open suitcase on the bed, her weak shout; the screwdriver. She and Maury would sit on her sofa, Maury's fingers on the back of her neck, and drink draughts of bourbon, without water, very icy. She pushed herself up from the tub's edge and went to his photo on the clipboard. Back-lit by the summer sun, he smiled at her, posed in front of a low-hung fringy tree. She looked at his arms, bare to rolled-up sleeves, with their veins and tendons and furry down, familiar by sight in the sun, by touch in the reassuring dark. It was strange that, never having needed Maury with any violence, her present need of him, violent enough, should be so grotesquely limited.

The lines of the clipping just to the right of Maury's picture read, ". . . and the good people of Boonesville know how they feel about Gerald Ford. It is gas, and gas alone . . ." It was the only thing in the room which placed her in time. At once she remembered a quotation she had used in her last article, not yet out, which she had embedded in a paragraph about proportion: "It is by dried cornflowers that we know that Tutankhamen died in April."

Definitely, the room was darker. She stood in the tub, so that she more directly faced the little window, and peered out. Everything was exactly the same, except that the wind, which had gotten higher, made the trees ride heavily, and small flocks of leaves sailed and skittered over the cinder path, beginning to heap themselves up against the wire fence. She thought that there were perhaps twenty more minutes in which someone might walk by. She propped her elbows on the tiny sill, which was always a little sooty. The wind blew in gusts, and traffic vibrated in the distance.

She whirled round, stepped out of the tub and picked up the little transistor; then, for fear that someone might pass the window at a run, she scrambled back. She switched on the tiny bevelled wheel, and immediately from the black leather case a babel burst out around her: contending voices, a scratch of music, a high-pitched blatting. A hair's-breadth turn, and a voice right in her hands said clearly "... by seven out of eight doctors." "Seven out of *eight*?" repeated a small delighted feminine voice. Her finger moved a fraction and someone said loudly "... and is bringing with it a low-pressure Canadian front. In the extreme northwest, snow is a possib—" merging a thousandth of an inch further with the hard, quick beats of a tango. She switched it off and put the small black object down hastily on the edge of the basin. Its outrageous magic struck her as inexplicable, as though the transistor had never been invented. What was, actually, going on in the stillness of this room? How could that babel, over silent lakes, and mountains and turnpikes, withhold itself? What else might be in the room? What was distance? What, above all, was closeness? She looked at the small black rectangle in horror, appalled by the naiveté of habit.

She stepped back to the window, and there, in the distance, on the short, visible section of sidewalk, were two women, walking slowly. One was short, both were bareheaded, and the taller had a poodle, straining against a leash.

At once Mrs. Glessner gave a mighty shout; the wind caught it up, whipping it about with a new cloud of leaves. The women disappeared, though the poodle, its muzzle poking at something, held back for a second, still in view. The sun, contracted and reddened, sent diagonal shafts through the tallest trees. The phone rang.

It rang seven or eight times—Mrs. Glessner was not sure which, she was listening so ferociously; and hearing it repeatedly shrill, she knew this was how it sounded in the empty apartment, in the dark of many evenings, echoing over the motionless objects. It stopped; and in the immediate silence, Mrs. Glessner noticed that she was hungry. This was really unlikely. She was used to little or no lunch, and she seldom had dinner before eight. It couldn't be six o'clock yet. Why was she hungry?

Two small boys came into view on the cinder path, directly below her, heads bent together, lingering. As though a switch had been thrown, a wave of heat went through Mrs. Glessner. Her throat felt raw: "Now," she said, "this is it," and thrusting herself as far as she could manage through the window, "Help! Help! Help! Help me!" she shouted into the wind. The boys moved slowly ahead. Mrs. Glessner seized the radio and, on tiptoe, flung it, with all her strength, out of the window to strike and shatter eleven stories below. Instead it disappeared into a heap of leaves behind the children. She saw it land. The boys rounded the corner, were lost, as the radio, the day, the room, the world were lost, as the planet plunged willfully away from light.

Like a monk adjusting to his coffin, Mrs. Glessner sat down in the tub. A conflict raged in her, the sense of remoteness, of isolation, of the gulf of galaxies between her and the woman with the poodle, the lingering boys, the stellar space; and the sense of sly immanence, the unknown tumult in this tiny room, boiling with voices, music, the uproar of contesting action, all utterly silent. The women were blocks away now, the boys, nearer. Georgia, Montreal, Havana raged in the bathroom. Mute now, buried in the colored leaves, the tiny box could not change or stop them; it could only deceive her. Perhaps Maury was in the room; perhaps she was in the sky, like her plane, over the dark ocean.

She got up heavily, stepped over the edge of the tub, took the toothbrush mug and drank some water. It was fresh and belovedly real. In the mirror, her face was so dim that she hastily switched on the light; all the porcelain glared and gleamed at her.

She picked up the dictionary. (What book would you choose to take with you . . . ?)

aback	*all'indietro*
abandon	*abbandonare*
abbess	*badessa*

absurd	*assurdo*
abuse	*cattivo uso*
barbarous	*barbaro*
barley	(as in late summer)
	orzo (base, base;
	how, base?) vile
beemaster	*Mischino alveare?*
	(a fringy tree,
	struck by the sun
	over her shoulder,
	July, July)
congeal	*congelare*
congenial	(what curious
	sequences)
	degli stessi gusti?
devotion	*devozione*
devour	(root cousin; or so
	she had always
	believed, wise she,
	wise, most wise,
	Maury) *divorare*
dearth	*carestia*
death	*morte*
debar	*escludere*
debase	*abbassare*

In the back of the dictionary was a series of situations helpful to the student: *alla spiaggia: le piace il mio vestito? in viaggio: Ho perduto la mia borsa.* Localities: *La sala da pranzo: la tavola,* the table; *la credenza,* the sideboard. Ah, here she was. *Nel bagno:* the basin, *il bacino;* the toilet, *la toletta;* the bathtub, *il bagno.* These letters were—or were they?—her terrible porcelain companions. But what was the actual connection between the letters and the porcelain objects close upon her? The translation from English to Italian was nothing to the other translation, from letters to matter.

She sat on the toilet lid. I am a writer, she said. For the first time, ever, she became conscious of what she knew. In her non-fiction, she never described things truly; not even as truly

as she could. She gave the article its shape, its stance. Whatever
weakened, whatever altered the neatness of that shape, that
form, lost its rights, was changed, was molded, disappeared in a
quiet wink between writer and reader. That was what gave her
prose persuasiveness, its dazzling quality, even. It was as though
intruders, whose identity might wreck the perfectly constructed
plot, were introduced by another name: the basin, *la tavola*; the
tub, *lo specchio*. "Jane Glessner," she said aloud, twice. "Jane
Glessner." What had been the name of Woman With Poodle?
Of Two Boys? If she had called their names, would they have
heard? She had read somewhere that tests showed that one's
own name carried uniquely to one's ear, could pierce a crowd,
or carry an unlikely distance. Maury was a name defined as
lover. Lover: *il telefono*.

She raised her eyes to look uneasily around. The hamper with
yesterday's clothes heaped like discarded costumes. The cabinet,
holding possibilities behind the world's most ambiguous object,
a waiting mirror. The purple fish, dry and motionless. Over the
fish hung the Haitian painting, a small rectangular canvas, a
woman's head, skin the purple of a ripe plum, long, judging
eyes, thick firm lips. A yellow bandana. When Mrs. Glessner
had chosen it, the Haitian artist said in her impeccable French
that she was a bad woman, that one. Fantastic bones. "A tough
one?" Mrs. Glessner had echoed. *"Elle faisait des anges,"* the artist
said simply. Unfamiliar with the phrase, Mrs. Glessner had at
once understood the succinct cynicism. Now, far from the hot,
green light of Haiti, the abortionist's long eyes stared patiently
over Mrs. Glessner's shoulder.

It was quite dark outside. "What shall I do next?" said Mrs.
Glessner. "I could take a bath," she said. This struck her as a
bit of gallows humor, and she actually began to undress, hanging
the navy-blue jacket of her now-rumpled suit on a hook, where
it covered the empty knob-hole. "The shroud: *il jacqueto*," she
said brashly, stepping out of her slip and peeling off her pants.

The sound of the stopper dropping down was thunderous,
but when the hot water fell in its own steam, the gentle familiar
vapor brought tears of self-pity to her eyes. Never did she say in
her mind, *starvation . . . death*. She was saved by the low comedy

of the situation. Men in Arctic crevasses, in their four minutes of consciousness, could think of a great single phrase; men in disabled submarines could write, with their last weak gesture, a message. But a message, in lipstick, on toilet paper . . . She knew this night had its special message, but she could not translate it.

"This is a bath," she said. "When I have finished, I will open the door and walk out. Or I will leave behind me silence. Because of the difficulties of translation." She knew it was the silence she could not direct. It all led up to the quality of the silence.

Naked, extended in the tub, she looked down at her body, still so useful, cut off from motion, from food, from love. The cell, she thought, what are the letters for that? Tonight a hundred thousand lived that word, but what were its letters? c-e-l-l meant nothing. She reached out a dripping hand, but *cell* was not there; the little dictionary's uses anticipated neither biology nor crime. She replaced it on the hamper.

It was time to get out of the tub, but as this bath was obviously going to be the night's one activity, she lingered. Drops fell from the tap at intervals; somewhere a dog barked, barked, barked. Perhaps it was the poodle. Or Barnie's dog. Barnie had a bony charmless mélange of setter and several other breeds, with caved-in looking sides, and a ratty plume of a tail. Tendentiously scrupulous where the tenants' cleanliness was concerned, Barnie showed an appalling indulgence toward the dog's less attractive habits. Constantly, it soiled the sidewalk and deposited feces on the pachysandra by the door. Perhaps this was Barnie's revenge. Mrs. Glessner loathed the dog; it always looked starved, though she knew Barnie gorged it. But she disliked even more the organized hostility of the tenants. There was a move afoot to force Barnie to do away with it.

The water was cooling. She shuddered a little and stood up, wrapping herself in a thick, blue towel; the water sucked and whirled away. It reminded her of something, and she looked at the little yellow capsule, now dry and stuck to a Kleenex. Much help that would be.

Well, she thought, with this awful sort of mirth which kept rising in her, I shall have it for supper. Was this the rumor of hysteria?

The little radiator poured out heat; it was always too hot. Mrs. Glessner did not dress. "That is sensible," she said; "nothing, absolutely nothing, can happen tonight." She discarded her blue towel, and gradually the heat in the room made small beads of sweat appear on the face of the Haitian woman, on Maury's forehead. The two syllables of Maury's name, that name by which she identified him, formed and then escaped in a clutter of images: ticket stubs, restaurant checks, a pair of trousers over a chair. She tried to visualize his body, then his eyes, his nose; but they had gotten translated into wavery lines, into foggy shifts. Deliberately, she tried to remember his entry into her body; but it was less real to her than the silent clamor around her. *l'amante:* the silence.

Once, hours later, the phone rang again. Eight times.

The quarter moon, pitted-looking and incomplete, appeared in the narrow window. Mrs. Glessner had heard conversations from below. People had talked, back and forth, calling each other by name. The moon stayed in the casement space a long time, apparently without moving, and then it was gone.

Rewrapped in her blue towel, Mrs. Glessner lay in the tub. She put a small lavender towel behind her head and got down on her spine, propping her feet against the waste-end of the tub. She had swallowed the yellow capsule, scraping off the fuzz of the Kleenex, and drunk a glass of water; she did not expect to sleep at all. But in some sort of perverse exhaustion, she fell asleep at once. She woke in a misery of discomfort, and shifting, lay flat on the bottom of the tub, her knees crooked, her head on the little purple towel.

When she woke up for the second time, the light in the bathroom was a curious dilution of street light and pre-dawn thinning of the dark. For an instant, utterly bewildered, she knew only the awful sinking sensation with which the waker, knower of intolerable news, resists focus.

She sat up in an agony of stiffness, the full, ludicrous, unbelievable, locked misery drowning her. She clambered to her feet, turning around to look out over the ragged, hanging screen. The wind had died. The faintest lemon light stained the treetops.

A great gust of furious hope and rage rocked her. She took a breath, held it, let it go. Though she was quite dry, she began to rub herself hard with the big blue towel. She stepped out of the tub, switched on the light and put on her underclothes. There was a comb in the cabinet, and she combed her hair, dragging the teeth savagely across her scalp until it tingled. She chose a lipstick and colored her parted lips. For a moment, a stomach cramp seized her and made her bend over the basin; then she splashed toilet water over her neck and arms and pushed her feet into the black pumps. She hesitated before her suit. Should that be an event for later? But impelled by a pressing haste, she buttoned the blouse, stepped into the skirt. She switched out the light, and the room was filled with a watery visibility of the palest gold. Preternaturally strong, she sat in an attitude of expectancy on the tub's edge.

Beyond her preparations was a sheer cliff. She could see its rim, but she sat there with her stomach cold and contracted and her eyes bright with knowledge. She knew the names of things. Perhaps she would never write another word, but she knew which words to write and which illusory silences to allow for. She would not see Maury again, perhaps, but she knew what a lover was, and was not. She would not see Italy, perhaps, but she knew what distance was.

The traffic sound had swelled. A point of very thin sunlight struck a cluster of purple undersea foliage.

A short, broad man with a dog on a leash came into view from the right, and moved below her on the path. She stared at him, as at a grounded flying saucer, shocked by the apparition. The dog paused by the wire fence, lifting its leg as the squat man patiently stood waiting. Mrs. Glessner put her head, softly, softly, like a bird-watcher, out of the window.

"Help, Barnie! Barnie!" she cried in the thinnest voice. The dog lowered his leg. "Barnie!" she cried.

Uncertainly, the man looked around.

"Barnie! Your name is Barnie!" she cried.

He pivoted slowly, his head tilted. Suddenly he saw her. He called something, some amazed inquiry.

But her throat froze, and no sound came. He gave the leash a little tug, still staring up; they disappeared from view the way they had come, the dog hanging crossly back.

Mrs. Glessner stood just where she was, an awful tearing

sensation in her stomach. It was as though she were being split directly into halves. Something was rushing away, rushing away, and in came the other flood—the rooms beyond the door, the elevator, the streets, the misnamed objects of her life. She stayed perfectly still.

The bell rang, her front door bell, this time; rang again. Barnie was not very bright.

It must have been ten minutes that she stood there without moving at all. Finally she heard the front door slam and heavy steps creaking in the little hall. "Barnie!" she called, and amazingly, tears began to pour down her cheeks.

"Mis' Glessner?" asked Barnie's voice, baffled.

"The handle's off!" she sang out. "I'm locked in! I've been here all night!"

"My goodness," said Barnie with distaste. After a little pause he said coldly, "You got a screwdriver?"

"Yes, yes," she said. "In the kitchen, in the toolbox. In the broom closet."

One half of her mind said, Barnie walked the dog there because of the tenants. Barnie heard me because the wind had dropped. The other half said, These are steps I hear. That hush-hush is the swing door to the kitchen. When I think of this, it will be the way it was. I will not change it. Barnie heard his name.

Trudge, came Barnie back. Metal scratched on metal, the door shook. There was a sucking click, and it swung in, Barnie with it, the screwdriver still in place. He looked at her, displeased.

"How you do that?" he asked.

She neither flung her arms around him, nor told him the secret. That was the first modification. She stepped, very slowly, over the threshold, past him. Everything waited, noncommittal, balanced.

Watch it, she said to herself. What actually happened? You got locked in the slapstick bathroom. But what would happen now?

The suitable spoke the first words for her, after all.

"Just wait a second, Barnie, let me get my purse," she said, and she crossed another threshold, Barnie stooping with a martyred sigh to pluck the glass knob from the hamper.

The Inner Path

————

W HEN HE BEGAN the walk, Peter Vail was tired, but freshened as he went. He had three days now, altogether, and this was the second. Yesterday, waking heavily at noon, he had simply lain in bed, the waves of fatigue curdling over him, until it was almost time for a drink, and dinner as early as he could get it, after the day's fast. The fatigue was a sodden accumulation, mental and emotional even more than physical; the wearing and tearing of tiny teeth; indignation, frustration, endless effort; the initial effort of clearing himself from instant imputation; the slow, dangerous, laborious attempt at the winning of confidence, the hoarding of facts.

Already, yesterday, the beautiful nightmare of the long drive here to the high posada had seemed remote; he could not recapture its quality, though he could still at least see, pressing his eyelids shut, the wild dark mountains, dropping below him as he helplessly climbed curve on curve of the black night, which an immense moon had suddenly illuminated.

He had been late in starting; a final rather furtive conference with the priest of the small village had taken much longer than he had planned; then he had missed his road and driven rutted, humped and useless miles in the wrong direction, blowing a tire before he turned. It was already dusk when he took the right turn for the climb. The priest would have told him that it was stupid to try the drive by night over the unfamiliar and unrealistic road.

The fact that he found he dared not stop, or even slow his climbing speed, was dismaying. The headlights kept picking out precipices for which he was immediately headed, so violent were the curves. The grade was precipitous, and constantly he stared straight onto first, blackness, and then, the moon having shouldered itself around a peak, onto a vast jumble of lightless mountains; lightless, endless, huge. The grade was ridiculous; he felt that if he braked once he would never start again, unless backward. Most unnerving of all, there was absolutely no sign of habitation; he passed two shrines, one with fresh and one with faded flowers, and four or five empty roadside stalls, where fruit and flowers must at one time have been heaped.

The skin across his knuckles felt constricted; he felt that if he blinked he would sail straight into nothingness. Had there been a choice, a turn possible anywhere, he would have guessed he had missed the road; but round and round and up and up the car panted, the only sound in all the world of the great Guatemalan night.

The first faint lights ahead had seemed dreamlike, the first cobbles of the street like sand below the feet of a drowning man. Then, incredibly, half an hour later, he was in front of a blaze, in a highbacked wicker chair, with whiskey in his hand and his suitcase and typewriter beside him, as though it was any normal evening. The slim dark boy, with the slanted eyes that had at first surprised Vail in so many Indian broad-boned faces, had slung a splash of kerosene, unstoppering a rag-stuffed bottle on the bricks, over the thin tough fiber of the wood, and an instant blaze had leaped before Vail's eyes and overhead in the shadows of the whitewashed ceiling.

Yesterday, lying luxuriously in the wide low bed, he had savored every slow second of the hours of early afternoon. It was the first day in a month in which he had not been in purposeful motion. Even the strawberry beds of Panajachel, the great secret depths of Lake Atitlán, under the pointed cone of the volcano peak with its tethered cloud, had been peripheral to his dogged intent. Perhaps it was ironic he had learned so little he hadn't known already when he came ... but he knew it now quite differently. Then it had been a matter of facts, of events, of statistics, however violent and bloody and inhuman. Now those events had the smell of the air of a country above them, and its rich steep soil underfoot.

The total beauty of the place shouldn't make any difference to the truth of his report; but it did. He had read a poem about Guatemala just before he left New York; the book was in his bag. Death, death, violence and torture, was what he was writing; but the poem had talked of another sense of death: an immersion, a sense of the numberlessness of the dead, of the tiny moving group of the living. He had had something of that feeling always in Mexico, but it was far stronger here. It was mingled here also with an invincibility of life, with the soft deep voices, the lovely clash of color in cloth and clothes; it was the invincibility of the tiny terraced ledges of maize and vegetables down the steepest slopes, where a man must move all day on uneven legs. It was in the forward movement of the figures on paths, almost horizontal under loads that in Mexico would have weighed down a burro.

He had got the book out, over his early whiskey—he was starved by then—and reread the poem; the offerings to the dead *... the tiny huddle of the living cautiously closes / the old bargain, paying candles, copal, and roses.* Watched over by the Lord of Crevices, the Masters: Masters of Rules, Masters of Masons, Masters of Lead, Masters of the Knives. All under the aegis of the dead: the corn climbing the barrancos; in village festivals, the marimberos and the tambereros; in the sky, remote and black, coasting, the purifying vulture. And at night ... the flutes, *wandering, linking, tiny and pure.*

And that, waking at some small hour, was exactly what he had heard. He had gone to the window, beyond which the moon, still full, flooded the vast landscape; and there had come from somewhere faintly to his ears the sound of a distant flute. He imagined it, the bare fine wood, the stops just holes for the fingers. It meditated, thin, clear, full of neither sadness or solace, but of an enduring question. His own fingers were used to keys, those of his piano, those of the typewriter that ate his hours. Above the piano keys, he loved the lingering lift of the hand, drooped from the wrist, of the last single note. The keys of the typewriter grinned at him, always hungry: give me, give me, give me; something to eat. His fingers could do without neither.

In this past month he had fed the typewriter keys doggedly, persistently, feeling his own fiery frustrations faintly eased by the lines that would express them, turn them into galleys, into pages between covers, for those, he thought in fatigue at night, who already knew and cared, or for those who did neither, to put aside or deny.

Now today, coming out into the high sweet air on which trailed a faint scent of copal, he wanted to think nothing. He wanted to walk, walk and breathe the air; to watch, to smell, to listen.

He turned the corner and came straight on the church. He remembered then that it was Sunday afternoon. The high steps up to the church doors had charred embers, and the smell of copal was stronger. He went up the pitted stone, and pulled open the heavy door. Inside it was colder, and near the door, the floor wavered and blazed with candles stuck in their own wax. He had seen them so often; and the Virgin, doll-size, in bright threadbare robes, attentive in pose, glass-jewel-crowned; and the Indian-cum-Spanish tortured figure over the altar, where the red light swung from the ceiling. He remembered friends' comments, faintly scandalized, faintly amused, on the melding of pagan and Catholic—the permissiveness of that tough and strange marriage.

It was the priests—the priests, the students, and two teachers and a nurse—who had spoken to him most freely—and they too were desperately cautious—don't name the village, don't name the source, don't describe too accurately—the soldiers will be sent, the advisers are quick. But how can I seem authentic? How can I defeat challenge? That, of first importance to him, did not, he saw, weigh equally with them. The death squads were alert as ferrets. "For your own sake, never discuss with a stranger." Men, women, children also, would pay. Round and round, in a circle without exit. At several times, in several places, he learned, a young priest had slipped away, into the jungles, into the hills, a breviary left, a rifle fresh, in a sort of generous despair.

The last priest he had seen spoke Spanish and Quiché, quite laboriously, but he could communicate directly, which was more than Vail could do. At first, and sometimes still, he had found the peasants' smattering of Spanish incomprehensible. He had wanted above all to talk to the peasants, to the village leaders. But the peasants were profoundly distrustful of his national origin, and the leaders, when difficult contact was made, had each time to believe that he was a maverick in what they regarded as the forces of evil, the obscene confederate of Authority.

Now he simply walked. The true part was over, the job he had come to do. What came next, in another world, what was bound, sold, read, was all ahead, was part of the everyday life of his profession.

The cobbled street had stopped almost at once. He was on a path with trees so high on either side that at last he had a sense of shelter. The grand speechless views were hidden.

He walked slowly. He had all the afternoon, and seeing an even smaller path (looking about him first to remember direction), he struck into real woods. The air was aromatic; there seemed no sound anywhere. Once, straight out from the tangled growth, trotted a pariah dog, across his path. It stopped ahead, grinning back at him, with the snarl, at once aggressive and cringing, he had come to know well. He stooped as for a stone, and the dog vanished soundlessly. A few moments later, around a curve, came a tall woman in dusty splendid colors. She wore a sort of broad woven turban on her head held high. Vail stepped aside and she passed him with a murmur, her eyes down, her tough brown feet rapid and even.

He was now so far from the posada that he thought he should turn, but he kept on as though he were in search of some destination. And indeed, around the next curve, narrowed by great tree trunks, he was suddenly in a small clearing. Beyond it, at the path's edge, lay a huge log, fallen from a rotting tree trunk, and on the log a man sat, carving something small.

He wore the loose white cloth of the region; beside him lay a wide-brimmed hat with a low crown and a brilliant band, and at his feet lay a bulky string bag, secured at the mouth with a length of thin bright cord. He was, evidently, on his way elsewhere.

Vail saw that an awkwardly carved animal in a light bright wood lay at his feet. Perhaps a jaguar? But the face held in the man's left hand as he looked up was far from awkward. It had almost but not quite completely emerged—pointed chin, beak-like nose, the grim slash of the mouth—yet the face had a kind of inner hilarity, sardonic, ambiguous. It was a small mask, such as Vail had seen for sale many times, but far more interesting.

Halted, meeting the man's dark bright eyes, he said tentatively, *"Buenas tardes."*

He saw that the man, whom from his stoop he had taken to be old, was not old at all, merely used-looking, and very thin. He put his hands on his soiled white knees, the knife in his right hand, the mask in his left, and looked at Vail. There was such a silence that Vail felt curiously embarrassed. He gestured slightly toward the mask, and said in his Manhattan Spanish, "That's very beautiful."

Still, the man looked at him. Then he stood up and held the mask out at eye-level.

The dog, or one just like it, had reappeared, at some distance. It sat grinning, and panting within its jutted ribs.

"Norte Americano?" said the man. He had a deep muted voice, curiously expressionless. Vail nodded *si,* and the man asked, as though it were a different question, *"Estados Unidos?"* His Spanish was thick and uncertain. They were not going to talk much. Vail, trying to form the Spanish words in separate clearness, asked, "May I see it?" indicating the mask.

The man handed it to him, whether in response to the words or gesture, Vail did not know, and Vail saw the raised cords of his hands, the grimy curve of the blunt squared fingers. The wood of the mask felt very light and very dry; the planes of the cheeks were carefully carved.

The man stooped to his bundle, and at the motion, the dog flinched back; but he was only untying the bundle's cord. From within he now produced a slightly larger carving—an animal, a bear or perhaps a rearing bird, in a human pose. The dog sat, panting.

Vail felt an urgent desire to communicate. In the little clearing, in the total silence, it was as though they were emissaries. It was just such a man he had consistently sought.

He asked, a little hesitantly, "Are they for sale? I would like to have one. I would like to have the mask when you have finished."

He could not tell if the man understood the words, but he held out his hand for the mask. Vail handed it back to him. He had not brought his wallet but he knew that he had some loose quetzales in his trouser pocket.

Still standing, the man began carefully, slowly, working on one of the cheeks of the mask; the cheek grew narrower, unequal. Then the fingers shifted and the knife bit delicately into the other cheek. As Vail stared at the brown fingers, the man blew gently on the mask and held it up. He had finished.

"May I buy it?" asked Vail. Everyone understood that: *Puedo comprarlo?* and the next question, *"Quantos?"*

"Diez quetzales," said the man, holding out the mask.

Vail's fingers took the light ambiguous wooden face from the man's hand, its lines etched in dirt. His own hand was in his trouser pocket when he was knocked down.

Breath gone, his face in the harsh stubble, he felt his arms wrenched behind him and immediately the bite of thin tough cord. The man's knee, sharp as a bone, pressed into his back and Vail could smell *aguardiente* and feel his breath, panting a little. Then a pain like a drill went through him so violently that for an instant it was unlocatable. It was in a hand. A sawing was going on, rhythmic and steady as a butcher's; he felt warm stickiness steal over his thumb, his wrist. There was a tearing jerk, and he was rolled over by a sandaled foot.

The man was holding up, as he had held up the mask at eye-level, two-thirds of a finger. He smiled and, still holding the finger, sketched in the air a brief pantomime—a rifle of air. The man crooked his index finger and his elbow snapped back. He said one word in Quiché and once more pulled the trigger of the gun of air. Then he said, shaping his lips: *"Dedo de gatillo."*

Wrists tight behind him, armlessly, Vail struggled to rise. The man stared at him without expression; then he smiled and flipped something in the dog's direction. The dog was on it in a grab, but it was so small a thing that the jaws turned it furiously, with a gulping motion.

The man put the mask, the bird, and the animal back into his string bag. He put on his hat and slung the bag over his shoulder. Then, with the knife in his hand, he bent over Vail. The sandaled foot pushed him over again, there was a sharp upward jerk. Vail's hands fell apart, and he saw the stump of his right index finger. Then the clearing was empty, except for himself and the dog, distant, still making its dissatisfied snatching motion. . . .

He got first to his knees, then to his feet. He leaned against the closest tree, gripping his finger's stump in his left hand. A tide of nausea rose in him, and he leaned over and vomited, still clutching his finger stump.

His brain seemed dazzlingly clear, as though an antiseptic white light had been switched on inside. Afterward, as he remembered it, every move was direct, however difficult, without pause. There was a light sweater tied around his shoulders and it was hard to get his shirt off; blood of course got on it. It was hard to rip, too, but a seam gave, to his teeth and nails, and he wound the strip as tightly as he could around and over the stump. He couldn't get his sweater on, so after he stuffed his ripped stained shirttail into his trousers, he carried it hanging from his left hand, his right raised to his left shoulder as though in a sling. Around his feet were scattered the quetzales.

He began to walk cautiously but as fast as he dared along the root-rutted path. He was terrified of fainting, not from the pain but from a lightheadedness which he assumed to be shock. In his illuminated brain, nothing was ahead. Each moment was the vital one. Without hesitation, he turned left at the point where he had turned right. Between the trees, there were no landmarks, but the path widened, was broader still. Then the first lumpy cobblestones were under his feet.

With infinite care he worked his right hand into his trouser pocket. Blood would seep through, but perhaps not before he got to his room.

Avoiding the zócalo, he went around to the back of the posada.

Its door was propped open to the early dusk, and he could see, behind the desk, the mestizo clerk hunched over a thin news-paper. He did not even look up.

Enormous blessings struck Vail. His booster tetanus shot. The key in his pocket.

His feet were soundless on the hall's fiber runner. The key seemed more difficult than any major woe. It would not turn properly in his left hand's bungling fingers. Dizzy, he leaned his head against the closed door. Slowly, carefully, his fingers went back to the key, moving it delicately, like the tumblers of a secret safe. It turned, and he was in his room.

He washed his right hand in water icy from the tap and tied it in a clean handkerchief, over bandaids suitable for a child's cut. He got the Demerol and a bottle of antibiotics, both unopened, out of his case. Teeth and fingernails, he got them open. He had a vague idea that whiskey and Demerol were a bad combi-nation, but the pulse of pain was clouding that cold clarity, and he washed the pill down with a straight slug of whiskey which burned beautifully inside him.

He got a fresh, short-sleeved shirt from the drawer. Once in it, he went straight back into the hall, leaving the door ajar behind him. At the hall's far end, close to the little lobby, was the posada's phone. *"Si, Señor?"* said the clerk's voice, and Vail told him, *"Ocho, ocho, neuve, quatro, por favor."*

He waited for the phone to ring, ring, ring, in the small cold room with the chipped desk, but almost at once a voice, faint, yet in his ear, said "Aqui, el Padre Cooley."

"This is Peter Vail," said Vail. Every word seemed before him in separate letters. "Can you come up here?"

There was a little pause. Then the voice, close and faint, said, "What's happened?" When Vail said nothing, it asked, "Are you ill?"

"Not exactly," said Vail, "but yes."

He could hear the change of tone. The voice said, "Do you need a doctor?"

"Not yet," said Vail. "Not here. Two people. You and some-one."

"What will we bring?" asked the voice briskly.

"A driver's license," said Vail. "Someone with a driver's license."

The hall brightened. Lights had been switched on.

"I'll be there in an hour. More or less," said the voice.

"Not in the dark," said Vail. "In the morning. Early."

"Mr. Vail," said the voice with some annoyance, "I've driven that road fifty times."

"Not at night," said Vail.

"I know the road. Goodbye." A small click brought the hum of disconnection.

Vail leaned against the telephone's shelf. The clerk could have food sent to the room, but at the image of food his stomach lurched. He thought with love of his bottle of whiskey.

Back in his room suddenly full of dusk, he poured a straight half glass, added a spurt of water, and passing the bed's lure, went to the window with the glass, then returned for the wicker chair. Far below him, two lights, separated by miles, had appeared, one bright and hard, one flame-colored. He sat, his right arm up, propped by its elbow on his knee, his glass in his fine left hand. The dragged chair had knocked over his typewriter; it lay on its back, and he stared at it, staring through the case to the invisible keys. It was a new thought. It brought with it the black and white keys of the piano, the flat lovely delicate balance of the white, the shorter raised shine of the black. Well, there was that, too.

The keys of the typewriter spoke for him. The keys of the piano spoke, also, in a separate language. But a gesture spoke. The gesture needed no speech, not his, not anyone's. The palm outstretched; the fist clenched; the fingers drawn across the throat; the hand upon the breast; oldest, and without bounds. A finger crooked in air, around a trigger of air. A message to the American on the inner path.

He knew that something—shock, drug, whiskey—had shut him off from the future, from, even, the next hour. He had a wide bright acquiescence; he supposed he was on some sort of high.

A big drop hit the pane before his eyes, turned pear-shaped, ran down in shapelessness. Then a flurry of patter. The enormous leaf of some plant directly beside the window dipped, dipped, and shone in the light from the room. Outside it was almost completely dark, and with neither moon nor star, rain must be falling steadily on the road below in its vertical climb. Here the world beyond the window had no existence but in the sound of rain, now steady with a tranquil drumming.

The sound, ancient and familiar, held no position. It varied only from the surface which received it, the cobblestones, dusty, washed to mud; the jungle growth; the posada's roof; the street below his New York apartment; the sea. He wondered suddenly where the mask-carver heard it. Where was the dog? Dripping or crawled to shelter? And the bone, gnawed clean, small and shining in the undergrowth. He could not much have appeased the dog's hunger. The man's? Perhaps.

After the last swallow of his whiskey, he put his head back against the chair's high cushion, and with his elbow propped on the chair arm, closed his eyes. Beyond the rain waited problems, evasions, his body's wholeness violated. Lord of the Crevices, Master of Masons, Masters of the Knives. Could they accept a shred of bone, embarrassingly small, into the great blood-stained night, into the company of the vanished?

If there were a flute, he would never hear it, through the rain, speaking its changeless tongue in the Guatemalan night. He could not imagine how the past hours, the present minute, would show in memory's tricky records. But now, very soon, he slept.

The Company

———

E XACTLY AS THEY shook out their napkins, the oysters appeared. Succulent on their opalescent beds, the browns and grays and pearls seemed the room's tone, though not its colors, which ran to rose and dull gold.

"How many years is this?" asked Jimmy Simpson, the youngest of the four, and the one whose life might be described as least orderly. Dates in his mind tended to shift and blend with the emotions of memory.

"Seven," said Dan Pierce promptly. Factually, he was the soundest of men. Heavily, his face carried almost a caricature of authority.

A drop of squeezed lemon hit the party's *raison d'être* in the eye.

"Ouch!" said George. "Watch it! Well, I'm 67 today, so that's easy."

James Alyott, for a moment speechless with his oyster, then said with a fine glutted sigh, "I wish to God I knew how you do it, George."

This was not flattery. The three younger men, the three old friends, gazed at George for a minute. He sat there, utterly reposed, rubicund, friendly but not eager, bearing easily on his unobtrusively tailored shoulders board presidencies, trusteeships, fund sponsorships, the commitments of the city's arts, not to mention his own business on which he kept a paternal eye from the short distance of a voluntary retirement. Childless, wifeless, he had eluded capture, and retained the friendship of the hunters. Whatever secret ravages age may have been about, none was declared.

"Speaking of looking well," said James Alyott, who was always called James as Jimmy Simpson was called always Jimmy, "I was amazed to hear about Harris."

There was a slight pause, almost as of embarrassment. Then Jimmy Simpson said, "Well, he was a pretty heavy drinker."

"Actually, how bad was it?" asked Jimmy of no one in particular. There was a small pause, and then Dan said, "Actually, I haven't talked to anyone who's seen him."

"George," said James, "we really ought to talk about that meeting next week. The Museum meeting. You know, there's real pressure to put Ely on the board."

George, drawing inward and downward his last oyster, looked benevolently at him. "That'll be no problem, James, it really won't. It just has to be handled."

Ely, a younger man, known to be somewhat quarrelsome by nature, had succeeded in insinuating himself into the Museum's affairs by criticisms of its displays—two published in the major paper—and by antagonizing its director. Now, purely it was felt through a ruthless desire for controversy, he had developed a party of his own which desired to see him on the board.

"I think that can be done perfectly gracefully," said George. He looked at their attentive faces. "As a postponement. As something promising, but not quite ripe yet."

Ah, that was the line. Before they could develop it, here was Henry, holding the wine, slantwise, out to Dan, like a sacrament which he hoped would be found valid. They all waited, though they knew exactly what it was; and after Dan had nodded gravely over his sip, it flowed brightly into their glasses. Since standing toasts in the Club's dining room were regarded as ostentatious, Dan pushed his chair back slightly and the three men raised their glasses in a gesture of real emotion.

"To George," said Dan. "That's absolutely all we have to say."

Now George had lifted his wine glass. But he stared suddenly at something and leaned gently to the left until he rested on Jimmy Simpson's shoulder. The wine glass toppled to the table-cloth, and the wine soaked George's elbow.

More drastic things had happened at the Club and, as at many busy luncheon tables, talk was unbroken.

George's stroke was "on the light side," as James nervously put it to Jimmy Simpson on the phone two days later. In the first hours, both speech and movement on the right side were affected, but already the improvement was marked. Every hour he was making himself understood more clearly, and already he was up in a wheelchair.

The news ran through its own community like a puff of wind, and the hospital was foundered by calls and flowers. The former, George's nurse noted down; the latter, except for a proud huge flock of birds-of-paradise, George had sent to the patients' lounge. To their surprise and indignation, he refused to see even the three companions sealed into intimacy by seven years of bi-monthly luncheons.

George felt a reasonable conviction that he was going to re-cover, practically totally, as he phrased it to himself; and he preferred waiting for that to happen prior to any efforts and protests of helpless affection.

He did indeed continue to improve, and ten days after the wine wet his elbow, he left the hospital, taking with him a marked limp in his right leg, uncertain fingers on his right hand, and an inability to seize the exact word at the exact moment he wished.

David came and got him in the Olds, which looked blessedly familiar. His nurse wished to cram it with flowers, but George knew how many more there would be. And sure enough, three great masses waited silently in his bedroom—a sunny burst of yellow chrysanthemums, an elaborate arrangement of African daisies with some rather malevolent-looking lilies, and a dozen flaming red roses from Jimmy's, well, fiancée. Jimmy, ageless in optimism, was between divorces. He and Shelby were going to be married shortly but shrank somewhat from the publicity of a status far from unique for either. The roses were brilliant and flawless, and George's heart warmed toward Shelby, whom actually he had encountered only twice.

George owned a duplex apartment and was looked after by what he referred to as a couple. They were a couple in the sense only of two people employed by a third. David was a large, squat, black, intelligent man, with a remote face of great strength and a rapport with the interior of cars. He slept in a small apartment next to Quincy's room and was regarded by George's envious friends as a sort of nocturnal guard or security agent. This was inaccurate, as David had an intense and unflagging night life. After he disposed of George, his return to his own quarters was late and erratic, and his subsequent slumber profound. The other half of the couple was Quincy.

Quincy's name was Margaret Quincy Snow, but having for private personal reasons an intense dislike for the name of Margaret, she had never in all the years of her employment by George been called anything but Quincy. She was an heirloom from George's mother, when Quincy herself must have been unimaginably young.

She was very small-boned and fragile, with a rather fierce but humorous face, veiled eyes, and tiny hands and feet. Her name suited her to perfection—her face, a pale bright yellow, had the faded luminosity of a fruit slightly past its prime, a little wrinkled, a little dried.

She had been there ever since George remembered, except for one brief astounding period when she had suddenly left to be married, no trace of a suitor having been previously observed. Six months later she returned, uncommunicative, her down-turned lips set firmly against any question, her eyes more than ever veiled by contemptuous lids.

She and David moved in close juxtaposition, but austere as planets. David spoke well enough to be a bank manager or bureaucrat. Quincy kept the speech of her working rural child-hood. Now and then it struck George that he had no idea how either felt about him. It seemed to him that there was nothing he could do about that, one way or the other. It was a serene and functional ménage.

Though the phone rang incessantly in the first days after

George's return from the hospital, he preferred to have messages taken—he was waiting for his pinpoint delivery. David, whose job as chauffeur and general factotum had at the moment boiled down to transporting Quincy's marketing, and doing slight services for George in the long afternoons, was good at this. Quincy was horrible.

She would listen silently, the receiver clapped to her ear like a hearing aid, and "Yes'm, yes'm," "Yessir," she would say. Replacing the receiver she would tell George with cold conviction that Mr. Pleats say please let him know he can come see you. He say, call him tomorrow. Or, Mz. Fodd say, can you eat calf's foot jelly, let her know. George knew, of course, no such persons, and would close his eyes, reflecting that he and Quincy at least had communication problems in common.

Finally, sick of procrastination, Jimmy, James and Dan arrived en masse at the front door. Quincy would have shut it in their faces and made leisurely inquiry, but David, who thought all this isolation ward nonsense and dangerous to the spirits, ushered them suddenly into George's room.

He had not yet moved to the big armchair which he could now reach unassisted with David at his elbow, but was propped on pillows, staring straight at the door. That perhaps brought them up a bit; at all events they hesitated a moment. Then they were all over him, hands, jests, chairs pulling up.

They stayed a short time, reminding each other that they mustn't tire George on the first visit. Conversation, so wandering and overlapping at the Club's lunch table, seemed curiously stilted. With care, George asked a few questions; his visitors answered eagerly but seemed disinclined to amplify. George wanted to ask about the meeting of the Museum's trustees, coming up on a day he had laboriously ascertained to be Thursday.

"George, don't have that on your mind," said Dan. "It won't be a proper meeting without you, anyway. We'll monkey around with a few practical details. The other things can wait till you're back."

Eyeing him closely, George saw that he was perfectly sincere.

"Well, look at you!" said Jimmy. "Already! At this rate . . ."

He seemed to George rather jumpy. This was perhaps natural

in next week's sixty-two-year-old bridegroom, but one might have thought that practice . . .

They wished to do errands for him, bring him books—not heavy ones at the moment. They thanked God for David. Quincy behind the kitchen's swinging door was no more than a name and a satisfactory meal, but on David they enviously doted. When he now appeared, bearing a UPS package, they all rose together like starlings, and told each other they had stayed too long.

George, stately with two pillows propped behind his head, denied this. David said that it did the patient good to see his friends, and helped Dan on with his overcoat, while Jimmy and James humped into theirs.

In the elevator on the way down there was a kind of pause, as though gears were being shifted.

"How do you think he looks?" asked Jimmy, and Dan spoke for all of them.

"Wonderfully well, considering," he said. "He'll be back throwing his weight around before you know it."

It was November, and as they stepped out into the dark, lights had appeared in all the buildings; the moons of the street lamps lit their faces.

"Next week as usual?" said James. There was a little flurry of exchanged glances.

"I won't be here, you know," said Jimmy, and Dan said, "Why don't we just postpone it for once? George is liable to be back this time next month."

George's second stroke came just five days later—actually, the day of Jimmy's wedding. It was more serious than the first. It left him temporarily unable to move alone, and with only the approximate and stripped speech of a very young child, though oddly with his brain clear. It was difficult to prove this, and he was not absolutely sure himself. He was in the hospital for a considerably longer period, and when he was able to return home, David had left. He did this in a perfectly open and friendly way, coming to see George in his hospital room and explaining he felt that for some time in the future he would be of small use to George. He was untrained for a sickroom; his skill was as a chauffeur and makeshift barman, and at the moment those abilities wouldn't be what George wanted. He had found a place where he was needed, but—he added—any time George wanted him back and could really use him, there he would be. Though he meant it, it seemed to him a perfectly safe remark.

Actually, David's words and his familiar smile over his shoulder as the big door hushed-to behind him were the first things which brought to George a sense of actuality.

George's doctor arranged for an attendant, trained as David was not; a thin, tall, tan man with liver spots and slightly protuberant eyes, named Harold. During George's recuperation, of which the doctor spoke easily, Harold would be his day attendant, and he would sleep where he could be called. Quincy, her cooking skill largely wasted, had agreed to sit with George in the evenings until he was ready for sleep. She wanted to take the phone calls.

When Jimmy got back from his honeymoon, the very first thing he did the next morning was to call Dan to ask about George. No one had marred his month with news of the second stroke, and it was a nasty shock.

"Oh God, I guess that's it," he said in dismal tones.

"Well of course you can't definitely say," said Dan, who had had time to adjust. "As James says, sometimes the recoveries are absolutely miraculous."

"Have you seen him?" asked Jimmy uncertainly.

"He doesn't want to see anyone yet," said Dan. "He won't be home till next week, you know."

"How about—about lunch?" asked Jimmy, still uncertainly.

"Oh God . . ." said Dan. "We could plan to stop by and see George afterwards."

But on the day of lunch, George still had the No Visitors sign on his door above the paper Christmas wreath.

The Club dining room looked very handsome indeed, with its great ropes of green strung from the central chandelier to the room's four corners and its holly springing up from each bud vase.

"You know," said James Alyott, "it's the damndest thing to

know what to talk about. The past is bad. And I guess the future is worse."

"That yesteryear bit must be as depressing as hell. And things coming up must be even trickier," said Jimmy, squeezing a slice of lemon; a drop shot straight up to a holly leaf. "Things *he'd* normally be doing, you know."

"Well," said Dan, watching the wine steward bearing his way. "I'm not sure that what's going on at the moment wouldn't be the most difficult."

"What was that thing of Harris's—about the laurel all being cut?"

"I thought of that the day of his funeral," said Jimmy affectionately. "Harris and his poetry." It had been a phenomenon.

"God, I miss Harris!" said James, as though suddenly lightened and freed, and they began talking of Harris, warm, and a real character, demanding nothing, embarrassing no one, alive and safe in their memories.

Quincy preferred sitting in the dusk. She either could not or did not care to read, and she sat with her little yellow hands, one over the other, as shadow softened the outline of everything, until George's imperative finger, and a sound she knew to be "Lights..." moved her from the big chair in which she was swallowed, to the room's lamps, blooming one after the other, and throwing their angled points on the high ceiling.

It was after the coming-on of the lights, and before the drawing of the curtains, that the thought of the Company first presented itself to George. He was lying propped on two pillows, his hands as peacefully crossed as Quincy's own, when its membership sprang, so to speak, if not to life, at least to whatever it was that George was living. It was Harris whose face formed itself. Actually at that point Harris was no longer a member of the Company, but this George did not know.

He wondered if Harris were awake, and if his light were on or not, and if he were alone. Harris had been a great companion, though tending in his cups to quote poetry—frequently French poetry.

But there was a period, mused George, lying face to the April evening, in which those who were neither in nor out of the living number waited.

A series of names now suggested themselves to him. Fred Allenby. Marsha Forte. Harris. What did they have to have in common to qualify as members? Well, they must be essential to no one. But that was not truly exceptional. They must be people so lodged in life and all its minutiae, so enmeshed in it, that their disappearance into some sort of immobility left tangled shreds, ruptures. They continued to exist, discrete, and persistently unredeemable. What a number they must be, constantly deserting, but constantly replenished: his peers. Behind windows, behind doors.

George summoned them to his midnight mind: the suspended, the long watchers between motion and escape, familiars of the last hours. Those of the limitless second and the horizon of minutes, unable to achieve or confer freedom; the innocent procrastinators. He imagined them, faces, attitudes, breathing presences in the room's quiet.

More and more lights bloomed in the immediate but remote buildings within George's view. He was fascinated. Which lights represented members of the Company, garrulous in their silence, inadequately exorcised from the minds of the movers and shakers. Quincy seemed like some presiding spirit. A mascot perhaps?

The Reverend Dr. Cartwright called on George. George had not sent for him, but certainly it was logic that he should visit a technical parishioner who had been generous to the church of his geographical choice.

Dr. Cartwright was an attractive man, with an absolutely beautiful voice. He was literate, and his Christmas and Easter sermons, those being what George had to judge by, were neither tedious nor lengthy.

Harold ushered him in, to where George had been established in his wheelchair, an effort becoming increasingly distasteful to the patient. The big window by the bed was open, and the curtains that belled softly in and out on the mid-April air showed a sky of blue but watery silk.

Dr. Cartwright was expert in sustaining a conversation which was necessarily largely a monologue. He skated dexterously among the dangerous and brittle objects of activity, and George waited a little nervously for the introduction of his professional specialty. But Dr. Cartwright, glancing about for his light topcoat, hesitated only when he stood. "Mr. Braydon," he said with a kind of simple friendliness, "I wish I could be of some use or other. Is there—could I—would you be interested in any—I've just finished a really remarkable book called *The Inner Spark*."

"Thank you," said George with care. "I'll be glad . . ." Suddenly, prompted by Harris, he essayed a smile, and added, ". . . laurels . . . You know, the laurels cut?"

Dr. Cartwright never ceased to astound his parishioners. Now he looked back at George and said cheerfully, "'We'll to the woods no more, the laurels all are cut'? Not *all*, you know."

But George shook his head and said, almost distinctly, in his awful accent, *"Nous n'irons plus aux bois / les lauriers . . . les lauriers . . ."*

Buttoning his coat, Dr. Cartwright reclaimed his way.

"Please let me know if there's anything I can do, anyone I can bring. And may God bless and keep you," he added a little defiantly from the doorway.

In the evenings of July the sounds from the streets seemed louder: the great breathing of traffic, the far clamor of firetrucks. In the evenings of August there were a number of sharp thunderstorms. The pane Quincy hastily lowered would be struck a rattling blow as of pebbles before she got it quite down.

An immense undemanding intimacy reigned in these evenings. Quincy's little pear-colored face, slightly averted, seemed to George indestructible as reality. Often he wondered about the Company's fluctuating members: its veterans, its desertions, its recruits; ah, its recruits. It was of them, in their first restless and incredulous evenings, that he most thought. Gradually he absorbed a great sense of membership.

If Quincy were disappointed that eventually she had no longer to relay the requests of Mr. Pleats and Mz. Fodd, she never mentioned it. Their proximity, George often thought—though it was less a thought than a consciousness—was a curious one.

All Quincy's secrets were kept in silence. They had scarcely exchanged a word, save on food, or her Delphic phone calls; yet, now in the hours and minutes and seconds of the indistinguishable evenings, they had merged into a vocabulary without alphabet.

He was glad, in an unformulated way, that it was she who could represent for him the liaison, the buffer between a member of the Company and the unenlisted, rather than one of the cut-out figures professionally representing humanity, where groups of the Company were mustered together in their joint solitudes.

The date on which the last person, save Quincy and Harold, saw George is uncertain in everyone's mind. George's desertion from the Company, by means of his third stroke, took place too quietly even for the doctor's ritual.

Dr. Cartwright's church was filled almost to crowding, and the relief of freedom to grieve and joy to remember lightened a number of hearts.

Selwyn Ely, standing in a little group between Dan and James Alyott, suggested that everyone needed a drink. This was undeniable, and Dan looked around for Jimmy. But Jimmy, whose marriage, it later developed, was nearing, though not yet on the rocks, was not there.

Instinctively avoiding a restaurant, just the three of them went to the Club. The first drink, serious as a libation, was truly for George, their warm, able, sensible friend, restored to their relieved hearts.

"We differed a lot, but he was a real *person*," said Selwyn Ely.

"God knows he *was*!" said Dan Pierce, and sudden glorious tears stung his eyes.

Season's End

"ALL RIGHT, Jimmy, what is it?" said Mr. Gaines; he could instantly tell that it was unpleasant. His partner's face was almost vague in the glare from the open door; he had set down his basket of tennis balls. "Want to sit down and tell me?" Mr. Gaines soothingly asked.

"No, I don't," said Jimmy shortly. Then he sat crossly on the edge of the closest chair. His tanned and exasperated face came clear.

"Arthur and Chico," he said, staring accusingly at Mr. Gaines.

"Oh God," said Mr. Gaines in disgust. He could feel tension gathering his scalp together. "This is simply ridiculous," he said.

"I told you," said Jimmy. "It just wouldn't work out."

"Well, it's just going to have to work out," said Mr. Gaines through slightly gritted teeth.

From outside came the amicable *pock,* pock, *pock* of strongly stroked balls.

"It's something you just can't force," said Jimmy. "Water and oil," he added, inspired.

"Which is which?" asked Mr. Gaines for diversion.

"Look," said Jimmy. "You want *everybody* made miserable?"

"But nobody's miserable but Arthur," said Mr. Gaines. He added hastily, "We're running a tennis camp. Not an encounter group. Arthur can just adjust."

A short silence followed the magic verb. Jimmy reached in for a ball, began turning its friendly fuzz in his cupped hand. "I just don't see why they have to *room* together for another ten days."

Mr. Gaines jumped up, then came round to sit on the edge of the desk. "A total of three weeks," he said, looking slightly down at Jimmy. "They can live through it. In the first place, imagine the whoop-de-do a shift now would cause. Everyone wanting to room with Chico. Jimmy, lead is light compared with Arthur. In the second place..."

"Well?" said Jimmy.

Mr. Gaines stared moodily through the open window to the court nearest, where the Medford twins, forbidden always to partner each other, supported respectively, Arthur Sayles and Teddy Joyce. "Arthur doesn't get any fun out of anything," he said.

"Algebra?" suggested Jimmy.

"Well, he's going to skip a class, as we've been told, and he's at it every spare minute; but fun..."

"Well, Chico has enough fun for everyone."

"Do you grudge him that?" Mr. Gaines heard himself ask rather sharply. "Has Arthur been complaining again?"

"He let drop that he doesn't like Chico's language," said Jimmy unwillingly.

"Oh for God's sake," said Mr. Gaines. "His language. He doesn't use it in the office or on the courts. Who but Arthur..."

"Arthur *says* he borrows his things without asking."

"Well," said Mr. Gaines mildly, "they all do that. And Chico isn't outfitted exactly like Arthur. That silly racquet. Arthur's parents ought to be committed."

"Sir?" Teddy Joyce had appeared in the doorway. Beads of sweat sat limpidly on his pink forehead. "Sir, we need new balls."

Jimmy tossed his into the basket and stood up. "See you, William," he said to Mr. Gaines, and out he went into the August morning with Teddy trailing.

Patting for a cigarette, Mr. Gaines stayed on his desk edge. At the moment he practically wished he had never heard of tennis, let alone a tennis camp. Camp? Eight boys. How well it had worked, though—the summer-empty school, three courts in perfect shape, quite a lot of money, really, and things he liked to do—did well—cope with boys, coach tennis. And a rest from French grammar.

And luck. Third summer. Three three-week hitches. Seven well-heeled, civil, solidly raised boys, one talented dark horse. Through his window Mr. Gaines couldn't see the blackberry shine of the eyes, or the cut of the lips, but nobody out there moved like Chico.

Arthur was intolerable. He radiated an invincible pomposity. This, Mr. Gaines had hoped to penetrate by exposing him to his antithesis—the one tennis scholarship which lent an air of civic purpose to an otherwise steadfastly prosperous summer. Last year, the first scholarship—a gentle, uncommunicative Jewish boy from Brooklyn—had worked out well.

In the case of Chico, Mr. Gaines had dealt with an athletic priest and a voluble grandmother. Chico was a cat of a different breed. He was a board member of what Mr. Gaines had always contended was the world's most pitilessly exclusive club—that of the charmers. Nobody could help you there, parent, teacher, banker, priest. Product of the public park courts, a complicated ethnic background, and fifteen years (he seemed older to Mr. Gaines), Chico had promptly showed up Mr. Gaines's carefully prepared schemata for his period-of-adjustment. There was, it turned out, to be no such period. Chico had nothing to adjust to, bar perhaps a rather intense popularity. But then Mr. Gaines had a feeling that that would not call for adjustment. Chico had that most seductive of qualities—total enjoyment. He *must*, Mr. Gaines reasoned, be sometimes bored, fatigued, discouraged. But to believe this was an act of profound faith. Could Mr. Gaines say all this after ten days? He could, and did to himself, and almost to Jimmy. How temperament did show up in games. Arthur, totally fair, took nothing unlawful, conceded not an inch. Chico, having a low boredom-threshold, called only "No kidding?" as a form of doubt.

Through his window, Mr. Gaines saw figures at the drinking fountain; the doubles were over. Clinic in how many minutes? But his wrist was bare. He stood up; and here in the doorway was Arthur. He was carrying his preposterous racquet, and his rather blank face was set with purpose.

"Sir, could I speak to you for a minute?"

"Yes, sure, Arthur," said Mr. Gaines, adding quickly, "Clinic coming up. I forgot my watch . . ." he ended rather tentatively.

Arthur raised his wrist. "I forgot mine, too, at home. My decent one. I got this crock downtown at Thurston's," he explained with contempt. "Ten minutes to ten."

"Well, we've got five or six minutes anyway," said Mr. Gaines briskly. "What's the problem?"

Arthur could be seen assembling himself. "I'm going to be here almost two weeks longer, sir," he said with a touch of gloom. "I'd just as soon not room any longer—er—just as I am now."

"Well, what's the problem, Arthur?" repeated Mr. Gaines, with the naiveté of surprise.

"We—we just—" Arthur came to a halt. Then he produced, "I guess I'm just not familiar with someone like that."

"Like what?" said Mr. Gaines in a changed tone.

"Any of the other boys would be all right," said Arthur, superbly.

Mr. Gaines stared at him. "How do you mean, 'all right'?"

"Well, everyone wouldn't keep borrowing my things and playing a lot of junk while I'm trying to work. And horse around all the time," added Arthur vaguely.

"Look, Arthur," said Mr. Gaines with an ominous gentleness. He stood up. "Part of being here is getting a little more experience. If you want to do your algebra, that's fine, but there's the library. You don't have to like Chico. Perhaps he doesn't like you—I have no idea. But it's important," he approached Arthur and passed him, "to learn to get on, for brief periods, with people with whom you're not congenial." At the door he paused. "You and Chico come here from different backgrounds, different experiences behind you (Could Arthur possibly have said "I'll say!" under his breath?), and I think you can learn something from each other. It's not a nine-month term, you know," he finished crisply over his shoulder. Though what Chico was to learn from Arthur, unless he took a sudden fancy to algebra, he couldn't for the life of him have said.

This time Arthur didn't even bother to say, "Yes, sir," as Mr. Gaines, with a flip of his hand, stepped onto the scorched grass.

Dewy mornings, each a fraction later, but the rains held off as the lawns bleached; evening brought a trace of coolness. It was always hard for Mr. Gaines to remember that the day span in late August was like that of early April. Somehow the summers seemed to Mr. Gaines to get shorter; or else their brevity had made more impression this year. In the evenings, as Jimmy drove the boys back from the village, the air smelt of a faint infusion of autumn. (Thank God none of them was old enough to drive, Mr. Gaines thought. It was one of his reasons for staying within the twelve-to-fifteen bracket. Chico, who had, he said, a sixteenth birthday coming up, had got under the rope by days.)

The movie changed only twice a week. There was an Atari parlor. The soda fountain in Thompson's drugstore stayed open until ten. There was a pizza parlor and a McDonald's. That was it. The first summer, Jimmy had nervously chaperoned the evening group. It had proved quite unnecessary—whether due to admirable upbringing or limited opportunity was unclear. There was one extraordinarily pretty girl behind the soda fountain— Jenny, Jenny whatever; and, as in the matter of driving licenses, Mr. Gaines was happy to have his *in loco parentis* status unstrained by emotional hazards. Now he or Jimmy just dropped the boys, and picked them up at ten-thirty at Thompson's, or eleven at the movies if it was the second show. Some stayed at school and played cards, or watched tennis movies, anyway. Now and then Jimmy went to the movies with them, but he understood perfectly that they preferred him not to. He went to see *E.T.* "You should see it," he told Mr. Gaines.

"I don't want to," said Mr. Gaines. Nothing physically unattractive interested him.

Of this summer's final group, Tim Leveridge and Chico had made the most progress. Tim was as accurate as a small machine, and Chico had developed a tight aggressive net game. The others, struggling mildly and enjoying it, at least held their own, trimming down major weaknesses.

But *l' affaire Arthur*, as Mr. Gaines found himself thinking of it, would not lie dormant. Jimmy complained, rolling his eyes, that Arthur had testified that Chico foot-faulted "at least four inches. Arthur would have measured it if he could."

"And does he? I hadn't noticed it."

"A bit, now and then," said Jimmy. "He's working on it so hard now he's way back of the line, and it's disrupting his service."

Chico came to see Mr. Gaines about his birthday. He wanted permission to have supper in town. "I can walk in," he said. He had, he said shyly, a date. Mr. Gaines gaped. It seemed a perfectly simple request; he just hadn't expected it. Where on earth, and when, had Chico gotten her?

Gleaming with anticipation, Chico stood across from him in a shaft of late afternoon sunlight, his racquet against his shoulder. It had been a gift from Father Cassidy and was not a very good one.

"Well," said Mr. Gaines. "I don't see why not. Where would you go? There's that seafood place . . ."

"Oh, I couldn't hack that," said Chico promptly. "The pizza parlor'll do us fine."

Feeling odious, Mr. Gaines said, "Do you mind telling me who your guest is?"

Chico for a moment stared. "My—oh," he said, "it's a girl works at Thompson's. Jenny Day. Is that okay?" he asked with sudden anxiety.

"Well, of course, why not?" (But she must be seventeen if she's a day, thought Mr. Gaines.)

There was a little pause. Chico looked at, into, Mr. Gaines's eyes; his small mobile face seemed, as it often did, lighted up.

"Hey, Mr. Gaines!" he said. "I really buy this place. You know? I really do."

Mr. Gaines was surprised by his own pleasure. "I'm glad you do." They both hesitated for a moment, then cautiously Mr. Gaines said in a noncommital tone, "How's it going with Arthur?"

Chico grinned at him. "I try not to bug him. I don't mean to. Arthur's a real solid citizen," said Chico. Seriously, or not?

Rising, Mr. Gaines said, "Right, Chico. I'll speak to Mr. Tufts. That overhead's coming on fine."

"See you!" said Chico and was gone.

Then, the next day at noon, Arthur came to Mr. Gaines and told him that Chico had stolen his watch.

He stood across the desk, a small triumphant smile in place. Mr. Gaines looked at him in silence. Then he said, "Sit down, Arthur."

Arthur sat down.

"Please answer me carefully," said Mr. Gaines. "Have you the slightest evidence of any kind for what you have just said?"

"My watch is gone," said Arthur.

"So your roommate must have taken it?"

"Who else would?" asked Arthur with real insolence. It was as though he had crossed a border.

Mr. Gaines looked at him. "You couldn't, of course, have lost it? You have done so several times, as I remember."

"When I did, I've always found it. Or someone else has," he added.

"But you have no reason to make this—this extraordinary charge except that you can't find your watch?"

"I had it yesterday, yesterday afternoon, before supper," said Arthur with an air of forbearance. "It's gone. I've looked, and I've asked everybody."

"Including your roommate?"

"Yes, sir. He said, 'Don't let it get you down.'"

"Arthur," said Mr. Gaines, "your watch has been found any number of times. You've been consistently careless with it."

"It's a piece of junk," said Arthur.

"That is not the point!" Mr. Gaines yelled. They both looked startled. "On one occasion, do you remember leaving it in the post office?" said Mr. Gaines in more subdued tones.

"I was going to set it," said Arthur, "after I posted my letters and looked at the clock."

"You realize, of course, that I will have to speak to Chico about this," said Mr. Gaines heavily. "It's a very serious accusation, and I can't ignore it. Though, really, I have no doubt whatsoever that you have made a mistake. Have you mentioned this to any of the boys?" he asked apprehensively.

For the first time, Arthur faltered. His blond face flushed.

"They're boobs, actually," he said. "I'm not the most popular person here, you know!" He threw this at Mr. Gaines, who lowered his eyes, acutely embarrassed.

"We'll talk about this later, Arthur. In the meantime, I—I'll have to make different arrangements."

Sheltered by good fortune, Mr. Gaines had not before in his professional life had anything as difficult for him as framing his opening sentence to Chico, poised, sweaty, and cheerful, across the desk.

A dive is a dive.

"Chico," he said, "this is very difficult for me to say to you, but you have the right to hear it. Arthur Sayles has made a very serious accusation."

Without anxiety, Chico looked at him.

"He can't find his watch—and he seems to think, for no reason that I could ascertain, that you might have taken it."

"Taken it?" Chico repeated. The blackberry shine of his eyes darkened. "He thinks I stole it?"

Mr. Gaines made a small unhappy sound in his throat.

A tiny smile lifted the corners of Chico's lips, less bitter than mocking. "Well, well, well," he said. "What do you know?"

It seemed to Mr. Gaines a different and mature reaction.

"Do I have to tell you I didn't?" he asked.

Struggling, Mr. Gaines said, "You wouldn't have to tell *me*, Chico. But you have to reply to a charge like this, yes. However outrageous you may find it."

"I—did—not—take—his" his lips shaped and abandoned an adjective, "his—watch." Then he looked away. "I guess Arthur thinks it figures," he said.

It was the first hint ever of what he might have been thinking. By now Mr. Gaines was so angry that he did not dare touch Chico, for fear of an emotional gesture. He did stand up and come around the desk. Chico waited.

"I'm moving Arthur tonight, Chico," he said. "Please try to remember that people sometimes say silly and offensive things when they are upset. Just try to put it completely out of your mind." His words sounded even sillier to him than they must have sounded to Chico.

"I'll work on that, sir," said Chico, deadpan. "Okay if I go now?"

By the next morning, and even without Jimmy's data, Mr. Gaines admitted to himself that some punishments did fit, or even exceed, the crime. Mr. Gaines's speculation as to what could be done to most impress Arthur with the heinousness of his conduct faded before the atmosphere that descended like a cloak of invisibility about Arthur. He might have been translated into the thinnest air.

Mr. Gaines reflected that had Arthur had even the basic chicken brain to confine his accusation to Mr. Gaines's ears—but Mr. Gaines knew well that Arthur could not, and never would, conceive that his cause was less than righteous, or that righteousness was not, in itself, lovable. Nothing would crack that or even mar it.

That night there was a full load for the movies. Mr. Gaines foresaw grimly that Arthur would take to algebra instead, and indeed the station wagon went off without him.

But before nine, at a tap on his door, Mr. Gaines found Arthur on the threshold. Unsympathetically, Mr. Gaines noted that he looked tired. His eyes, perhaps from having stared at a tennis ball all day and at algebra for another hour and a half, looked red.

"Could I speak to you for a minute, sir?"

It seemed to Mr. Gaines that he must have listened to Arthur saying that one thousand times.

"Come in," said Mr. Gaines with an effort at hospitality. He went back to his armchair, but Arthur did not sit down. Standing, he regarded Mr. Gaines with cool hostility.

"I just talked to my parents, sir," he said. "I told them I wanted to come home."

With mixed emotions, Mr. Gaines rallied to his duty. "I think you should think about that a little longer, Arthur," he said. "What you've said has caused a bit of a mess. But I think forgetting the whole thing would be helpful now. There's barely a week to go. You're doing excellently in your tennis, and now that you have a room to yourself, you'll be more relaxed. How's the algebra going?" he asked into Arthur's blue stare. Although professionally opposed to the idea that words existed for which there was no equivalent in one's own language, the verb *dévisager* now occurred to Mr. Gaines. It was as though his face was under actual attack.

"I'd prefer to go home, sir," said Arthur. "I've explained to my parents, and I think *they'd* prefer I didn't stay." Then, with a tiny sneer, he said, "There wouldn't be any need for a refund, you know. They're not interested in that."

Immediately on Arthur's departure, the weather took a curious turn. It might have been November, instead of nearly Labor Day. Sweaters were pulled over heads; at night trousers covered bare legs; there was a fire in the common room.

Though Mr. Gaines did not think often of Arthur, when he did it was with a small sinking. It was simply that, until now, no boy had ever left. Often he did worry that Chico might store this up as a cautionary experience; but he prayed that the instant and unanimous reaction of his fellows had taken care of any tendency to make a hateful little incident into some kind of moral.

On Chico's birthday, there was a cake at lunch; it was the only birthday of the summer. Jimmy was on final paperwork, and Mr. Gaines himself dropped Chico in town, though he repeated his willingness to walk. *E.T.* had finally reappeared, and Mr. Gaines, restless on the next-to-last night, fretted. It was a damp foggy evening; most of the boys were packing, and Mr. Gaines was feeling a curious depression, rooted in what, he could not imagine. He wasn't going to build a solitary fire; Jimmy was sealed up. In the end he went to the movie, getting in a bit late and nearly sitting in someone's lap.

As he had feared, Mr. Gaines found the picture cute. He planned to accuse Jimmy of faltering discrimination. When the lights blared up, stretching, he turned to see, far in the back, Chico and Jenny moving into the aisle. Even at this distance she looked very pretty in a red dirndl and an off-the-shoulder blouse; and Chico, a shade shorter, looked somehow older, as though his birthday had suddenly moved him up a notch.

In the aisle, Mr. Gaines was glad to be behind them; he felt instinctively that Chico would be embarrassed by triple amenities. Ten minutes from now, he and Chico would ride back through the fog, the autumnal night, for the last time. Mr. Gaines had a sudden attack of old age and winter, neither of which had arrived.

They inched up the aisle and scattered a bit in the foyer, Mr. Gaines hanging back. At the swing doors, Chico and Jenny halted. They discussed. Chico's left wrist flashed up and was lowered. He had consulted his watch.

Then the couple swung through the glass doors and turned left.

Mr. Gaines was disconcerted to discover that he was nauseated; it was as though the brightly lit pavement under the marquee was slightly, treacherously, heaving.

He picked Chico up as agreed at the parking lot. As Chico reached to close his door, his jacket sleeve—too short for him— disclosed his naked wrist. Close to Mr. Gaines, his profile was lit by pure pleasure.

"You know what? I really had a great night," he told Mr. Gaines, who did not reply. After a few comments on the movie, Chico shut up. One of his gifts was adaptability. The fog parted and streamed before their headlights.

Up the driveway, Mr. Gaines let Chico out at the door, but leaned after him. "When you go in, wait for me, Chico," he said, and in the door's light, the boy stared at him.

Walking back from the car, Mr. Gaines found he was breathing as after a wicked rally. Inside the door, Chico stood. There was a bench in the narrow hall, and Mr. Gaines sat on it. There was an instant's silence.

"Where's the watch, Chico?" Mr. Gaines said.

Chico's eyes widened a fraction; then, after what seemed a bottomless pause, to Mr. Gaines's consternation, they moistened. He said nothing.

"I wasn't spying," said Mr. Gaines as if defensively. "I was behind you coming out of the theater. I saw. I saw you look at your watch. Where is it now?"

Chico's hand went into his right pocket, came out with the watch, laid it on his left palm. The wristband glittered in the bulb's light. He looked expressionlessly at Mr. Gaines.

"You think it's Arthur's," he then said.

"I do," said Mr. Gaines, but not quite so breathlessly.

Again Chico waited, as though controlling—pain? fear? anger? Then he said, "It's not. It's mine."

Mr. Gaines continued to stare at him.

"I bought it yesterday. For my birthday. I bought it at Thurston's. They're cheap. As Arthur said," he added.

They were speaking softly, as though it had been a conspiracy.

"Why did you hide it?" asked Mr. Gaines. Looking at Chico's face, he was beginning to feel a sick sense of the approach of an awful guilt underpinned by joy.

"Because I felt funny about it after—after... Though I never thought you..."

A silence fell on them. As though Mr. Gaines were a stranger at whom he no longer cared to look, Chico lifted his eyes to the wall above the bench's back. He said impersonally, "My grandma gave me some cash when I came. For my birthday. Everybody had a watch. Those things at Thurston's were cheap. But then—it was like his. And I just didn't feel like flashing it around. That's not so tough to understand?" he suddenly, passionately, added. Then he permitted himself a short sentence. "You can ask them at Thurston's, you know."

Mr. Gaines got up. He did not touch Chico, but he forced himself to meet his eyes full on.

"I'm sorry," he said. "I'm sorry. It was your taking it off... I should have known better..." But as Chico did not move, he went down the hall and into his room, and at the click of his door, he had still heard no sound from the hall.

He switched on the light and went to the window, which was rattling a little in the wind. He stood there, looking out to the invisible courts, soon to be covered in drifts of leaves.

He said aloud, "Yes, I can ask at Thurston's." Then he added, "I could."

He switched off the light and lay down, still in his suit.

The Edge of the Sea

T HEY CAN HEAR the sea in the darkness near them; when the music stops, it turns out to be breathing there, with a soft rush and a brief silence, and another soft rush. It is quite near.

Caddy is sitting at a table close to the thatched wall, with Dan, and Lily, and Gina. Caddy is twenty. She is a junior at college, but she is here on a sort of vacation, because she has been ill—which is a fair enough way of describing it. She is not pretty, exactly, but a tide of charm flashes in her face, withdraws and leaves it pinched. She is a little too tall, and much too thin. She is the youngest of them.

Dan is her second cousin. He is twenty-nine, and he is on a real vacation. He is a man who is beautiful without embarrassment; his beauty is uncriticizable. He affects people as sunshine does in winter. Children, who hate and fear the ugly, love him, even from a distance. He is married to Lily.

Lily, a few years ago, was as beautiful as Dan, with something added. Eight years ago, she was beautiful in the way that fable has implied. Now she is just quite beautiful. She is thirty-two. Gina is her half sister.

In less dazzling company, Gina might seem beautiful. The half sisters' dead father has given them a ghost of resemblance, a high curve of eyebrow, a lower lip's push, and a characteristic movement of the hands. Gina's possible beauty will show as a little coarser, richer, riper, more vital. Intelligence is mixed with it, too, and it is quite empty of Lily's gentleness. Gina is getting over a divorce as Caddy is getting over a kind of illness. She is twenty-six.

To Caddy they all three look so beautiful as to embarrass her. As a couple, Dan and Lily look unreal. With Gina added, and the moon riding high, and the brass of the mariachi players alternating with the sea's breath, and the long thin elegant stalks of the three rosebuds, and the fact that they are in Acapulco, Caddy feels that they seem like one of those shameless advertisements in thirteen colors that invite either to sun, or sand, or sea, or to all three. But instead, she knows that they are simply beautiful, and good, beloved, and loving.

It is the night before their last day, before old snow and old schedules, and the disappearance of all three of them from Caddy into their own lives. They have saved her life, she believes, mostly by being themselves—by their ease, their golden ease.

Lily's brown long fingers hold her leggy rosebud—there is one for each of the ladies. The buds are red, still tight shut, but the very outside petals are curled over at the top, to show that they are about to loosen, to open, to reveal. The long, bamboolike stems are dethorned, powerful, slick; spraying fronds of leaves.

"But isn't it awfully far out?" Lily asks.

"No, I don't think so," says Dan. "Twenty miles, maybe. A piece of pie."

"Have you ever been there?" asks Gina.

"Never. Someone showed me a picture, an enormous beach, nearly empty."

"How long ago, nearly empty?" asks Caddy doubtfully, and then there is a tiny halt, as all three women think at the same instant that perhaps Dan saw the picture when he was here with Eloise.

"Oh, six or seven years," says Dan. "I think..." But they can't hear what he thinks as the mariachi throw back their heads and wail, and blow their bright trumpets, the clear brassy sorrow coming in on the end of the wail like a second wave, spreading clearly.

They are all a little in love with each other, their intimacy heated by the sun, refreshed by the tide, in a stunned satisfaction of margaritas, burned by *molé*, softened by wine. It is a circle, Caddy thinks, of just the few hours left, and she wants it never to be broken; but directly outside it lies her own jagged time to be picked up. And separations: Gina is going far away on a cruise, Dan and Lily back to Detroit.

Here is the check.

It is Gina's treat; and it is one evidence of their ease, of their loving ease, their lack of angular vulgarity, that they enjoy it, that no one minds, and rich Gina can treat and treat, and nothing is owed or balanced.

"Shall we have another drink?" asks Gina, dawdling, but they all say no, no, having reached the perfect pitch between the drunk and the sober.

For the second time the players launch *"Coo-coo-curoo"* on the air, the leader smiling, smiling at Dan, and they all sit, dreamily, as the bright swelling wave pours over them, until the final throb; and then all the chairs go back together, and in a jumble of smiles and sighs they move between the tables, and out over the hard sand, and jostle a little at the foot of the wooden steps.

Caddy slightly hangs back, and Dan laces his fingers in hers, and pulls her smiling up the steps beside him, beyond the pale rising heads of Lily and Gina. Caddy and Gina fall smiling into the back of the car, and it is only minutes later, curving up the cliff, that Caddy remembers the roses and shouts in dismay. But no one wants to go back for them, and Caddy wonders if they will be inherited, opening for people she has never seen.

Caddy has eaten so much, drunk so much, swum so much, that she falls into sleep as if it were a hole, and when she does wake up, though it is perfectly dark, she still knows instantly that it is a minute before dawn.

For months, she has been afraid of waking up at night, but now that the tide has turned, nothing closes over her. This is, at last, her depth, and she is not out of it.

A very faint breeze rocks the jalousie, not enough to stir the great pale scoops of the calla lilies on the bureau, in the wicker basket. Here too the sea breathes, but in its place. There is the edge of the sea, Caddy thinks, and there is the foam at the false edge. There is the invisible sand on which one walks out into the salt water; this is land, covered by the nets of the sea, the celestial chicken wire of light. But at a shifting moment, just somewhere, the foot cannot find the sand below, and the edge is crossed, the sea's edge, into the sea's power.

She understands the edge, she thinks; it is there for a bull fighter; for an artist; for a racing driver; for age, she supposes: the moment when the foot can no longer touch sand, when authority moves to the tide and the current.

She has crossed that edge, and floundered back. Eloise crossed it, and did not get back, did not wish to.

Caddy has not gotten back to the same place, however; she knows this. She wished to come back to where Jimmy had been, but he has moved, too, and she is carried in the opposite direction; and she cannot see how they should have moved back to their foothold.

The very light breeze has died, and a loud cock crows close at hand, and then another, and one more, far off. There is a diluted air to the darkness; and suddenly huaraches go slap slap on the pavement below the hotel, get louder, fade and pass.

Caddy gets out of bed and, barefoot, walks out on the balcony.

It is an inexpensive hotel. Dan and Lily haven't much money, and Caddy has added this trip to the expenses of college, so this is a good thing; also, that it is beyond the city. Pushed up and off, at the far end of the crescent, it looks over the bay, on which now the lights of sleeping boats still float and stir. The bay's indestructible curve is powerful and pure, and the ugly city is still under a tide of dark. Now Caddy can make out the spigot opposite, by the sidewalk, where on her first morning, watching like this from the balcony, she saw the Mexican girl wash her face, and pin up her hair, and fill her pail.

It is the beginning of their last day, and for the first time in a year, Caddy stands in absolute peace, accepting all conditions. It is as though the last faces, figures, words are sucked out with the tide of darkness, to the dark bay, to the sea that will be blue.

The facts are the landmarks that will not go; but the debris is gone, the heavy debris that the beach trucks scoop up if the tide does not; wrack, sodden, sunk into the iridescent sand, wedged; packed up by the sea's action and pried loose by the sea, bobbed and pushed by the highest arc of the tide. Facts are never unusual, they are always repetitious. Only Caddy is unique.

Caddy had a lover. He was a cheerful, active, sensible boy, without theories, radiating honesty. Caddy is neither, by nature, especially cheerful nor especially sensible. But then sensible can mean, also, responsive to stimuli. Caddy had kept looking at the pictures, or seeing them when she did not look. It seemed to her that the pictures followed her, were thrust at her from kiosks, from photographic displays in museums, from newspapers abandoned on sofas. Always the eyes had the same monotonous expression. They looked, from a disaster fresh and final, to nothing at all. Usually the bodies, fallen in odd attitudes, clutching babies, or a fragment of something, were bony, but not always. The bones were, in general, small because most of these seemed to be small people, but age and sex and gesture were blotted out by the identity of the eyes.

People get over obsessions, or often they do, Caddy knows that now; but that obsession, with the eyes, was a hard one. The eyes looked through everything, and everything they looked through came apart. Nothing held. So that the matter of truth got involved. When the eyes looked at people, at cosmetics, at billboards, at speedometers, at blackboards, these objects came apart like wet tissue. Caddy knew that in reality this was impossible. She decided she was sick, and she looked around for someone to help her. Obviously, it must be someone with whom she had not been previously familiar. She looked around, and there was Jimmy, out of the army, sound as an apple, seeing exactly what he looked at. They slept together with great affection and pleasure, and with no coordinated intention; first, in summer, somewhat precariously, and then whenever he could manage a New England weekend.

It was not that Jimmy did not understand about the eyes. He did. But he placed them, most intelligently, in a context of antiquity, in which they lost their appalling newness. They looked at him, whenever he happened to meet their gaze—and he did not avoid it—not just from the debris of villages, and smoking huts, and gun-raked streets, and dry land, but from the original caves of time. In a way what they lost in immediacy they gained in stature. It was as though they could keep on lasting, and that gave one some time. Jimmy was majoring in astronomy, which perhaps gave him patience.

Immediacy was what you could do that minute, in or out of bed. Caddy, finding something which did not shred apart, got on better, and they fell in love eventually. Perhaps that was what Jimmy's fondness and pleasure and Caddy's frantic grasp could be called. It must have been exhausting for Jimmy; and as luck would have it, there was already a girl in Baltimore with whom Jimmy had been on happy terms—a very pretty and cheerful girl, who was funny too; hours, by night and day, provided her with irresistible and perfectly valid occasions for hilarity. To her beautiful credit, the hilarity was contagious rather than jarring.

Nothing could have been less serious than this association, from which Jimmy intended to withdraw to more impersonal ground. He did, actually; but after one weekend with Caddy in which he still felt she saw something over his shoulder and was uncertain what he could do about it further, he temporarily relapsed with a sigh into Mary's laughter; and by a fluke, on a home weekend, this came to Caddy's attention. Her mind did not find it greatly significant; but having concentrated all permanence and all nonshreddable salvation in Jimmy's luckless shape, Caddy wrote Jimmy three affectionate lines, went into the family garage at 2:00 a.m., shut the door, climbed into the Pontiac, turned the passport key and, amid rakes, flashlights, kindling, and hoses, drifted away.

She couldn't have been less successful: missed, followed, rescued.

After that she spent some months talking and talking to a large kindly man with uneven eyebrows and a fatigued mouth, from whose professional understanding she defended herself with intelligence and agility, while Jimmy transferred to, and settled down in, San Fernando State University. When the doctor said she could go back to college, she said she could and would.

But there was some mutual hesitation, into which stepped a friend of the family whom Caddy admired and enjoyed, a very old lady, a widow named Mrs. Brounlow. Mrs. Brounlow, who had given Caddy formally her first cup of tea (and music box), thought Caddy should first take a holiday, and Caddy thought so too. In earlier years Mrs. Brounlow had been addicted to Mexico. Her great-niece, Lily, who had married Caddy's second cousin from far Detroit, was going to Acapulco. Why not also Caddy?

"Acapulco," said Mrs. Brounlow over her teapot, "is a disaster. But it is perhaps the most beautiful site in the world, and the sun never stops shining."

As a twelve-year-old, Caddy had been dazzled by Lily before she disappeared into Detroit. There was a gentleness, a lovely credulity about Lily which had nothing to do with stupidity. Benign is the word for Lily.

Caddy leans over the balcony. She is not thinking of all this; it is only there as a nugget of knowledge lodged in the memory. She has made a fool of herself, terrified her parents, annoyed the college, martyred Jimmy. To Caddy, her suicide attempt lacks all drama; it is only horrid to remember, shameful, like throwing up on a bus. She doesn't know if this is because of its failure. Eloise's shadowy exit seems quite different. In any case, she looks back on that year as a purging, a revolting purging.

Visibility has shifted through all the air; the lights go out, there and there. On the faintest apricot in the east, shadowy masts appear. The light continues to swell.

From Caddy's left, a girl comes down the abrupt hill of the street. She has a pail in her hand, and Caddy, delighted, sees it is the same girl she saw the first morning, the only other morning she has come out at such an hour onto the balcony. She decides the girl comes every day; so that Caddy knows in one leap a fact of a secret life. The girl is tall and moves victoriously, swinging the pail a little. When she puts it on the ground beside the spigot it turns out to be three pails, one within the other, which she sets at her feet. She turns the handle of the spigot, and in the dawn air Caddy can hear, just across the street, the water fall, making, finally, a long finger pointing and advancing down the street. The girl slips off her huaraches, cups water up over her legs, runs wet hands up her arms. She takes something from a pocket and begins to pin up her hair, across, across, behind, in a pile on top. Her hair safe, she bends down her face and raises it, dripping.

Caddy stares, ravished. This is the metaphor for the new last day: an early, fresh beginning. The girl starts to fill the pails, the largest first. Now she has all three full. With a quick swing one is on her head. Carefully, carefully, she raises one in each hand, her feet find her huaraches, she goes up the hill, straight, in a tide of confidence.

Caddy leans on the rail, trusting the day. In the next small room, Gina, red as a lobster with sunburn, is sleeping; across the hall, Caddy imagines Dan and Lily, tangled together in sleep. The threads of rescue go far back, she thinks. Lily frightened me when I first saw her. I was twelve. If that's how people can look, I thought, how ugly I am. But Lily's smile of utter trust—trust especially that you would be like her—promised Caddy honestly that she need not be afraid. Now Lily has brought Caddy into these days, healing without instruction. And Gina. And Dan. Had Dan ever needed to be healed too? It seemed impossible that he had ever needed anything. Even from the shadow of Eloise, unknown Eloise, forever clutching her empty vial.

Suddenly there is an arrow of sun across Caddy's hand.

At Recuerdo Beach there are no umbrellas for the sun, only a weather-frenzied thatch, supported by poles, with battered chairs beneath it. But the shade is the same. Planks are laid across the sand to walk on, but it is too early to need them. There is almost no one yet on the great beach (they came early, Dan said they must have a whole long day): a Mexican family with three children and a sand-colored dog, under the next shelter; the chair renter, in soiled white, with considering eyes under his frayed hat; and a small Mexican girl, in long skirts, her arms hung with necklaces of colored shells, trudging through the high loose sand. A long way behind them, a distant fence is fringed with palms, but whoever lives there has not come out yet. It is high tide.

Far out, the waves break; they are big ones. To the left, the beach curves around a headland and disappears; to the right, a long way down, are huge rocks, stranded. Dan says they must go down there and see the crabs.

"How do you know there are crabs?" says Gina.

"Dan always knows what there is before he sees it," says Lily, from the sand, her voice muffled by her huge hat. But also her asthma, which comes and goes, has been worse.

"They're appropriate," says Dan. "I believe in the appropriate."

Suddenly the neighboring children, who have disappeared, come plunging up the sand, plunging and screaming: *"Tiburónes! Tiburónes!"*

Everyone turns, looks, some jump up, but doubtfully. The children fall in the sand, coating their wet bodies. *"Tiburónes!"* they gurgle, pounding the sand in mirth. Angry looks greet them, and the fat man, their father, gives them a ritual shove each, but laughing too, he says loudly, *"No hay tiburónes!"*

"Fake shark alert," says Dan, grinning at his monolingual women.

A squat man, with his sombrero far back on his head and a guitar slung over his back, toils up the sand towards them.

"Canciónes?" he asks, bringing his guitar over his head in one swing.

" 'Coo-coo-cooru'?" says Dan.

"Si, si, cómo no!" says the man. He plays *"Rancho Grande."* *"Ai, ai, ai-ai."* Then he wipes his forehead and picks a chord and looks at them expectantly.

"Do you know *'Chapala'*?" asks Caddy with diffidence.

"Si," says the man with a rapid smile. He throws back his head. *"Espera un poco, un poquito más ..."* he sings. Well, it's really nicer than *"Chapala"* anyway, thinks Caddy.

They do not ask for anything else. Still reading, Gina fumbles with her left hand in her hanging bag, and the man says, *"Gracias, Señora, muchas gracias,"* and goes on to the Mexican family.

"No, no, no queremos nada," says the fat father, and the man turns down toward the firm dark sand nearer the sea and walks, slowly, away in the direction of the appropriate crabs.

There are a number of bathers now, mostly standing bemused

in shallow water as the waves' fringes rush around them. "Wouldn't you think they'd get *away* from each other," says Caddy. "All in a little group like that."

Finally they go to see the crabs, except Gina, who stays in the shade. She is reading *Under the Volcano* for the second time, and will only say to them, "The hands of Mano! The hands of Mano! *You* go look at the crabs."

In her red face her eyes are shining with excitement. Gina explores books as a conquistador explores a treasure chest. She is restless for treasure. The sunburn has made her look more than ever like ripe fruit.

Dan, standing, dusting sand, looks down at Gina, laughing. Caddy sees that in this light his eyes have exactly the sunlit quality of the sea. "What a greedy face you have, Gina!" he says.

But Gina only makes claws and repeats, "The hands of Mano!"

Now it is so hot they put on sneakers and huaraches to walk along the beach; the planks are only in a small area. The children from the next shelter are shouting and flipping in the dirty lace of foam. One looks up and says slyly, under his breath, *"Hay tiburónes!"* as they pass.

An enormous woman is sitting on the wet sand in a few inches of going-and-coming foam. A black bathing dress falls below her knees; it has small cap sleeves, from which huge arms descend to compact hands, peaceful on her thighs. From her massive Indian face, her bright small eyes look out to sea, un-blinking. Her gray hair is screwed neatly back by a tortoiseshell comb. She neither moves nor looks as they politely skirt her.

Here is the little girl, in the long green dress, with the shells over her arm. She stops them. "No, no," they say smiling; but she suddenly puts her soiled brown hand on Dan's arm and says something angrily in Spanish as they move ahead.

"What did she say?" asks Caddy, taken aback.

"She's outdone because we don't want any," says Dan.

Caddy looks over her shoulder, and the girl is staring after them, and Caddy turns back quickly. But it must happen all the time.

At last here are the rocks, from which the tide swings out with a sucking sound. It is in retreat. The rocks are an enormous jumble, great almost smooth slabs at the bottom, huge ones tossed on top, and a few poised at insecure-looking angles higher up. On the sea side, life pullulates on the soaked rock surface; their tide has just left them: tiny crustaceans, a green-gray, sharp-edged coating, minute breathers, and a sort of lucent moss. Great swags of seaweed have been stranded.

A limber veer at her foot makes Caddy jump. It is the appropriate manifesting itself. An enormous crab vanishes between slab and rock, into wet darkness. Now she sees, with a slightly tightening sensation, that the boulders are alive with crabs. Gross things, like overdeveloped spiders, sink, rise, veer; small, menaced-looking popeyed versions rear, fiddle, vanish. It is a community, older than the rocks themselves.

Dan sits on a boulder, stretching out his legs, crinkling his eyes against the light, and Lily sits just below him.

"I can't sit down," says Caddy, ashamed. "There are so many crabs!"

"They won't come near *you*," says Dan scornfully.

Caddy perches, rigid; the rock is warm.

Lily rather breathlessly says, "Oh oh oh it's so *hot*!" In the brilliance of the light, she looks stripped.

Dan smiles straight at her. "We'll go in a minute," he says, as to a child.

"From here?" says Lily.

"Why not?" says Dan. "It's a piece of pie."

They are silent, the consciousness of this last day, this particular salty sunny instant perhaps taking all three.

"Look!" says Lily. "Is it an eagle?"

There is a black speck high over the bluff beside them, very high in a blue so bright it is almost white to the eye.

"An eagle!" says Dan, laughing. "That's no eagle. That's a *zapilote*."

They look at him docilely, but before he can tell them, Caddy cries, "A vulture!"

The speck is circling, but moving behind the bluff, and as they stare up, it disappears.

"Did you see the three yesterday, sitting on the Chesterfield neon sign by the hotel?" says Caddy, beginning to laugh. The sun is making her dizzy.

"Oh for God's sake let's get in the water," says Dan, sweating

lightly, and he pulls Lily to her feet. They waver together, and
start down the rocks with caution.

"What am I supposed to do? Sit here and get sunstroke?"
calls Caddy, but Dan on the lowest slab calls back callously,
"You could always walk back!"

Lily kicks off her huaraches and starts to run, and Dan, hopping on one leg, struggles with a knot in his sneaker lace, cursing.

Lily plunges in a dolphin arc, and starts her strong stroke
straight out.

"Wait for me! Wait!" yells Dan, hopping, but of course with
the waves' roar, how can she hear him? With a wrench the
sneaker is off, and he shades his eyes, but Lily's head is already
gone into the dazzle of sea. Dan jumps down to the last slab,
then he too plunges.

Morosely, Caddy climbs down and gathers up the flung
huaraches and sneakers, putting them side by side. She does
not wish to stay with the crabs, and she starts back, with a
curious feeling of desertion. Men do not have to miss their last
day in the sea. It is just the golden mixture of Lily and Dan,
extended, warming her, and Gina, that she has loved; but now
up the baking beach she is alone. And it will be hard to remember
the inside of the circle of gaiety and love, as hard as to warm
herself by last year's fire. But, she says to herself, looking unseeingly at the huge unmoving figure of the Indian lady ahead, I
have seen that happiness exists.

She walks on, using the head of the big woman as a landmark,
and suddenly the head turns toward her as if listening.

Then she knows she has heard a shout, very faint, dispersed
on the waves and air. Now stronger, it is "Help! Help!"

It is Dan. Whirled about, screwing her eyes, glaring, she sees
his hand go up, plunge and go up.

She runs.

People run past her, the chair man, pounding on bare feet,
a young Mexican in white trunks running fast, and at the edge
of the rocks Gina catches her. The young Mexican, shouting to
someone behind him, has plunged in. She sees his arms flash
flash. Caddy runs into the water, Gina runs, Caddy begins to
swim, raising her head desperately for direction. Someone yanks

her shoulder, grabs her. It is the chair man. *"No, no, no! Demasiado peligroso!"* shouts the chair man, struggling for a foothold in his dripping clothes. Now she is held from behind: the fat father has miraculously arrived.

Beyond her in the glitter the young Mexican and Dan are gripped in a sort of furious embrace. The chair man struggles, peels off his clinging blouse, strokes out, his empty blouse hissing out behind him on the wave's suck. The embrace has broken. In the hard glitter Dan is dragged slowly, steadily, between four brown hands. He is sobbing in great plunging sobs. He tries to free himself, and they let him go and he falls to his knees in the froth of foam.

"Oh Jesus, oh Jesus," he says. "I couldn't get to her. I couldn't get there. I saw her go. I saw her go round the bluff. Oh Jesus. Why didn't you tell me?" he shouts at the young Mexican. "God damn it, why didn't you tell me?"

The young man looks at him with dignified pity. *"No puedo hablar inglés, Señor,"* he says. *"Usted mismo tiene mucha suerte. No se puede nunca nadar alla."*

As predicted, Lily shows up on the beach of the Indian fishing village five miles down the coast, at the following high tide. A number of people are there to meet her. Dan has tried to send Caddy and Gina back to the hotel, but they stay close to him, to each other. It is two of the fishermen, in a boat, who spot Lily. Back on shore, they lift her out carefully, and lay her on a blanket on the sand. Now she is wrapped in a coarse cloth like a sail, which the doctor replaces. He has come as a special favor to strangers; in the late afternoon heat he has on a string tie, a jacket, and a wide hat. Now Gina, her eyes puffed in her red face, is allowed near, and stoops to loosen the cloth, but the younger of the two policemen catches her elbow. *"No se debe mirar,"* he says in a soft voice. *"Los pesces . . ."*

Although she does not understand the words, Gina understands not to look under the cloth. Caddy has moved up. She looks down at Lily's small hulk and sees that she is wrack. Embedded in death, she is sodden, she is debris. Yet the bones under the cloth are familiar. The bones are familiar to Caddy. They are like the bones in the pictures. She can hear the doctor's low voice, saying in English what everyone has said, "not even the *clavistas* . . ."

It is Dan's face which is unrecognizable. It looks to Caddy older than the crabs' history, distant and cold. It is as though the sea still has him. The doctor is saying one more time, "There was nothing you could do, *Señor*. That someone reached you before you were further, you yourself are most fortunate. When the tide goes away, around the cliff, no one, not the *clavistas* of the Quebrada," he says, "could stay, could come in."

Caddy remembers the little groups, close together, far up the beach.

Dan has stopped saying "For Christ's sake why didn't someone tell us? Why isn't there a sign? Why . . ." It is a country beach. The sun is at an angle, it is almost four o'clock.

The group of children has been shooed away twice, but it follows them at a distance; but not to the ambulance at the edge of the sand. One boy holds a red kite with a long tail that trains.

Dan says roughly to Gina, "Can you drive? I'm going with . . . I'm going in that."

"Yes," says Gina, "I can drive." After the ambulance begins to move, she puts her bare foot on the accelerator, and they begin to follow. Through the open window Caddy sees the doctor, receding, raise his hat.

Caddy goes back to college. Her parents, terrified for her, wait for results. The early spring comes, all mud and pale skies.

Caddy works hard. In June she is on the dean's list. As if by common consent, she does not write Gina or Dan, and she does not hear from either. Gina does send a small snapshot taken by Dan: it is at La Roqueta, on their next-to-last day, on the day that ended with the beach restaurant, with the mariachi players, and the long-stemmed roses. Behind the three linked figures, laughing at Dan, can be seen a fat baby seated on a rebozo, and the head and feet of a small boy buried in the sand. Gina is leaning forward, and Lily, who in the picture looks older than Caddy is sure she looked, has a strand of Caddy's hair tugged in her fingers.

Jimmy will not be coming home for the summer; someone says he has a job in an observatory.

When Caddy gets home from college, she does, and does not, want to see Mrs. Brounlow. But Mrs. Brounlow has been very ill, ill for months, and cannot see her; she has two trained nurses, and when she cannot see her, Caddy realizes that she wants to sit in a room and speak to, and look at, Lily's great-aunt.

But it is mid-July before Mrs. Brounlow's nurse calls and says, yes, come, come over and see Mrs. Brounlow. Don't stay too long. Mrs. Brounlow says, come to tea.

Caddy's mother is afraid that seeing Mrs. Brounlow will upset Caddy, but Caddy will not be upset. She has a kind of steadiness, a serenity of sorts, a possession of experience, of herself.

The ferocious sun is shut out of Mrs. Brounlow's rose-and-gray living room. She is still a large old lady, but she seems to have become hollow. Her skin, mottled lightly with brown spots, seems stretched over hollowness. Her thin white hair is softly brushed, and shines, and her hands, lifting the bright bumpy repoussé teapot, have authority; precarious, but present.

Carefully, Mrs. Brounlow has said nothing about Mexico; but Caddy, on her second cup, says suddenly, "Mrs. Brounlow, I can never tell you how glad I am you sent me. How glad. No matter what. How glad I am."

Mrs. Brounlow puts down the milk pitcher and folds her hands. "Have you heard from Gina?" she asks now.

"No. No," says Caddy. "We . . . we waited. We didn't write."

"Then perhaps you didn't know . . . Did you know that Gina and Dan have married?"

Neither of them says anything for a while after that. Mrs. Brounlow swallows tea, sets down her cup.

Finally Caddy blurts, "I'm glad. I'm glad." She has no idea if this is true. "When?" she says.

"Just last week," Mrs. Brounlow says. "I had a note from Gina. They were just leaving Ischia."

"I'm glad," says Caddy. There is a buzzing sound around her head. But suddenly she knows that she means it, in a painful, chaotic way. It is as though Lily has drawn her back into the circle. The Mexican girl comes into her mind, the thinning dark, the finger of water reaching down the street, the early morning strength of the girl's walk. The beginning of a day.

"I would like to see Mexico again," says Mrs. Brounlow. It is as

remote, as without the hope of intention, as though she spoke of
Ur. Now Caddy is glad that Mrs. Brounlow thinks Lily died of a
heart attack brought on by asthma. But why, why, she had cried
to her parents, it's not true, why can't she know the way it was?

"Because the way it was was horrible," said her mother crisply,
"and Mrs. Brounlow is too old and too sick, and she loved Lily
very much."

"Mexico is very beautiful," says Mrs. Brounlow again, without
complaint. As she says this, Caddy sees Dan, smiling down at
Gina, dusting the sand from his arms.

"Dan is the most beautiful man I have ever seen," says Caddy
to Mrs. Brounlow, who has never called a man beautiful. Mrs.
Brounlow looks at Caddy and says doubtfully, "Was he so
beautiful?"

"Oh yes," says Caddy.

Mrs. Brounlow gets slowly up; it is an accomplishment. She
looks down at her feet, settled on the floor. Moving them, she
goes heavily over to the knobby desk, opens the top drawer,
pokes about, then lifts out a red leather album. Dr. Brounlow
taught Dan at Johns Hopkins.

Mrs. Brounlow comes back slowly, as though on a deck, and
sits down with a little pant. She opens the album, sorts over
plastic-sheathed leaves, finds one, and Caddy sets down her
cup and comes and stands beside her. They look together at a
picture of four people: an old gentleman whom Caddy recognizes
vaguely as Dr. Brounlow, two strange women, and flanking
them at the other end from Dr. Brounlow, Dan. His arms are
folded lightly before him. He looks at once so young, and so
familiar, that Caddy makes a little sound.

"When was that taken?" she asks, leaning.

"Oh, long ago," says Mrs. Brounlow. "Eight years? Nine
years? Before he and Lily got married. Long ago, when I was in
Mexico." It is so long ago, Caddy sees, because it is sealed away.

Caddy watches her shut Mexico into the red album, which
she lays on the floor beside her soft black shoes. Shut out also
from that permanent sunlight, Caddy says, "Where were you,
all of you?"

"That was the winter we had our cottage near Acapulco," says

Mrs. Brounlow. "It was a hot winter there. Dan came, and stayed two weeks. Eloise hadn't been dead very long. He used to take walks, walks, even at night. He looked better, I remember, when he left. He was very handsome. But beautiful . . . ?"

Yes, Mexico is beautiful, Caddy thinks, and it all falls over her: the slick leggy rosebuds, the children crying *"Tiburónes!"*, Dan's fingers laced in hers, pulling her up the gritty steps.

"Where was your cottage?" asks Caddy. "Was the picture taken there?"

"Yes. We had a little cottage, very simple, and quite far out. At Recuerdo Beach."

There is an absolute silence around Caddy, a stillness like a wave's arrest. Then she says, "But Dan couldn't have been there!"

"Why not?" says Mrs. Brounlow, surprised.

"Because—" says Caddy, "because—I just don't know," she says.

The wave breaks, and in its splinters she thinks, I will call, I will go, I will go to Gina and tell her, I will go . . .

But they are married, and the tea is at the rim of the cup, and she does not know where they are, or who they are, and the tiny figures recede, the crabs run. Lily strokes straight out, the little shell girl scowls, watching them move toward the rocks, Dan wrenches at his sneakers, the teacup is full, she starts alone up the beach, here is her cup, the huge woman turns her head.

"There," says Mrs. Brounlow handling carefully the empty cup that Caddy sets down. "I'm glad you still drink tea." Over the empty cup she smiles at Caddy. "I don't think I shall get to Mexico again," she says.

The Gesture

T HE SUN ON THE BALCONY, even under the largest of the parasols, was like a stoked furnace.

Guests, emerging from the cool cavern of the big room, all bare floor and beige wicker, blinked and murmured, clicking the ice in their drinks, pushing on dark glasses. Most of them had retreated. Anabel, inured to that sun by hours over her sketch pad, leaned on the cement balustrade, which was hot under her bare arms. Beyond the sea wall, the Caribbean glared and glittered.

Still the speeches were going on. A very tall, very thin man, bright with sweat, lifted his harangue in a singsong rhythm. The square full of dark faces, turned like sunflowers, churned with motion. People shoved through, pushed their way to a friend, left the fringes, came and rose on their toes to try to see.

Anabel and Mr. Hothboy were the only people from The Plumbago at the party, and Mr. Hothboy, after one comprehensive look from the balcony, had retired with his planter's punch into the dim interior, where he was talking to a stout, mahogany-colored man in gold-rimmed glasses, the assistant manager of Barclay's Bank. Invited, the Partridges had just said succinctly, in the person of Mrs. Partridge, "No. No."

"But you usually like that party," said Mr. Hothboy, good-humoredly.

"Not with the whole island of Boudina milling in the streets," said Mrs. Partridge, in her low, bird-clear syllables, looking over the early lawn at Ezekiel, shifting the sprinkler. "Imagine getting there. And leaving."

But Mr. Hothboy had been ept: Amos, in the Inn station wagon, had deposited them a block from the big house, where they were allowed to walk down a street cordoned off to cars; and now they would soon be going, from the back door to the back door of another garden, into a side street.

Only Mr. Singh had been apprehensive about the afternoon, the crowd, the speeches. "It is a very fine time to stay out here," he had said strongly, at breakfast. He pushed his coffee cup a little away. "You do not know. You cannot tell. We are, after all, strangers."

This in itself was a strange statement. Mr. Singh had lived in Boudina for eleven years, traveling from its vantage point to other islands on his business; Mr. Hothboy, for seven. Nor was "we" a true inclusive. Mr. Singh, and Mr. Hothboy, and Mr. and Mrs. Partridge, and Anabel were no more "we" than they and the crowd seething below were "we."

"Mr. Singh," said Mr. Hothboy pleasantly, as became the Inn's owner, "I thought you understood that all this is an internal problem. It's economic. It has nothing to do with 'strangers.' With nationalities. Or race," he added, with a touch of reproof.

Skeptical from antiquity, Mr. Singh pulled his coffee cup back and took a tepid swallow.

"With crowds," he said, "you do not know what the next minute will have to do with. We are strangers."

When he went off to pack his suitcase for Grenada, Mr. Hothboy and the Partridges exchanged glances. The Partridges and Mr. Hothboy, emanating respectively from Surrey and Kansas, each made different allowances—the former for an expected taint of barbarism, the latter for the occasional touchiness of Empire declined. Their minds conversed in an ethical esperanto.

Anabel, not long ago from Philadelphia, had established herself in the Partridge's international experience as a sport, genetically speaking. She had referred, over last Sunday's drinks, to the Mad Hatter. The Partridges stared at each other, too confounded for tact.

"The Mad *Hatter*?" repeated Mr. Partridge, stupefied.

"Well," said Anabel, taken aback, "You know . . . 'no room, no room!'"

But Mr. Partridge was exalted. "My dear," he cried to the speechless Mrs. Partridge, in a transatlantic glow, "Mrs. Avon is familiar with the Mad *Hatter*!"

Anabel said very crossly, "That's not really unusual, you know."

But Mr. Partridge would have none of this false self-abasement. From America, like a rare planet in the surrounding fog, she shone.

Now, sun-dazed on the balcony, Anabel wondered if she wanted to go in for another drink. Suddenly a roar went up below, and immediately half a dozen guests emerged, drinks in hand, to see. Down in the square, the mass heaved closer together; the tall man had jumped down from his Coca-Cola box.

Two policemen, natty in red-striped trousers and white gloves, shoved and pushed amicably, trying to clear passage on the narrow sidewalk. That must be the end of the meeting. Had they decided on the strike? No one knew. Beneath the figures now lining the balustrade, the crowd milled and tunnelled. Anabel caught a glimpse of Ezekiel's squat figure. He had on a red shirt with a white heart on it, and a sailor's cap. Then she lost him in the crowd.

At that moment, directly below Anabel, there was the faintest high tinkle and a woman screamed. Anabel saw her, frozen in an attitude of angry shock—a baby on her shoulder had a thin red line down its cheek. A glass, a glass from high up, had smashed on the sea wall and flung up a splinter.

For an instant it was like an exchange—the woman's hand, curved by her baby's cheek, arrested. Anabel could see her eyes, fixed on a hostile and threatening line, up and into the leaning faces; directly, it seemed to her, into her own gaze.

"My God!" said someone behind her, "That was close!"

A swelling murmur rose; the two police bored through the crowd, staring up.

"Glad I've got *my* glass right here in my hand," said Mr. Hothboy's cheerful Kansas in Anabel's ear. In a quick, almost furtive glance, Anabel saw hands clasped around their drinks. The woman had not moved her hand, nor her eyes, starkly trained upon them.

The taller policeman, shouldered to the woman's side, stared up, shading his eyes.

"Who did it?" he shouted.

No one had seen.

"No one see it? No one at-tall see it?" the policeman shouted, in angry skepticism.

"I think it came from lower, the next balcony down," said a woman in yellow, peering over the balustrade. "What an awful idiot thing to do!"

"Where's *your* glass?" asked Mr. Hothboy's flat friendly voice of Anabel. "I wouldn't be in your place!" He leaned alongside of her in perspiring jocularity. But seeing her face, he pushed up off his elbows. "Oh come *on*, Mrs. Avon," he said, shaking his head. "Don't look so tragic. Nothing happened, really."

"It nearly did. It did. The baby had a cut."

"So! No one see!" shouted the policeman. He swept the balcony with his truculent gaze, but the urgency was gone. The woman, in a tight cluster of bodies, moved away, down the square, a handkerchief, or something white, pressed to the baby's cheek.

The whole crowd was loosening; gaps appeared. Somewhere off the square, faintly, a steel band started up.

"*That's* an old tune," said Mr. Hothboy. "Well, I guess we might as well . . . where's our host?" And he plunged ahead of her into the cool gloom singing softly,

> And everyone call she
> Ma-dame *Drac*-u-la. . . .

As they went through the garden, still raw with the flare of ixora and poinsettia, Anabel said, "That's what Mr. Singh meant, I suppose. 'With crowds you don't know . . .' How did he say it?"

"Oh sure, sure," said Mr. Hothboy, rather impatiently. "It *could* have been nasty. If the baby—or the woman—had really been hurt. . . ."

"But maybe it was. The baby. I could *see* blood."

"Believe me," said Mr. Hothboy, shoving her gently ahead of him through the iron gateway into the side street, "we'd have seen something then. It was a scratch. And by now, nobody believes the glass was thrown. Some damn fool with too much rum had sweaty fingers. *There's* Amos."

But that night Anabel woke from the flash of raw sun, pouring down into the blast of eyes fixed in infinite accusation. She realized very clearly that, had Boudina not been Boudina, Mr. Singh's apprehensiveness might have proved wisdom.

Her feeling about Boudina was strong; she just might come to live here. But immediately the thought of living anywhere, of putting the injured nerve ends back into the stuff of commitment, set her back on her heels. At the moment, the essence of painlessness was still detachment. She was grateful to the gently alcoholic drifter who had sent her here. "The Plumbago's too small for me, you know—they can't help keeping track of you. But they don't *try*. Hothboy's strange—I don't know *what* he thinks. He keeps his head down, and he's friendly. The Boudinians seem to like him. *He* likes the Boudinians. Which is the point, I mean. Try it."

Now for three weeks she had tried it, coming thankfully in the off-season when it didn't cost a worrying amount, and staring vaguely, as she bicycled about with her sketch pad in her basket, at small cheap-looking pastel-colored houses, wondering how much they would cost and if she could possibly live here.

Other people got divorced with brio, with upper lips of undefeated stiffness, or noisy and relaxing vengeance; indeed, it seemed to her that most of the women of her own age whom she knew, had been divorced. She had behaved in the least acceptable—to herself—of manners, repeating scenes like a stuck projector, tearing up promising sketches, still having violent fits of weeping in the smallest hours.

Now, pressing heavily on the prospect of her first one-woman show, on her response to Boudina, she supposed that she was coming round. She slept better, in spite of the ghastly courtings of an itinerant cat below her window; and the island, dazed and dazzling by day, spice-ridden and intimate by night, lifted her up like the whisper of good news.

The Plumbago was just right. The only real hotels, two on the other side of Porte Lucie, she had not even seen. There was another inn, the Morne Jaune, run by a lustrous Boudinian beauty, and some rather tatty-looking guest houses scattered here and there over this less desirable section of the island. Next month The Plumbago would be full, mostly with refugees from an English winter; twenty sun-starved faces, turning to a more decent coloring slowly, slowly, on the distant swooning curve of the beach.

Anabel did not go to the beach often, walking instead over the short grass iridescent from Ezekiel's sprinkler, down the slope to the slippery rocks and coral of the sea's edge. In the old sneakers earnestly recommended by Mr. Hothboy, she minced out, propping her palms on bearded stones until she could cast herself into the salt blueness that climbed the huddle of rocks in little washes, or retreated to leave plum-black sand, sopped with prostrate seaweed.

Sometimes she and Mr. Singh fed the fish, saving perhaps a whole piece of breakfast toast, which vanished in a violent flush of darting bodies, wavering like light-strokes; colors, shapes, sizes too quick to be properly seen; there, wherever a crumb was flung.

"No birds are that quick," she said to Mr. Singh.

"Fish are very quick," he agreed seriously. "Even the big ones."

"You mean sharks?"

"Many big fish. Sharks never come in here."

"I saw a fin one day, out by the Point. Twice, actually."

"It is easy to think you see fins, in the bright sun," said Mr. Singh. He was by nature and experience a skeptic.

Although it was not what she looked at that she drew, so far she had sketched mostly in two places. One was her small balcony, which faced slantingly out over the coastline, and directly, though distantly, on an accidental pool, trapped by roots and rocks. Here children came, naked, or in ragged underpants, or in trunks, yelling faintly, sailing driftwood, sometimes retreating in a rage to throw sand at fellow swimmers. In the very early morning, when she took her thermos of coffee into the pale light from which the island, dark and gleaming, later emerged, she would see a man who came to bathe. He wore some sort of trunks. These he removed and washed. Then he washed himself. She could not see the water, cupped in his hands and streaming over his body, but she could see the gesture, the gesture of raising, and pouring, and laving. It was like a rite, distant, dignified, renewing.

The second good place was the Point. It was hot there, on the spiky growth of coarse grass, wild herbs, stubble, pebbles, and usually she went in the late afternoon. But the view, less conventionally tropical than anciently and durably shaped and cut—headland, blank and dazzling sea, the tip of the lighthouse, and far away, the clear first white of the beach—drew her back. She was obsessed with gestures, and each of these made its own, translated as a line, a blocking out of space, an arrested motion. She found that its magnetism was as much the isolation as the view—the smell of dusty sun and some crushed aromatic plant; the pulse in a lizard's throat; the shield of light on the water, that corroded to bronze, to copper, to lilac as the sun focused itself into a huge ball, round as a blood orange, touched the sea's rim in one sensual gesture and slid—slid actually as the eye watched—below the world.

It had been by a gesture that she knew her marriage was ended; in response to words, a small, final movement of the hand. It flicked on her screen, flicked on her screen, flicked, when she tried to move on to other gestures, other words, which she herself might make or speak.

Gestures were the real language, the ancient one. The sculptor, the dancer, the priest understood this. Actions, too, were gestures, deeper, simpler, than they seemed. On the spiky grass of the Point, her sketch pad baking on a stone, she sat in a pose of arrestment, in itself, she knew, a gesture of fatigue, not yet even a gesture of waiting.

Here the breathless Caribbean afternoons were motionless. When lizards came they thrust their antique profiles on the air. The cliff, stretching in each direction sheer and sharp, was too high for her to see any passage under the brilliant surface directly below. Now and then a distant sailboat shivered over the glare, or a white steamer inched along the horizon; and once a school of flying fish, pursued by some invisible hunter, leaped into an arc of sun and spray as though their terror were exuberance. Almost nothing ever seemed to pass on the dust path a hundred yards away, though if she were late, once or twice she would see Ezekiel, pedaling home.

She was convinced that Ezekiel hated her.

This conviction was so bizarre, so unlike her own mind, that she felt it must be the projection of some submarine guilt, some shame or inadequacy under the surface. But there it was.

Ezekiel was The Plumbago's gardener. He was broad, and rather squat, with a wistful, stupid, wide face, and anxious eyes. He spoke the rich rhythm of Boudina, but he was American, Mr. Hothboy said. At least, his parents were Americans, come finally to live in Boudina; and Ezekiel had left The Plumbago to return to the country from which he had come as a child. For four years he had saved his pay; and then he had said goodbye, for good, to Mr. Hothboy and gone away on a freighter, to Trinidad, and then to New York. He had stayed there, or somewhere, for almost two years. Then one day he had turned up at the kitchen door of The Plumbago, asking for Mr. Hothboy. During Ezekiel's absence he had been replaced by a series of teen-age boys, random and inexpert, and Mr. Hothboy, a little unfairly, had promptly demoted the incumbent to fish-cleaning and car-washing. Ezekiel never mentioned anything whatsoever about his stay in the United States, not even to answer questions. But Mr. Hothboy was not a great questioner.

"There's something strange about Ezekiel, isn't there?" Anabel boldly suggested to Mr. Hothboy after her first two weeks.

"How?" he said, looking at her a little cautiously.

"I don't know. A sort of, a sort of *general* hostility. Not to me," she hastily added, though she did not believe this. "Like a conversation with himself."

"Yes," said Mr. Hothboy, propping his blue sneakers against the white wrought-iron railing of the little pavilion. They stared through its rigid network to the deep lilac of the sea. "I know what you mean."

It was nearly time for drinks. Ezekiel, going up the soaked concrete path between the hibiscus bushes, bound for his bicycle and home, had set Anabel off.

"He was different, a little, before he went to the States." Anabel heard the distance from that locale in Mr. Hothboy's voice; it was as though he pronounced "Cathay" or "Nome." "Not *that* different. I mean, he always seemed to be turning something *over*, you know. But it was more like, oh, eagerness."

"Did he have a bad time, do you suppose?" asked Anabel. "He might have."

"He might have," agreed Mr. Hothboy, without much speculation. "He was always death on being an American—it gave some of the Boudinians a pain."

Anabel looked at Mr. Hothboy, his head against a red cushion, his leather-brown sockless legs pushing the white iron. She realized just then that she and Ezekiel were the only Americans The Plumbago had to offer. Kansas and all, Mr. Hothboy was transplanted, for good.

Well, she thought confusedly, Ezekiel and I should do better than we're doing—we're both refugees of, and from, one place. She started to try to describe to Mr. Hothboy Ezekiel's expression when he looked at her, but she thought that might get him into trouble with Mr. Hothboy (though she doubted that), and anyway, at that moment, they were joined by Mr. Singh. He never drank with them, or without them, as far as she could see; but he stopped by often, in these minutes distempered by rich and flowing colors, to watch the sun touch the water.

The swallows were here. Soon the bats would hunt, swift as swallows, but elliptical and wider. The tide was out; there was no sound at all. Over the sea, nothing moved.

"How still the sea is," said Anabel, watching the swallows' interlacing dart.

"There are many things alive in the sea," said Mr. Singh, as one imparting information. Anabel, who had fed the fish with him, stared. He saw her and said quickly, "They are moving down there now, just as they rush on the surface when we feed them. Many beautiful things, under the surface. Ugly, too. But all hungry."

"But so are the things in the air," said Anabel argumentatively. "Bats. Birds."

"Yes," said Mr. Singh. "Cousins. But the birds sing, and make nests. Their temperature is high as fever. Their blood is warm. The sea-things are cold. You would not think appetite could be so high, and blood so cold. Don't you think it is strange?"

Anabel had not particularly thought so. Now she visualized her toast crumbs, the demented maze and flicker of hunger.

"All that stuff about sharks," said Mr. Hothboy, looking rather derisively at Mr. Singh. "When the boys dive for lobster—what we *call* lobster—they hit the sharks on the nose, and they go away. The sharks."

"Those are the small sharks," said Mr. Singh severely. "No big ones near the shore. Further out."

As the Partridges came down the path, Amos, transmogrified and white-coated, slipped behind the little bar, with a red ice bucket.

"If there's no blood," said Mr. Hothboy, removing his sneakers from the railing and pushing himself upright, "the sharks really aren't interested." He raised a hand, and a clear flute note of "Good evening" reached them. Mr. Singh looked mutinous. He was going, anyway. But, "Hunger is very important," he said portentously before he left. Then he went up the path, bowing to the Partridges as he passed. The Partridges smiled at him, with the courteous, switched-on brightness of the experienced.

Then Ezekiel stopped looking at her, altogether. Her painter's eye had noticed it at once, probably, but she did not think about it until, a day or so after the strike meeting, she met him head on, by the water tap on the lawn. He had bent over to turn on the hose, and raising up, his face was brought within a yard of hers. He put his eyes on his shoes, the toes swollen from moisture.

"Good morning," she said.

In inescapable response, he made a low sound in his throat.

Why on earth do I *care*, thought Anabel. Mordecai at the gate. But she stayed where she was.

"That's not our cat, is it?" she asked, staring at his lowered lids. "The big ginger one, that makes that awful noise every night now. Right under my balcony," she added, to the silence.

He raised his eyes over her head, to the lower branches of the soursop tree. After a while he said, "No. That cat is come from somewhere."

Suddenly Anabel felt tired. "Well, I wish it would go back away," she said, and went past him.

Should she actually look for a house? She had a harried feeling that before her return, or visit, or whatever it was going to be, to New York, for her show, she would like to strike down a taproot. But did one grow on command? Mr. Hothboy had accomplished it. He liked Boudina, with an undemanding and relaxed appreciation. Most of his friends were Boudinians; and she had caught, in his bland blue eye, a sort of amiable derision for the discrete quality of Mr. Singh, and the Partridges, habitués in sanitary suits. He was, she saw, internally more patient with wide-eyed ignoramuses, askers of naive and preposterous questions, than with those who gave the air of "managing" their relationship with an island they "understood." Mr. Hothboy did not profess to understand anything, or indeed that there was anything in special terms to understand, other than getting from day to day as the island offered; though he was endlessly knowledgeable about customs, habits, tastes, the shaky present and the blood-soaked past. He loved, in an unpossessive way, the small island, its smells, its contours, and voices. Did she? Could she, in that way? She doubted she was cut for it. What *did* she now enjoy?

At the moment, she seemed to love absolutely nothing—not the marvelous shifts of the sea; not her work; not—she almost said, held back by shame of melodrama—her life. But was she, in her last two weeks, going to, or not going to, make a move?

Perhaps her bizarre obsession that she was an object of acute aversion to The Plumbago's gardener, was the reddest and oddest of herrings, used to divert her from reality. But she knew that she was right: she represented something to Ezekiel, and whatever it was, gave them a strange sort of intimacy—that of hostility, so weirdly comparable to its opposite; a word, a gesture, was noticed. She was conscious of his back, bent over the

herb bed, of his hands tying tough pink hairy cord about the
sprawling young hibiscus; and he, of her afternoon reappear-
ance, when she came home early, disheartened, pushing her
bicycle behind the variated hibiscus, to its resting place. But this
relationship, this now undeniable relationship, had been honestly obvious to her only in recent days.

In a burst of guesswork, she wanted to ask Mr. Hothboy if
Ezekiel could hate her because they were Americans. But the
verb was embarrassing, and he had never responded to her first
blurted-out statement. She did, truthfully, not want to make
trouble, least of all trouble fabricated out of no speech or action.
Finally, one night at the foot of the curving concrete steps that led
up to her room, as she was about to say good night, she did ask
Mr. Hothboy, "Do you get many Americans here, in the season?"

Mr. Hothboy considered this, as though wondering what sum
was many. "A few," he said. "Not so many. They're a bit more
luxurious, in general. Mostly English. Things are a bit tight for
them, at the moment." He reflected. "You're the first American
this year."

That night the cat returned. Uncompleted, his affairs renewed
themselves in yowls like drawn-out pain. They burst forth,
hushed, burst out again. Anabel, burrowing, tried to laugh. It's
Ezekiel. He's a werecat. But no. The cat was all for love.

It was early the next morning, as she was drinking coffee on
the little balcony, watching the distant bather, stooping, rising,
vanishing into the sea, climbing back over the far rocks, that
she decided she would try it. She would *rent* a house. For a year
and a day. And just see.

Resolved, she swallowed a final mouthful of now tepid coffee.
She shook the thermos. Yes, there was a little more, possibly
hot. With her habitual gesture, she shot the cool coffee over the
concrete rail into the invisible growth below. But the handle
skidded from her fingers, and the cup flew away too, disappearing silently into the green tangle. It didn't make a sound; it just
disappeared. Annoyed, she went in and found a glass. She
tipped the thermos, for about a tablespoonful of coffee; it was
now only a little warmer than that in the cup whose flight had
left a sprinkle of drops on the balcony's ledge.

Dressing, she decided to ask Mr. Hothboy for concrete suggestions on a house—concrete, she thought rather glumly, being the *mot juste*. As she pulled on her jersey, there was a single knock on her door.

She went over and opened it. Ezekiel was there. In his right hand he had a coffee cup; earth was clotted on its brim and there was a green stain on its curve.

His eyes, this time, looked straight at her and she saw that now his dim strong face was not expressionless. It was inner-lit by some triumph.

"I find your cup," he said.

Uncertainly, she stretched out her hand. But he did not hand her the cup.

"Your cup," he repeated. "Your coffee cup that you did throw at that cat."

She gaped at him.

"What cat? Oh! *That* cat. But I didn't throw it."

He looked at her.

"It did not come close," he said. "That cat is very, very quick."

She wanted to laugh, but not very much. She reached out her fingers for the cup, but his retained it. She would not pull. The conversation was insane.

"Well," she said, mustering hauteur, "give the cup to the cook. I don't want it. I was throwing out cold coffee, and it slipped," she then heard herself explain.

He still looked at her, almost in collaboration, as though together they had solved a nagging problem with finality.

"That cat is very, very quick," said Ezekiel. "*He* can move, of heself. No one carry *he*."

Anabel shut the door. There was no sound at all for a moment or two, and then Ezekiel's steps went down the concrete stairs. Through the window, she saw him steadily carrying the cup to the kitchen door.

She sat flat down, the connection made. Ezekiel had been carrying at the center of his attention the glass flung or dropped from the balcony the day of the party. It had expressed, in a perfect gesture, a scorn and hatred looking for its body. He had believed it, cherished it; but only now, by the fey logic of the obsessed, did he have his proof. At a cat, at a baby, the betraying gesture of the evil heart, the embodiment of something he had already come to know.

She saw the woman's deep accusing glance. She had forgotten the entire episode. Here there was friendliness everywhere. For all its staggering economy, and the tensions boiling in neighboring islands, Boudina was the green heart of all sanity. She was dealing with a madman. No; not really. A searcher for some distorted face of justice, of gentleness; against the launchers from heights, the viciously arrogant.

It suddenly made the concrete house impossible. She understood perfectly that this was reasoning as perverse as Ezekiel's own. Of what possible difference could the warped vision of Mr. Hothboy's self-exiled American gardener make to her separate, part-time life in Boudina? It made a difference. Like a sharp pebble in a shoe, a faint bitterness on the tongue.

Well, she would go no earlier, and stay no later, than her last two weeks. Ezekiel was neither the army, nor the law. As he well knew.

Whatever he was avenging, would go unavenged through her. And yet he did have a kind of vengeance, after all—on her work. She felt an ardent urge to pack up her paint, her rags, her brushes, her palette, to make no statement, extract from herself no intuition. She would lie in the chaise longue, under the soursop tree, and stare up through its massive foliage, finding out its fruit. She would feed the sea's ravenous denizens, with Mr. Singh. She would exchange accents with the Partridges. As soon as the fifth sketch was finished. When she bicycled off to the Point, after her long nap, she was resolved, and already light, disengaged of work, of house, of, indeed, Boudina.

She did finish, too. The fifth and final sketch should have filled her, as usual, with the peace of sated energy. Instead, she was heavy and tired.

She sat with her back to the ruined tree, to the goats, to the face of landscape that confronted the sea, and faced instead out over the water, still a blind dazzle, but deeper in color, ready to turn to the Caribbean evening. The sun was low, not yet contracted into its huge ball, but beginning to concentrate itself, lower itself, over this speck floating on the busy depths of the sea.

Facing out like this, she did not hear Ezekiel at all. His shadow was behind him, and his feet were bare, so there had been no sight or sound. He had her wrists before her breath came again. A band of tough pink cord locked them behind her back.

He stood up and she looked at him, he was between her and the distant path, the empty landscape. There was no one any-where. Only the goats moved, shifting ahead.

He had on the soiled red shirt; his machete hung against the stiff blue cloth of his earth-stained trousers.

The settled loathing on his face disposed of her hope. They'll kill him afterwards, she thought, but he doesn't care. But she said in the strangest voice,

"What will happen to *you*?"

"Nothing," he said. "Nothing is going to happen to me. You did go, back, back, and so, to look. I have seen you, going back. It did happen like that: it happen to she going backwards, to look at she paper. Stones and grass and all went down. They can see."

He had honed this preposterous plan to an edge. But weirdly, he took off his machete, and bent down and nicked her bare brown leg with its tip—a little blood spurted over the skin.

A scream might carry on the air. Hers seemed to be soundless as he pulled her up. She stared in wild confusion at her leg. Then she understood.

"Please, please, please," she tried to say. "Not alive. Your machete, please, your machete . . ." But they were moving, hesi-tant as the goats, she on her knees, dragging over the spiky stubble. The cut still bled a little. Fool, fool, the blood will be on the grass. But what he knew was that it would spread, too, in the water, diffusing itself, a message better and clearer than toast crumbs.

Suddenly fury brought her to her feet. Their faces, hers turned up, his bent down, almost touched.

"I did not throw the glass at the baby," she said clearly, right into him. "I did not have a glass. I did not throw the cup. The cup slipped and went. But I did not have a glass. And I would not . . . I would not."

His face drew back, staring at something in hers. He stared

and stared. His eyes slid away. They stood there, their shadows interlaid. Then his eyes came back to her face, forced, held. It was as though his own machete had gone into his ribs; his body sagged. She saw with her physical eyes truth strike his target, his careful, blessed, hard-formed target.

Then he said, "It is too late. What am I able to do now? It is too late to change it," he said to her, like a co-conspirator.

"I will never tell. Never, never." She tried to lock his eyes, but he slid them away again. His face had loosened, darkened.

How can he possibly believe? she thought, without hope.

"Listen, listen," she said rapidly. "Listen. You thought it. Something made you think it. Something you knew, about people. But listen, I would not hurt a child. I have not tried to hurt anyone, not a dog, a cat, not a woman. Ezekiel, Ezekiel, I did not throw the glass from the balcony. I will not tell. I am going away. Let me go. I did not throw the glass."

He dropped her onto the stubble, as though she were suddenly worthless. He stood staring at her upturned face.

"I am telling the truth," she said. She saw his hope die.

His hand reached blindly for his machete, the tip split the cord. He looked dully at the marks on her wrist, the blood drying on her leg.

"I slipped, on the stones," she said. "I backed, I backed, as you said. I nearly went over the cliff. I cut my leg, on the stones." But he still looked at her wrists.

"I have a smock, look, I was sitting on it." His face seemed to be growing smaller, contracting, as if it were being drained. "I will leave tomorrow," she said.

He turned and left her, moving slowly on his bare feet, back to a distant glitter. The sun had struck his handlebars.

She lay flat on the stubble. He picked up the bicycle and stood astride it, turning his head in each direction, so long that she waited for him to drop the bicycle and turn back. He got on. He rode off, smaller and smaller, and around the first bend.

It could not be because he trusted her. How could he? But he was an executioner, not a murderer. Something had gathered and broken. He was paralyzed by what truth had taken from him.

She began to touch her body—her face, her breasts, her legs.

It was two things: it was wet meat, the bloody bits of a food torn, cold and bobbing, by hunger. And it was her warm existence, her senses, her motion. She tried to stand up, then she did. With a glory of motion, she moved, stepping forward, tentative as the goats.

Ezekiel had left the pink cord where it had fallen on the stubble. She picked up its hairy length, and when she had pulled on her paint-stained smock, and fastened the cuffs about her wrists, she went uncertainly over to the cliff's edge, and threw it out into the air. It fell very slowly, and then she saw it, faint, coiled in a slight motion on the water.

When she reached her bicycle the sun had gone into an oblong cloud, but the handlebars were hot.

Late Fall

U NDER THE FLAMING trees of fall, Father Consadine drove, feeling the sun in his face, precious with its imminent weakening. The sky was a sharp blue; on the mountain crests last night's snowfall still shone. Down here, it had been cold hard rain, and the trees were thinned; but a sun warm almost as summer had burst out, and the sky blazed blue over all this uproar of Vermont color.

The list on the seat beside him had four of its five items checked. At the top of the long hill down into the village, he nearly paused: the white houses, the three steeples, the clock over the firehouse represented something always lost when he turned left into the circle around the common; a village, a parish, a promise. To counteract this tendency, he accelerated slightly, taking the downgrade at a smart rate. He had never had an accident, properly speaking, but now since he had twice (in six months!) backed into other cars, from his dreadful habit of leaving his car in reverse, and then forgetting, he compensated by a new sense of caution. The rectory sat on the steepest hill, and he distrusted his emergency brake. Now twice his car had leaped backward on innocent bumpers. No damage done, his sense of guilt had been silly; in fact, he was experienced enough to know that it was a drop running into a reservoir. Guilt he felt now day by day. In other years, bouts of it, normal bouts. But this autumn, he argued pro and con almost every moment, when not vehemently occupied. He knew Father Haggerty's presence to have aggravated this, but he also knew him blameless.

As he turned left, a car shot by him, its top exuberantly down in a final fling, its small red body gleaming. In it, Mrs. Vance and Father Haggerty disappeared rapidly from sight even in his rearview mirror. Father Consadine sighed, pulling on his brake in front of Doakes Notions, shifting the gear to reverse. He liked Mrs. Vance. In a practical way, only good could come from her talks with Father Haggerty. But would it really have been impossible for her to discuss her problems in the angular chairs of the rectory? Acute her problems were, he was sure of that.

As he set off the door's bell, his guilt growled like an ulcer. Exactly: he *liked* Mrs. Vance; not, alas, so much as he *dis*liked Mrs. Doakes.

She came forward with an obese alacrity, her pasty jowls contracted into a smile. He wanted pens, and as she fussed above the glass divisions between an F 25 Fine Point and an #M 19, her gimlet eyes kept pricking his. She malingered in her worry. Finally he almost snatched two pens, and poured change into her hand, wheeling like a nervous horse toward the exit; but he knew she was going to say:

"Have you a minute, Father?"

"A minute is about what I have, Mrs. Doakes," he paused with a smile as false as her own. That there wasn't a soul in the store did not prevent the conspiratorial sweep of her glance.

"I'd have come to the rectory, Father, but I never know whether it'll be you or Father Haggerty'll be in."

He could feel his glance chill as he stared at her. That the postcards and potholders might not eavesdrop, she lowered her tones.

"It's the statues, Father. If they're gone, they're gone, and I just have to get on with it. But it's hard, Father. I have tried; but it's like two big holes when I go in there."

" 'Holes,' Mrs. Doakes?" His hypocrisy was strong; he knew exactly what she meant.

"Holes, Father," she said with vigor. "One on each side. I

never went in church that I didn't pray there. To St. Philip, and then St. James. They were *friends*, Father."

This he knew to be false. He did not for one moment believe that this foggy and malevolent woman was a friend of St. Philip *or* St. James, although he reminded himself sharply that they might be—nay, were, of course—friends of hers.

"Mrs. Doakes," he said gently and, he hoped, with finality, "we decided, during the renovations, on simplifying the altar. The church is small, and the statues weren't really good ones, and they crowded the altar. They were distracting. You don't, of course, need them, to pray to our patron saints." They seemed to be in a contest of dishonesty; "we" had not so decided; he had reluctantly approved Father Haggerty's passionate reasoning. There *were* two holes, for him as for Mrs. Doakes.

"Well," she said, suddenly sullen, "it seems to me, when there's no room for the images of the Holy Saints, it's a small church, all right. There's plenty feel as I do. Murray's mother tried to tell Father Haggerty how the people feel, but he's here and there so fast..." Another name trembled on her lips and was suppressed.

"We can form our own image of those we love, Mrs. Doakes," he said, feeling sententious, and letting in a burst of cold sunny air. "Good-bye, then."

Outside, he attempted to escape from the hovering aura of Mrs. Doakes. Did he and she really share a reaction? What did he feel about the dismantled, red-robed, gilt-bordered statues, helpless as outmoded dolls? What on earth could they possibly have meant to him? But he knew what they had meant. They had been grotesque representations of objects of his love. Rather, he glumly thought, like offensive passport photographs. It all came back to that wretched necessity of his for contact as immediate, as personal, as a human body.

When he opened the front door of the rectory, Elsie popped her head in from the kitchen.

"Any calls?" he asked.

"Four. For Father Haggerty," said Elsie. "Mrs. Doakes called you, early, but she said never mind. And Murray never came. If I don't get rid of this trash today, it'll swallow me alive."

Father Consadine went into his room and closed the door. He sat down in the chair by the window and shut his eyes. He did not wish to pray or to meditate. He wanted to be perfectly still. But stillness, unfocused, was always invaded. Now here came the lion and the desert.

The lion and the desert had recurred in other years, but at long intervals; and they had come and left without shame, though never without uneasiness. In the past weeks, the sense of shame —fundamentally rejected—had accompanied their appearance, and doubtless accounted for its frequency. As a young priest, Father Consadine had found that the lions of Roman history were real to him in a curious way. They seemed to symbolize the majesty, and danger, of a brute force, inescapable, terror-striking, and innocent of malice. Tawny, hot-breathed, the feline metaphors of death, disgrace, loneliness, and ferocious doubt.

At that period he had had what now and then still wracked him with delight, the immediate and passionate sense of the presence of God. How this penetrated flesh and circumstance was the bright mystery, and he thought a great deal about that precious thinnest thread, connecting the senses *in extremis* with that Sense. At that last moment, did anyone believe, so confronted? Yes. But—and here was the crux—did they, could they, know they believed? Facing that hot maw and the impersonal ravening gaze, could they hold that thread?

Father Consadine had always thought that the Roman crowds would help; all those turned-down thumbs and avid eyes would pull the flesh together and support it. So that was not the ultimate encounter. The ultimate encounter would take place in the desert, with no observer but the high wheeling vulture, the bleached rocks, the yellow seedless sand. With no human consciousness to watch, however cruelly; absolutely alone with the reality of flesh, and blood, and death. Could that soul hold communion with God, assert itself in worship? Wasn't it Teilhard who had said that he hoped, not to die while communicating, but to communicate while dying?

The fascination of this speculation, though secret, did not seem strange to Father Consadine, for many years. It was a metaphor, like another; his especial metaphor, set by God knew what early cause. He had tried to apply it to the incredible sufferings of the tortured, but these were different. Between torturer and tortured, human consciousness existed; the actions of the tortured registered on the mind of the torturer. There was missing the ominous innocence of the natural. It was in the absolute loneliness of innocent matter that the lion came.

Father Consadine's relations with all men, save for the few humans he spontaneously loved, came to any good at all only through his fitful intercourse with God. The mean-spirited, the cowardly, the bully and the knave, he knew, generated in God an inexplicable affection. Of this Father Consadine stood in genuine awe. *(Who is it that accuseth? It is God that defendeth.)* But of Father Haggerty's glowing and inexplicable ability to love Mrs. Doakes and Murray, unsponsored by their mysterious attraction for the Deity, Father Consadine, thirst as he might, had tasted never a drop. With luck and grace, he might see them, valid as children, in God; but to find God through them, as Father Haggerty constantly preached and Father Consadine instructed himself, was beyond him.

This distasteful knowledge had begun to produce an abiding guilt. He might say to himself bravely and sensibly, that God had created him, and if he was mired in a personal, noncommunal, channel toward God, that was as it was. The unique, the private, the intensely personal, was the stuff of his nature; perhaps, if it thence expanded into a reflected charity, there was room for it. In the meantime, abashed before his curate, neither leading nor following, sixty next week, he grew dubious, irascible, and inwardly unforgivably satirical.

He heard the door slam now, and Father Haggerty's cheerful, "Elsie! Did that Murray turn up?"

"He *did* not," said Elsie's distant voice. "If I don't get rid of this trash today, it'll swallow me alive."

"If that young slob doesn't turn up after lunch, *I'll* take the trash. Look at the length of the grass, too, will you?"

When Father Consadine came out into the sitting room, Father Haggerty was leafing through notes. Father Consadine knew exactly what he was up to, rejoicing in the coming Sunday's text, as only a homilist can rejoice who has got his teeth into congenial meat. He had been waiting for the 27th; no dragging about this Sunday in search of fresh angles. All the way from three days ahead, Father Consadine could hear Father Haggerty's voice ring out, reproaching the donors of pews and windows, the devil's smug. True there were not, in the winter parish, so many of the wealthy and powerful as he would wish to reach, but no matter. A text it was to his heart: *"You rich, weep and wail over your impending miseries. Your wealth has rotted, your fine wardrobe has grown motheaten, your gold and silver have corroded and their corrosion shall be a testimony against you. It will devour your flesh like a fire. See what you have stored up for yourselves in the last days. You lived in wanton luxury on the earth, you fattened yourselves for the day of slaughter."*

Father Consadine was irrepressibly reminded of certain mission sermons, of another day, in other small villages, preached by towering, roving Redemptorist friars, on unnatural sex acts, missing Mass, and consorting with heretics. Well, one had to strike out, and Father Haggerty's was a worthy target.

"Well," said Father Consadine matily, "Mrs. Doakes was after us about the statues."

"Mealy-mouthed old bag," said Father Haggerty heartily. In saying this, he managed to convey an affection for Mrs. Doakes which tightened Father Consadine's skin with envy. "As for Murray, it's not just that he doesn't show up for the jobs. Do you know, Elsie can't find her second watch, and I've my own ideas."

"Her *second* watch?"

"The one she keeps on the shelf over the sink."

Father Consadine had never known of its existence. Murray had been employed by Father Haggerty on the strength of several small thefts, proved or suspected. "Well, we can't be sure," Father Haggerty pursued. "I expect him to show up. He *likes* to go to the Dump. He kills rats with a slingshot."

"Did you hear it's got to the point where they're going to have to fill the Dump in?" said Father Consadine. "They'll mess up somewhere else now." He knew this to be a topic congenial to Father Haggerty. But the latter surprised him. "Well, the Dump's got its own fascination," said Father Haggerty, who wrote poetry. He had published two poems, one in *Foxfire* and one in *Lillabulero.* "Do you know Nemerov's poem about a town dump?"

One of his most engaging qualities was his speed. He disappeared now, and was back in a wink, book in hand. "I was reading this this morning. Listen:

> *But I will add*
> *That wild birds, drawn to the carrion and flies,*
> *Assemble in some numbers here, their wings*
> *Shining with light, their flight enviably free,*
> *Their music marvelous, though sad and strange.*

It *was* beautiful . . . *music beautiful, though sad and strange.* "But the rats," said Father Consadine, against his will, "he doesn't mention the rats."

And at a slammed plate and a muffled shout, they moved in to lunch.

"You know," said Father Haggerty, on the last syllable of Father Consadine's grace, "in spite of Ma Doakes and her ilk, there *is* a new spirit in this community." He looked hopefully at Father Consadine, who looked briefly back. "They've stopped worrying about their souls—" ("If they ever did," said Father Consadine) "and are beginning to worry a little about the people to whom they've never given that cup of cold water in their lives. Some of them are finally getting it into their thick heads that if they don't make it through their neighbor, they won't make it at all."

"Not all the saints had that temperament," said Father Consadine, defensively. (He resisted, strongly, the temptation to introduce the great contemplatives.)

"And some of *them* were very oddballs *indeed*," said Father Haggerty, helping himself to coffee and waving the pot at Father Consadine, who shook his head. "Roosting on poles, and crawling into caves in the desert."

"Did you ever read *The Ascent of Mount Carmel*?" asked Father Consadine, in what he hoped was a bland tone. "There have been encounters, so all-absorbing . . ." It sounded wrong, and he bogged down.

"So 'all-absorbing' that they lost sight of everything but themselves. The Bible's full of the most ghastly egomaniacs, doing the most ghastly things, and in right with *their* God. Did you," he asked suddenly, countering St. John, "read recently about the Levite, and his concubine, and the men of Gibeah?"

Father Consadine treated this question as rhetorical. *"That,"* said Father Haggerty, enflamed, "is an example of self-righteous cruelty for you. That's how much women counted. There's nothing more savage in the whole thing. 'And with her hand on the doorsill, she died.' In right with the establishment laws of hospitality and his Deity, *he* was."

"The manners change," said Father Consadine at last, "but it's the contact with God that changes them."

"Elspeth Vance is a woman who cares about other people," said Father Haggerty suddenly. "That oaf of a husband, for one."

"And Dr. Mike Brown, for another," said Father Consadine, looking hard at his curate.

There was a small silence. They had had one unprofitable discussion, in which Father Haggerty had analyzed what constituted a spiritually consummated marriage. If a marriage could be annulled for lack of a physical consummation, why then, etc. Father Consadine had borne down, on that occasion, and now they skirted the issue made vivid by the predicament of Mrs. Vance.

"I ought to be off," said Father Haggerty. "What an afternoon. First, the hospital horror-floor." (A group of geriatric patients were kept on the top floor, lest they depress the more juvenile patients.) "Then those poor old tabbies about the Guild. And I suppose, the Futchers. He was worse last night. Then Mrs. Lamoine—God between us and all harm! She told me, straight-faced, yesterday, she'd told her Mary she'd come to no harm if she ejaculated 'Jesus, Mary, Joseph!' four times a day."

Father Consadine said, not without malice, "Pope John laid great faith in that."

"In what?" said Father Haggerty, startled.

"In that ejaculation," said Father Consadine. It was his theory that for all his worship of Pope John, there was much about him Father Haggerty chose to be ignorant of.

"I doubt *that*," said Father Haggerty, now rising. "Well, here I go."

"You needn't," said Father Consadine, "doubt it." Since the development of his preoccupation with the personal and communal problem, he had fortified himself with ammunition. "Page something or other in the middle of *Journal of a Soul*."

"Well," said Father Haggerty over his shoulder, "as I always said, he had a great sense of humor."

This was too much. Father Consadine, unsmiling, shut his door smartly as Father Haggerty's rapid feet drummed on the porch steps.

He sat down at his desk and pulled out his sermon notes. On top were the notes of his sermon of Sunday before last. He reread his text. Sept. 6th: *Say to those whose hearts are frightened: Be strong, fear not! . . . then will the lame leap like a stag, then the tongue of the dumb will sing. Streams will burst forth in the desert, and rivers in the steppe. The burning sands will become pools, and the thirsty ground, springs of water.*"

This Sunday, the reading was all about cutting off your hand, and tearing out your eye, as prophylactic measures. He stood up restlessly. His chair toppled and he caught it.

He went out, and through the empty sitting room, and across the cement walk, past the small grotto of the Virgin and its scarlet geraniums, and through the sacristy and onto the altar. There he hesitated; then, genuflecting, he went and sat down in the third pew from the altar rail.

It was absolutely quiet. The small red flame, hung high, indicating the presence of the Host, wavered in its glass. Though the window next to him was opened, the altarcloth and the curtain of the confessional hung unstirring. The big golden crucifix over the altar presented its skewered feet and open palms in a pale clear streak of sun. Then the streak slowly deadened and paled, and the altarcloth lifted in a gust. The radio had said rain or sleet tonight.

Father Consadine slid his knees down onto the wooden bench and put his head in his cupped hands. He made no effort to pray, but simply waited; perhaps for the thirsty ground to yield the spring. It did not do so. Something heavy—a logging truck?—labored uphill; its gears changed with a short howl. *Say to those whose hearts are frightened, Be strong and fear not.*

He put his hands down and sat back in the pew. For any acknowledgment of his presence, he might have been back at his desk. It was all wrong; he had lived by personal encounter, by grace of the experience of grace. That encounter, that sense of grace, had become rarer and rarer. Suppose finally it never came again? Well then, he would wait.

Who was he to be disappointed, to dictate the occasion of meeting?

As he got up, light footsteps came down the aisle. A girl he had never seen before, in green corduroy trousers, her hair strained back under a scarf, came past him, genuflected, and knelt at the altar, laying her purse carefully on the step beside her. Father Consadine left her kneeling there, rigid with attention. Asking for something or other, he thought; to have this removed, changed, granted, spared. Then he thought, Why couldn't I assume she was at worship?

Elsie was on the porch, looking for him. "It's Mrs. Vance on the phone!" she called.

At the moment the receiver reached his ear, as though she could see him, Mrs. Vance's deep rich voice said, "Father?"

"Father Haggerty's away for the afternoon," he said. It was as though Mrs. Vance was Father Haggerty's patient. "Could I give him a message?"

"No," said Mrs. Vance. "I don't want to see Tom. I want to see you."

"Well, of course," said Father Consadine. He was very surprised. "Would you like to come here, to the rectory?"

"Will you be there about half past five?" she asked.

"Yes," he said. "Yes, that's fine."

There was a pause, then she said, "I'll only be a minute. I want to say goodbye."

He did not ask her where she was going, having a sudden clear idea what she was taking leave of. He only said, "I'll see you then."

He went back to his room and finished his sermon notes. It was getting grayer, and the wind blew far off somewhere with a high

whine he hadn't heard since March. Through it, he could hear
Elsie, slamming the lid on the trash can. He went into the kitchen.

The can was brimming; the lid wouldn't fit. No Murray. There
were Father Haggerty's flattened tin cans, and two round empty
Minute Maid tins. Father Haggerty, haunted by ecological problems, made Elsie cut the bottoms out of the empty tins and then
step on them. He explained that the village wouldn't be thinking
about opening a new dump if everyone had done this five years
ago. Thousands of tins, protecting empty air and devouring
space. The small Minute Maid tins, which had been the only
ones Father Consadine could get at the A&P this week, wouldn't
yield their bottom lids to the can opener; there they both still
were, wasteful and round.

"Don't put that thing back, Elsie," he said. "I'm going to take
it over there now."

"It's a shame and a sin," she said. "Father Haggerty telling
me if we fire him, he'll only steal again. Telling me that as
cheerful as you please. And now that father of his'll have gone
to the dump already today." Murray, when moved by the spirit,
wheeled their trash to his father's house, on a board contraption
supported on the wheels of roller skates. His father had a truck.

After he pulled the car up to the kitchen door, Father Consadine went and put on a heavy sweater; the temperature had
dropped. He manhandled the big can onto the rear seat, accusingly watched by Elsie; in the driver's seat, he called out to give
her a message, in case Mrs. Futcher phoned, but she had shut
the door in protest against this self-humiliation of a cleric. Father
Consadine knew his action to be unseemly, but he was in a state
of rebellion. He was unsure whether he was indulging or punish-
ing himself.

The Dump was two miles out, and when Father Consadine
turned into the dirt road that led there, he saw that yesterday
had blasted summer's traces. The goldenrod that had glowed
everywhere forty-eight hours ago had withered; suddenly
brown, it jerked in the wind. The omnipresent evergreens looked
almost black, and though there were still bright leaves, they were
thick only on the road and the roadside grasses, where they lay
deep, freckled and crisping. When he passed Mrs. Rapicault's,

she turned, with the tin pot of chrysanthemums she was carrying in from the saggy porch, and waved as he bowled by.

The mountains ahead, darker for their snowy crests, drew in so that he lost all but their lower slopes. The road wound left, then right, and curved sharply upward. He turned off it into a wide dirt space, bumping over ruts.

The smoke of a damp and constant fire, far below, hung in the autumn air. Debris, fallen from arriving trucks, lay around: tires, a child's two-wheeled wagon. He drove on, made a wide turn, and then backed cautiously near the rim. When he got out, he stood for a minute, listening to absolute silence.

Then he walked to the back of the car and looked down over the lip of the ravine. Chaos lay below, in heaps and mounds and giant curves. Exactly as he looked, a cold bright lance of sunlight struck through the cloudcover of the sky and a blue patch widened. At the foot of the ravine, the Dump glittered in a dazzle of brilliance. The sun's torch found and lit all the splendor of rejection: smashed bottles flashed and sparkled; cans blazed; jagged hunks of mirror rayed out a fan of colors; tins, unflattened, sent a cosmos of suns jetting into his eyes. Burst-open cushions, plastic shards of yellow and red, a wheel's dented hubcap. Then, as smoothly as it had struck, the sun glided under, and Father Consadine stared into that abomination of desolation spoken of by the prophet; in this case, the raw remains of the once-possessed, the shards of personality. It was disintegration, visible. "Jesus, Mary, Joseph!" said Father Consadine, with a small smile for Father Haggerty.

He undid the tailgate, scrambled out the can, and cautiously avoiding the brim, tore off the lid, and with a swing that wrenched his shoulder, sent a volley of bright debris hurtling down into the depths. He noticed three of Murray's targets in the quick motion of alarm. There was a twisted poker still in the can, and he flung that far out. It fell with a faint tang on something metal, and then everything was quiet. He put the can back in the car, slammed the door and went round to the driver's seat and got in.

He sat there for a minute. Something had tensed the air. A feeling of extreme happiness, a lifting, a lightening, surrounded him. A sense of presence in a vast and vigorous hush. He sat in it, perfectly still.

In a few minutes, he realized he was cold. Whatever had come, had gone; but he had a feeling of leeway, from which he looked at his day (now lost in early dusk), and his days. Those days were composed, not of the question, the lion and the desert, but of hours. Inevitably, Father Haggerty, who longed and prayed for a ghetto parish, would depart for brighter fields, and he himself would have a new and, by the law of percentage, less endearing curate; or, for his sins, a clerical Mrs. Doakes. There would be no climactic encounter; there would not even be the grotesque, the faint shadow of Peter with his feet in the air and his eye at ant-level. He would die in bed, anointed, and murmured to rest.

He rolled down the window, and looked at the Vermont sky, darkening, lowering itself toward the land. Night already was falling, as snow had fallen on the mountains, as leaves fell and were covered, as winter fell on the earth.

He would be late for Mrs. Vance. Father Consadine briskly rolled up the window and, turning the key, tromped on the gas. Once more in reverse, the car shot easily back, over and out. It sailed freely, smashed on the slope, sailed, flew over and over, hit, and burst into a small bonfire. But Father Consadine, like an elaborate toy, had been ejected, and at the bottom he lay peacefully, in a rag-doll attitude. He did come to, for a little while, and had his chance at the question, though nothing large moved in the Dump, and the bird wheeling above was an autumn starling that, frightened, did not come to rest until it was completely dark.

Help

"Help!" cried Mrs. Cloy. "Oh help!"

"Yep," said Mrs. Gruber, "the rest are mine.... That's the rubber, Agnes."

"Well, so it is," said Mrs. Haines, in a tone of no surprise.

Violet, ironing behind the swing door, couldn't hear Mrs. Harker say anything at all. Last time, the talk after the game had gotten a little sharp, and everybody had agreed that next time, when the game was over, it was over.

"Lily," cried Mrs. Cloy in a cheerful wail, "we'd better quit this. Someday we're going to lose our pants."

Violet set her iron on the heel, to go and get some more ice and the sandwiches. Drinks were for during play, but the sandwiches were for now. She took off the wet cloth and started running warm water over the back of the ice tray. While she was doing it, Mrs. Harker came in with the empty ice bucket. She had stomach trouble, and at the moment Violet thought she looked awful. She was always white, but sometimes, like now, there was a green tinge, and the dark spot, where she had told Violet the cabinet door had struck her eye, made it clearer.

"We're ready for our sandwiches, Violet," she said, louder than need be. It was the same at the bridge table. Violet could hear every word, yet Mrs. Harker believed herself to be far distant. She had the illusion, or fomented it, that the apartment was the size of a barn instead of a mousetrap. With Mrs. Harker came her perfume. It was a brutal jasmine and marked everything she touched—cigarette stubs, playing cards, kleenex; Violet could have traced her through a labyrinth.

"I'll bring 'em right now," said Violet. She dumped the cubes into the ice bucket, and Mrs. Harker went into the living room where the players had shoved back their chairs, crossed their legs and taken out their compacts.

"Seven and four, six, is fifty-*four*...," said Mrs. Gruber, still figuring. "That's eleven dollars you owe us. Boy oh boys, what am I going to do with all that money—five dollars and fifty cents of it!"

Mrs. Harker had lost again. She had distinctly told Mr. Harker that she would tell her friends that it was more fun to play for fun. For over four weeks Mrs. Harker had lost money through not playing for fun. Though herself no gambler, Violet had considerable sympathy for Mrs. Harker, largely because she contrasted her own circumstances with those of Mrs. Harker—meaning mostly Mr. Harker vs. Lester. All other qualifications aside, Mr. Harker lacked a good heart. Violet knew a mean man when she saw one. She had met shame in Mrs. Harker's eye. Shame was something Violet knew about, from a former period. When Mrs. Harker told her about how she had struck her eye on an open cabinet door, Violet had immediately said, "I did exactly the same lone thing myself, the other day."

"So," said Mrs. Gruber, "that's five-fifty apiece, and then Lily's six dollars from last week, makes eleven-fifty, and half *that*..."

"You're lucky your Girl does your ironing," Mrs. Haines, who had not been paying attention, said to Mrs. Harker. "If you can *get* Help now, they won't do anything but this, or that."

"Most of Them you *can* get, I wouldn't have in my house," said Mrs. Cloy, annoyed by this ostentation. "Well, Happy Days!"

"Happy Days!" said Mrs. Gruber. "Don't I know. Dress to kill, and then steal the gold out of your teeth. I had a friend had a Girl clean for two years, walked off finally with all her jewelry, six pair of hose, and two transistors."

"Well, she was a fool not to lock up," said Mrs. Cloy tartly. "I wouldn't trust one while I winked."

Mrs. Harker at last spoke. "Well, now, Milly," she said, "I think there's some are perfectly honest. Help like Violet has a lot of self-respect."

"You leave your stuff laying around?" said Mrs. Haines, derisively.

"Well, naturally, I keep an eye out," said Mrs. Harker.

"I ought to get out of here," said Mrs. Cloy with a swig and a sigh. "That steak's going to be hard as a brick when his nibs gets home if I don't take it out of there."

"Don't go yet," said Mrs. Harker. "Come on, it's early."

Violet, who had heard this conversation duplicated a number of times, knew they would be there almost until Mr. Harker came home. She folded his last silk shirt and placed it on top of the pile on the kitchen banquette. Today she had gotten so much ironed that there was just about room for her own pile of belongings: her good shoes, her purse, her market bag and her new green coat. Every time she looked at the coat, it was as though Lester had grabbed her and laughed. She began to whistle under her breath, and went to see if the refrigerator had finished defrosting itself; every week it was immensely furred and ridged with ice. Lord, yes, the glass bowls were swimming and the ice pans were naked. When she came back from the bathroom she would just about have time to clean it out.

She went and got her cigarettes out of her purse; they were underneath everything, of course; she paddled through the lozenges, her handkerchief, the bills for the down payment on Curt's bicycle, bound with an elastic band and rammed into one of her wool gloves, a head scarf and two pencils, and the matches. To use the bathroom she went two flights down, to the ground floor, and then another into the warm dry humming bowels of the apartment house. On the whole, this struck Violet as a good idea; it got her away from Mrs. Harker and what she regarded as a rather cheesy set of rooms, and she always had a cigarette before she came up again. Also, if she had had to use the apartment bathroom, she might have been in it when Mrs. Harker wanted to throw up. Violet thought that it was possible that, among other things, not being married, or at least, not being married to Mr. Harker, made Mrs. Harker nervous. Violet had no idea how she knew that Mrs. Harker was not married to Mr. Harker. It was just one of the things she knew. She had a feeling that that was partly why playing bridge with Mrs. Cloy and Mrs. Haines and Mrs. Gruber, and having her Girl there that day, was so important to Mrs. Harker. Mrs. Harker never seemed to be sure, when it was her week, that they would come; each time, she called them up. She didn't really seem sure about anything. She would change her dress two or three times a day, frequently for the worse, Violet thought. There was no way Mrs. Harker could keep her eyes from looking too wide open, or her skin from having that white, plucked look. Violet wondered if she had been a finer-looking woman quite a lot of years ago when she was young.

"Now when Lily gives us what's coming from her, from last week, we're all square," said Mrs. Cloy.

Violet opened the apartment door, took it off the latch, and shut it hastily behind her as a mist of sawdust went in her face. The carpenters were still in the little hall of the apartment next door. The exterminators had come and gone, and now there was this sawing and planing, and a sawhorse stuck right out into the main hall. The pimply-faced boy who had already been here last week was still here. He grinned at Violet as though she were a huge joke. Violet did not like his looks, and refrained from amenities. Instead, one flight down, she suddenly wondered about leaving the door off the latch. But if she latched it, and rang, Mrs. Harker would not like having to come and let her in, and anyway, what mischief could even the pimply-faced boy get into with four people in the living room. Violet, on the second flight down, smiled rather derisively because she was talking just like Mrs. Cloy.

Before coming up, she sat on the toilet lid and smoked her cigarette. She found some of her best thinking was done here: perhaps it was the concentrated space. Violet did not approve of smoking, but she had taken up this vice at her worst time, for the sense of luxury. Long before she met Lester, when she was so poor she worked evenings after leaving her day's work, when

she often felt she could never make enough money to raise Curt
and give him one pair of shoes after another, and kept being
afraid of getting sick and not being able to work for weeks on
end. To persuade herself that she had excess money, money to
burn, she started buying a pack of cigarettes a week, even when
they still made her think of a badly lit fire. But she would say
to Curt, "I think I'll have a cigarette . . . ," and immediately this
made her a queen of whim. And though then she would not let
Curt strike the match, she let him hold it to the tip, though he
sometimes breathed so hard he blew it out. Well, well, she
thought, Curt fifteen now, and I got a husband don't let me
want for *nothing*.

To think back now was partly fun—like bad weather after
you got inside the house. But she only wanted to think so deep.
It was like walking over a frozen pit without going through the
ice. For instance, last week, in spite of what Violet had said
about doing the same thing to her own eye, Mrs. Harker's eyes,
looking out of her white, pinchy face, had slid away; and that
was shame. To have someone see your shame, and know it,
was hard to bear. Violet was very good now at not thinking
about a thing or two in the past, but seeing Mrs. Harker's eyes,
she had had to push away some things that had come up through
the ice over the pit. She was right now thinking of one that had
got out: Mrs. Raney's little boy, Joey Raney, that had called Curt
a dumb nigger right by Mrs. Raney's kitchen sink. When she
had taken Curt to the undertaker's wife who looked after him
on Saturdays, the undertaker's wife was sick, and she had to
bring Curt to Mrs. Raney's house. She didn't look for any good
to come of it, but she was dead scared of losing the job, and
she threatened Curt hideously about the penalties for not doing,
quick, what she told him to do. Mrs. Raney was then her only
Regular, and Violet went to her four days a week. Curt was five,
and he played out under the tree, all right. But Mrs. Raney's
little boy, mean as they come, was home from school, too, and
he had a fight with the boy that had come over to see him, and
the boy went home, so then he went out, even though he was
seven, and started playing jacks with Curt, who was smarter
than Joey, and five minutes later into the kitchen they charged,

Curt sweating with rage, and Mrs. Raney's little boy with a nervous fat smile on. "Ma! Ma!" shouted Curt. "He called me a dumb nigger! You hit him, Ma! Hit him!"

"You ought to be ashamed of yourself, Joey," Violet said. "You don't talk like that. Not to Curt, or nobody else!"

Howling, Joey flew through the swing door; he was very sensitive to admonition. And the next minute, Mrs. Raney was there. "Now look here, young man," Mrs. Raney said to Curt with a hearty small smile, "all this nonsense. Joey called you a nigger, and that's what you are. There's nothing wrong with hearing that, or with being that. There's no cause for offense, and the sooner you accept it, the better for you."

It seemed to Violet that Curt was huge, enormous, that he towered over her like a god. But she would not look. "He didn't mean nothing, Mrs. Raney," she said.

"Well, I should hope *not*," said Mrs. Raney.

That night, before he went to bed, Curt was so rude to Violet that she had to slap him; but when he cried, his crying was different, and so fierce that she was scared.

That was ten years ago; a world away. It was something she never deliberately thought about, as she thought, with pleasure, of a checked coat she had had which had become disreputable-looking before she could get rid of it, or of the street Curt and she had lived in right up to the time she married Lester.

Violet got up and flushed her cigarette stub down the toilet; it was queer that Mrs. Harker's face would make her think of that time when Curt had been too large for her to look at him. She went back upstairs.

The workmen were gone. The door of the empty apartment was shut, but they hadn't swept up the sawdust on the hall floor. When she got in the apartment the company was gone, too.

Violet emptied the refrigerator pan, and then she went into the living room to get the used glasses. Mrs. Harker was standing at the window. It was January, and it had gotten dark, and the window reflected her face instead of letting her see what was outside.

"I'll do that, Violet," she said. "I'm going to get your money now. I'll rinse those out later."

Violet would have rinsed the glasses, but it was after five now, and the bicycle shop closed at six. This was Friday night, so, on Time, Curt would have the bicycle tomorrow and ride it all Sunday. So she didn't say no. When she came back from the kitchen she was carrying the laundry and she went back to Mr. and Mrs. Harker's bedroom. Mrs. Harker had taken a ten-dollar bill out of her drawer.

"Violet," she said, "I hope you can come some other time. In the future. I'll call you sometime." She was in a hurry for Violet to leave, and Violet knew this was because she didn't want Mr. Harker to know that Violet had been here. She looked furtive, like a sickly child.

"Yes'm," said Violet, looking at her with a sort of kindly contempt. "You call me. Goodbye, Mrs. Harker."

As she left, Mrs. Harker lay down on the bed.

Violet put on her green coat which was almost brand new, and got out her head scarf. She poked around, feeling for her gloves. It took her a minute to believe it: the roll of bills was gone. She got hot and then very cold. There was no chance she had lost it. She hadn't taken it out. That open door. But it couldn't be true. She snatched open the hall door as though the workmen might have come back. A radio was playing faintly in the apartment down the hall. She ran to the kitchen window. The carpenters' truck was gone. They had *seen* her go downstairs. "Mrs. Harker! Mrs. Harker!" she called.

The bedroom door was shut, and she knocked on it, calling, "Mrs. Harker! Mrs. Harker!"

Mrs. Harker opened the door, her face so close to Violet's that Violet jumped.

"Mrs. Harker," she said, "I been robbed. Somebody stole eighteen dollars out of my purse while I was downstairs."

Mrs. Harker stared at her, appalled. "You *sure*, Violet? You *pos*itive?"

"Yes, I'm positive," said Violet furiously. "When I went downstairs, I left that door open. I had eighteen dollars, in a elastic."

"That boy!" said Mrs. Harker. She stared at Violet, her eyes enormous. "'A drink of water'!" she said bitterly. "He came here to my door asking for a drink of water, because the water in that apartment was turned off. I was mixing a drink, and I left him at the sink. And he thanked me, from the kitchen, and went back out the door."

Violet was surprised at her own fury. It wasn't a hundred dollars. But she couldn't ask Lester for it, right after the coat; and saving five a week for it, for four weeks... "What's the name of those carpenters?" she asked.

"I don't know. But I'll get after them Monday, if they come back here," said Mrs. Harker. "I certainly will. I just don't know how we'll prove it. But I'll certainly call you, Violet."

"Nothing meaner than a thief," said Violet. She went back to the kitchen, forgetting to say goodbye. She tied her scarf over her head with a yank, snatched out her gloves. She held one in her teeth, to pull on the other, and it smelled like all the harems of the world.

Violet sat down hard on the banquette, and after she sat down, it was still a good two minutes before her mind straightened out. She had two things before her: something could not be, and it was. The carpenter's boy could not possibly smell of jasmine. Mrs. Harker had been into her gloves and taken her money while she was downstairs. While the company was there? Maybe. Now that she accepted the impossible, it became hideously clear. Mrs. Harker hadn't paid up on the game last week, and she couldn't ask Mr. Harker for the money—that Violet understood immediately. She must have taken the ten-dollar bill she had saved up for Violet and given it to her company. Then she had to have ten dollars again. But of course if she was going to lay it onto a sneak thief, she would have to take all eighteen dollars. Nothing meaner than a thief. Violet was suffocated with fury. That popeyed, pasty-faced slut. "I'll call you, Violet." "I don't know just how we can prove it." She and her fat boyfriend, with his sweaty shirts and his stingy ways.

Violet knew at once that there was absolutely nothing she could do, and that was why she was so purely furious.

She sat there listening, listening, for a sound from the thief. But the apartment had not one sound in it.

Then suddenly Violet began to feel better. A sweet cruel sensation crept from her stomach to her throat. She got up and looked around her. There was no paper anywhere. She opened the slandered cabinet door and tore a yellow strip off a half-empty sugar bag. She got out her pencils, took the sharper one, and began to write slowly and carefully.

> I know you took my eighteen dollars. I would be ashame if I was you to steal from your own Help. I know Mr. Harker hit you and that it was not no cabinet door. I know he is so mean you cannot pay your gamboling debts. There is nothing meaner than a thief. You should think about that.
>
> Violet Johnson

She read this over. She took the strip of paper to the refrigerator, reached down the red tea canister from the shelf above it, and propped the strip against the redness. It was bright as a Shell sign. It was very conspicuous. Perhaps Mr. Harker would see it before Mrs. Harker did. She reread it, but this time she did not go all the way to the end.

She started to put on her wool gloves; but she didn't want to, and she stuffed them in her pocket. Then she put back her pencils, changed her shoes, tested her head scarf and got out her carfare. She looked around the kitchen. The kitchen sink seemed to step out at her and then go back. She went to the front door and found herself shutting it with great softness behind her.

The janitor had not turned on the lights yet, and the steps gleamed dimly below her. Violet went downstairs quietly as though she were scared of waking someone up. On the second flight she stumbled and had to grab the railing. She pushed open the heavy door, and the dank cold of the city dusk struck at her. The street lamps Mrs. Harker had looked down at from the window sent a naked light onto the pavement.

Halfway down the block, Violet turned around. She did not expect to do it, and she had purposely not thought about anything. She turned around, however, and went back to the apartment house door. Here she stood quietly, not thinking of anything at all. Then she opened the door and began to climb the stairs.

It was only when she got to the door of the apartment that

she thought enough to realize it might be locked now, and it was. She stood there looking at it. It settled everything, big and dark, with an angled glass doorknob. Relieved, she turned around and went back to the steps again.

At the head of the steps she turned back and stood in front of the door.

After a minute she lifted her bare hand and pushed the bell. She could hear it ring quite loudly in the kitchen close at hand. But nobody came and she couldn't hear anything except the voice of the man talking and talking on the radio down the hall. She pushed the bell again.

This time she heard a sound in the apartment, a faint slow sound of heels on the floor. They came up on the other side of the door and stopped. After a minute the door opened a little and a small portion of Mrs. Harker's teased hair, and nose and mouth, appeared in the space. She made a quick move to shut the door, and then opened it and looked past Violet.

"What do you want?" she said.

"My list," said Violet. "I forgot my list."

Mrs. Harker stood back, and Violet went past her into the kitchen, past the kitchen sink to the refrigerator. The strip of paper stuck up in front of the red canister. She took it and put it in her purse. She put the canister back on the shelf and went back to the front door. Mrs. Harker was standing up against the wall and Violet did not look at her.

"Well, goodbye, Violet," said Mrs. Harker.

"Goodbye," said Violet at the head of the steps. She saw as she said it that Mrs. Harker was leaning up against the wall. All the way down the stairs, she did not hear the door shut.

When she got to the apartment house door, she was ready to think. And the first thing that came was a heady sense of excess. Something she did not need, that she could throw away if she chose, she dropped lightly. She watched it splinter with a fine, mild contempt, pity, and a curious cool sense of fun not devoid of ferocity.

As she stepped outside a boy flew past her on a bicycle, weaving like a happy bat. Violet pulled her green coat around her, and pulled out her wool gloves and put them on her hands.

Vocation

D R. LOGAN AND HIS CREW boarded the ship of her room every morning at relatively the same hour.

She had formed an attachment to Dr. Logan—perhaps that of a lifeboat passenger to its captain. But she knew it wasn't quite that. They had had, in the one long quiet explanation of what she faced, the congeniality of strangers who, finding themselves in a sticky situation, pick up signs that the shared predicament will be lightened by trust—trust in the way mind and reflexes will respond to the event.

Dr. Logan had drawn terrifying but reassuring diagrams—flattering her ignorance with the confidence that it could be modified. Dangerous? (Of death, of course, they meant.) No! Unless one wanted to say that any five-hour operation was tricky by definition. Major? Yes. Drastic. And—this was important—with a long and particularly unpleasant convalescence. Worse than all the tests? Oh yes. Much worse.

So be it. They smiled at each other, figuratively hoisting knapsacks to their shoulders.

Set at last, it would be tomorrow morning. The past two afternoons, each time looking very fallen-away from the freshness of the morning, Dr. Logan had come by and sat down in the armchair. They talked, mildly, about irrelevant things, while his rather misted blue eyes rested on her, or on his own long fingers, clasped at the knee. Mrs. Curtis thought that giving her this unnecessary time was strange but pleasant.

The whole week she had been quite alone, except for the normal staff forays. She was divorced, so there was no anxious husband to worry about. And she wanted no visitors. Not one. That was her privilege.

The room had piled up with so many flowers that Miss Converse, the head nurse, had suggested passing others on to the patients' common room where Mrs. Curtis, in her paced prowl along the corridor and back, could see them peacefully wilting in the antiseptic air.

Now the immaculate figures gathered around her bed, as though she were an unexpected golden egg laid by a provident goose during the night. Dr. Logan and, slightly behind and around him, Drs. Carmody, Hanson and Brade. Dr. Brade, always to the rear, had never spoken yet. Nor had he smiled—certainly something she didn't require, but the absence of which she had noted. His gaze, at once speculative and expressionless, seemed to look at something slightly to the left of her head. But once their eyes met, and a curious—what? wonder? jolt?—went through her. He couldn't possibly dislike me, she thought. That's ridiculous. He sees me five minutes each morning. He wasn't even involved in the tests.

Now they shouldered away through the wide door, Dr. Logan looking back over his shoulder with an appraising smile. She smiled back, feeling nearly as cheerful as she looked.

The day, however, like a cat stretching, suddenly lengthened itself. When lunch, her final preoperative meal, had been taken away, she unexpectedly wished for company. Almost she put out her hand to the unused phone, but she couldn't imagine making, at long last, that kind of demand. And in any case, what at the moment did she want to say? It was just that the knowledge that her familiar and unbroken body was to be immensely violated, in protracted rearrangement, had become suddenly immediate.

She pulled up the coarse white shift and stared at the curved, familiar flesh. Inexplicably, she thought suddenly of Dr. Brade. Would he be a standby?

At dusk, she hadn't turned on the light. The head of Miss

Converse, for whom she had earlier obediently swallowed two unfamiliar pills, appeared in the doorway.

"Mrs. Curtis," said Miss Converse, "we'll be giving you a Little Sedative tonight. You'll be awake so early tomorrow, we want you to have an extra good night's sleep. Don't you want some light in here?" she said, peering over at the bed.

"Yes, yes really, I do," said Mrs. Curtis, and she reached over and switched on the crane-necked lamp.

"There!" said Miss Converse happily. "*That's* better! Anything you want?"

Somewhat to her shame, Mrs. Curtis heard herself ask, "I suppose Dr. Logan's left?"

She had had the conviction that this afternoon he would be sure to come. It was, of course, quite unnecessary.

"Oh poor Dr. Logan," said Miss Converse with relish. "After all his day, he's got an emergency. He's at it right now. The poor man probably won't get home till all hours. Now you relax!" she threw kindly over her vanishing shoulder.

After the student nurse had watched her take her pill, and she had again turned out the light, Mrs. Curtis lay, taking deep breaths. A sense of not totally ominous excitement had grown in her—a good sense of powerlessness. She was launched.

She was asleep when light blared, switched on at the door. Her eyelids flew up. Dr. Brade, a clipboard in his hand, was illumined.

Without greeting, he came over and sat on the edge of the hard slick straight chair.

"Here's some information I have to give you, Mrs. Curtis," he said. "It's a formality. Just a release, to be sure you understand everything. Risks, et cetera."

Five minutes later, his clipboard complete, he rose, but he paused by the foot of the bed.

"I suppose Dr. Logan's talked to you personally about the operation?" he said. He seemed to Mrs. Curtis somehow to be blocking her from the door.

"Oh," she said, "Dr. Logan couldn't have been more helpful."

Dr. Brade looked at her, and she realized it was the first time she had seen an expression invade his face.

"Well," he said, "Dr. Logan's the Chief Surgeon. They can

afford to be pleasant." He spoke as of a group.

To this, Mrs. Curtis said nothing. A sense of some familiarity with Dr. Brade's expression had come to her, but it was utterly unidentifiable.

"It's we who have to tell the patients the truth," now said Dr. Brade. "They never tell the cancer patients what they found. That's our job. They come in later and do the cheer-up."

She was dazed by what was happening. Dr. Brade's eyes were now familiar, but as in a dream.

"Dr. Logan has been very frank with me," said Mrs. Curtis rather louder than she meant. "He took great trouble to go into details."

There was a little pause while Dr. Brade tapped twice on his clipboard with his chained pen.

"Yes. Well," he said. "They do the preoperative cheer-up, too." He turned toward the door. "I just think it's fairer that you shouldn't count on anything. Do you want this light out again?"

She looked straight at the familiar gaze and said, "Yes, please," and the next instant the door, closing with a whoosh, stood outlined by the hall's light.

For a moment, in the renewed dark she was still in the constriction of a dream. Then, emotion began to boil away the mist— outrage, confusion—above all, anger. What on earth was behind the words? And how on earth did he dare, in his circumstances? What immense pressure must have forced up that speech? But the answer was as clear as it was impossible. He was angry because he was afraid I wasn't frightened. He was trying to make me believe, tomorrow morning, that Dr. Logan has been lying to me. He needed my fright.

She pushed back the smooth sheet top and switched on her crane-neck lamp. The small metallic room sat there, the flowers' rainbow, the armchair from which Dr. Logan's misted tired blue eyes had met hers.

Now she was frightened, by what had just occurred. She was hot on a trail. But to what?

And then, as though a trap had been sprung, she knew why Dr. Brade's eyes were familiar. She had seen them, late at night, in a great railroad station.

It had been almost two years ago, just after her divorce. And it had never really totally left her mind; something seemed constantly to refresh it.

She had missed her late train back to Baltimore, arriving breathless five minutes after it had pulled out of the station in a self-righteous glide, exactly on time. Now she had two and a half hours of which to dispose.

She glanced around mournfully, but she was not destitute. She had a book in her bag. She was not being met.

She sat down on one of the yellow-brown hard benches and gazed around her at the vast station. How strangely different it had looked when she had arrived at midday, two days earlier. It had been like a miniature city—or an anthill, if you like. In any case, a hive of activity—lit-up shops everywhere; orange juice and hamburgers; the more austere glass doors of the restaurant whose bar shone faintly from within; bookstores, stacks of magazines; bright ticket windows with lines of feet that pushed suitcases in front of them, step by step.

Every bench was crowded—people sat on suitcases, stood, shifting feet, by some luckier companion. Children slid, and screamed, and were snatched back. On the high black lists, white figures winked in and out; and somehow-felt mass movements sent converging waves of people to numbered gates even before the sonorous echoing announcement. Everyone had an intention, was traveling toward it. Perhaps it was already pre-Christmas rush, or perhaps an ordinary day. Outside there was a cold thin blue December sky.

But tonight it was as though the wind that was sucking up mean sleet-crystals and flinging them about the bitter air, had sucked the station clean. A handful of travelers was dispersed around it—sprawled on benches, with flung-back heads, reading captured newspapers, or just staring ahead. These are people who have to travel tonight, she thought.

She felt cold and tired and somehow uneasy. She thought of hot water and, lugging her small suitcase, went down the long flight of dirty steps to the Rest Rooms. Following the arrow above that bland euphemism, she came to a row of white bowls. She bathed her face in cold water—there was no hot—combed her hair, and went back out through the swinging door. She had evidently failed to notice, when she came in, the figure against the wall. It was an old woman, with a thin gaunt soiled face and a high, hawk nose. She lay against the wall, her head, in its torn green scarf, resting on a string bag. She might be dead, or ill, or drunk. But coming nervously closer, Mrs. Curtis saw that she was merely asleep. It was not sleeting here. They'll never let her stay, she thought; but two women, arguing, passed the figure without a glance.

Upstairs, Mrs. Curtis slapped her suitcase on a bench, opened it, and got out her detective story. But something had jarred its reality. She closed it for a moment and looked around. The station passengers had dwindled even more.

On the bench directly opposite her, huddled up, lay a figure so small and curled that at first she thought it was a child. Then she saw it was a very small, very old, very dirty man, as fast asleep as the figure she had left below. A stained gray cap was pulled over his face, almost to the gray stubble of the caving chin. His hands, tiny and fleshless as the claws of a bird, were curled at the knuckles. He had no overcoat and no shirt, but his little stick-wrists protruded from the frayed cuffs of a jacket that had probably been blue. His sneakers, laced with string, were mismates.

Mrs. Curtis's eyes were drawn back to him as by a magnet. She wondered if she could stick a bill in the sagged pocket without arousing him. The monumental uselessness of this paralyzed her.

Then, as though a wing had shadowed her page, she looked quickly up at a figure coming down the aisle between her and the benches opposite. He was not a policeman, but he wore a tan uniform and he carried a policeman's nightstick. As he passed Mrs. Curtis on her bench, she saw his eyes, and at the anticipation in them, she was struck as by the sleet itself. He passed her without a glance, all his attention on the minute, disreputable figure. His eyes had the glutted look of one kind of importunate desire. They were full of the lazy yet eager look of total power.

He poked the man, not hard, with his stick. The claw hand flew to its cap and revealed eyes staring straight up.

The guard brought his nightstick full force against the pitted soles of the cracked shoes. There was only a sort of deep strangled grunt. Almost before it was out, the tiny figure was yanked to its feet, the twisted collar in a firm grip. The expression on the small sunk-in face was curiously passive, as of one who has no responsibility whatsoever. Off they went, fast, between curious eyes, frogmarch, toward the entrance beyond which the sleet did or did not fall. The whole thing could not have taken three minutes.

To her own surprise Mrs. Curtis, in her train, in her apartment, going about her ways, found that when the scene recurred to her, which it decreasingly did, the picture of the tiny dirty man grew vague as that of the woman stretched by the wall. But, mysteriously, the eyes of the man in the tan uniform seemed not to fade.

Now, from this bed, she had seen them in this room, and deadly cold, she seized the blanket at her feet and snatched it up around her shoulders, chills coursing through her like ripples. From the healer's uniform, those eyes had been bent steadily on her—brimmed with power, eager for its use.

She found, without much shame, that she was shivering with fear. She rang her bell. A little red eye glowed, and a voice said softly, "Can I help you, Mrs. Curtis?"

Without clear purpose, she said quickly, "Could I speak to the resident for a minute?"

"I'm sorry," said the voice soothingly, "Dr. Carmody isn't here. Dr. Brade is on tonight. Would you like him to come to you? You oughtn't to be still awake, Mrs. Curtis," the nurse's voice added reproachfully, to her most stoic patient.

"No, no. No, thank you," said Mrs. Curtis a little breathlessly. "Just a small question. I'll see Dr. Logan in the morning."

She lay still as a rabbit; surely, surely, Dr. Brade was drawing his loved power from some secret knowledge. Suppose Dr. Logan hadn't told her the truth. Suppose he thought it useless to frighten her.

Bitterly ashamed, she pulled out the phone book. She ran her fingers jerkily down the Logans—how many there were! Here it was, Eustace R., M.D., Office 687-4111. Residence 223-4322.

She dialed the last softly, and almost at once the bell began to ring and pause, ring and pause. Just as she was about to drop the receiver with a kind of relief, a heavily muffled voice, up from what depths of sleep and fatigue, said, "Yes?"

Mrs. Curtis couldn't speak. Why, in God's name, was she calling? With what purpose? "Yes?" said the voice, a trifle more clearly. "Dr. Logan here. What is it?"

Mrs. Curtis did the unforgivable. Softly as a thief she let down the receiver into its cradle. The phone, returned from instrument to object, sat slick under her fingers, which she hastily withdrew.

You have a sadist loose here. Not loose. Knit into your structure, wearing the uniform of power. He is one of Those.

Did you lie to me, Dr. Logan? Do you foist all evil news on your assistants? But no, no, even in her midnight fear, that was not it. She knew truth in her bones when she met it. She would stake her life (well, hadn't she?) on Dr. Logan. But the mystery, the old bad mystery, how could she have met it here in its crisp white? The power to instill fear, to hurt; and the deep visceral joy in that hurt. They chose, and deformed, the insignia of power. Suddenly, all over the world, eyes shone at her, steady in their useless, cureless, idiot priesthood.

When, around dawn, Miss Converse came in with the razor, hot water, and soap, Mrs. Curtis was quite awake, and gave her a wide, clamped-on smile.

Mrs. Curtis's convalescence was exactly as hateful as Dr. Logan had predicted; indeed, it changed several small things permanently—brands of patience, definitions of pain.

The afternoon before her discharge, she sat on the corridor's balcony, reading. There she was joined by Dr. Logan. He sat down beside her and they smiled at each other.

"Saying goodbye to you is the only unjoyful part," she told him formally.

The early May sky, slightly veiled, was a good enough match for the satisfied gaze he gave her. "Don't forget, I'll see you six weeks from now."

"Oh, that," she said, dismissing that date as irrelevant.

"I haven't seen Dr. Brade in days," she said suddenly. She had never mentioned the night of her aborted call; but there had been something now and then in Dr. Logan's manner, and she had wondered. It had been the part about Dr. Logan which had hushed her.

"Oh, he's on another floor this month," said Dr. Logan.

"Does he have a clinic?" she asked. "Poor people, who come in, I mean."

"Oh yes," said Dr. Logan, looking at her over the faint yellow-green of the new leaves.

Without the slightest foreknowledge, Mrs. Curtis said, "He is a sadist."

To her surprise, Dr. Logan did not at once reply. Then he shifted a little to face her directly.

"He came in to you late, the night before your operation. And you called me."

She gaped at him.

"It was something he said to me later," went on Dr. Logan in a detached tone. "Something about your being excessively nervous that night. It seemed natural, but uncharacteristic."

She looked at him mutely.

Then, amazingly, "They slip through, you know," he said. "It's the one thing we can't screen ahead of time. Unless we're shown it. And we aren't. You can test for brains, skill, application, industry. Whatever you want. But not that. He came and frightened you, late that night, didn't he? And you called me. Why didn't you speak?"

"I couldn't," she said, and he did not argue that.

He stood up and looked down at her. It was the time of day he looked most tired. "Tinker, tailor, soldier, sailor," he said. "It's an odd vocation. The tinker and tailor have to make their own chances. Not so the policeman, the soldier, the security guard."

"The doctor," she said.

"Yes," he said. "Few."

"You can catch them at it," she said.

"With help," he said, and she averted her eyes.

Often he had patted her shoulder. Now he put out a hand formally. "Goodbye, Mrs. Curtis. I'll see you at the office."

"Goodbye," she said. She looked after him with something to do with love.

How well we know each other, she thought.

And Dr. Brade, wherever he and his siblings were, came before her eyes, steadfast, unsmiling; ancient.

The Night the Playoffs
Were Rained Out

I T WAS IN THE MIDDLE of the third inning, with two men out, a
runner at second, and two and two on the batter, that the bliz-
zard erupted. Across the screen swept a dazzle of jerking spots.

Mr. Plessy sprang to the set, while Mrs. Plessy groaned. But
every station was the same; all was obliterated in that horrid
motion.

The prospect of the game had sustained the Plessys—baseball
fanatics both—in the foggy rain through which they had doggedly and dangerously plunged toward the laced letters of the
Jersey Turnpike for hours in the afternoon, blinded by the spray
from oil trucks, mesmerized by the fairly fruitless windshield
wipers. "It shouldn't be raining *there*," Mrs. Plessy said.

They had had a leisurely lunch, deliberately prolonged. Mrs.
Plessy, in whom forty years had not truly impaired the optimism
of her natural bent, had cheered up, after being as usual somewhat sunk by the noon news on the radio. Particularly grim, it
had struck both the Plessys—as it increasingly did—as making
normal private good cheer vaguely vulgar. Mrs. Plessy, over
onion soup so ropy that she had frequently to shut up, com-
mented as she often but not boringly did, on the apparent impos-

sibility of hacking away at the ancient roots of rancor, hostility, and profound uncongeniality that wound like iron through the earth. Mr. Plessy, who much admired his wife, believed her capable of a profound amity. Though not stupid, she had so resilient a trust in humanity as sometimes to seem so, and she tended to personify countries as children personify animals.

The day had started out with the blandest of blue skies; but that had altered rapidly, and before the green and white JT signs had altered to the thing itself, wisps of a sullen brown fog had begun curling over the immediate air.

Bound back to Potomac, the Plessys had planned to drive straight through to Philadelphia. They would reach home by midday and in good order. But in a louring October dusk, Mr. Plessy's hands on the wheel showed slick white knuckles, and Mrs. Plessy was very tired of racing, totally blind for instants on end, alongside thundering trucks.

"The next, the absolutely next exit," said Mr. Plessy. But a Holiday Inn and a Ramada were both behind them, and who could be sure what a rudimentary knife, fork, and spoon stood for?

When, finally defeated, they took an unfamiliar exit, the brightly lit motel looked cheerful; but also the parking lot looked perfectly full. "This is ridiculous, at four o'clock," said Mr. Plessy. Simultaneously, their thought leaped to the game. Were they to hear it crudely translated for the radio as they rushed, homeless, on and on through the night?

Mr. Plessy finally found a weedy margin at the far end. "You wait here," he told Mrs. Plessy. His report came back that it wasn't much of a motel, whatever that dim criterion implied; but they had exactly one room left. "Of course, it'll be next to the elevator," said Mr. Plessy, reversing the car and pulling up to the entrance with the relief of a night-beset pilgrim.

It wasn't next to the elevator, but it made up for that in general dreariness. The only spurt of excess was in two beds, one large, one enormous, in which the Plessys might alternatively revel. Everything gleamed and was brown; and Mrs. Plessy felt that mild sinking of the heart which afflicted her at the idea of the invisible presence of hundreds of nameless travelers, suffering proximity without purpose, scurrying like ants in bizarre directions. And why was there always that faint humming sound in the halls?

When Mr. Plessy went to get ice, he was gone so long, Mrs. Plessy decided that he had forgotten his room number or discovered the ice was all gone. But he returned with a heaped carton, and in mild exasperation. He had been waylaid at the ice machine by a talker who seemed, Mr. Plessy said, to think ice was made of marbles. He now poured the martinis carefully from glass to glass, chilling but not diluting them. "Jovial type," said Mr. Plessy, in muted tones. "Wanted us all to see the game together. Instant pal. Little bitty eyes."

"Why are you muttering?" said Mrs. Plessy. "Is he under the bed?"

"No, but he's next door, 108," said Mr. Plessy, with a grin, handing her her martini.

Mrs. Plessy shuddered slightly and took a cold lovely sip. "Check the TV," she suggested.

A rainbow blazed. The bright orange face of an anchor man yelled at them "... body was found by some homecoming children ..." Mr. Plessy hastily reversed the sound, "... who were taking a short cut..." Mr. Plessy snapped it off. "Well, the umpires might look a little funny," he said, "but maybe I can adjust it."

Luxurious in dressing gowns and pajamas, the Plessys had survived two threats by tarpaulin, when, in the middle of the third inning, everything ended in a dazzling flash.

After three minutes of frantic struggle, Mr. Plessy took to the phone. When Mrs. Plessy heard him cry, "But that's impossible!" she knew at once that it was not only possible but true.

Mr. Plessy slammed the receiver—a wildly untypical gesture —and they stared at each other. "They haven't got an extra, and The Man isn't on at night," he said in absolute despair. They continued to look at each other.

"That guy," suddenly said Mr. Plessy. "The one at the ice machine who wanted us to all hear the game together." There was a wretched pause.

"I'm Luther Gombrecht, and this is Minna. Here, here, here," said Mr. Gombrecht, shoving a chair behind Mrs. Plessy's knees and taking to the edge of a giant bed. "They got him out. It's still 3 to 2."

In 108 the fundamental hint of disinfectant was powerfully overlaid by the strength of perfume. Mrs. Gombrecht had a fat strong face, from which eyes of a bright ceramic blue, after a good stare at Mrs. Plessy, returned to the screen.

An unnatural intimacy enveloped everyone. Clothes, tossed about, had the air of being still warm. A fifth of Chivas Regal, half full, sat on the bureau top, and curls of smoke shifted over the TV.

"One more inning and it's a game," said Mr. Gombrecht. "That's still rain coming down, a little."

"That's the TV," said Mrs. Gombrecht. "Sure you won't have some Chivas Regal?"

"I don't think, on top of martinis," said Mrs. Plessy, who had never had any.

"Well, we don't happen to have martinis," said Mrs. Gombrecht, looking hard at Mrs. Plessy.

"Well, just a little," said Mrs. Plessy, stronger on hope than backbone.

Mr. Gombrecht handed her a paper cup, half full, in which a small eye of ice floated, becalmed.

"Well, *that* wasn't much of an inning," said Mr. Gombrecht. He appeared injured. "You a lawyer?" he suddenly asked Mr. Plessy, who was surprised.

"No, no. No, I'm a teacher," Mr. Plessy said, giving, he found, a propitiatory smile.

"What you teach?" asked Mr. Gombrecht, withholding judgment.

"English," said Mr. Plessy apprehensively.

"English," Mr. Gombrecht repeated, ruminating. The ladies silently drank.

"I'm in rayon," said Mr. Gombrecht. No development followed this. "You take teachers," said Mr. Gombrecht. There was a little pause while they were taken.

Mrs. Plessy gazed hard at the lead-off batter; viciously he swung three bats, slash, slash, slash. Each player on the screen was now accompanied by his ghost.

"They should get paid more," said Mr. Gombrecht. "Teachers."

"Well, that's why you don't get your executive type going for that," said Mrs. Gombrecht, raising her voice over the batter's history. "If you want to make something of yourself—in the practical way, of course—you don't go for the dead end."

On the diamond, twins were now everywhere. Mrs. Plessy looked miserably at this *corps de ballet*. She had an inarticulate belief that baseball, like bad news, should be shared with the loved. Or with hordes, as in the ballpark.

"Anyone else, before I kill this?" said Mr. Gombrecht, hospitably waving the Chivas Regal. "Look what *these* guys get paid— and most of them morons. Half of them can be fixed, and the other half are potheads."

Speechless, Mr. Plessy swallowed the rest of his drink in a gulp.

"Well," said Mrs. Gombrecht, "the money picture changes all the time. You can't count on any rules, really. Our apartment house neighborhood has changed—changed very greatly. A Hebrew gentleman moved in this week," said Mrs. Gombrecht genteelly. "And now the Colored are about five blocks away."

Mrs. Plessy attempted a strange little smile, to show that on the whole this was good news.

In an effort to drown the announcer, Mrs. Gombrecht said earnestly and a little thickly, "Well, I just wasn't brought up that way." Her ceramic eye pondered how Mrs. Plessy had been brought up.

In one motion the pitcher whirled and threw to first, where the runner sprawled in superhuman extension. This attracted Mr. Gombrecht's attention. "He was off base!" he shouted.

To Mrs. Plessy's alarm, her husband said in a tight voice, "He was not! His fingers were right on the bag!"

"Well, pardon me," said Mr. Gombrecht obscurely. "Just an opinion."

There was a long hard fly to the outfield. It curved over the warning pad, headed fast and away. The center fielder leapt like a lizard, clung like a lizard, espaliered to the wall, staggered off with the ball in his hand. Pandemonium. For a second, total grace descended on the room, conspiratorial smiles curved their lips. It began to rain fluently.

"Oh Jesus," said Mr. Gombrecht. "Now look."

Hastily Mrs. Plessy rose. "Well," she said, "we must go. Thank you so much . . ." Mr. Plessy was at her shoulder.

"You can't tell yet," said Mrs. Gombrecht, with some hostility. She seemed less anxious for her visitors to stay than affronted by their departure.

"We have to get up early," said Mr. Plessy firmly, by the door.

But a sudden tide of pure color had flooded Mrs. Gombrecht's face. "I must say!" she shouted, but for a moment was unable to formulate the essence. Then she directly addressed Mrs. Plessy. "We invited you to share our room. You lap up our Chivas Regal. And then you—you *sneer!*"

"That's ridic—" began Mrs. Plessy, but her husband, with the door open, gave her a little shove. Unquestionably, the door behind them slammed. They stood, a little breathless, in the fluorescent glare of the empty hall. There was the faintest unlocatable hum.

At the door of 110, suddenly Mr. Plessy recoiled.

"Oh God, oh God," he said, "the key."

They stared at each other, appalled. "I'll have to go in there and get it," said Mr. Plessy into Mrs. Plessy's silence.

Instantly, Mrs. Plessy said, "You can't. You can't possibly."

The greenish light shone down on them. Behind the long row of closed doors the invisible crowds were silent.

"They'll have another key at the office," said Mrs. Plessy. "They have to have."

"In my *pajamas?*" said Mr. Plessy.

"Well, you can't get in to take them off."

The sallow youth at the desk couldn't help wondering, gazing at Mr. Plessy's pajamas, what they'd done with the one they had. Was it locked in their room? Mr. Plessy explained, adding with a desperate sanctimoniousness, "We can't go back and wake people up at this hour."

The youth reasoned with Mr. Plessy. "If you just came out of there, you wouldn't think they could possibly be asleep yet."

"Will you please get me a duplicate key to 110," said Mr. Plessy in a low vibrant tone. "I'll return them both in the morning."

Perhaps at this very moment Mr. Gombrecht in a drunken rage was attacking Mrs. Plessy in the hall. He turned his back on the desk while the boy rooted in an invisible drawer.

The empty lobby looked like a tatty station. People would pass through; no one would return to linger between the outstretched arms of the chairs. The rusty ferns sprang motionless. The room waited, isolated and claimable.

"There," said the youth without pleasure. He pushed the plastic oval across the counter to Mr. Plessy who said stiffly, "Thank you."

In the vast bed, Mr. Plessy took Mrs. Plessy's hand, which was cold.

"Just forget the whole thing," he whispered.

"It was so *silly*," said Mrs. Plessy, doubtfully.

"Well, just go to sleep," said Mr. Plessy, soothing.

"It didn't *have* to turn out like that..."

"*Please* go to sleep," said Mr. Plessy. "God knows what time it is." In the filtered light he could see their dim familiar clothes, amicable identities, heaped here and there.

Suddenly a voice began speaking quite loudly in the next room, and a confused clamor rose behind it. Play had resumed.

Mrs. Plessy burrowed in her pillows, and then placed one lightly over her face, while Mr. Plessy pulled the sheet over his head. There was a quick enduring roar.

"Home run," said Mr. Plessy softly. Over the uproar, the excited voice gabbled.

Mr. Plessy took his head out from under the sheet and looked, first upside down and then right side up, at his luminous watch. Twelve twenty-five. "*We* can't complain," he said.

They plunged almost simultaneously into their separate sleeps. Mr. Plessy's minute hand had moved only a short distance when there was a blow on the door. The Plessys shot up, in attitudes of confused terror.

"Now, what..." Mr. Plessy swung his legs over the bedside to stand up. Mrs. Plessy, at last out of control, hissed, "It's him! He's drunk and he's going to attack us!"

Mr. Plessy, caroming off the bureau edge, unlocked and flung open the door. A small glinting object hurtled past his head. Mr. Gombrecht, listing, was already half through his own doorway. "Anything else?" he cried, and vanished.

Sun struck in long points on the carpet when the Plessys walked into breakfast. The dining room looked unexpectedly cheerful: there, the hanging plants in good green shape, triangular red napkins on white cloth, and a round-faced, round-eyed waitress, who brought them coffee without asking.

After a furtive glance around them, the Plessys, who had spoken little up to that point, took companionable sips and smiled tentatively at each other. Mr. Plessy's smile broadened into a grin.

"Well, Mary, honestly, it had its funny side," he said, persuading. But Mrs. Plessy, her smile lost, looked at him dolefully.

"It was so *awful*," she said.

"Oh come on," he said. "Not that awful. Have the eggs with sausage."

The waitress, expectant, had returned. As Mrs. Plessy continued to gaze mournfully at him, Mr. Plessy said cheerfully, "We'll both have the double orange juice, and the eggs and sausage. And some more coffee, when you have a moment. Mary, you're taking this whole ridiculous thing too seriously," said Mr. Plessy, draining his coffee.

"If I hadn't had *any* drink, would it have been different?" asked Mrs. Plessy uncertainly.

"Of course not. They probably do that every night somewhere."

"But at first they must have been trying to be hospitable."

"They were just dogs looking for cats." But he saw it wouldn't do. "What *on earth's* the matter?" he reasonably asked.

"Tribes," she said obscurely. "Clans. Borders."

"Oh, *that's* it," said Mr. Plessy, enlightened. "No sight of Peace Now. Mary, don't you see—" he broke off, paralyzed. She would not turn her head, but the back of her neck stiffened.

"They're not up *yet*?" she pleaded.

"Oh sure," said Mr. Plessy jauntily. "I told you, they do it every night."

But when Mr. Plessy picked up his change and glanced at his tip, a resolve which she dared not share rose in Mrs. Plessy.

Her husband got up, humming very faintly, and turning, she instantly located the Gombrechts, seated in a thick silence, between the Plessys and the door.

Mr. Plessy, walking slightly on the balls of his feet, as if ready for whatever, looked high in front. But Mrs. Plessy, preparing a womanly after-all-how-silly smile, tensely rigid, at close quarters caught the eye of Mrs. Gombrecht. Mr. Gombrecht, rapidly stirring his tidal coffee, concentrated. But Mrs. Gombrecht met Mrs. Plessy's eye full on. Bright, blue, her ceramic gaze hardened, shone. With a fixed, china hostility, she sent a look straight into Mrs. Plessy's tentative eyes.

Over the early turnpike the sky had the tenderly fresh blue of rain's aftermath. Mrs. Plessy leaned her head back quietly. Mr. Plessy switched on the news, and after a minute hastily switched it off again. He reached over and put his hand on Mrs. Plessy's knee, and regardless of the thunder of oil trucks, drove that way in silence right up to the toll plaza.

A Walk with Raschid

WHEN THE MUEZZIN began to call, James got out of bed and went to the window. Tracy shifted as he did so, murmuring and giving a light shiver, and he pulled the sheet over her body, which looked bright in the moonlight; the iron grillwork barred it.

The call, a rough, unhuman, melancholy, hornlike sound, fell and rose, with a breathstopping pause between phrases. It appeared to take up, in a strange tongue, an unsettled theme. That it referred to a god could never be doubted. It insisted, accused, identified, summoned. No matter that he couldn't get so much as his toe into Moule Idris, shoeless or shod.

They had turned off the fountain just below, and the tiled courtyard, where he and Tracy and Mr. and Mrs. Neeson had sipped mint tea at noon in a daze of color, was absolutely still. The bone-blue of the medina slept; anyway, was silent. Not a bawl, not a bark. That extraordinary voice, not like a reed or a ram's horn, but more like both than a voice, proceeded powerfully up and down its ways. Were the tanners asleep, bright yellow and red, peacefully stinking? Did the single-toothed coppersmith rise and kneel to the east? Did it wake Raschid? At the thought of Raschid asleep or awake in that visible bone-blue city, James thought immediately of Oliver, asleep or awake in a home once as familiar to James as his fingers, now distant in a variety of ways. This had happened three or four times. Beyond the fact that Raschid and Oliver both belonged to the human species and were ten-year-old males, it was hard to see a connection.

Shivering a little in the three o'clock air, he heard the phrase end, on a wild deep braying gasp; a pause, and then a high climb. He stared through the grill at the blaze of moonlight; all the dark seemed to have contracted into the cypresses. A small dizzy sense of ridiculousness wafted over him: James Gantry, naked, immaculately shaved, hearing the news of Allah and his Prophet, while his wife, bright as a minted penny, slept behind him, and his honeymoon rose in the blanched Moroccan night. Here every known thing seemed to have its alien echo: his feet, the brilliant geometry of the tiles; Tracy, the carved and gilded and painted bed; his son's pale square-set image, Raschid.

Raschid wore a striped djellabah; it was too small, but looked dignified. He never (when James had seen him) raised the hood. He had small bones, extended eyelashes, and a left thumb flattened in some mishap. His eyes (differing in this from his face, which was somber) were light-hearted in their darkness; unlike those of Oliver, which were of a pale and steadfast blue.

Hastily choosing the lighter confusion, James pressed down on the thought of Raschid. He didn't understand Raschid. Political prejudice aside, he did consider Arabs decorative; and then, Oliver's lack of childish charm had only lucklessly sharpened James's love of it. So he was prepared for that aspect of Raschid. But although he was gloomily convinced that the man who wasn't a scoundrel was apt to be a boob, he didn't want to be a boob, and he was alert for Raschid's angle. It could hardly be other than money, and when James found it apparently wasn't, he was thrown into unease. The whole of Fez contributed to this.

Fez was all there, close, breathing, smelling and moving, and yet he felt unsure what was real, where, exactly, the fraud began. The dyers and tanners were real; standing high above the stench, on narrow pitted steps with Tracy gamely clutching his elbow, the guide waiting, and Raschid gesticulating one step below, he saw them, inside their own lives; but, too, in some circle of Dante's. And in the cavern of trays the coppersmith, with his one tooth and serene eyes, looked at once like a tourist's artisan and a disguised and saintly magician.

Raschid had cut himself out from the horde of children by an incident common between the sexes, and not unknown between adults and children strange to each other—a sudden wordless intimacy, based on a mutual attraction solid as an electric shock.

Raschid's reaction, James perfectly well knew, was inevitably rooted in a lack in the past, and a hunger for the future. His own, he faced with a familiar stale qualm, was at least the former. The future, now, was Tracy. He had never been truly equipped to love Oliver, if love entailed satisfaction. But, unrejected, he would have offered as fine substitutes as his nature would provide and guilt could prompt. But he *had* been rejected; first somewhere in secret, and then verbally. It was odd how clearly he knew that it was he who had been rejected, rather than Louise who had been chosen. If Louise had never found their son a very interest-compelling subject, she had maintained with him, during the periods when he attracted her attention, a mild-mannered friendliness. There were children who *did* interest her; but any comparison which she may have made in silence, or in dreams, never resulted in maternal animosity.

It had always been hard for Oliver to speak; and it was Tracy who had got him through the ordeal of his decision, by her ability to listen, an ability as native and as finely honed as her tennis game. How a child of his and Louise's could be that inarticulate passed James's understanding. Though he secretly thought of Louise's articulateness as facile (perhaps because it worked so well on her newly privileged kindergarten listeners), there it was. Oliver gave, always, the impression of weighing. He was a sort of small, human, heavily constructed pair of scales, the results of whose balances were never disclosed. After the permissible baby age, he had been caught now and then telling stories, all involving possessions, material or animal; but until James had looked at them in the light of Tracy's sunny honesty, he had not called them lies. Like Tracy, he spontaneously believed lying to be the meanest of the vices. "Know the truth, and the truth shall make you free." It was Tracy's only biblical quotation.

One hot September afternoon she had said it to him, running her cool fingers over the pink shells of her toenails. James, waiting in his brown hateful bed-sitting room; Oliver, redelivered to the house which for twelve years had been James's home. Tracy had been standing at the window; he thought she appeared like Mercury, the gods' lissome and terrible messenger. She came over to the daybed, kicked off her pumps, curled up and seized her toes. Over them, half humorous, half tearful, she quoted her maxim.

"Well?" said James.

"He wants to stay with Louise."

The curious shaft, like dry ice, that burned through him, he could not have diagnosed for his life.

"I don't believe it."

"He told me so. In so many words."

There was a silence. Tracy kept it; she never blundered.

"Well," he said at last. "How hard was it—for him, I mean?"

"Very, I think," said Tracy softly. She looked, for her, tired, and James rushed toward her in his mind's eye. How much she gave, how little, without denigrating herself, she asked. She had not demanded commitment. Now that she had it, she would have shaped herself to another woman's heavy and taciturn child, if that was what James and Oliver wanted. Oliver had liked her at once. He was always looking for a new thing to belong to him, James glumly thought, and it was Tracy who had lifted from all three of them that most savage incident of a split marriage—self-declaration by offspring. Louise, conditioned to consult, in her warm-soup voice, finger-painters versus block-builders, had kindly said, "Oliver should choose, himself. He's ten. It's only a limited choice, it's not as though he'd never see the other."

"A child that age, even a *frank* child," Tracy had said as she and James turned it gently over and over, "can't get words around huge things, the things its life is made of. If you ask him about motorbike parts, or batting averages, it's a piece of cake. But fool, awful questions, like 'do you love your mother?' 'are you mad at your father?' . . . What we've *got* to have is the truth, that's the only thing that'll hold up. He can say to me 'my father' or 'my mother.' To you, or Louise, he'd have to say 'you.' That's where, perhaps, I helped. Getting 'loyalty' out of it. Poor Oliver. Christ, the things people do in the name of loyalty. Pulling live tissue apart. I said it was a temporary pattern; just that. No great, permanent decision. That you and Louise wanted to stand enough aside to give him room to breathe and think. This way, he needn't say to either, 'I don't want to live with you.'"

"It's just," said James lamely, "that he seems so remote from Louise."

Tracy laid her weary head back against the brown cushions of the daybed.

"Louise really only likes them at the prejudgment age," she said astutely. "It makes her nervous to be sized up. Children are death on that."

"Did he say anything about me?" he after a while asked.

"Bang!" went knuckles on the door. James rose; it was their ice. Conveniently later she said gently, "He was embarrassed. He's only ten. And he sometimes finds it hard to be honest. This was one of the hard times."

James raised his amber glass and drank. Tracy, too, raised her glass. "To Oliver," she said slowly. They drank. Suddenly a wild relief—the die cast, that inn of decision in which the mind sleeps well—flooded James. "To Morocco," he said. But the second toast was too soon for Tracy. She set her glass softly by the icebucket, and closed her green eyes.

The chanting had stopped. The muezzin had gone back to wherever he had come from. The moonlight had withdrawn; Tracy was only a dark corner. James, who had sat down on a sighing hassock, got up. A light burst out in a kitty-cornered window in the lower garden, and Mrs. Neeson, in flamingo chiffon panels, went across it. How very gorgeous, James thought meanly. Mrs. Neeson was too much for him. The effect was flawless but, though effortless in appearance, seemed to spring from a vast hidden machinery. Surely Nubian slaves must have toiled for centuries, computers made hairline decisions, sleep, reading and eating have been forsworn for plans. Was Mr. Neeson the machinery?

Mrs. Neeson's references were too oblique and intimate to be name-dropping; nothing so cut-rate fell from her lips. The Palais

Jamai, reprieved by quaintness and the lovely tokens of old Moorish lusts, amused her in an endearing way. "How we do envy you dear old number seven," she had said at once. "We cabled just too late." Tracy, with her candid gaze, had subsequently reexamined their small lustrous room. "Well, now we have the Good Housekeeping Seal," James said nastily. It had amused him that Mrs. Neeson should cause Tracy to reassess anything.

Did that flamingo vision arise, from the first sweet sleep of night, to perform esoteric rites of beautification? Or was she merely en route to the bathroom? The light still burned. The medina still slept. In an orgy of pre-dawn slackness, James wondered, abashed, if Raschid dreamed of the American who spoke French, who, infinitely powerful, infinitely just, was an enormous sudden friend. James was as beautiful as Raschid, though at thirty-three it would never have occurred to him that this was true.

In the morning, the courtyard tiles shone from the hose. The fountain, released, sprang up and fell, and distant noises came from the medina.

Raschid came to the outer entrance about ten o'clock. James, who had gone out to treat with a taxi driver, saw his striped djellabah swerve out of the medina alley. The taxi driver said at once, "The guides will get police if he keeps does so. He can't guide. Beggars, beggars."

"He is not a beggar," said James shortly. He decided to ignore the taxi driver's opinions. "At eleven-thirty, then," he said haughtily, and turned toward Raschid.

Day before yesterday, when he had first joined them (doubling their steps quietly along the stony way, regarded sideways by a James enchanted, apprehensive, waiting for the story and the brown small palm), he had worried about James's French. "*Vous comprenez?*" he asked, drawing up his short nose as though smelling language deficiencies. "*Vous comprenez ce que j'ai dit?*" Then he began to worry about Tracy, but not much. "*Expliquez à votre femme,*" he said once or twice rather perfunctorily, as if she might be dangerous if too much excluded.

He made the stale standard joke, pushing a donkey aside,

"*Ce sont les petits taxis de la medina!*" and his eyes laughing at James, at himself, at the donkeys, at the prostrate jest, took James into a dazzling intimacy.

At the end of their stroll through the bleak biblical landscape of stones, bare earth and bleached sun, James extracted a handful of change. Instantly a cloud passed over Raschid's brown eyes, muddying their color. He put both hands behind his back and looked sullenly down at his feet under the djellabah's dirty edge.

"*J'ai voulu faire votre connaissance,*" he said. "*C'était tout simplement ça.*"

Amazed, pleased, uneasy, James had returned his dirhams to his pocket.

"What did he say?" asked Tracy, smiling at Raschid.

"He said he wished to make my acquaintance, that was his only purpose."

They shook hands with him, first James, then Tracy, and he asked James when he would care to go through the medina. They were going the next morning, said James, but with a guide, it was already arranged. Raschid murmured something in Arabic. Then he lifted his head and said clearly in French, looking James straight in the eye, that he would like, once, to take them himself into the medina. They would go to certain places the guide would not have time for; then, when that was finished, they would go to *un restaurant typique, très typique, très petit, très bon,* and there they would *prendre le déjeuner ensemble.* "*Demain, peutêtre?*"

That they could not do, Tracy, easily snared, having committed them to lunch with the Neesons. "*Alors, le lendemain...*" said Raschid.

"*Hélas, nous allons à Meknès.*"

"*Alors, le jour après ça...*"

"But that's our last day," said Tracy, guessing.

James said to her in rapid English, "We could go in the afternoon, late, and have supper instead of lunch. I'd really like to. That would leave practically the whole day free."

"Good," she said instantly. She grinned affirmatively at Raschid; but his face, direly balanced between their glances, stayed dark until James committed them: "*Eh bien, d'accord. À quatre heures et demi. Après, nous pouvons dîner ensemble. Le jour après le lendemain.*"

The next day he came with them and their outraged guide. He pointed now and then, but did not speak except to say, with taciturn authority, *"Moule Idris, c'est le plus beau de tous."*

As they peered over the shoulders of a picture-snapping compatriot, into that vast, ordered, brilliant coolness, Tracy said a little crossly, "I don't see why they let people take *pictures* and not go in—if they take their shoes off, I mean. My husband went into one in Alexandria," she told the guide.

He gave them a bland frown. "Fez is a more holy city," he said. "Very holy." Raschid stared at James to see how he received this statement.

Disoriented, they trudged behind their towering and animated guide: coppersmiths, tinsmiths; souks, weavers, tanners, dyers. They debouched, helpless, into lavish rooms at the end of sinister entrances; undesired rugs, glowing like radiant signals, unfurled by rapid boys; mint tea; unstuffed hassocks, cast upon the floor to sink in gorgeous slow motion; mint tea. They flattened themselves against stone to let donkeys pass. The donkeys' aristocratic legs supported immense piles of planks, towering baskets, piles of colored cloth. *"Ce sont les petits taxis de la medina,"* said the guide.

Tracy, golden, in white linen, stayed cool and happy. James was battling a sense of disequilibrium. It seemed to have darted like a shadowy fish in deep water ever since the hour when he had heard the muezzin's raucous wandering call, when he had been alone at the window. He was summoned, yet he was not. He could touch people at any minute—indeed, it was impossible not to; but he should have been closer, or more distant. This way, it needed to be a travelogue, a chapter: the medina, Fez. The place hummed, milled, teemed; all the travelogue words. But the eyes that met his, over yashmak and under turban, slid over human material borne past them by a guide.

His elbow was jerked; on his arm the soiled brown hand with the smashed thumbnail rested, pressing. *"Voilà! C'est notre restaurant futur. Quand nous faisons ensemble notre promenade."*

He could see nothing but a blind darkness beyond an open doorway; and they were past it, anyway. But it was an engagement; and it was as though at last he were identified.

They had not gone to Meknès, after all. Something had upset

Tracy, and she lay all day, qualmish and languid, not even much reading. She urged James to go anyway, but he suddenly realized how much he did not want to. He wanted to stay still. The Neesons *had* gone to Meknès, causing Tracy to remark, childishly, that if she *were* going to be sick, it seemed like a good day.

James sat in the shadow by the fountain and read *The Tale of Genji*. Ravished by a paragraph, he stared from his shade into a daze of sun. He jumped up, and went in to read to Tracy about the little maids going into the dim early garden, carrying their cricket cages; but she had fallen asleep, her pale hair lightly snarled on the punched-up pillow. He stared at his future, awed. The simple, unambiguous, exquisite, and here-present future. He went back, through the cool splendors of the hall, into the courtyard, sat down and read the passage again. But this time it had thinned out. He shut the book, and then as two couples paused, staring lovingly around them, raised it.

He had not heard his muezzin again, except the night before, when, a semicircular foursome, they were having coffee in the small bar. Then, though faint, the hard distant wail had caused them slightly to raise their voices.

It annoyed James that he did not enjoy the Neesons. He credited them with being out of the run; *more* of something, if not of something different. Mr. Neeson, who looked as though he had had his blood painlessly extracted and then been sealed again, had a small, pungent speech. It admitted of no qualifications, but it was lively. Mrs. Neeson, whose anecdotes, never blasting, were pleasantly penultimate, glowed and breathed. Perhaps Mrs. Neeson had all that blood?

A friend of hers, a more-than-promising young French film director (formerly a Godard protégé, but now intransigently individualistic), was, or might be, at Marrakesh; the Neesons were waiting for a call. Against the embroidered cushions, Mrs. Neeson appeared to have been incarnated from an absolutely first-class original. Lustrously, she leaned toward James, with a luminous-lipped air of barely pre-coital chic.

"He's very ready," she said. "Very open-ended. But there's a terrific thrust. He used color-change for mood long before Antonioni."

"Film is exciting," said Tracy. James saw with love that she felt uncertain, but not totally docile, in her habitual self-underestimation.

"It's the camera. It's knowing how not to interfere with what the camera sees." A turbaned head appeared at her shoulder; it was the Mamounia, calling from Marrakesh.

The Gantrys were halfway up the stairs when she returned. "Jean-Paul!" she cried softly after them. "It was! His art man is going to do some sketches of a palace in Meknès, and we're going back to Meknès, and meet him at a friend's place outside, where we can go for cocktails, and then drive on late to Rabat, all of us."

Back at the foot of the stairs again, the Gantrys glanced at each other, reapproaching the bar. Could she mean "all"?

"I've told him about you both." So she did. "And you were going to Rabat anyway, the next day."

James said at once, "How nice of him, and of you. But tomorrow, we can't." He saw Tracy's eyes cloud. "We're tied up," he nevertheless said. It sounded lame. Somehow he could not get a grip on Raschid which could produce him for the Neesons in the guise of an engagement.

But Mrs. Neeson was incurious and easy. "Oh dear, if we'd only known a bit sooner."

Behind the big carved door of Number 7, James said guiltily, "Why on earth don't you go? You can take a car back here."

Tracy had crossed to the window grille. The fountain was still playing. "Darling, don't be ridiculous. 'Jean-Paul' doesn't want to see me. It might have been fun—but not just me, with them."

He joined her at the window. The cypresses pointed straight at a great many stars.

"I mean," said James, "he's been counting on it for three days. A kid that age . . ."

"Heavens, yes," she instantly agreed. "We couldn't change him to lunch, you don't suppose?"

He was somehow relieved that evidently it wasn't that she hankered for the Neesons in exchange for Raschid, as that she had a generous appetite for both. "We can't get *hold* of him. I've no idea where he lives, in the medina. Do you know," he said, surprised, "I can't even remember his last name. He told me twice, but Arabic names . . ." But it still seemed to him strange.

"Oh well," said Tracy mildly, and taking her kimono she disappeared into the bathroom, through whose open overhead arch he could hear her running the shower and cheerfully whistling.

He dreamed of Mercury. The god's heels, conventionally wing-tipped, barely rested on the kindergarten floor. The small black faces stared, not truly frightened. "And *this*," said Louise's breathy voice, "is *Mercury*. He is a messenger. He is the gods' *messenger*. He is a god, too. He is the god of lovers, and of thieves. We will draw that thing on his head. With our crayons. It is a helmet. A *golden helmet*. Oliver, will you turn him sideways for us, please." As Oliver moved to do so, James woke, coldly clear. Mercury had been beautiful. The small black faces had been beautiful; open, dark, turned like royal pansies toward Louise's sun. Louise's son. James's son. Not that pale, really, not in real life; not that squat, not that shut.

He had had one tantrum, Louise wrote. Only one. He bought a snake, sent from an unscrupulous snake farm in Florida. It had to be fed live mice. Regularly. The whole thing was psychologically wrong at the moment. Cruel, stupid and inefficient. She had returned the snake, collect. Oliver had exploded. He had called her a white mouse. A white rat. For the snake to eat. He wanted to live with his father. His father was, actually, coming to take him away.

Louise, rancorless, and encouraged by this purging, had reminded him of his choice. It was a lie. He began to weep. He had never never said that, never, never. She had not said, "Then why hasn't your father come to get you?" And a little later, when she came back to the room he hugged her violently and explained that he had said it because his snake had been returned. He had chosen her because he loved her. Since then he was friendly, and was saving for a Siamese kitten.

For an awful day James had wondered if, in his rage and frustration, Oliver had lived through minutes of believing his own invention; that he had summoned a father who, silently, never arrived; received a disprized home, nursed a secret he could never admit. Tracy had gone quite white over this story.

But she did not think that, even in his rage, Oliver believed it. "That's his weak spot. It's because he's inarticulate. I'm sure. He lies sometimes, like about the raccoon—because he can't fully express things."

Faces such as Raschid's did not, basically, need words; but he had them, correct, lucid, formal. It was a curious rendezvous; beyond the afternoon, the walk, the dinner, the farewell, what did Raschid want? A different memory? A promise? A bond outside his arc? Yes, he had brothers, he had answered. Six. Two sisters. No father. (Gone? Dead?) An aunt. A mother.

What sort of present could Raschid be given? He was extraordinarily intelligent. He spoke well. He had fire, grace. He was dirty; but small boys got dirty. But this was settled dirt. And the djellabah was mildly ragged. Would he like James to meet his mother? To what purpose? Was this really a friendship? Wild as that seemed. What would they eat? What on earth would the restaurant through that dark doorway be like? But then the inner shops . . . He felt a tremendous hot gaiety, a sense of some light-hearted reprieve, that spilled into his sleep. He was amused to find he was thinking in terms of "not letting Raschid down."

Their last day came over the gardens like a single jewel. After lunch they went down to the lower level to say goodbye to the Neesons, later departing for Meknès and Jean-Paul. The Gantrys had an hour before Raschid's arrival. The lower garden was cool and dusty; the Gantrys, faced with a long, sunny trek, slumped peacefully in wicker chairs. Tracy thought of the postcards she had meant to get. "I could do it now," she said. "Oh sit still," said Mrs. Neeson affably, but Tracy went on mournfully remembering that she would *not* want to write them tonight, and God knew, not before leaving early in the morning. Finally, she went to get them. When she came back, some time later, she was dissatisfied. Having searched, she had ended up with pictures taken from curious angles, denigrating the courtyard and its views. Nevertheless, she scribbled laxly, stopping to sigh, in the fragrant heat.

At quarter past four, James rose. "Well," he said, "have a fine trip. I hope . . ." But the Neesons were coming up, too. At five, the car for Meknès would be there; they would wait by the fountain. "Those streets must be death, in this sun," said Mrs. Neeson. It was hotter in the upper courtyard, an intimation of outside.

"You go and see," said Tracy to James. "He mightn't be there yet."

James secretly had a feeling that he would have been there for some time. He went out through the flower beds, past the lily pool, along the tiled way, to the outside glare. Raschid had not yet arrived. There were two taxis (neither the one driven by Raschid's foe), a motorcycle, loiterers in the narrow shade thrown by the wall. He went back to the courtyard. Tracy had finished her cards. She stuffed them in her purse, slung it on her shoulder, and looked ready.

Suddenly James was anxious. It was like one of those dreadful, contrived stories in which at the last moment someone is run over, his mother falls dead, he is arrested, or locked in a window-less room.

"He *must* be there now," said Tracy. She had evidently explained things to the Neesons, since they looked only interested. "If your small Arab doesn't show, you'll get to Rabat with us yet," said Mrs. Neeson amiably.

"It's twenty-five to five," said Tracy. "You know he'd be there by now. Go see."

One of the taxis was gone. The shade along the wall had widened. He could not see Raschid. Perhaps the boy had come during James's return to the courtyard and dashed away for a minute. His breath felt odd. I am *not* meeting a general to negotiate for peace, he reproved himself, a little amused and puzzled. The taxi driver stared at him. James looked fiercely at the ground; the man knew perfectly well that his cab was not wanted. Then he raised his eyes quickly to his watch. It was a quarter to five, and a weight like a concrete block fell on him. Something *had* happened. And he would never know. That was the only part that was really bad. The truth, he thought, joking, can't make me free if I don't know it. Couldn't Raschid have sent him word? But he knew that an alley tart would have had more chance of penetrating the late sultan's harem, than Raschid or a friend, of penetrating the courtyard.

A taxi drew up, and two black and enormous women got out,

one magnificent in royal blue, the other towering in a bone-crushing pink. They were mammoth, handsome, ferociously powerful. They began pulling bundles from the taxi, roped huge mounds, baskets, bags with knotted necks. Their driver had disappeared into the medina. James looked gratefully at this diversion. Raschid had no watch. Time, to an Arab child . . . But he did not believe it.

The taxi driver reappeared from the medina entrance, followed by a man in a soiled white djellabah, leading two donkeys. The man and the driver began to load the bundles onto the donkeys, higher and higher; last came a roped trunk. Finally, when only the huge heads and delicate legs were visible, the man struck each donkey a blow with a large stick and they lurched, and then swayed, sagging, forward down the sloping alley and out of sight. The taxi backed, ground gears, rushed off. The driver of the parked taxi addressed James.

"Berbers," he said. "Berbers. No damn good." He spat from the taxi window. "Bad people around," he said.

James looked at him. The man stared into his eyes. "Bad boys, too," he said. "That boy, he kicked your wife."

"What?" said James.

"He kicked her," repeated the driver. "Police fix him soon, I say it. She speak to him nice, and he yelling, *Non, non, non.* And then she try to give him something. Give him American money. Goddam fool, he kick and yell."

"I don't know what you are talking about," said James.

"Not one hour gone by," said the taxi driver with care. "Not one hour. He yelling at her, *menteuse, menteuse!* That's 'liar' he says. In French, crying and yelling. Then he pull up his hood, and kick her leg and run away. She smile at me, this way," he lifted his shoulders to his ears. "Very nice lady, not to get police."

James went over to the alley and looked down it. The Berbers and their donkeys had disappeared; other figures, other donkeys, strode and swayed. Hooded heads turned corners. Under a djellabah hood, dark eyes, now turned a light, steadfast blue, raced away, raced away. The wall had cut off the sun, and a faint fresh coolness rose from the stones. As the taxi driver watched him, he turned back and went toward the courtyard.

The Friends

———

A CROSS THE CITY, Rosie's phone began to ring. Mrs. Perkins could hear it, right in her ear, with that strange tone, at once patient and imperious. After the fourth ring, she knew what had happened, but she kept the receiver at her ear, as it rang seven, eight... when she hung up.

Rosie hadn't gone out at night in twenty years. Tiger would be wild with rage and confusion. God knows who would have fed him, thought Mrs. Perkins, snatching at the smaller panic. But Dr. Cutler had promised, *promised*, to call if there were a change —had he lost the number? Staring out over her still unopened suitcases, Mrs. Perkins dialed again, and after three rings, a woman's voice said, "Patient Information."

Assertion, not question; she had cut a lot of red tape that way. "You have a patient there, Mrs. Rose O'Shaugnessy. I want to inquire for her."

"Hold on," said the voice. Mrs. Perkins could see the vast tiled hall, the heavy mahogany counter before the switchboard. "Hello? Hello!" she said.

"I'm just checking," said the voice patiently. "No, ma'am, we have no Mrs. Rose O'Shaugnessy registered."

"I am a patient of Dr. Cutler's," said Mrs. Perkins untruthfully. "Could you let me speak to him please?"

"Dr. Cutler is out of town," the voice said promptly.

Father Gilbert answered on the fourth ring. Though she had never seen him, she had a number of times heard his voice. "It's Susan Perkins, Father," she said. She wished violently she hadn't called. Until tomorrow. "I've just got home—I've been away for three weeks. Rosie doesn't answer her phone."

"Well, no," said Father Gilbert. "She's gone into the hospital. I took her yesterday."

How many times had terrified Rosie told them both she would sooner be dead?

"It's bad then."

"Well, yes, bad. She'd never have gone, except for the pain. But we've both known it was coming, haven't we, Mrs. Perkins? It's been a long time."

"But Dr. Cutler said there might not *be* any pain," she said childishly.

"Do you know of anyone who could take that dog?" asked Father Gilbert, in a tone of urgent doubt.

Mrs. Perkins was getting very frightened, quite as if she hadn't been prepared.

"No, no, I don't—Tiger . . . what on earth can we *do*? How long has he been shut up there?"

"Well, all his life, you know," said Father Gilbert relentlessly.

"No, I mean without food."

"Well, I only took her yesterday—she left him a great pile of food. I've been trying to reach you. I could call the Pound, but . . ."

"Oh, we can't!" cried Mrs. Perkins.

"Well, she'll never see him again. We don't have to tell her, do we?"

"No, no, Father Gilbert. I'll call my vet. He'll keep him. I know he will."

"But Mrs. Perkins, you know that dog."

"I'll call him now. They'll pick it up." She had to ask, "Does the doctor answer, I mean . . ."

"Well, they can't exactly say." The experienced voice was ahead of her. "I think it might be a matter of days. Or weeks. Not more," he added as encouragement.

"I'm going over now," she said.

"Hadn't you better wait a bit? After a night's sleep?"

"No," she said. "I'm all right. I'm fine. I'm going." She said, "Goodbye, Father," before she hung up.

The vet was helpful. But must she describe Tiger? Right now?

"Gloves. Gloves and a net," she said. "I'll leave a key under the mat. I'm on my way to the hospital. Just feed him and keep him for me. I'll call back."

After three weeks of neglect, the car kept stalling stubbornly. Susan drove right through her darkening suburb; the lights bloomed as she turned east. They showed row houses, increasingly dingy—there were fewer traffic lights and innumerable stop signs. She swung left into Hargrove Street and pulled up by Rosie's peeling steps. As she mounted them, key in hand, Tiger landed against the inner door with a crash, snarls loud as a dog fight. His claws raked the panel as she slipped the key under the rubber mat. Rosie's begonias pressed themselves against the window pane. Not a soul was in sight.

Amazement seized Mrs. Perkins as she drove as fast as she dared. Why was she so surprised, undone? But things had been changing so little, or at least so slowly, that she had ceased to believe what she knew. Eighteen months ago, Dr. Cutler had set a rough date—but it had come and gone, and still, each morning, the key turned softly in the lock of the apartment's front door, and Mrs. Perkins had heard it, or not heard it, and there was Rosie, peering in the bedroom, to see was she awake. Some mornings Mrs. Perkins got up very early and made her coffee and took the paper back to bed.

If she were still in bed, "Have you had your coffee, then?" Rosie would say. For thirty years she had said that, in the exact intonation.

"Turn on your LIGHTS!" bellowed a passing voice.

On her left appeared the towering old hospital, deep rose, set in meager grounds, flanked by its newer progeny in liver-colored brick. Everything was lit up.

Since it was now night, there was space in the first tier, though she could see the glitter of cars up and up the rising ramps. In the elevator her insides sank. The plastic cover of the plane's lunch, ripped off, had released a blotting-paper piece of pressed turkey, limp and faintly bluish, and a slice of tomato, barely flushed. She had had weak coffee in a doll's cup.

Across the covered bridge, she stepped at once into the curious air of a nocturnal hospital, at once hushed and busy; all muted noises, distant voices, faint metal, figures turning corners, and the sudden blast of a repeated name. At the desk, as the large girl came forward, Mrs. Perkins asked herself, had this been the voice on the phone? Again she tried assertion. "Would you tell me the number of Mrs. Rose O'Shaugnessy's room?"

The big fresh-faced girl with projecting teeth looked at her doubtfully. "Did you call just now?" Mrs. Perkins hesitated, and the girl added, a little nervously, "We don't *have* a Mrs. Rose O'Shaugnessy."

"She's here," said Mrs. Perkins. "She came in yesterday."

"We don't *have* her," the girl repeated.

At bay, Mrs. Perkins made a leap. "Look under 'S'—under Shaugnessy. Please," she said.

At last the girl looked genuinely irritated. She went over and swung the flange of a metal file. She came back with a pencil between her teeth, took it out, and said "Oster 8, 471." Then she added quickly, "No visitors at this hour."

"I'm not a visitor," said Mrs. Perkins. "I'm her employer." The word here sounded strange. "I've just gotten home. Her doctor is expecting me."

"What doctor would that be?" It was as though she wished to make up for the hospital's inaccuracy by its authority.

"Dr. Cutler's assistant," said Mrs. Perkins instantly. She had no idea who that might be.

When she left the elevator at Oster 8, clutching her soiled visitor's card, it was as though for the first time in all the activity, she realized that in a moment she would see Rosie.

The nurses' station was behind her; she walked quickly away from it along the hall—461—463—471.

The door was ajar and she slipped through. She was looking down at a small old man, brown with age, asleep. Beyond him, next to the window, was a second bed. On the pillow was Rosie's head.

Mrs. Perkins went over stealthily. Rosie was asleep. There was a straight chair against the wall, and lifting it carefully, Mrs. Perkins put it by the bed and sat on its edge to look at Rosie. Her first thought was of starvation—was it possible so to drop away in three weeks? Steadily Rosie had been losing weight, but the skeletal arm, the skeletal hand with its loose wedding ring, the high cheekbones jutting over hollows . . . The wrinkled lids covered the small defiant familiar eyes. Mrs. Perkins could see the scalp, onion-pale, through the thin hair.

She sat there, third in the utter silence of the room. A quick, light squelch of rubber soles went by. A ray from somewhere faintly lit Mrs. Perkins' watch.

Then Rosie's face contracted, like a child's, in distaste, and she made a sound, half grunt, half moan, and opened her eyes, stared at Mrs. Perkins' knees, and focused. Her hands leaped up, and she gave a kind of shout. "Missus Perkins! Missus Perkins!" she shouted as if from a tremendous distance. "Oh, Missus Perkins! You're here, then! Oh I'm so glad, so glad," the voice retreated. Tears flew out of Rosie's eyes, and the light went on. A tall young intern in the doorway stared at them, Mrs. Perkins low in Rosie's bony clasp. He came over and said good-temperedly to Rosie, "There now, she's here! I told you she was coming!"

In Rosie's grip, Mrs. Perkins stared back at him. "See me before you leave," he said. He touched Rosie's shoulder, and she jerked a little away. He switched off the ceiling light as he went out.

"I'm here, I'm here," Mrs. Perkins repeated.

"I've got a pain," said Rosie. "I just came for the clinic, and they couldn't fix it, at all. I'm going home in the morning. Tiger . . ." she suddenly stopped, looked sideways at Mrs. Perkins.

"He's all right, he's fine," said Mrs. Perkins. To her amazement, no question came to this manifest lie; she felt the weight give way and shift to her. Rosie, who had turned her head aside, turned it back. "You tell them to give me something for the pain," she said. "They don't care, at all, at all."

In the hall, the tall young man turned out to be sallow-faced, and briskly kind. "That was very touching," he said seriously.

He might have been speaking to a child grieving over her puppy's frantic joy. "I'm Dr. Hotchkiss. She's been asking for you about every five minutes. She's been with you for a long time."

"Thirty years," said Mrs. Perkins shortly. In a false composition, she saw them: herself and the young intern: physician, concerned employer of an ancient retainer. As in the script, she asked, "How bad is it?"

"I have Dr. Cutler's notes on the case. So . . . as you know, it's the terminal stage. You've known about it for some time. When was it she refused the operation? Ten months ago . . ." he answered himself.

"Over a year. The pain . . ." said Mrs. Perkins. "What can you do about the pain? Dr. Cutler thought there might not be any . . ."

His eyes examined her carefully, politely. "Well, yes, that was a possibility. That it would terminate before this happened. We're giving her morphine, but since we don't know how long . . . You just got back, didn't you? I'd go to bed now and come tomorrow. Or the next day."

In the apartment, the flowers had been watered; Rosie must have come until a few days ago. The begonias, ancestors of those pressed against Rosie's pane, were covered with small, glazed, rose-colored blossoms. The pink geraniums had two great puffs of bloom, and the giant philodendron had thrust out a still-curled lighter green shoot.

Mrs. Perkins switched out the lamp by her bed and laid her head on the fresh pillow slip; when Rosie put one on, she smoothed it three times. Thirty years, said Mrs. Perkins in the dark. But they were jumbled, without sequence; events flung into a bright chaos, as though a toy kaleidoscope had been shaken. When Mrs. Perkins, then Susan Sloan, was twenty-two and just married to her first husband, Rosie Ryan, homely, neat, stubborn, nineteen years old, with a brogue so strong as to be almost inaccessible, had come to keep things clean. There was a cook—then, though not now—and a series of one-day-a-week cleaning women; it was Rosie who looked after things. Mrs. Perkins had had a job then; she had liked it, as now she liked to cook. But the sheer perversity of deterioration was Rosie's to deal with: surfaces that sprouted a film of dust from nowhere; inner curtains that changed from ecru to dingy; fingerprints which appeared on fresh paint; buttons which flew off and disappeared in the thinnest air; tumbled beds that wanted fresh linen; and the faint first miasma of tarnish breathed on brass and the silver service.

It was that shining metal, that silver service which first ravished Rosie. From day to day Mrs. Perkins had let its bright bloom lapse until it faded so shabbily in its neglect that it nearly landed in the storeroom. What on earth must Rosie think of bothering with that, she wondered. But Rosie, once and forever, lit its lamps; under her stubby fingers it shone bright and brighter, until a stray bit of sun fired it to a blinding dazzle. She was never sure whether Rosie's passion was that of power or of joy.

At that time Mrs. Perkins was in the early days of a bad marriage, and Rosie, of escape from a drunken father. A shattered wrist, crooked forever, was one memento of his wrath; and when Rosie went to his funeral, she turned him over, for good and all, to the Blessed Mother who could do with him as she saw fit. Rosie disliked men. But when she was twenty-eight, solitary, suspicious as always, quick for a quarrel, unshaken in a baseless opinion, an Irish longshoreman managed to marry her, savings and all. It was the good old days all over again—a black eye, a swollen lip, money for bail. Rosie got pregnant about the time of Mrs. Perkins' divorce and was knocked down the stairs the day she got her decree. That ended the baby, and six months after that a brawl in a bar sent O'Shaugnessy to a state hospital instead of to jail. With lips parted, head lowered, and extinguished eyes, he hulked in a wheelchair for fifteen years. Each week, Rosie went to see him, taking three street cars and bringing him something special to eat. "Are you sure he knows you're there?" asked cynical Mrs. Perkins. Only the Blessed Mother knew, Rosie said, but she herself had a notion he did. To Mrs. Perkins' joy he suddenly but predictably died two weeks after she married Sam Perkins.

By that time, a very tough alliance had rooted itself. Like someone spun into a web so imperceptibly that freedom is lost before being valued, Mrs. Perkins found that an awful interdependence had established itself. Whether Rosie had been born suspicious, isolated, or whether those protective qualities had been knocked into her, Mrs. Perkins was never sure. Rosie regarded men—all men—with active contempt; women with deep suspicion. Even priests, who technically came within the bounds of abstract approval, made her uneasy. Of her pastor, Father Shuster, she said grudgingly, "He's a fine priest, and all . . ." in a tone of minimum acknowledgment. As far as Mrs. Perkins could see, the Blessed Mother had created the universe, and any subsequent, prior, or peripheral manifestations of divinity were secondary if not incidental. In Mrs. Perkins—so that recipient found to her strong dismay—Rosie had invested all her reserves of approval and, finally, trust. She could do no wrong. Rosie fiercely disapproved of divorce, but she hated Joe Sloan, was so barely civil to him that even his wife's disillusion was dismayed. Always, Mrs. Perkins knew Rosie managed some sort of private exemption, some sort of special indulgence lefthandedly provided by the Blessed Mother.

Since Sam made Mrs. Perkins happy, Rosie, she could see, struggled with her natural instinct and achieved a sort of watchful tolerance. When a speeding truck, running a light, finished Sam, and the private sector of Mrs. Perkins' happiness closed down, it was, it seemed to her, through Rosie that she survived. She discovered then that lack of verbal communication could be water to thirst. Her friends rallied round—Sam had been a prince, a love, one in a thousand; they knew just how she felt. She must take time off for peace and rest; she must step up her work and her play to fill the empty corners; she must—they did not say, marry again—they said she must remember she was only forty-one, she was still, honestly, perfectly beautiful, she mustn't morbidly assume certain things were behind her.

Rosie never mentioned Sam. Simply, she suffered in Mrs. Perkins' misery. She abstracted his silver-framed picture, of which she had always to be reminded, and polished the frame until it nearly extinguished his face. In the nights, in the days away from work, face thrust into her sodden pillow, Mrs. Perkins heard the phone ringing, in a distant country, in another age. She discovered that Rosie was repeating, "She's not here now, then. Who will I say was calling her?" And later, Rosie would tell her that Mrs. Wad, or Mrs. Coton, or Mr. Avil, none of whom Mrs. Perkins had ever heard of, had called. At that time, it gave Mrs. Perkins the comforting sensation of being a newcomer into a city where blessedly everyone was a stranger. When she returned to the apartment, "Plees call Missis Hose," Rosie would have written. "Mr. Glumb says he's expeking you."

Her friends complained mildly about the problems of communication, but long ago they had accepted Rosie as a character. "How's Rosie these days?" they asked with derisive amity.

Rosie had viewed her landlady darkly. Eight years ago she had resolved on a house of her own, a move Mrs. Perkins considered little short of insane. She tried to show Rosie the pitfalls. The house she chose was decrepit, in a neighborhood declining from shabby to suspect. It had a coal furnace and two steep flights of stairs, not counting those to the cellar. Mrs. Perkins might as well have spoken against the Blessed Mother. It was at this point that Rosie had acquired Tiger as protection.

Reprieved at his last breath from the pound, Tiger either possessed or acquired Rosie's deep suspicion of all things. Once up her three steps, his paws never touched them again. At first, Rosie let him out briefly into the packed dust of her back yard; but someone tossed over the high wire fence a piece of poisoned meat, which Rosie discovered as he flung himself upon it. After that she went with him, for a minute or two. So summer, winter, day, night, he guarded the sagging house with single savage intent. On the rare times when Rosie's bell wheezed, he was dragged, struggling, into the kitchen, where he snarled and snatched in a fever of frustration. In eight years he had never seen another human, let alone another dog, though at night, staring through the pane into the wicked street, he saw faintly a staring dog he found to be inaccessible. Trusting no one in the world but his sufficient mistress, unmated, he patrolled his cell world. Then something had arrived which passed Tiger by.

Rosie called up at six one morning, scaring Mrs. Perkins out of sleep, to say she wouldn't be leaving home that day. The pork chops had disagreed with her. Three weeks later Mrs. Perkins had pleaded, argued, and finally denounced Rosie into an examination. She had gone to the clinic—the woman at the desk had no idea what she was doing at all, and the doctor was worse yet. For a little thing like a bit of indigestion, they would cut her up? Mrs. Perkins had already talked to Dr. Cutler, and Rosie was manhandled into his office. It might of course be benign, he said, but we've got to do a section. Unconditionally, beyond hope of conversion, Rosie refused. "Missus Perkins, they'll never take a knife to me. Indeed, I'm fine. There's no man going to cut me, that I can tell you." She began to lose weight.

In the coldest weeks, implacably, Rosie arrived, escaped from solitude into familiar warmth. "I'm as well as ever I was in me life," she repeated. The cool, antique surfaces of the silver glittered like mirrors.

At home, Mrs. Perkins was suddenly blind with fatigue. Her suitcases still untouched, she crawled between the sheets and laid her head on Rosie's fresh pillow. Retired six months ago, there was nothing to wake her except Rosie. In the dark she lay straight; the lamps outside opposite the window lit faintly the shapes of plants. She felt her fingernails digging into her palms, and relaxed her hands.

Like a spring of underground water, Rosie's curious love had renewed the days, refreshing roots, unfailing. They spoke of fresh linen, of a glove lost, of which canned dog meat Tiger preferred, of the heat, the cold, of Rosie's wicked landlord, of the mysterious death of a plant. Rosie had forced her to speak to the landlord, Mr. Jones, an ancient, patient man, with an old, light voice, of whom and to whom Rosie constantly complained. "People aren't like yourself," she reiterated to Mrs. Perkins. "You wouldn't know at all the meanness there is to them." Heavily, sweetly, the weight of Rosie's total approval had settled forever on Mrs. Perkins. Disapproving deeply of divorce, of an unfamiliarity with the Blessed Mother, Rosie had somehow managed a private exculpation of Mrs. Perkins—some arrangement, perhaps, with the rosary she carried in her change purse.

Lying in the flawed dark, Mrs. Perkins knew it was not Dr. Cutler, not Dr. Hotchkiss, not Miss Cox (they don't know what they're doing, at all . . . said Rosie's voice in her ear), but herself, the self Rosie had created, who had Rosie's case in hand. At one o'clock she was still awake. She dared not take a sleeping pill, but she wandered out to the sideboard and poured herself a neat whiskey. By her elbow the silver teapot, cream pitcher, sugar bowl, slop jar gleamed in faint splendor.

For the next three mornings, Mrs. Perkins sat in the straight chair by Rosie's bed. There was an armchair with an extra pillow, but she wanted to be instantly visible. Sometimes she stood for moments at the window, staring down into the street, and twice she found herself smoothing the pillowslip three times. Much of the time Rosie slept, her swollen stiff lips open, the arm with its i.v. cord slack by her side, her breath inaudible. But the pain, sucking strength as Rosie diminished, woke her at shorter and shorter intervals. She continued to request that Mrs. Perkins do something about it, stand up for her against the doctors' and nurses' sinful ignorance. Though she called now and then on the Blessed Mother, it was Mrs. Perkins who dallied and malingered.

The small brown man was named Mr. Malone, and though Mrs. Perkins drew the curtains between the beds, he was made frantic by Rosie's sounds.

"Can't you do something with her?" he asked Mrs. Perkins furiously as she passed the foot of his bed. "There's others sick, you know."

Mrs. Perkins, waylaying Dr. Hotchkiss in the hall, asked about the morphine. It wasn't working, she said childishly. She had thought they knew how to control pain. (You would think anesthesia had still to be discovered.)

Patiently, Dr. Hotchkiss explained that they were giving her as much as they dared—a little held back, for the possibility of worsening hours. "But it can't go on like this!" cried Mrs. Perkins in a hushed voice. Dr. Hotchkiss looked at her, with the mingled patience and impatience of the veteran for the rookie. "Yes, it can, Mrs. Perkins," he said, turning away to catch a passing orderly.

Mrs. Perkins was frightened because Rosie's voice, weak as a thread, never mentioned Tiger—it was her form of despair, her final surrender.

Her rosary was under her pillow; on the bedside table a small soiled missal with a frayed red ribbon rested. The nurses' attempt to remove the impediment caused as much protest as Rosie could make. Mrs. Perkins doubted that Rosie could read any but the simplest words. Once Mrs. Perkins opened the missal and knew it might as well have been Greek. Where she had opened it, the little book showed a long list of characterizations: Ark of David, she read, Tower of Ivory, House of Gold, Singular Vessel of Devotion, Ark of the Covenant, Morning Star . . . It was out of the question. "Missis Pont cal. Pleas cal back."

Mrs. Perkins cancelled her engagements. On the third night, she had a wild impulse to go to a friend's dinner party to which she had been committed; and she called, inexcusably, to say she would, after all, come. When she arrived, walking into the room filled with laughter and lamps, she felt giddy, as on a heaving ship. The faces, the voices seemed hung in a haze of distance. Later, her dinner companion, a pleasant, sharp-faced man, looked at her strangely, and she realized she had lost a conversational thread. She left at an uncomplimentary hour. On the way to the door, the hostess, an old friend, asked, "And how's Rosie these days?"

"She's fine," said Mrs. Perkins.

"Well, Susan, don't you let anything happen to her. Things being what they are. Did you *notice* my silver?" she said despairingly, for Rosie was famous.

On the way home, Mrs. Perkins was beset by an awful sense of unreality; it was as though the world she had left, of old friends and good food and common topics, had shot away like a retreating comet, and that other world, of the half-room, and the metal bed lamp and the sounds of Rosie's struggle, was the only reality—had never begun, would never end, had always been. At home, she rummaged through the bathroom closet, searching for a sleeping pill. There were none. But she went to sleep at once and dreamed of Rosie. In a happy light, she was sitting at the kitchen table, and in her hands was a wickedly tarnished teapot, covered with a creamy smear. At her feet, here in the apartment, lay a tranquil Tiger, his head on his paws, at Rosie's feet like the lap-dog of the rubbing between the dining room windows, and his eyes on Rosie's elbow, moving back and forth like a piston. A great burst of joy bloomed along Mrs. Perkins' veins and she woke up. She was appalled by the simplicity of the dream's pleasure.

When she got to 471 next morning, Mr. Malone's bed was empty. But he couldn't have died; he wasn't even very sick. The curtain between the beds was drawn back, and at first she thought Rosie was conscious because of the sounds coming from between her parted lips. She sat down in the chair, the chair, the chair, and put her hand cautiously close to Rosie's. Instantly, without opening her eyes, Rosie gripped it; the ring sliding on her finger bit into Mrs. Perkins' palm. Rosie opened her eyes and stared straight at Mrs. Perkins, with a look older than memory. Then she closed her eyes, but she said, "I can't, then. I can't, at all . . ."

"I'll be right back," said Mrs. Perkins, releasing her fingers. In the hall, she flagged down hurrying Miss Cox.

"Could I speak to Dr. Hotchkiss? Just for a second," she said hastily, at the frown.

"He's on rounds," said Miss Cox shortly. "Can I do something?"

Mrs. Perkins, uncharacteristically timid, asked, "Could you possibly give Mrs. O'Shaugnessy something stronger? At this stage—I mean . . . there doesn't seem to be any *point* . . ."

"She's getting the maximum possible," said Miss Cox, squinting down the hall.

"But surely you could keep her unconscious . . . asleep . . ."

"She's getting the maximum," said Miss Cox. "She's less conscious than you think. Father Shuster brought her extreme unction," she added.

"Oh, did that frighten her?" asked Mrs. Perkins involuntarily.

"They call it the Sacrament of Healing now," said Miss Cox on one foot. "It didn't upset her, no."

Mrs. Perkins walked down the hall to the little waiting room. Two years ago she had stopped smoking. Now she thought she would go to the shop downstairs for cigarettes. She got up, started for the elevator, turned and came back. Then she saw Dr. Hotchkiss coming out of a room far down the hall. He was coming in her direction, and she met him half way, her question like an echo in her ears, as was his answer.

But she repeated angrily, "The maximum? Really the *maximum*?"

"Short of a lethal dose," said Dr. Hotchkiss, tapping his stethoscope lightly against his thigh.

"Is there any chance," said Mrs. Perkins rapidly, "any chance at all, of a remission? In the pain, I mean."

He stared at her. "At this stage, no," he said.

They looked at each other. Then he said, tiredly, the inevitable words. "Are you sure she knows you're here? I don't think you should stay here hour after hour like this."

She didn't answer that. Instead she said, "What happened to Mr. Malone?"

"He had a rough night with Mrs. O'Shaugnessy. We've an extra bed at the moment, and we moved him."

Before she reached the open door, she could hear Rosie.

The next morning Mrs. Perkins could hear her though the heavy door was shut. The sound in the hall was faint, a dire animal sound, divorced completely from speech, from intent.

When Mrs. Perkins went in, Rosie was lying straight on her back and did not move. And when Mrs. Perkins bent over her saying as to a small child, "Hush, dear, hush now, hush..." Rosie's eyes, in the crater of her face, did not flicker. The cries were weaker but more regular, as though they were a kind of pulse, a pain in the very blood.

The sound of traffic came faintly through the heavy glass. In the hall someone laughed, and there was the jingle of a cart. Ten minutes to twelve. Mr. Malone would be having his lunch. She took a Kleenex and bent over to wipe Rosie's forehead and lips. As she did so, deep from Rosie's eyes, Rosie looked at her. "Missus Perkins," she said, "I've got a pain."

"Rosie," said Mrs. Perkins.

Rosie's glance broke and dulled, and she gave a cry of surprising strength, just as the door opened. A round-faced little nurse advanced on them, syringe in hand. Rosie's eyes shut almost at once, and there was soon only the smallest steady whimper after the door closed.

Mrs. Perkins stood up, a little stiffly. She went over to the armchair and came back, holding in her arms carefully the extra pillow. This she placed completely over Rosie's face and held it there, pressing with all her force. Rosie's feet walked a little under her sheet, and her hand lifted in a kind of gesture. Then it fell. But Mrs. Perkins stayed quite still, pressing down with all her strength.

After there had been no movement for many seconds, she lifted the pillow. Rosie's face had smoothed, but her eyes were open.

Mrs. Perkins took the pillow and put it back in the armchair. Then she went and stood with her back to the bed and her face to the window.

When the door opened again, it was Miss Cox, more friendly than usual, who said, advancing, "You know, you're just worn out. Why don't you get some lunch now?" Before Mrs. Perkins could answer, she gave a little smothered grunt, stepping between the patient and the visitor. Then she dropped Rosie's wrist, and came to put her hand on Mrs. Perkins' shoulder.

"She's gone," said Miss Cox, quite gently.

In the phone booth near the exit, the phone book had been ripped away; the chain hung free. She couldn't remember the number of Hanson's Kennels, and while Information checked it, the voices of friends said in hushed and sweetened tones, ". . . so we had to put him to sleep . . ." But the dog, asleep, woke up, shook himself, stretched, trotted off, nose to the ground. What a cheap lie, said Mrs. Perkins. So when Dr. Hanson finally answered, she said curtly, "This is Mrs. Sam Perkins, Dr. Hanson. Tiger's owner has died, my servant Rosie . . . you know. And I want him put down."

How relieved Dr. Hanson was. He was a nice man, and boarding Tiger must have depressed him.

When she circled down from the fourth tier, Mrs. Perkins drove north, straight through the city, and past her own avenue. She turned down the steep hill toward the little public park that had a small lake at its center. It was sunny and the day had turned quite warm. It was, Mrs. Perkins imagined, the first spring day of the year.

A weekday afternoon, so early in March, the place was practically deserted. There were only three cars parked between the white lines, and the voices of two children, shouting to each other, sounded especially distinct. The trees were completely bare, but their branches, stirred slightly now and then by small gusts, moved with the proud heavy burden of sap.

She walked along the narrow path, the small lake bright blue on her right, the slope steep on her left. A man was leaning on the railing, his back to the lake, watching two children who rolled over and over like barrels down the slope, and then trudged back up.

Mrs. Perkins walked all the way around the lake. Great peace bathed her like the sun. She had no thought at all but this sense of peace.

She walked quietly, not meeting anyone, though once a brown dog, its license jingling, galloped past her. In the air there was the sense of a busy, invisible, enormous expectation, and when she opened her car door, she saw in the grass beyond her right fender a small purple stain; it was a crocus.

In the hall, outside her apartment door, she could hear her phone ringing. She put the key unhurriedly in the lock, and since the phone still rang when she closed the door behind her, she stepped into the kitchen and took the receiver off the hook, letting it hang by the cord. She stood and listened to the tiny voice of ringing until it stopped, and then she replaced the receiver gently.

It was when she went and sat down in the first armchair in the living room that she said to herself, so that was why I did it. To feel better.

When she had said it, it seemed to her a false and wicked thing to say. No, it was all Rosie, she said. She looked at and past the framed rubbing, the little lap-dog perfect before the small turned-up feet. While she sat in the chair, the sun began to go down. It was, after all, early March.

She decided to draw the curtains, and she did—first in the living room and then in the dining room. That made it almost dark. She switched on the dining room light. The silver leaped out at her handsomely. She went over and picked up the sugar bowl. In the strong light she could see over its bright curve the faintest mist of tarnish. But when she held it higher, her face flashed back at her, though stretched and broken, into mysterious patches.

Motion of the Heart

T HE SNOW SQUEAKED under their feet; it had gotten so cold. Ahead of them, the winter-violet clouds were pricked suddenly by a shaft of light. It struck across Milly's eyes, and she lowered her head a little.

"That's the last of *that*, Noel," she said. "I just felt a flake."

"It's going to be quite a night, I think," said her father proudly. He took credit for snowstorms—their rarity and his house making a happy marriage.

Its windows lit, the house ahead of them rode like a tight ship. Larry, in front of the study fireplace, wouldn't see how secure it looked as small flakes multiplied in the stillness.

The walk was almost over, and Milly—annoyed, relieved—saw that Noel was no more able to say what he had intended than she was to speak for herself. Sooner or later, he would have to speak. And so, indeed, would she. She looked slantingly at his face, graved and grained by familiar assumptions.

Larry's face was constantly in change—looks passed over it; it was in shadow or light; it melted and sharpened. The restless element in Larry made Noel nervous. What charmed and liberated Milly affected Noel with a deep unease. The two men she most loved would never really like each other.

"Larry hasn't any arctic instinct, has he?" said her father now, but without malice.

"No more than a cat."

Were there three coming home, or two? Noel's grandchild was here—or perhaps not. Not his grandchild—a surgical prospect. Round and round and round. In a way, it was a comfort that her hand would be forced. Saturday night to the Monday morning return—that was her leeway. Then she was ashamed. What a weakling.

Beyond the hedge, past the lit window, Mrs. Farmer's heavy shape passed serenely. Out went a light as the curtains closed. Noel and Mrs. Farmer, she thought. They are survivors. Country gentlemen with housekeeper-cooks; were there others?

Oh good, kind, tough, wonderful Mrs. Farmer, tied to garden tomatoes, hot plates, sun at breakfast. Let Larry talk of surrogate mothers, of ancillary lives (parasitic, exploited, take your choice). Death, not craft, had produced this pair; her own shadowy mother, shadowy Mr. Farmer.

They were at the gate, and Noel stepped back a little to let her pass through. She could see Larry's grin.

Suddenly the snow set up a tiny whisper all around them. By the time they reached the door, they were butting against a scurrying wall.

Noel went upstairs to change. She was not really wet under her windbreaker, inside her boots. She discarded them, and went into the study. ("Will they find my body here, do you think?" Larry had asked.)

Moving silently on the rug, she frightened him. He gave a jump, and his face, which had just struck her as sad, definitely sad, broke into light-hearted reproach.

"Mrs. Farmer and I thought your bodies would be found, preserved, next spring. What a night for a stroll." But really he was questioning her: How did it go?

"Do you suppose we could have a drink?" she asked him, and as on a Mayfair cue, here was Mrs. Farmer with a shining tray of bottles. And, on cue, "Whiskey?" he asked politely as Mrs. Farmer shut the door behind her.

Milly took the whiskey, and by the fire stood rocking it gently in her glass.

"Isn't it simpler to get it over with?" Larry asked.

A small sip of whiskey burned satisfactorily. "I couldn't, until we decided," she said.

"But we *did* decide," said Larry. "Mrs. Farmer forgot the wine again. Oh well," he said resignedly, "whiskey let it be." There was a small splash; the snow seemed to have soundproofed the room.

He took her silence as half of a dialogue.

"Look," he said cheerfully, "we couldn't have given him *two* shocks, *anyway*. Not simultaneously. Of course, that's not a reason," he hastily added. But then he could not resist. "I wonder which shock would have been worse. Your marrying me . . . ?"

It must be maddening for Larry, she thought a little harshly. Every time he thinks it's settled, I do this. "I never promised you an abortion, Larry," she said, to her surprise.

"But we did agree," he said. "I mean, really agree. Not now. Not at this point. You don't know what you're going to be adjusting to, Milly. With*out* that."

"No Mrs. Farmer, you mean?" she jeered.

"No, my dear," he said seriously. "I do not mean Mrs. Farmer. I mean me."

"I think I can take that," she said more happily. But she saw the kind of shadow that had become familiar to her cross his face. It was as though he looked away at something. "Marriage can't be that difficult, Larry." They smiled at each other. People kept saying that being lovers in no way prepared you. She did not believe this.

Footsteps beyond the door. "Look, darling, for God's sake, don't cross us up now," said Larry rapidly. "Give us a chance. For a while."

Noel came in.

It was their sixth dinner.

Tomorrow's would be the last. And the small space in which Milly stood—again she thought of it as a train platform—would disappear. Double-lived as any spy, she sat between her child-hood and her choice, turning her head politely as each speaker staved off silence.

She could open her lips and release a word or two, and that platform would vanish for good. She felt suddenly a sullen resentment against the lives pulling at her: Noel, his windburned face turned dutifully toward his guest's (saying to himself, is it already too late? is this really going to happen?); Larry, his head cocked like an attentive dog, his every word strong with irony for her ear (asking himself, is she going to back out now? how *can* she?); and the quietly growing determined life shaping itself inside her, which in a few days would disappear from itself.

Bodies—how they chattered. Her own, out of her father, her ghost-mother; fed, and clothed, loved, and comforted; all the days and nights of Noel's shelter; of lessons, of measles, of tears and sprains and rainy walks; of the smell of fresh bread from the kitchen. Larry's, familiar as her hand, known for six months, timelessly. And now this brief spasm of unwanted and inappropriate beginning.

Deceit lay before her, like a desert to be crossed. Noel's bliss of ignorance; she felt fury rise against him. Did it honestly ever occur to him, after twenty-two years, that her life was not still safe and simple? Was she really going to marry this alien? was the only question that suggested itself, and she could see him straining to prepare.

". . . I imagine it's greatly changed," he was saying. "Milly was thirteen when we were there."

"I've never been out of the country. Sir," added Larry, daring Milly's eye.

"Let's have some coffee," she said with hostility, standing up. She swept past them, and as they followed her, the doorbell rang, a long peal.

They stopped as though the snow had spoken.

"Who on earth . . . ?" said Noel. He stepped to peer out of the window but saw only the race of flakes on the dark.

Mrs. Farmer, with an affronted air, came past them, bound for the door.

"Oh, let's sit *down*!" said Milly crossly, and Larry did, while Noel followed Mrs. Farmer into the hall. In case the bell hadn't rung, someone banged the brass knocker. A flurry of cold air reached them. From the hall a voice said, "I'm terribly sorry to barge in like this. I'm stuck."

"Where's your car? Come in, come in." The door closed.

"Three is a crowd, four is a rescue," said Milly.

Away went Mrs. Farmer, and Noel said, "Come in, come in to the fire. You must be frozen. Have a drink."

They appeared in the doorway. The wiry small man in the heavy canvas jacket had bright hair. He was struggling out of the jacket and, released, he turned on the room a face alive with gaiety.

"What a thing to do to you at this hour!" he cried to Noel. "I'm clean off the road, about a hundred yards down *that* way. In some enormous bushes. I don't think I'll get out this winter."

Pleased, Noel beamed at him. "It's quite a storm, isn't it? We'll try our service station—but I doubt... Oh. This is my daughter, Milly Gibbs, Mr. . . . ?"

"But Larry!" cried the visitor. "I don't believe it! Larry Sercombe! So this is where you've got to!"

On his feet, Larry said, "Well, well, well." He came forward and put out his hand. He looked very astonished. "How are you, Gill?" he said. "This is Gill Matchell," he said to the room in general.

"Absolutely marvelous now. Thanks to your father," Gill Matchell said to Milly. "I expected to hibernate in the bushes. In my car, of course."

Here came Mrs. Farmer, always with her air of entrance. The great tray went down on the coffee table. Noel pounced on it.

"Coffee?" he asked Gill. "Whiskey? Both?"

Gill, rocking back on his heels, looked at Larry. "There's something positively eerie about this," he said happily. "I stagger through the snow, like that Miner fresh from the Creek, and in a strange, gorgeous house, run slap into an ancient friend." He took the glass from Noel. "More and better storms!" he proposed.

Grouped around the fire, they decided it was less than strange —it was always happening, in airports, at counters, in subways. And New York was only forty miles away.

"But I'd lost track of Larry lately, so it's that much better," said

Gill with satisfaction. His very clear brown eyes went over their faces like light, gratefully, inviting their friendliness. Milly could see Noel warming—he liked the young when they allowed it.

The reaction from constraint eased Milly—it was as though someone had given her a shot of immunity.

Appealed to, in common recollection of names, of incidents, Larry said yes, yes, he did, didn't he? Yes, it was awful. For Milly there was a dreamlike air; as though they were a colored advertisement for a fine whiskey or a scent—handsome Noel; Larry and Gill, friends reunited by chance on a snowy night; she, with her feet lightly propped on the fender; the leaping fire, the curtained room. No problems, financial, surgical, familial.

For six months, she had continued to feel separate from Larry's life. "You'd think you were ashamed of me," she told him once, but he said reasonably—a caller having left early—"Do we really want one of those how-are-Milly-and-Larry-doing affairs? We'll get sucked in soon enough."

And she liked it, and that his apartment was new. It was as though she and Larry had been created when they met. She began to feel a faintly eerie quality about something so discrete.

Was that why they were marrying? No, there had also been the sense of playing together a slightly shifty children's game. And games, carried on too long, were boring, ended in fights.

Fresh from the semireality of her office, in the long July evenings, she lay in another country, in the point of sun that crept through the venetian blinds. At this minute, she could see Larry's wrist, the blue vein faint under the skin, the place where her fingers could find his mysterious pulse. Then it seemed to her that Noel's house was a stage set—her own office desk, a shift of scene. She lived here. The rest had been waiting.

This time a year ago, they had never seen each other.

"What am I doing here?" she asked Larry. "When did I know I would be here?"

"Don't try to analyze it," said Larry. "It happens. It's a motion —a motion of the heart."

She had put her finger on his breast and felt the faint steady thud.

"Yes," she said.

"What's he do?" Noel asked, at first. But the answer did no good. To Noel, "designing" might mean anything, but "free lance" meant one thing only. Work was in an office—or out-of-doors. Work that was neither was cousin to the riverboat gambler's frayed fortunes.

Noel was being the host incarnate.

". . . but how can I settle in on you like this?" Gill was asking.

"How can you not?" Noel had him there.

Mrs. Farmer, reporting, quenched all hope for the car; it must stay in its bushes.

Without warning, the shot wore off. "I'm dead," said Milly, standing. "Too much tramping about in the cold," she told Noel. "You'll be here for breakfast," she told Gill.

He said, pleased, "So it seems."

"Goodnight, then," she said to Larry. She touched his shoulder, passing him.

She didn't switch on the light in her room but sat on the edge of the bed, looking out where a pallid radiance vibrated through the glass. This was deceit, too, this room. Or was deceit's opposite, according to one's view. Or, it was fairness: household mores.

"'When in Rome'!" Larry said philosophically, "'Get fed to the lions,' it ends."

During the whole week, the week extorted from Larry, they slept in their separate rooms, discrete as nuns.

If she said to her father: I have been living for the last six months with a man you neither like nor trust. I am pregnant, but we do not wish a child now, though we are going to marry very soon. I will have an abortion; then I will marry; and move, fully, into the half of a life I have been living . . . , he would be there, as always, whenever she wished him to be. He would not be able, ever, to forgive her totally for having allowed him to be so mistaken, but the difference would be wordless and without action.

Though profoundly baffled by Noel's survival, she was never naive enough to accept an image of mindless rigidity. Instead, it would be that something living, organic, was being tampered with; a progression; an order like that of his planting—his setting of bulbs for spring, his pruning of autumn shrubs.

As to the abortion, it was hard to separate cleanly her own repugnance from Noel's. Well, hers was individual, highly personal (this body, this child), vulnerable to reason and suitability. His was tribal, societal, immense. His genes were incapable of forgiving her.

"I will do exactly what we have planned," she said aloud, and got up.

She undressed and lay down. But the rapid snow seemed to vibrate along her nerves. "I never promised you an abortion," she had said to Larry. Then Noel had come in. Then they had had dinner. Then Gill had arrived.

She knew what Larry wanted, considered essential. And she herself could not imagine changes so total, pinning her between them. Suddenly she felt a violent longing for peace—to be rid of her father, of this house, of Mrs. Farmer, of the strange thing taking possession of her body. I want Larry, she thought, and to be left alone by everything else. To be left *alone*.

She got out of bed and snatched up her wrapper. In a blade of light from the driveway lamp, she went straight to the door and opened it softly. The hall was black, but there wasn't an inch in the house she couldn't have traced, and she went along down the hall, past the room where Noel would put Gill, past the bathroom, its door ajar, and as stealthily as a thief, opened Larry's door.

The same lamp sent its blade across the bed, and Gill's hair was so bright it looked in the dimness like metal.

She must have said a word or made a sound; the locked forms parted.

All three of them stayed still for a moment, then she was out of the door and down the hall and into her room and sitting again on the edge of her bed.

She had a fear that Larry was right behind her, and she got up and softly locked the door, and stood listening. But there was no sound at all anywhere in the house except, through the window, the infinitesimal tick of snow.

Her mind was clear of any thought whatsoever; she simply

sat, with her hands palms-up on her knees. It seemed that everything except the room had sunk easily into the snow without a
trace. An anesthetic peace held the room.

Then a clock struck, endlessly, far away—twelve times, end-
ing the day forever.

Yes, of course, she thought.

Did I know, always? Was Larry too eager, too sad? Then she
thought lucidly, I was a program. A program that failed. Through
the numbness she wondered, with a sort of polite curiosity,
would it have failed if it hadn't snowed tonight? But it had failed
already; it had failed before it started.

She thought about that, sitting motionless on the edge of the
bed. If it had been a woman's head, in the pale blade of light . . .
With a kind of stunned relief, she thought, I *couldn't* have been
enough. There was no way I could ever be enough.

A wave of faintness made her bend her head. Well, that was
one question decided for her. Father, lover, child. She drew back
her mind, pitilessly, into her own private and controlled body.
The new invasion was over. She could scarcely wait to confirm
its absence.

Fingers brushed the door, the knob turned with a little sound.

"Milly," said Larry outside softly.

She stayed as still as if it were a burglar.

"Milly," said Larry.

She turned her head toward the door and began to weep
without any sound. She could feel the tears slide over her cheeks;
one dropped on her knuckle.

"Milly, I'm not going to beg you to open the door," the under-
tone went on, "but I do ask you to."

She got up, and again went faint and dizzy. She blundered
against the end of the bed, and then unlocked the door and
turned away.

Larry shut the door behind him, and when she went back
and sat down on the bed he came and stood in front of her,
blocking out the light from the window. He stood there, saying
nothing, and Milly, looking up, said, "If you want to talk to me,
why don't you sit down? But I wish you wouldn't. Talk."

He sat beside her, and for a curious moment she felt the

naturalness of his presence—they would lie down together in a minute.

"Larry, please, please, please," she said rapidly. "Please, really. Don't talk. I see. Really I see." Then a question came out of Milly, amazing her, "He didn't break down, did he? Accidentally."

"No," said Larry. "He didn't break down."

It was as though she had started on a steep slope, faster and faster. "You were together, before you and I . . ."

"Oh yes," said Larry. "We were together. For three years." He waited a moment, and then he said, "We were quite a famous pair."

"Why did you . . . I mean, what happened?"

He put up a hand, she could see it faintly, like a warning. "Yes," she said quickly. "It doesn't matter now."

"I haven't seen him. I told him no. When he couldn't reach me, he called your office. Then a friend told him we were getting married."

"And when he walked into the living room tonight . . ." said Milly.

"Yes," Larry said.

"'A motion of the heart,'" said Milly.

He made a little sound.

"I remembered that," she said.

They sat there, in a curious amity.

"What are you . . . ?" He bogged down.

"I'm going to have an abortion," she said. "I've got plenty of sick leave coming. I'll tell Noel I'm going for a visit—he doesn't cross-examine. I'm going back to my job. I'm coming up here on weekends. I'm going to eat Mrs. Farmer's pancakes. I'm going to get to be twenty-three."

The room darkened again as he stood up, facing her dimly.

"Gill and I'll leave before anyone's up," he said. "I'll take my car. We'll work something out about his."

"Yes," she said.

He leaned to kiss her, but instead put out his hand. She took it. It was cold, but totally familiar.

"Milly, Milly," he said. He might have been speaking of a

country. Then the door closed, quietly, behind him.

She went back to the edge of the bed as though that were her post. As she passed the window, she saw the snow had stopped. As she looked, a single flake sailed waveringly past her eyes. Mica-white was deep on one side of each branch.

Noel's face appeared before her eyes, so sharp that he might have come into the room. Breakfast, she thought. We'll have it at breakfast with Mrs. Farmer's cakes: the missing guests. But, in the end, he would be relieved. It would be as strange to him as an unsavory novel, but he would be relieved. And we'll take things up; Larry will just be a word we never use. Noel can keep that nice, grained look. No lover. No fetus.

She took off her wrapper, and lying down, pulled the covers up to her chin. In the total stillness, for no reason, she thought of a storm at sea, a huge storm. She and Noel had been on the Italian line, coming back from Barcelona. The ship, tormented, had wallowed and plunged. It was a three-force gale. Passengers stopped clinging to velvet ropes and clung to their bunks as cabins shuddered and creaked and suitcases shot out of closets. The wind worked freely across the great black water, hitting their shelter as the waves hit it, blow after great blow. The huge ship, down to a pitching crawl, struggling, sank and rose. There was a girl on the boat seven months pregnant, traveling with her husband. As the winds drove the waves up to towers crashing upon the decks, Milly had thought of her.

In the morning, with puffy clouds cruising through a bland sky and the sea a hypocritical blue, sure enough, there was bad news. In the worst of the storm, she had gone into labor. The baby had been born dead. Noel, up for breakfast, came into her cabin where she lay, still greeny-white. She closed her eyes, and he went away.

Later, Milly, with a curious tremor, asked, "Where—is it?"

"It was buried at sea," Noel said. "Much the best thing."

"Was it a girl, or a boy?"

He didn't know.

At some point, on each of the three remaining nights before port, she had thought of that, fascinated by the human life, so soon to turn into the full glare, blare, relationships, hazards, details of human hours, at this moment an infinitesimal bit of jetsam in the sea's dark enormous maw. N.G.I., the towels had said: *Navigazione Generale Italiana*. The girl's name had been Phyllis.

At this exact moment, and without any preparation at all, Milly saw what she intended to do—saw it before her. It was her undefined motion that had called up the storm. So it had been there right along, waiting. With all her will, she drew back, terrified. There would be no Larry. Though she failed to believe it, she knew it. Noel would be worse than gone; he would be there.

She felt rushing away from her the details of which her life was composed—lover, father, job, home. More mysterious than death in her body, life in its shelter furiously grew—and she looked ahead at the infinitude of hours and minutes coming toward her. They bore down upon her, full of voices and figures, of cycles of weather, and words, of all the veiled future, of an unknown face, approaching, approaching. Motionless on her bed, she stared at them as, in another world, the clock struck one stroke.

The Jungle of Lord Lion

I T WAS ON THE MORNING of the sprinkler debacle that Mrs. Pomeroy remembered that she had first noticed Mrs. Chubb —truly noticed her—over the matter of Lord Lion, a matter as small as Lord Lion himself.

Lord Lion's baptismal name was Hubert, and his feral quality would have struck no one. Indeed, Mrs. Pomeroy would never have known he *was* Lord Lion, had Mighty Vampire not sung "Island in the Sun" and "Yellow Bird" to their group, stopping as he trudged down the blazing beach toward the cruise ship floating white and racy on the blue water of St. Jude's harbor. Mighty Vampire had tramped off, followed moments later by two small donkeys with rope halters and swags of crimson bougainvillea around their necks, each donkey ridden, just over the tail, by a long-legged Boudinian. Behind them a tall, sooty, handsome girl toiled by in the soft sand with a basket on her head from which acid-green bananas, breadfruit and a springing swatch of gaudy croton sprouted.

Now, looking extra-small, as he especially did when driving, Lord Lion sat with his patient paws on the wheel. There was always the air of an admirable trick about his chauffeuring, as of a small monkey taking his pony through a paper hoop. When he had arrived at the beach house, the Marmows and Mrs.

Pomeroy had been ready. They had accumulated everything, and they stood in the frond-shade where Lord Lion had stopped the Morne Jaune's station wagon. They waited for Mrs. Chubb, who was still concerned about her ant bites, as was, necessarily, Miss Gilse.

"Yes," said Lord Lion to Mrs. Marmow. "I know the Mighty Vampah, and so." His forehead, always wrinkled as in distress, contracted further. "He sings songs by others, and like that. I sing My Own Compositions. I am the Lord Lion. I sing My Own Compositions. 'Beautiful Boudina,' and 'So Darling Come Shift,' and 'Boudina Jump-Up.' All my own."

As Miss Gilse patted Mrs. Chubb with a bathtowel and the palms slightly made their raining sound, Lord Lion amplified: he did not batten; he created. Every night he practiced. Eventually he hoped to go to Trinidad. The Mighty Sparrow had come from a small island, Grenada. Lord Melody—

Here came Mrs. Chubb, refraining from scratching; hot with the cross of self-discipline, she climbed in back. Miss Gilse followed with the thermos, towels, bronzite and the plastic headrest, and Mrs. Pomeroy joined them. Mr. and Mrs. Marmow rounded the car and climbed in beside Lord Lion.

Suddenly Mrs. Chubb said clearly, "Wouldn't they like to get back here? Couldn't we squeeze them in back here?" She addressed Mrs. Pomeroy, who stared. Mrs. Marmow, a small quick woman, looked nervously over her shoulder. "This is fine," she said in her muffled English voice. Mr. Marmow, elbow to elbow with Lord Lion, looked studiously ahead.

"That's why I like to have someone with me over here," said Mrs. Chubb, speaking to Mrs. Pomeroy over Miss Gilse's head. "In these islands. When you're one alone, they take advantage of it, and they put you in front. Right next to the driver." Her small unsagacious eyes rayed significance at Mrs. Pomeroy. No one said anything at all. They sped around a curve; a girl in a red dress leaped up the bank. A goat sprang away, chickens scattered. Here they were already. The kindly gates, dripping coralita, swallowed them, and Lord Lion, much more cautiously, curved under the green fountain of the mango tree and stopped.

Mrs. Heatherby stood on the steps. She always looked as

though she had been carved and, with fortunate taste, set down where she stood. She was a beautiful, tall woman. Her skin was a lustrous gold and she had ripe, cleanly shaped lips. Her hair, iridescent as feathers, gleamed black in a tower on her head, and she wore Chinese blouses and tailored silk shirts. The good modeling of her long narrow feet was interrupted only by the sandal thong between her toes. She was a recent widow with three children; two pale tall girls in a convent in Trinidad. Mrs. Pomeroy had seen their pictures, pleated skirts and Peter Pan collars. There was a little boy, Patrick, almost black, finely boned and thin, only four. Mrs. Pomeroy could see him now, dragging his wagon across the lawn toward the lily pond. Cynthia, the Marmows' blond fat six-year-old, trailed behind him.

"Hubert, go and get the ice," said Mrs. Heatherby to Lord Lion, and she smiled slightly as her guests straggled past her to their rooms.

After lunch, Mrs. Pomeroy, who every day now was really feeling much better, decided that as soon as she had spoken to Mrs. Heatherby about her breakfast trays, she would go to her room and lie down until the cool of the late afternoon. She felt that she had been unreasonably put out by Mrs. Chubb's stupidity; her own intense reaction had seemed more like the raw-nerve vulnerability of her last two weeks in New York than a part of the extraordinary fragrant peace that seemed to have descended on her as silently as dew in these days on Boudina. She understood that if she were not to ruin everything, she must take her fellow guests as they came, especially in so small a guest house as Morne Jaune. After all, the taking could be very minor— a few minutes en route to the beach; passing a table, the civility of a breakfast greeting. If she thought about Lord Lion, driving them so wildly well, incandescent with his Own Compositions, spattered by Mrs. Chubb's arrogant idiocy, it was possible to get angry; but Lord Lion must long ago have devised his defenses. He had a good place to live, she thought coming down the steps from the vine-hung concrete porch into the dazed, spicy, glittering air. Even the blackbirds were quiet in the heat. The African tulip trees near the gate blazed away, and as her foot touched the ground, one of the smaller gold and turquoise lizards flashed past her toe into the grass soaked by the sprinkler. "Lord Lion's jungle . . ." she thought. And then she thought, *They say the lion and the lizard keep / The courts* . . . and laughed quite happily to herself. She went along as far as the little conical dinner pavilion and hesitated. Mrs. Heatherby was nowhere in sight. She was almost always about, strolling quietly and terribly here and there. Everyone said that was why the place was so marvelously well run. Since Mrs. Pomeroy had decided that having breakfast in bed was to be part of her program of self-indulgence, she might as well say so now. She stepped under the shade of the roof and sat down in one of the deep cane chairs. It was very quiet. Down the slope of the lawn toward the sea was another sprinkler, and in it Patrick, in vestigial shorts, and Cynthia, in a red polka-dot bathing suit, jumped back and forth with faint shrieks of pleasure.

Just as quickly as her doctor would allow her to travel after the operation, Mrs. Pomeroy had come to Boudina. It was a long-held ambition and, amazingly, Boudina had disappointed in no detail. In fact, the special quality of its light, that light which seemed to live inside its flora and fauna, radiating from the great ragged banana leaves, the huge golden calyxes of the *coupe d'or*, the black gleaming skin of the fishermen moving over the turquoise and lilac sea, seemed to reveal to her not an island, but a planet, as though the plane from Kennedy Airport had never come back to earth at all. She was sometimes aware that this had to do with her uncertainty in regard to her going on living; security might have dulled it, or a definitive sentence have set it small and implacable before her. Whereas the uncertainty of her relations with life, like those of a passionate but insecure love affair, lit everything—was perhaps itself the Boudina light. She was happy as she had never been happy since her husband's death quite a long time ago. Waking each morning, in the smallest, cheapest room, to the bowing of fronds a few feet beyond the open glass louvers, to the languid explosions of the waves on the rocks below, she would move her hand, turn her head, prop herself on her elbow to stare more fully at the new day, one of an endless file which as yet there was no need to count. This holiday, extravagant but not ruinous (in case the news should turn out to be good), would not end for three and a half months; over fourteen weeks, over ninety-eight mornings. She had been delighted to find that she need spend virtually nothing beyond payment of her weekly bill. On what would she spend it? Lord Lion took them to the beach in the Inn's car. Certainly she had no desire for the boutiques and festivities of the two beach hotels. So that breakfast trays would be perfectly feasible.

There was a louder shriek from the lawn. Cynthia had sat down on the sprinkler; strangled, it jetted feebly in place, prickling her hair and water-speckled face. Elated, Patrick danced wetly about her; suddenly, unable to sit, too, on the sprinkler, he sat in her lap. A small local rainbow shimmered over them; they were bathed in bands of peacock blue and jonquil. Something in Mrs. Pomeroy's wrists and breast gave a queer lift. It was as though just there shone all beginnings.

"It is a calm day at sea today," announced a voice, and there was Mrs. Chubb, right beside her. For a minute Mrs. Pomeroy, gazing at her, thought she had come out with some pigmented and loathsome disease, the outward and visible sign of an inward and spiritual splotching. She looked like a nasty sea monster, all blubber and malignancy. "Violet Gentian," she said in her fat voice, noting Mrs. Pomeroy's dismayed fascination. "Those bites are poisonous, if untreated. I am waiting for my Captain." Mrs. Chubb was either unaware of Mrs. Pomeroy's sentiments in regard to her, or indifferent to them. She went on to explain. Two couples, friends of Mrs. Chubb's from New York, were arriving next week. They were, all five, chartering a yacht, and would take trips, cruising through the Antilles. Miss Gilse would stay here. Miss Gilse was a bad sailor, and indeed preferred her native Toronto to the slack air of the Caribbean. Mrs. Chubb did not bother to explain what Miss Gilse was doing here at all, in that case, and Mrs. Pomeroy considered it unnecessary. As the only iguana on the property suddenly emerged from a tree trunk behind Mrs. Chubb's head and flowed over the railing and down the lawn, Mrs. Pomeroy said to herself that if she ever had seen a dogsbody born, it was Miss Gilse. As though she were a thought-reader, Mrs. Chubb now said that Miss Gilse would remain here, and, very kindly, attend to any important mail. They would all, of course, keep their rooms between trips; the Morne Jaune was not yet full, but it would be, all ten rooms of it. "Will you be here long?" she suddenly asked Mrs. Pomeroy. "Oh yes," said Mrs. Pomeroy luxuriously, "until May."

"It is a sixteen-foot ketch," said Mrs. Chubb in answer to this. "But the Captain should be here now. It sleeps eight, and that means that five of us will be comfortable."

Still Mrs. Heatherby did not appear. At this moment, Mrs. Pomeroy had an intuition for escape. Exactly as she had it, Mrs. Chubb cried, "Look at that!"

The iguana had run up the little mariposa tree; its head stuck out, lifted from the bark, still as porphyry. Mrs. Pomeroy would never have seen it but by following the children's gaze. Ravished, immobilized, they crowded over each other, transfixed as the reptile itself.

"Doesn't it look old?" said Mrs. Pomeroy. But Mrs. Chubb, her voice slightly expanded by the intensity of her feelings, said, "This is a perfectly disgusting sight. It is cheap, and demoralizing, and it cannot—it *cannot* be tolerated." She was gazing, rigid as a pointer, to where the soaked and shining children clutched each other, motionless.

Just once in her life, Mrs. Pomeroy had been caught by a serious undertow, and now with a lurch of apprehension she recognized the violence and rapidity of what was pulling her: she knew also that it was the ricochet from something that had shone with life. But she could not stop. "What is cheap?" she said.

"You cannot have a white little girl and a black boy playing together half naked, unless you are a fool," said Mrs. Chubb. "If Patrick doesn't know his place he'll only be unhappier. Mrs. Heatherby must know that. She's intelligent. It's her white blood. Patrick is black, and she can't pretend anything else. She should have thought of that—it's too late now. In a place such as this you can't have niggers playing with the guests' children. She'll *lose* her guests, if she isn't careful."

With the awful detachment of a bystander, Mrs. Pomeroy heard herself speak. "I can't imagine," she said, "why *anyone* would want such a ridiculous and unpleasant person as yourself, anywhere at all."

As she turned, Mrs. Heatherby, materialized from the middle air, stood behind her. In her quiet sandals she stood a foot away; on her arm was a wicker basket of bougainvillea, and from her long fingers hung bright shears. She was looking past Mrs. Pomeroy at Mrs. Chubb, and even in her red-hot exaltation Mrs. Pomeroy gave a small shiver.

From the blazing blue water at the foot of the slope the conch sounded its hoarse breathy bellow.

"That's our fisherman," said Mrs. Heatherby, as Victoria emerged from the kitchen door, a basket on her head.

Nearly at sunset, Mrs. Pomeroy went down to the little ridge just over the tide. It was large enough to establish one chair. She had carried one of the feather-light aluminum and plastic affairs there last week and it had not been replaced on its proper stone terrace, so her habit seemed established. It was five minutes to six.

The sun, a large flame-colored disk, was just off the pure bare curve of the sea. Mrs. Pomeroy walked down slowly, in the curious leveling light. In the islands, sunset, rather than announcing the end of something, had the quality of an introduction. And like that of all introductions, its intimation was still undefined. Mrs. Pomeroy sat down gingerly; there was really very little room. Below her the tide plunged raggedly toward the rocks, broke with a seething hush, leaped up and fled back. The straight great palm to her left at the rim of the bank had lost its glitter; it darkened instant by instant. Warblers in very rapid flight darted erratically through the air, into which darkness seemed to be visibly filtering. The sea, almost totally gold and lilac, darkened, too. The disk was in the water. On the little mariposa tree clutching the ledge beside her, the leaves had folded thinly shut, thinned as the closed wings of butterflies. Once in the daytime she had tried to shut them by hand—they sprang open, of course; and once at night she had lightly forced one apart. With a delicate shrinking it had reclosed.

A deep rose, mixed with darkness, fumed into the sky in

silence; it struck Mrs. Pomeroy that all this was going on in silence. In silence a steel-sharp star pierced the last stain of color and on the instant the lighthouse at Pointe Orage flashed. It flashed again, vanished as the ray pivoted, recurred. The darkness, rather than quenching, seemed to have gathered into itself all the detailed brilliance, the coarse rich blossoms, the sea's last stains of lilac, the folded mariposa leaves. Suddenly, as though since last night it had never stopped, the liquid, high sweet pulse of the tree frogs, directionless in the dark, flooded the air. I am absolutely happy, thought Mrs. Pomeroy.

When this relief from fear, sharp as a starved appetite gratified, had first stung her, she had been differently frightened; it was almost an hallucination. The words *a terrible beauty is born* recurred insistently, to her embarrassment. There was something shaming in the equating of her precarious glance at life, with great words. But the words were as true as bone, and finally she understood that it had nothing to do with herself—it was life held up like a transparency to the blaze of loss.

Sitting on the ledge, she had not mislaid her knowledge of realities, it had only been assimilated. She tried now to exercise this knowledge of the unforgiving mechanism, and gradually, with effort, it became real to her. The birds, zigzagging a moment ago through the melting color, flew to hunt; they were death on the wing. Under the hyacinth surface, pop, lidless eyes cruised in a permanence of ravening. In the hills the mongooses had rabies; there were poisoned baits out for their hunger in the dark. And the cane-field rats could choose between bait and mongoose. But she might have been reciting a geometry formula. Knowing all this, she was now permitted to accept it. It was assimilated effortlessly into the scented dark in which at the core of the glass-green leaves the green throats of the tree frogs, compelled to exult, brimmed the night. The stars had all come out.

At dinner Mrs. Pomeroy found to her amazement that she was not in the least distressed or embarrassed by the thought of her unique, her unpardonable outburst. Even Mrs. Heatherby's outrage, the warning of her eyes on Mrs. Chubb's face in the pavilion, she recognized as something amply provided for in that lady's beauty and pride. She did wonder if her own serenity could be a token of the setting-in of isolation, but she felt only cheerful, and faintly curious as to whether Mrs. Chubb would remain cheek-by-jowl with a guest whom she must regard as a madwoman. After that look of Mrs. Heatherby's, a look whose grimness did faintly trouble Mrs. Pomeroy's vision, surely no one could stay. But then, she realized instantly, how could she assess the look seen through Mrs. Chubb's eyes? Could Mrs. Heatherby simply demand that Mrs. Chubb leave? She supposed not, and yet there was a dignity of toughness, of the ability to move, in Mrs. Heatherby which showed in her walk, in the strong turn of her superb neck. Just suppose Mrs. Heatherby *should* move, thought Mrs. Pomeroy; how bright would the lighthouse be then. She felt no qualm of mercy for Mrs. Chubb. Obviously she could manage either of the beach hotels without a quaver; it must have been some obscure thirst for pre-eminence that had led her to the economy of Morne Jaune in the first place. Mrs. Pomeroy guessed that Mrs. Heatherby *would* move, but not precipitately or naively.

Mrs. Pomeroy's book was exciting. By dessert at her little table, spooning her soursop ice cream unseeingly, she had only two chapters left, and the odds were beautifully balanced. The denouement would take place in bed—Mrs. Pomeroy's bed. After the last mouthful of coffee, she went out the screen door and, by the help of the light bulb lashed to the mango, along the side of the house toward the small separate square of her room. But she almost stopped dead, and had consciously to push forward. The open window of Mrs. Heatherby's office was lit. She sat at her desk, erect and absolutely implacable, and across from her stood an agitated Mrs. Chubb. Mrs. Pomeroy's heart rose in a pure and ferocious joy. She understood that this vindicated every blade, every frond and petal; the island, as though fed by an infusion, shone glossier in the dark.

Mrs. Pomeroy went softly along and into her room, and as she closed the door the rain struck. It fell, not as at home in a strident whisper, but straight, furiously, with a glorious din. In the dark she leaned against the single window's open louvers. Spray fumed in her face, the thick flowering bushes gave off a noise like drums; the palms steamed and strained. It kept on for almost a quarter of an hour. In her nightgown Mrs. Pomeroy brushed her hair. Abruptly, the rain diminished; but it was still dropping noisily when there was a light quick knock on Mrs. Pomeroy's door. She opened it, and there was Mrs. Heatherby.

Suddenly Mrs. Pomeroy knew that at the moment there were things she could, and things she could not, handle, and that Mrs. Heatherby's frank appreciation might be one of the latter. "Mrs. Heatherby! Come in," she said.

Mrs. Heatherby, a light raincoat over her shoulders, was gleaming with drops.

"Do sit down," said Mrs. Pomeroy.

"No, thank you," said Mrs. Heatherby, and her rich voice sounded fainter in the noise of all the drops falling and dripping. "I must tell you our trouble, Mrs. Pomeroy," she said, and she smiled without agitation.

"I know," said Mrs. Pomeroy, more impulsively than she had intended. "I'm extremely sorry. But it isn't really *important*, is it?" she said hopefully.

"Mrs. Pomeroy," said Mrs. Heatherby, "we are having some work done here—there is a threat of termites."

Mrs. Pomeroy stared, confused. "I'm sorry," she said again. "About the termites, I mean."

"Yes," said Mrs. Heatherby. "It is most unfortunate. I'm afraid the workmen must take over this room."

The sound of drops had stopped and in the stillness Mrs. Pomeroy said, with a slight sinking of the heart, "I shall have to move to another room?" She thought rapidly: But the others are all more expensive. . . . But perhaps as it isn't my fault . . . "Well, of course," she said. "How soon?"

"But this is the unfortunate part," said Mrs. Heatherby. Her face, in the lamplight, looked paler than Mrs. Pomeroy remembered it. "There are no other rooms, except the rooms which must be worked on. We are completely booked."

The two women stood there looking at each other. Then Mrs. Heatherby's gaze moved to the window. "I'm afraid your blanket got damp," she said. "These storms are brief, but so violent."

Mrs. Pomeroy had risen above nothing. Panic, fury, and a

total, childish grief raged in her chest, so that for what seemed a long pause she could not speak. Then she heard her voice from a sickening distance. "Of course, I see. When do you need the room?"

Mrs. Heatherby's eyes reached past her to the dark outside the window. "Tomorrow, if that's possible," she said pleasantly. "If not, of course the next day will be perfectly satisfactory."

"I see," said Mrs. Pomeroy again.

Mrs. Heatherby with a quick motion almost like anger slipped her coat from her shoulders. She flung it over her arm; bright drops flew to the straw rug. She looked directly at Mrs. Pomeroy with a curious urgency, like that of an accomplice telegraphing a hopeless message.

"Thank you, then," she said. At the door she turned. "It's been a pleasure to have you here," she said. She went out, closing the door lightly and surely behind her, and Mrs. Pomeroy could hear her quick heels receding on the wet flagstones.

Mrs. Pomeroy went to the window. The clouds were tearing apart in rapid silence; a star, three stars appeared swinging toward her through thinning vapor. Then, as the wind shook a small storm of raindrops from the heavy banana leaves, the whole golden configuration was framed again in her window.

Mrs. Pomeroy stood looking at it; and she remembered it. She had seen it from the ledge. It stood over the jungle, and contained it, as the jungle, wet and glittering in the dark breeze, contained tiny Lord Lion and beautiful Mrs. Heatherby, and the tentative future of her own body.

She could not remember her own anger or fear, though they were there, somewhere within her knowledge. She had understood the terrible components of joy. Alive, and breathing, Mrs. Pomeroy stood there in the wet soft air, looking into the darkness.

The Wreath

———

I T WAS VERY COLD today; tonight, though actually it must be
colder, there seems more warmth, because the snow is still
falling thickly and consequently the house has a sheltered air.
I can see the gold wedge of my light, thrown through the window, on the snow by the box bush; at twelve it's always quiet
here, but this is snow-quiet.

It wasn't snowing yet when I drove the Ladies out to Pine
Mount early this afternoon. The sky had a tight hard look, and the
cold was the Baltimore kind that goes through flesh like a knife.

The Ladies were carrying wreaths to decorate the place for
the Christmas party; big springy circles of greens with gilded
cones and bells; some of them were sprinkled with artificial snow
and had satin-soft bows of red ribbon.

There was so much of the stuff in the back of the station
wagon where a seat had been taken out that, when we got to
the parking lot by the broken fountain, Miss Raney, who had
the most confidence (though they all had quite a lot), stopped
a patient who was going back to the kitchens and asked him to
help. I suppose she thought if he was going to the kitchens
alone, it must be all right.

He was delighted. His slack lips drew back from his big yellow
teeth and his little eyes honestly shone. We all loaded up with

wreaths, but the man took the most, and we carried them all
the way up the ramp of the dingy corridor to the small room at
the head, by the nurses' desk. Theoretically, the driver isn't
supposed to have anything to do with that part, but I couldn't
sit and freeze in the station wagon, and it seemed stupid to
mince along under nothing but the weight of my car keys.

Pine Mount was like most of those places—clean where scrub-
bing would do it, and dirty where only paint and money would
help. When we got to the top of the ramp the man didn't want
to put down his wreaths—he wanted to go right on carrying
them somewhere else—but Miss Raney was there with a hand
on his shoulder, crying, "We can't monopolize you! How do
you know people aren't out there just *waiting* for your help?" It
was effective, anyway. He dropped the wreaths just there and
loped off down the ramp toward the parking lot.

The nurse at the desk had blue eyes in a tidy face; she said,
"Driver, wouldn't you like to wait in the reading room? It
shouldn't take the Ladies more than an hour to distribute."

I could imagine that the reading room was the pick of the
rooms I might have entered, and I said, yes, thank you, and
she called a snub-nosed nurse with a comfortable air who was
thumb-tacking notices onto a plywood bulletin board and said,
"Take this lady to the reading room, will you, Miss Ertz?"

Miss Ertz unlocked a corridor door with a key from the bunch
at her waist and we went past more locked corridor doors to a
glass door which swung free. We went through that and down a
hall which looked as though it had been painted in the last five
years. You could hear people talking in the distance, and a radio
was going somewhere—a quiz program, with periodic roars of
remote laughter. Miss Ertz stopped and pointed. "To your right,"
she said. "That little room to your right. Just beyond Women."

She went back briskly, humming to herself. I kept on down
the hall and turned into the doorway she had shown me. The
reading room looked good to me at first, by contrast. It had
curtains, which toned down the bars, and a red leather chair
and a potted orange tree. It was warm, too; there was a smell
of steam and a little hissing sound. Rows of the book shelves
went round the walls, but they were about half empty and most

of the books looked beat up. Only one person was in the room, a stout young man, in a straight-back chair near the orange tree.

He had a comic book open on his lap, but he wasn't looking at it. He was obviously a patient, though a top-echelon patient. I wondered why he didn't sit in the easy chair; but when I took off my trench coat and sat there myself, it was easier to understand. Every spring was hysterical.

Somehow I didn't like to get up again, so I took out a cigarette and lit it and sat there watching the smoke attentively. The fat young man's attitude never altered. He just stared at an invisible point; about the time I finished my first cigarette he got up, placed the comic book carefully on a lower shelf and went out.

I could still hear, more faintly, the quiz program and the unspontaneous laughter; the steam hissed a little and now and then voices swelled for a minute as a door opened or shut. I got up to get a book and actually got one, with a bright blue binding, but when my fingers closed on it I didn't want it.

I'm no good at that kind of place; I'd have happily left when Miss Raney put her hand on the man's shoulder and sent him out to the broken fountain. I sat down again, still in the sprung chair as though I had a license to use it, and looked at the orange tree. It was hanging on, but it had had it; the tips of the leaves were rust-colored and the two wizened oranges were arrested. It was, somehow, a funny thing to see there. The tropical touch it was supposed to give the room had gone sour—that Valencia gold had left only its mummy.

I hadn't opened the book, but my hands held it; for some reason the right hand had grease on it where I'd tested the emergency after I took off my glove. Maybe that's why I decided to wash it. Anyway, like the fat young man, I replaced my unread matter carefully and went out into the hall and opened the door marked Women.

Hot air and a smell of disinfectant shut me in. Miss Ertz was standing by the closed door of one of the toilets with an annoyed, patient look on her fresh face. The doors of the toilets had no fastening, but this one was closed tight. When Miss Ertz saw me she raised her eyebrows and drew down the corners of her mouth, indicating semi-humorous outrage.

"Now come on, Lily," she said, addressing the invisible occupant. I tilted the glass soap-holder and let the cold yellow slime cup in my palm.

"She's got it tied with a piece of string," softly said Miss Ertz in her small capable voice. "I could *crash* it, of course," she added, "but that would frighten her, and she'd sulk all day. Lily, will you come on out now?"

I soaped my hands and watched in the mirror. There was a shuffling noise and below the door I could see a pair of down-at-the-heels brown pumps shifting stubbornly, as though someone on the other side were silently listening.

"Lily!" said Miss Ertz with a new briskness in her voice, "if you *don't* come out, you can't possibly go to the carol-sing tonight." She said to me softly—though dropping her voice seemed a technicality as we were all within six feet of each other—"She hates noise. I'll have to make a noise. I don't like to." I dried my hands on a paper towel that let the water run miserably up my wrist, smiled hastily at Miss Ertz, and opened the heavy hall door. As it whooshed slowly behind me I could hear Miss Ertz begin a sharp tattoo on the fastened door with her knuckles.

When I turned back into the reading room it was occupied. A visitor (or a staff-member?) had joined my wait; a pretty girl in a black dress and red pumps was sitting in the straight chair by the window, reading. Though I certainly hadn't thought I needed her, I was glad she was there. *I* can't read when someone near me is just sitting, so I got out a notebook and a pencil stub from my purse and began to jot down some last-minute Christmas chores.

The room was very quiet—just the little hissing sound from the steam and the busyness of my pencil stub. When I finished my list it was so quiet that I was bothered; I realized that it was taking the girl a long time to read a page, then that she wasn't reading. She—as a matter of quick glance—was looking past the arrested orange tree, through the bars to the frozen lawn. Her expression was cheerful to the point of anticipation.

Suddenly she turned her head and caught my eyes squarely. "Is it going to snow?" she asked. Her voice was attractive, but the accent was genteel.

"Any minute," I said.

"I hope it snows for Christmas," said the girl. "I'm going home day after tomorrow—Christmas Eve."

I could feel the surprise printed helplessly across my face. "That's nice," I said. If I'd had a week to think, I still wouldn't have known the proper response. Now, of course, with hindsight, I thought I noticed what I'd missed: the pressed-down eagerness, the careful dignity.

She looked through the window and smiled; her smile had an extraordinary sweetness. It seemed to me that her imminent departure sent a breath of good air through the jaunty bitter little room. "At three-thirty, day after tomorrow, I'm on my way home," she said. "My boyfriend's coming to get me." I couldn't repeat "That's nice." I smiled back at her and her face brightened abruptly. Still I could not really see her here; I had so immediately placed her among the free. There was a look of soft injury about her, though; she made me think of a bruised peach.

"Christmas list?" she asked.

"Yes," I said. "I thought I was through, but you never are, are you?"

Struck by something, the girl sat forward and looked at me tentatively. "I wonder," she said, "if you could possibly do me a big favor?" I made an encouraging sound. "Well," she said, "really, I have a problem." She wore drop rhinestone earrings and the one nearest me was missing its center stone. "Being here," she said rapidly with a small embarrassed smile, "I haven't gotten a chance to do anything, and trying to shop Christmas Eve . . ." Her eyes held on to mine with a sort of horrified shyness. "I was wondering if you could *possibly* phone Hutzler when you get home, and order some things for me—to be sent—so's they'd get there in time for Christmas?"

"Well . . ." I said. "I don't see why not." I saw very clearly why not, having no illusions as to my desk officer's reaction. There didn't seem to be the slightest reason for anyone's knowing. You could see the tissue-paper wrappings bringing the whole bright world. "They could be charged," the girl went on quickly. "I could make out a list now, and I'd certainly greatly appreciate it. I haven't a thing to wear," she added; she looked down at the spotted black dress. Suddenly it seemed to me very exciting that this should happen today; it seemed, as a matter of fact, absolutely wonderful.

"I'm sure I'll be home before the store closes," I said. "You should get the things by Christmas Eve morning—afternoon, I mean." I took my pad and pencil stub over to her and she reached for them with a sort of tender caution.

I went back to my crazy springs and she began to scribble earnestly, balancing the pad on her knee. Every now and then she would stop for a second and stare through the orange tree leaves to the barred window. I lit a cigarette and figured my chances of getting home before five-thirty. It had become very important. I figured that if the worst came to the worst, I could call from a pay station after I dropped the last of my Ladies.

The pencil stopped. The girl stared at her list for a minute, came over and handed it to me. "I don't know if you can read it," she said. "My writing's awful." She smelt faintly of perspiration and cheap powder. Close up, the prettiness of her face dissolved, like an oil painting held close to the eyes. She read off, as my eyes followed the words:

1 Black petticoat, horsehair ruffles
1 Cup-bra, size 34—(cut low under the arms)
1 Ceinture belt
2 Peasant skirts
4 Scoop-neck blouses
6 pair sheer hose, size 9½
1 pair red high-heeled slippers, double A size 7

I could feel her breath on my neck; looking up I saw her eyes dilated as a child's with pleasure.

"All right," I said. "We'll be taking a chance on the skirts. And any particular color for the blouses? And who do I charge them to?"

She straightened up and looked at me. "Charge them to my boyfriend," she said. "He's a great artist. He wants to give me the things for Christmas." We looked at each other. "Those things I wrote," she said, and she smiled brilliantly at me, and with the smile the pretty face recomposed itself. Suddenly she said with great rapidity: "And some furs. And jewels. And some real good perfumes. And charge it to Great Artist, Norwalk, Connecticut."

There was quite a long pause. Her soft, round, bruised-peach face watched me; the defective earring swung slightly.

"All right," I said. I had no idea how it sounded; evidently not too well. She drew back a little. "You're going to do it, aren't you?" she said. "You told me. You said so."

"I'll do my best," I said. I got up and for a minute there didn't seem to be a doorway anywhere. "Well goodbye," I said.

"Merry Christmas," she said, and smiled and watched me. "You'll do it, won't you?"

Like a parrot I said, "My very best." I went out of the room and down the hall, with my coat over my arm and the crumpled list in my hand. The tones of my desk officer ticked off in my mind like those level, uncadenced calls in a hospital which repeat, "Dr. Forbush, Dr. Forbush, Dr. Alan Forbush": *"Of course you understand that at no time whatsoever do you take any communication given you by a patient out of an institution; hand it directly to the attendant, even if it is about her. Whether you like it or not. It's very important for the sake..."*

I went through the glass door and down the long hall. There was no one at the desk. I stood there for a moment, but no one came. I put on my coat and buckled the belt. Still no one in sight. I took a nice deep breath and crumpled the list. As I did so Miss Ertz came up the ramp from the outside door; I could see a little cluster of people she had admitted. I got out the list and smoothed it. "Miss Ertz," I said. "A patient gave me this. In the reading room."

Without looking at me she extended a quick hand, glancing at the empty desk and down the hall. "O.K.," she said. "I'll look at it later. Thanks. Know who she was?"

"A dark girl," I said. "Pretty. Has on a black dress and red pumps."

She smiled. "Oh, Lenz. A shopping list?"

I nodded and went down the ramp. Halfway, I flattened against the wall, meeting the arriving group. Up the incline was being led an old, old woman, with thin, cotton-white hair. Her face was emaciated, with a great hooked nose and terrible black eyes. It was set, like a mask of implacable rage and grief. "Just a few more feet, Auntie," said the pale plump girl who had her arm, and behind came an embarrassed, kind-looking man in a brown suit. The old woman, like an ancient, yellow-taloned, wounded eagle, glared and crept.

Outside across the cement yard and over the parked cars, snowflakes had started to float. It was already dusk. I walked over to the station wagon and got in. I turned up my coat collar and put my hands in my pockets. The snowflakes were still melting as they struck the ground, but I noticed that a few were beginning to lie on the mat of dead leaves in the bowl of the fountain.

The building bulked very solid and very gray. As I sat hunched behind the wheel, two white-sleeved arms appeared at a window almost opposite, lowering a big wreath, evidently on cord. It had a huge bow; it swung a little; then the arms withdrew and it hung still. The bars quartered its bright green-and-red circle. And by some queer sudden movement, as though the ground beneath the station wagon had shifted, altering every proportion just a little, its broken circle seemed to me beautiful and strong and appropriate.

Jack Frost

MRS. TRAVIS was drinking a sturdy cup of tea. She sat in the wicker rocker on her back porch, in a circle of sun, after picking Mrs. James her flowers. Exhausted, she felt a little tired, and she rested with satisfaction. Mrs. James's motley bouquet sat by her knee, in one of the flower tins.

Mrs. Travis wore a blue cotton dress with a man's suitcoat over it, and around that a tie, knotted for a belt. Her legs were bare, but her small feet had on them a pair of child's galoshes, the sort that have spring buckles. Since several springs were missing, she wore the galoshes open, and sometimes they impeded her.

Half of her back porch, the left-hand side, was clear, and held her wicker rocker with its patches of sprung stiff strands; but the other half was more fruitful, a great pile of possessions which she needed, or had needed, or in certain possible circumstances might come to need: a tin footbath containing rope, twine, and a nest of tin containers from the insides of flower baskets; a hatchet; a galosh for the right foot; garden tools; a rubber mat; a bee-keeper's helmet for the black-fly season. Nearby, a short length of hose; chunks of wood. The eye flagged before the count.

There was a small winding path, like the witch's in a fairy tale, between cosmos so tall they brushed the shoulders. To its right almost immediately, vegetables grew: the feathery tops of carrots, dusty beet-greens, a few handsome mottled zucchini, the long runners of beans. Last year there had still been tomatoes, but the staking-up and coaxing had become too much; she said to herself instead that such finicking had come to bore her. To the left of the cosmos, below a small slope of scratchy lawn, was the garden proper—on this mellow September afternoon a fine chaos of unchosen color, the Mexican shades of zinnias, the paper-cutout heads of dahlias, a few grown-over roses, more cosmos, the final spikes of some fine gladioli, phlox running heavily back to magenta, and closer to the cooling ground, the pink and purple of asters. There were even a few pansies, wildly persisting in a tangle of grass and weeds.

Until a few years ago her younger brother Henry had driven over two hundred miles, up from Connecticut, to help her plant both gardens, but Henry had died at eighty-two. Mrs. Travis herself did not actually know how old she was. She believed herself to be ninety-three; but having several years ago gone suddenly to check the fact of the matter in the faint gray handwriting of her foxed Bible, a cup of strong tea in her hand, she had sloshed the tea as she peered, and then on the puffed, run surface, she could no longer read the final digit. 3? 7? 1883? Just possibly, 1887? For a moment she felt youth pressing on her; if it were, if it possibly were 1887, several years had lifted themselves off. There they were, still to come with all the variety of their days. Turn those to hours, those to minutes, and it was a gigantic fresh extension. But she thought the figure was a 3. It was the last time she looked in the back of the Bible.

Tacked onto the porch wall was a large calendar; each day past was circled in red. Only three such showed; she would circle September 4th when she closed the door for the night.

Now before she could swallow the last of her tea, here came Mrs. James's yellow sweater, borne on a bicycle along the dirt road outside the hedge. Dismounted, Mrs. James wheeled the bicycle up the path and leaned it against the porch post. She was sweaty with effort over the baked ridges of the road, and, half a century younger than her hostess, she radiated summer-visitor energy and cheer.

"Oh Mrs. Travis!" she cried. "You've got them all ready! Aren't they lovely!" She was disappointed, since she had hoped to choose the picking; but she and her summer friends regarded Mrs. Travis's activity as much like that of Dr. Johnson's dog walking on its hind legs.

Mrs. Travis looked with satisfaction at the jumble of phlox, gladioli, dahlias, and zinnias which, with all the slow, slow bending and straightening, had cost her an hour.

"Oh, it's so *warm*," said Mrs. James with pleasure, sitting down on the step at Mrs. Travis's feet.

Mrs. Travis had so few occasions to speak that it always seemed to take her a minute to call up her voice, which arrived faint with distance. "Yes," she said, almost inaudibly. "It's a very good day."

"Oh look!" said Mrs. James, pleased. "Look how well the rose begonia's doing!" She had given it to Mrs. Travis early in the summer, it was one of her own bulbs from California, and she could see its full gorgeousness now, blooming erratically beside the path, hanging its huge rosy bloom by the gap-toothed rake and a tiny pile of debris: twigs, dead grass, a few leaves.

Mrs. Travis did not answer, but Mrs. James saw it was because she was looking at the begonia's gross beauty with a powerful smugness. They sat companionably for a moment. Mrs. James seemed to Mrs. Travis like one of the finches, or yellow-headed warblers, which frequented her for the warmest weeks. Exactly as she thought so, Mrs. James said, suddenly sad, "Do you know the birds are all going, *already?*"

"No, not all," said Mrs. Travis soothingly. "The chickadees won't go." But Mrs. Travis did not really care; it was the flowers she created out of nothing.

"I hate to see them go so soon," said Mrs. James, stubbornly sad.

"But you'll be going, too," said Mrs. Travis, faintly and comfortingly. Mrs. James, lifting her chin, looked at Mrs. Travis. "Are you going to stay here all winter, *again?*" she asked.

Mrs. Travis looked at her with stupefaction. Then she said, "Yes." She was afraid Mrs. James was going to repeat what she had said for the past two autumns, about Mrs. Travis moving into the village for the winter; here she was, no phone, no close neighbors; nothing but snow, and ice, and wind, and the grocery boy with his little bag, and the mailman's Pontiac passing without stopping. But Mrs. James said only, "Look, here comes Father O'Rourke."

There was the clap of a car door, and Father O'Rourke appeared between the cosmos, surprisingly wearing his dog collar, his black coat slung over his white shoulder. Mrs. James stood up, pleased that Mrs. Travis had a visitor. "I've got to get these flowers back," she said. Now came the embarrassing moment. "How—er, they're so lovely; what...?"

"That's three dollars for the pailful," said Mrs. Travis with satisfaction. Mrs. James, whose grandmother, as a little girl, had known Mrs. Travis in Boston, continued to feel, no matter what she paid, that the flowers had come as a gift from Mrs. Travis's conservatory. She laid three dollars inconspicuously on the table by the oil lamp, and Mrs. Travis watched her and Father O'Rourke saying hello, and goodbye for the winter, to each other in the hot slanting sun.

As Mrs. James wheeled her bicycle away, Father O'Rourke replaced her on the step. He did not offer to shake hands, having noticed that such gestures seemed to distract Mrs. Travis, as some sort of clumsy recollected maneuver. He had just come from making the final plans for the Watkins wedding, and fresh from all that youth and detail, he looked at Mrs. Travis, whose pale small blue eyes looked back at him, kindly, but from a long distance. The purpose of Father O'Rourke's visit embarrassed him; he was afraid of Mrs. Travis's iron will.

"What a lot of flowers you've still got," began Father O'Rourke, obliquely.

Mrs. Travis looked out over the ragged rainbow on the slope. The sun, at its western angle, was still a good bit above the smaller of the big dark mountains behind which it would go. "Oh yes," she said, "they'll be here for a long time. A couple of weeks, probably." He saw that she meant just that.

"Well," he said, "you know, Mrs. Travis, after five years here, I've found we just don't know. Things may go on almost to October; and then, again, a night in late August will do it."

Mrs. Travis did not reply to this, and Father O'Rourke

plunged. "I saw Mrs. Metcalfe at the post office this morning," he said, looking placatingly at Mrs. Travis's profile. "Did you know that she's finished making that big sitting room off her south porch into that little apartment she's going to rent out?"

Mrs. Travis, who had had enough of this for one day, indeed for one lifetime, turned her head and looked him straight in his hazel eye.

"I'm not going anywhere," she said, surprisingly loud, adding from some past constraint, "Father O'Rourke."

A final sense of the futility of his effort struck him silent. They sat quietly for a few seconds. What on earth am I trying to do? he thought suddenly. Why *should* she move? Well, so many reasons; he wondered if they were all worthless. He knew that before he was born, Mrs. Travis had enlisted in the army of eccentric hermits, isolates, writing their own terms into some curious treaty. But she was so much older than anyone else that the details became more and more obscure; also, more romanticized. There was even doubt as to a dim and distant husband. A fallen or faithless lover appeared, along with factual but tinted tales of early privilege. But the Miss Havisham motif he tended to discount; it was so widely beloved.

All he knew for certain was that, with Mrs. Travis, he was in the presence of an authenticity of elimination which caused him a curiously mingled horror and envy. At times he thought that her attention, fiercely concentrated, brought out, like a brilliant detail from an immense canvas, a quality of some non-verbal and passionate comprehension. At other times he saw a tremendously old woman, all nuances of the world, her past, and the earth's present, ignored or forgotten; brittle and single, everything rejected but her own tiny circle of motion.

With a fairly complex mind, Father O'Rourke combined a rather simple set of hopes, not many of which were realized. One of these was to enter Mrs. Travis's detail, as some sort of connection with a comfort, or even a lack of finality. The bond between them, actually, was a belief in the physical, a conviction of the open-ended mystery of matter. But since Mrs. Travis had never been a Catholic, that particular avenue wasn't open to him. Her passion was in this scraggy garden, but he distinguished that it was coldly unsentimental, unlike that of most lady gardeners he knew. He was not sure just how Mrs. Travis did feel about her flowers. He considered that, in homily and metaphor, the garden-thing—Eden to Gethsemane—had been overdone; nevertheless, in connection with Mrs. Travis, he always thought of it. He had, on a previous visit last month, brought up some flower passages from the Bible; but the only interest she had shown was by a question as to which type of lily the lilies-of-the-field had been. She had at least five kinds, lifting their slick and sappy stalks above confusion. But when he had said they were most like anemones, she had lost interest, having forgotten, after fifty years in the New Hampshire mountains, what anemones looked like.

"I have to go back to the Watkinses again tomorrow," said Father O'Rourke. He knew he should have been back at the rectory half an hour ago. Here he sat, mesmerized somehow by the invisible movement of the sun across the step, by the almost total stillness. It was cooling rapidly, too. He picked up his coat and hunched his arms into it. "Can I bring you anything, then?"

"No," she said. She was sorry to see him go. She turned her head to look fully at him. "Do you want any flowers?" she asked.

He hesitated, thinking of Mrs. Metcalfe's pious arrangement, three pink gladioli in a thin-stemmed glass on each side of the altar. "Well," he said, "how about some zinnias for my desk? I'll pick them tomorrow," he added hastily, as he saw her eyes cloud, rallying for action. On the step he lingered, smiling at her. Oppressed. "Well," he said idiotically, "don't let Jack Frost get your flowers."

She watched him attentively down the path. Just as his starter churned, the sun left the porch and, looking up to the mountain, Mrs. Travis saw that it had gone for the day.

She went in at once, forgetting her rake, lying in the garden, her empty teacup, and the three dollars on the table, but carrying a short chunk of wood under each arm. She took at least one each time she went into the house. She never turned on the furnace before October, but there was a small chunk stove in the corner, by the lamp table, and it warmed the room in a matter of minutes. She decided to have supper right now. She had a chop, and there was still some lettuce. She had picked a fine head this morning; it was right in the colander, earth still clinging to its bottom.

By eight o'clock it had got very cold outside. But the room was warm. Mrs. Travis went to sleep in her chair. Sleep often took her now with a ferocious touch, so that everything just disappeared; and when she woke up, she found that hours had passed. On a warm night in July she had slept in her chair all night long, waking up, disoriented, to a watery dawn.

Now she not only slept, she dreamed. An unpleasant dream, something extremely unusual. She was in a dark huge city lit by thin lamps, and she was afraid. She was afraid of a person, who might be coming toward her, or coming up behind her. And yet, more than a person—though she knew it was a man in a cap. She must get into a house before he found her. Or before he found someone else. A strange-looking girl went by her, hurrying, very pale, with a big artificial rose in her hair. She turned suddenly into an opening on the dreamer's right; it was the darkest of alleys and the dreamer hurried faster than ever. Ahead of her, in the fog, she could see the dimly lit sign of an inn; but as she hurried faster, a terrible scream, high and short, came out of the alley. It woke Mrs. Travis, her hands locked hard on the arms of the chair.

She sat quite still, looking around the familiar room. Then memory handed her one of the clear messages that now so seldom arrived. The Lodger. That was just it. She had suddenly, after all these years, had a dream about Jack the Ripper, as she had had several times when she first read of his foggy city streets a very long time ago. But why this dream should have escaped from the past to molest her, she could not think.

The little fire in the stove was out, but the stove itself still ticked and settled with heat. The wall clock said two minutes to eight. Stiff from sleep, Mrs. Travis reached over and turned the dial of the small discolored radio under the table lamp, and immediately a loud masculine voice said, ". . . front, all the way from the Great Lakes, throughout northern New England, and into Canada. Frost warnings have been issued for the mountain areas

of Vermont and New Hampshire. Tomorrow the unseasonable
cold will continue, for a chilly Labor Day; but by Wednesday . . ."
Appalled, Mrs. Travis switched off the evil messenger.

Frost. It was not that it was so strange; it was so sudden. She
could still feel the heat of the sun, on the porch, on her hands
and her ankles. Two weeks, she had thought.

As she sat, staring for a moment straight ahead, a brand new
fury started up, deep inside her. Two weeks. It was an eternity
of summer. The long nights, the brutal chill, the endless hardness
of the earth, they were reasonable enough, in their time. In their
time. But this was her time, and they were about to invade it.
She began to tremble with anger. She thought of her seeds, and
how dry and hard they had been; of her deathlike bulbs, slipping
old skin, with everything locked inside them, and she, her body,
had turned them into that summer of color and softness and
good smells that was out there in the dark garden.

She turned her head, right and left, looking for an exit for
her rage. Then suddenly she sat forward in her chair. An idea
had come to her with great force and clarity. It grew in the room,
like an enormous plant covered with buds. Mrs. Travis knew
exactly what she was going to do. Her intention was not protective, but defiant; her sense was of battle, punitive battle.

She stood up carefully, and went and got the flashlight from
the shelf over the woodbox. She went to the porch door and
opened it, and then closed it hastily behind her, protecting the
room's warmth. There was no sound or light in any direction,
but there was a diffused brightness behind the mountain's darker
bulk. She tipped over the pail that had held Mrs. James's flowers,
so that the leafy water poured down the sloping porch. Then
she began fitting the tin flower-holders into it. She could not
get them all in, and she took her pail into the house and came
back for the last three. She arranged the pail and the tins on the
kitchen floor, and then she attached a short length of hose to
the cold water spigot, dropped the other end in the pail, and
turned on the water. She filled the big tins the same way, and
then lifted the small ones into the sink, removing the hose, and
filled them. Turning with satisfaction to look through the doorway at the clock, she was disconcerted to see that it said five

minutes after nine. She stared at it, skeptical but uncertain. It could *stop*; but surely it couldn't skip *ahead*. Perhaps she had mistaken the earlier time. She began to move more rapidly; though she was so excited, all her faculties had come so strongly into one intention, that it seemed to her that she was already moving at a furious pace.

She went over to the kitchen door and took off its hook a felt hat and an ancient overcoat of Henry's. She put the hat on her head, got carefully into the overcoat and stuffed her flashlight into the pocket. She took down from the top of the refrigerator a cracked papier-mâché tray Mrs. James had sent her several Christmases ago; its design of old coins had almost disappeared. At an open drawer she hesitated over a pair of shears. Lately she had found them hard to open and close, and after standing there for half a minute, she took a thick-handled knife instead. She went to look at the empty sitting room and then moved back through the kitchen faster than seemed possible.

Out on the porch, a square of light came through the window, and looking up, she could make out a cloud over the mountain, its edges stained with brightness.

She lit her flashlight, and went cautiously down the step and along the path, carrying her tray under her arm. Faces of cosmos, purple and pink, loomed at her as she went; but even in her tremendous excitement, she knew she couldn't bring in everything, and she went on, the tops of her galoshes making a little flapping noise in the silence. She turned carefully down the slight slope, and here were the zinnias, towered over by the branchy dahlias. She laid her tray on the ground.

But now, breathing more rapidly, she saw that she was in trouble. To cut with her knife, she had to hold the flower's stem, and she had to hold her flashlight to see it, and she had two hands. Fiercely she looked about for an idea; and at just that moment, a clear thin light streamed over the edge of the cloud and lit her. The moon was full. She might have known; that was when a black frost always came.

Mrs. Travis made an inarticulate sound of fierce pleasure and dropped the flashlight into the tray. Then she began to cut the flowers, working as fast as she could, giving little pants of satisfaction as the shapes heaped themselves up below her. Inch by inch she moved along the ragged rows, pushing, with a galoshed toe, the tray along the ground before her. She cut all the gladioli, even the ones which were still mostly flaccid green tips; she cut all the dahlias, even the buds, and every zinnia. She felt light and warm, and drunk with resistant power. Finally the tray was so full that blooms began to tip over and fall into the cold grass.

Very cautiously indeed she got the tray up, but she could not hold it level and manipulate the flashlight. It made no difference. The moon, enormous and fully round, had laid light all over the garden; the house's shadow was black, as though a pale sun were shining.

Teetering a little to hold the tray level, Mrs. Travis went up the path, carefully up the step. She set the tray on the table, knocking over her dirty teacup and saucer, and each broke cleanly in two pieces. She stepped over them, opened the door on warmth, and went back for her load.

First she filled the pail; then every tin. There was a handful of zinnias left, and a pile of phlox. Threatened, Mrs. Travis looked about the kitchen, but saw nothing helpful. She could feel her cheeks burning in the room's summer, and with a little noise of triumph, she went through the door to the bedroom and came back with the big china chamber pot. It had a fine network of fractured veins, and on it was a burst of painted magenta foliage. When she had filled it under the tap it was too heavy to lift down, so she stuffed in the flowers and left it there. A small chartreuse-colored spider began to run up and down the sink's edge.

Then, just as she was turning to look at all she had done, like a cry from an alley, like a blow between the shoulders, to her mind's eye came the rose begonia. She could positively see in the air before her its ruffled heavy head, the coral flush of its crowded petals; from its side sprang the bud, color splitting the sheath. The bulb had thrust it up, and there it was, out there.

Though she felt as though she were drunk, she also felt shrewd. Think of the low ones you can't stoop to tonight, she thought, the nasturtiums, the pansies, the bachelor's buttons, the ragged robins. But it made no difference. She knew that unless she took the rose begonia, she had lost everything. She looked at the clock; it was half past ten. She could be back in ten minutes; and she decided that then she would sit right down by the stove and sleep there, deliberately, and not move into the cold bed and take off bit by bit so many clothes.

There were four sticks of wood by the stove, and under the lid the embers were bright. She put in three sticks; then she went empty-handed to the porch. It was very cold and absolutely still. The moon was even brighter; it was almost half way up the sky. She found a terra-cotta flowerpot on the porch corner, and she rooted in the footbath until she found her trowel. Then she went, as fast as she could go, down the path to the halfway point, where she came upon the rose begonia, paled by the chill of the light. As she bent over, her head roared; so she kneeled, and drove the blunt trowel-edge into the earth.

When the roots came up in a great ball of earth she pressed them into the pot, stuffing more clods of fibrous earth around them. Then she started to get up. But with the pot in one hand and the trowel in the other, it was impossible.

She dropped the trowel. She did not even think that she could get it tomorrow. Suddenly she was cold to her very teeth. She thought just of the room, the hot, colored, waiting room. Holding the pot in her left hand, pushing with her right, she got herself upright; but it made her dizzy, and as she lurched a little to the side the rake's teeth brought her down in a heavy fall. The flower shot from her hand and disappeared into the shadows and a bright strong pain blasted her. It was her ankle; and she lay with her face close to the cold dirt, feeling the waves of pain hit her.

Mrs. Travis raised her head, to see how far away the porch was. It was perhaps ten or eleven yards. Another country. Things seemed dimmer, too, and wrenching her head sideways and up, she saw that the huge moon had shrunk; it sat high and small, right at the top of the sky.

Mrs. Travis lowered her head gently and began to crawl, pushing with her hands and the knee of her good leg. She went along, inch by inch, foot by foot; she had no fear, since there was an absolute shield between one second and the next.

The porch was so shadowed now that she nearly missed it;

the step struck her advancing hand. It took her three tries, but she got up over it, and went on, inch by inch, toward the door. A sliver of china bit her hand. Bright light came through the keyhole. She reached up and easily turned the doorknob; then like a crab she was across the sill.

She could not, she found, turn; but she pushed out with her left foot, and miraculously the door clicked shut just behind her. She felt no pain at all, but there was something forming under her ribs.

In the room's heat, the foliage of the marigolds gave out a spicy smell, stronger than the fragrance of the phlox. A dozen shapes and colors blazed before her eyes, and a great tearing breath came up inside her like an explosion. Mrs. Travis lifted her head, and the whole wave of summer, advancing obedient and glorious, in a crest of color and warmth and fragrance broke right over her.

On the Island

––––––––

A FTER DINNER the Driscolls sat for a while with Mr. Soo, by the big windows looking out and down over the bay. There was nothing to close: they were just great oblong unscreened openings, with all that fantasy of beauty spread straight before them. Mary had not learned to believe in it, any more than she had learned to believe that the shadowy, bamboo-furnished, candlelit room behind them wouldn't be invaded by insects—even perhaps bats, or one of the host of hummingbirds. For storms, there were heavy shutters. But nothing ever seemed to come in; only the air stirred, faintly sweet, against their faces; it grew spicier and more confused with scent as the dark strengthened.

Mr. Soo, in his impassive and formidable way, seemed glad to have them; or perhaps he was only acquiescent, in his momentary solitude. The inn was completely empty except for themselves, Mr. Soo, and the servants. This was rare, she gathered, even in the off-season she and Henry had chosen—and, indeed, their room had been occupied, only the day before yesterday, by another couple. A party of six would arrive after the weekend. Being here alone was part of their extraordinary luck. It had held for the whole trip: in Port of Spain they had got, after all, the room facing the Savanna; on Tobago they had seen the green fish come in, the ones that were bright as fire in the different green of the water; they had even seen, far off, on the trip to

Bird of Paradise Island, a pair of birds of paradise, dim and quick through a great many distant leaves, but unmistakable in their sumptuous, trailing plumage.

This still, small place was their final stop before the plane home, and just as they had planned it, it was beginning as it would end, hot and green, unpeopled, radiantly vacant. "It's the closest we'll get to real jungle," Henry said eagerly. And the jungle was no way away. The inn sheltered in cocoa bushes, shaded by their immortelles: Mr. Soo's plantation was a shallow fringe stretching for acres and acres, with the true jungle less than half a mile behind it. Mr. Soo, she felt sure, had never read one of Henry's books, but obviously was aware of his name; and this perhaps had led him to offer them brandy and sit by them in one of the gleaming, cushioned chairs, as they stared out to the disappearing sea. He did not look to Mary like a man whose pleasure lay in fraternizing with guests. Pleasure? His hair, in short, shining bristles, clasped his head tightly, giving the effect of pulling his eyes nearly shut by its grip. His face was the agreeable color of very pale copper; the mouth straight and thin, the nose fleshy. She and Henry had secretly discussed his age: thirty-eight? forty-four? thirty-seven? In the exhausted light he appeared now almost as though he had been decapitated and then had his head with its impassive face set, very skillfully, back upon his shoulders.

Mr. Soo had been born in Trinidad, but had come here to the island almost fifteen years ago, to raise cocoa. Mary was sure that the friends who had told them about the tiny inn had spoken of a Mrs. Soo, but she was not here and there was no reference to her. Arthur, the major-domo, had said only, "No Mrs. Soo," in response to an inquiry if she were away. Dead? Divorced? A figment of friends' imagination?

"Yes," Henry was saying, "'like it' is too mild; they can't wait to come again. They're very bird-minded."

Mr. Soo looked at him in astonishment. "Your *friends*?"

"Yes. Very. Why?"

"They seemed to me," said Mr. Soo, obviously shocked, "very nice people. Intelligent. Not bird-minded."

Henry now gaped, baffled.

"Bird-*minded*, Mr. Soo," Mary said nervously. "I think you're thinking of how we sometimes say bird-*brained*. Bird-*minded*. It means thinking a lot about birds. Anxious to see new ones, you know."

Mr. Soo still had an offended air. "Very intelligent people," he said.

"*Very!*" said Henry and Mary simultaneously.

A rush of wings veered past the window, in the new darkness. "Very few here on the island, intelligent people," said Mr. Soo. "Just natives. Blacks."

There was a short pause. A faint yattering, like the rapid clack of unskilled castanets, came dimly from the upper reaches of an invisible tree.

"Haven't you any Chinese or Indian neighbors?" asked Henry, noncommittally.

"Fifteen miles," said Mr. Soo, "is the nearest. I do not like Indians," he added. "But they are civilized. They come from civilized country. On Trinidad, all the shops, the taxis, all mostly Indians. They have an old civilization. Very few criminals. Except when they are drunk. The criminal classes are the blacks. Every week, choppings."

Oh, God, thought Mary, here goes our jungle holiday. Well, she decided immediately, we don't *have* to talk to him; we can go to our room in a minute. She caught Henry's glance, flicked to his wrist.

"Good heavens, it's after ten!" he announced like an amateur actor. "If we're going to get up early for the birds..."

Mr. Soo said quickly, "Lots of birds. Even at night. Pygmy owls. They fool the other birds," he explained. "That honey creeper, green honey creeper. The pygmy owl fools him. Like this." He suddenly puckered his lips and gave a tremulant, dying whistle; afterward, he smiled at them for the first time. "And you see cornbirds. Tody-tyrants, too. And motmots, with long tails..." He sketched one with a quick hand on which the candle-light caught jade. "They pull out their own tailfeathers. And the kiskadee. That's French, corrupted French. *Qu'est-ce qu'il dit?* Means, what's that he says? Over and over. The kiskadee."

The Driscolls rose, smiling. Are the birds part of the inn, like

the soursop drinks and the coconut milk and the arum lilies?—or
does he like them? It seemed to Mary that he did.

"There was a bird this morning," she said, "on the piles..."

"A pelican," interrupted Mr. Soo.

"No," said Mary rather shortly. "I know pelicans." (For
heaven's sake!) "A little boy told me what it was. But I can't
remember. Like 'baby'..."

Henry and Mr. Soo said simultaneously and respectively, "A
booby! That's what it was, a booby!" and, "A little boy?"

"The *nicest* little boy," said Mary, answering Mr. Soo. "He
showed me the fiddler-crab holes and all the live things growing
on the big rock, on the sea side."

"What was his name?" asked Mr. Soo unexpectedly. He had
risen, too.

"I haven't an idea," Mary replied, surprised. "No, wait a
minute..."

"A black boy," said Mr. Soo. "With a pink scar on his cheek."

Mary was not sure why the words she was about to say—
"*Victor*, I'm sure he told me"—seemed suddenly inappropriate.
In the little silence, Mr. Soo surprisingly bowed. "I am sorry,"
he said with obvious sincerity. "He is, *of course*, not allowed
there. He has been told. This will be the last," he said quickly.
"I am *so* sorry."

"Good heavens," said Henry, rather irritably, "he was fine—
we enjoyed him. Very much. He was a bright boy, very friendly.
He showed us how he would fight a shark—imaginary knife
and all, you know."

"He was in the *water*?" said Mr. Soo with a little hiss.

During this contretemps, Arthur had approached; his dark
face, lustrous in the candlelight, was turned inquiringly toward
them over the brandy decanter.

"No, really, thanks," said Mary. She managed to smile at Mr.
Soo as she turned away, hearing Henry say, "We'll be back for
breakfast about eight," and then his footsteps behind her across
the lustrous straw roses of the rug.

Later in the night she woke up. Theirs was the only bedroom
in the main building except for Mr. Soo's apartment. Earlier,

massed poinsettia, oleander, and exora had blazed just beyond their casement windows in the unnatural brilliance of the raw bulb fastened outside—now, by a round gold moon that was getting on for full, blue and purplish hues had taken over. The bunches of blossom were perfectly still.

She could see Henry's dark head on his pillow; he was spread-eagled with one foot quite out of bed. Very soon, familiar pressure would swallow them. Henry, even here, was immersed in his plots, manipulating shadowy figures, catching echoes of shifting dialogue. It had nothing to do with happiness, or satisfaction, but she knew that increasingly Henry's mind veered from hers, turning in patterns whose skill she admired. Henry believed in his plots. His cause and effect, lovely as graph lines and as clear, operated below all things. This island, which seemed to her full of hints flying like spray, yielded itself to him in information of tensions, feathers, blossoms, crops. More and more, like a god let loose on clay, he shaped and limited. She loved him for this, too: for his earnestness and the perfection of his sincerity; but sometimes now, she knew, her mind seemed to him disorderly and inconsequential, with its stubborn respect for surprises.

A breeze had begun to stir. The blanched crests of blossoms nodded beyond the broad sill and there was a faint rattle of palm fronds. Also, something moved in the thatch.

I will go to sleep if I think of the right things, she said to herself, and she set about remembering the misty horses, galloping easily over the Savanna track in the Trinidad dawn; she'd stood in her nightgown on the balcony to see their lovely, silent sweep. And the fern banks on Grenada: hills of fern higher than towers, deep springing hills of fronded green. And the surf, the terrifying surf, when they'd launched the little boat off Tobago for the trip to Bird of Paradise Island. The turquoise water had broken in a storm of white over the shining dark bodies and laughing faces of the launchers, the boat tipping and rocking, flung crazily upward and then seized again by dripping hands. She'd felt both frightened and happy; Henry had hauled her in and they'd plunged up and down until finally they reached deep water and saw ahead of them, beginning to shape up in the distance, the trees which perhaps sheltered the marvelous birds. "Nothing is known of the breeding habits of Birds of Paradise," her *Birds of the Caribbean* said. She repeated this, silently, sleepily. Nothing is known of the breeding habits of Birds of Paradise. How nice.

Suddenly, she heard water, a seeping sound—though, on her elbow, she could see it wasn't raining. She swung her feet over the bed, but not to the floor. Luck had been good here, but in the dark she wouldn't walk barefoot and her slippers she kept under the sheet. She felt her way cautiously to the bathroom door. Inside, she lighted a candle—the generator went off at 11:00. The bathroom was immaculate, but water shone by her feet and seeped toward the depression which served as a shower floor. The toilet was unobtrusively overflowing in a small trickle. Eventually the floor would be covered and water would ooze under the door. What on earth could they do about it tonight, though? Move in with Mr. Soo? She began to giggle faintly. But it was a bother, too; in remote spots things took forever to get themselves fixed. She put Henry's sandals on the window ledge, blew out the candle, and closed the door softly behind her. Henry hadn't stirred. She got back in bed, thinking: It's a good thing I saw those sandals—they were *in* the water! The words set off an echo, but, as she remembered what it was, she fell asleep.

By morning, the water was in their room, reaching fingers in several directions; the heavy straw of the rugs was brown and dank. When they came out into the pale, fragrant sunlight of the big room, Arthur was throwing away yesterday's flowers from the two big blue vases on the low tables. Henry, dropping his binocular-strap over his head, stopped long enough to report their problem. Arthur looked at them with an expression of courteous anguish and ritual surprise and said that he would tell Mr. Soo.

When they returned two hours later, hungry and already hot, Mr. Soo had come and gone. His small table, with its yellow porcelain bowl filled each morning with arum lilies, was being cleared by Arthur, who brought them a platter of fruit and told them that after breakfast he would transfer them to Mr. Soo's room. They were astounded and horrified in equal proportions. "That's absolutely impossible," said Henry. "We can't inconvenience him like that. Why can't we go down to one of the beach cottages? Or up on the hill?"

Arthur, who at the moment represented all help except the invisible cook, did not say: Because I can't run back and forth and still do everything here. He said instead, "Mr. Soo did tell me to move you after breakfast."

Henry was anxious to talk to Arthur. Wherever they went, he absorbed gestures, words, inflections, as a lock-keeper received water, with the earnest knowledge of its future use. He was very quick at the most fugitive nuance; later it would be fitted into place, all the more impressive for its subtlety.

Arthur had poured their second cup of coffee. Now he reappeared from behind the red lacquer screen, carrying one of the big blue vases. It was filled high with yellow hibiscus and he set it gently on one of the teakwood stands.

Henry said, in his inviting way, "You do a bit of everything."

Immediately, Arthur came to the table. "Only I am here now," he said. "And the cook. Two boys gone." He held up two fingers. "Chauffeur is gone."

On short acquaintance, Mary did not particularly like Arthur. He had a confidential air which, she noticed, pivoted like a fan. At present it was blowing ingratiatingly on Henry. "Mr. Soo had a lot of trouble with help," said Arthur. Mary saw with a rather malign amusement the guest's breeding struggle with the writer's cupidity. The victory was tentative.

"Now we're upsetting things," said Henry, not altogether abandoning the subject. "It's ridiculous for him to move out of his room for us."

"Won't upset Mr. Soo," said Arthur soothingly. "He can shut the apartment off, sitting room, library. Another bath, too, on the other side. Used to be Mrs. Soo."

Mary could see the waves of curiosity emanating from Henry, but he gallantly maintained silence. "There is a sleep-couch in the sitting room," Arthur went on. "Mr. Soo does want you to be comfortable, and so." He pivoted slightly to include Mary in his range.

His eyeballs had crimson veins and he smelled of a fine toilet water. "Mr. Soo is very angry with that boy," said Arthur. "Mr.

Soo does tell he: Stay away from my beach, ever since that boy come here."

In spite of herself, Mary said irascibly, "But that's ridiculous. He wasn't bothering anyone."

"Bother Mr. Soo," said Arthur. "Mr. Soo is so angry he went last night to go to see he grandmother. Told he grandmother, that boy does come here again, he beat him."

"May I have some hot coffee, please?" asked Mary.

Arthur did not move. He swept his veined eyes from one to the other. "Mr. Soo does not own that beach," said Arthur. "Can't no mahn own a beach here. Mr. Soo's beachhouse, Mr. Soo's boat, Mr. Soo's wharf. But not he beach. But he don't let no mahn there, only guests."

"Why does he like this beach so much?" said Mary, for it was small and coarse, with plenty of sharp rocks. "The boy, I mean."

"Only beach for five miles," Arthur told her. "That boy, Victor, come with he brother, come to he grandmother. They live top-side. Just rocks, down their hill. Very bad currents. Seapussy, too. Can't no mahn swim there."

"May I have some hot coffee?" Mary said again.

Arthur stood looking at her. At this moment a considerable clamor broke out in the kitchen behind them. Voices, a man's and a woman's, raised in dispute, then in anger. The woman called, "Arthur! You come here, Arthur!"

Arthur continued to look at them for about two seconds; then, without haste, he went away, walking around the screen toward the kitchen.

"All right, all right," said Henry, answering a look. "But you know perfectly well we can't come here for five days and tell Mr. Soo who he must have on his beach."

"It isn't his beach."

"It isn't ours, either."

Something smashed in the kitchen. A door banged viciously. Outside the window went, running easily, a tall, big boy. His dark, furious, handsome face glared past them into the room. He dived down the wooden steps past the glade of arum lilies. His tight, faded bluejeans disappeared among the bushes.

"What was *that* in aid of?" said Henry, fascinated.

Arthur appeared. He carried the faintly steaming enamel pot of coffee, and coming up to them, poured a rich stream into Mary's cup. Then he said: "The big brother of Vic-tor, he's a bad bad boy. Daniel. Same name as the man fought the lion." He bowed slightly, thus reminding Mary of Mr. Soo, turned to the other teakwood stand, lifted the empty blue vase, and went off with it behind the screen.

"'*Fought* the lion'?" said Mary, inquiringly, to Henry.

"Well," said Henry, "I suppose Arthur places him in the lion's den, and then improvises."

That was the last of the excitement. They were transferred quickly and easily from their moist quarters; the toilet was now turned off and not functioning at all. Mr. Soo's room lacked all traces of its owner, unless a second bed could be seen as a trace. It had a finer view than their abandoned room, looking all the way down the series of long terraces to the small bright rocky beach.

Greenness took over: the greenness of the shallows of the bay before it deepened to turquoise, of the wet, thick leaves of the arum lilies, soaked each morning by an indefatigable Arthur, of the glittering high palms, and the hot tangled jungle behind the cocoa bushes shaded by their immortelles. Mary had—unexpectedly to herself—wanted to leave before their time was up. She had even suggested it to Henry right after breakfast on that second morning. But Henry wanted to stay.

"It *isn't* Mr. Soo," she said, trying to explain. "It hasn't anything to do with that. It's something else. There're too many vines. Everything's looped up and tangled. The palms rattle against the tin and give me dreams."

"Don't be fey," said Henry rather shortly. "We'll be away from palms soon enough."

Mr. Soo continued cordial in his immobile fashion: he talked to them from his small table when, at dinner, their hours coincided. Once, he had Arthur make them each a soursop, cold and lovely as nectar, when they came in brown and sweaty from the beach rocks. But by some obscure mutual assent, there were no more brandies. After dinner, the Driscolls sat on their tiny terrace, watching the moon swelling toward fullness, and drank crème de cacao in tiny gourd cups provided by Arthur. They knew they were destined to share their final hours on, and their first off, the island with Mr. Soo. He too would be on the biweekly plane to Trinidad. Mr. Soo said he was going to Port of Spain to procure plumbing fixtures. Arthur said Mr. Soo was going to procure a number two boy and a chauffeur. Where on earth did Mr. Soo wish to be driven, over the narrow, pitted, gullied roads that circled the island? Through and through his plantation, perhaps. Arthur took no note of coldness in relation to his comments on Mr. Soo; also, Mary felt, the most ardent questioning would have led him to reveal no more than he had originally determined. His confidences went by some iron and totally mysterious autodecision. She was uncertain how his sentiments stood in regard to his employer.

On their last afternoon, the Driscolls went for a walk. Just before dusk, they decided to go deep along the jungle path. This was the hour for birds; all over the little island they were suddenly in motion. Almost none, except the hummingbirds with which the island fairly vibrated, flew in the golden hot midday, but at dusk the air was full of calls and wings.

Mary and Henry went along the middle ledge, above the lilies. Down on the beach, the fiddler crabs would be veering, flattening themselves, then rearing to run sideways, diving down holes into which fell after them a few trembling grains of sand. From here, the Driscolls could only see the white waves, leaping like hounds up at the rocks. They went along slowly, musingly, in the fading heat, up the steep path back of the garden sheds, below the giant saman, the great airy tree with its fringed, unstirring, pendent parasite world. With its colony of toe-hold survivors, it was like the huge rock on the beach, half in the tides, to whose surface clung and grew motionless breathers.

They turned up the small, dusty road toward the solid wave of tree crests towering ahead. They had been this way twice before; they remembered a goat tethered up the bank at eye-level, a small scrubby cow standing uncertainly in the ditch. They would pass a cabin, half up the slope, with its back to the bay far below, its straw roof smothered under rose-colored masses of coralita.

They walked in intimate silence. The road was daubed with the fallen blossoms of immortelles and their winged pods. Once, two laborers passed, stepping quietly on their tough bare feet, the shadows of leaves mottling their bodies and bright blue ripped trousers, machetes swinging gently from their heavy belts.

Around a curve, they came on a dead, long snake, savagely slashed. Just before their path struck off the road, there was a jingle and faint creaking, and around a tangle of scarlet blackthorn rode two native policemen, their caps tilted against the sunset, their holsters jogging their elbows. They pulled their small horses, stained with sweat, into single file; one raised his hand easily in a half-salute and both smiled. These were the first horses the Driscolls had seen on the island, and the first police. Of course, there had to be police, but it was strange how out of place they seemed. When the hushed fall of the hoofs in the dust died away it was as though horses and riders had melted.

Later, sitting on a fallen tree in the bush, Mary thought idly about the snake, the laborers, the policemen. Henry had gone further in, but she had felt suddenly that she couldn't walk another step. She sat on ridged strong bark coursed by ants and thought about the policemen, their faces, their small dusty horses, on that peaceful, hot patrol. Surely there must be almost nothing for them to do. And yet the idea of violence, she realized, had come to the air she breathed. Not violence as she knew it in Henry's books, or in the newspapers at home—riot, rape, murder, burglary. This violence seemed a quality of growth—the grip of the mollusks on the wave-dashed rock, the tentacles of the air plants flowering from the clutched saman. It oppressed her with its silence, its lack of argument. Perhaps she responded in some obsure portion of her feminine heart. An ant ran silently and fast over her hand. She shook it off and stared into the green that had swallowed Henry. His preciousness to her appeared not enhanced but pointed up by her sense of the silent violence of growth around her, as if, among the creepers, windfalls, sagging trees, his face, clear to her love, defined itself as the absolute essential. Of the rest, blind accidents of power, and death, and greenness, she could make nothing. Nothing they might do would surprise her.

There was a wild cocoa bush not ten feet away, dropped into this paroxysm of growth—thin, tall, struggling for light. She could see the pendulous gourds in their mysterious stages of ripeness: cucumber green, yellow, deep rose-bronze, and plum-brown. That plum-brown was on the voluptuous poles of the bamboos, the great, breeze-blown, filmy, green-gold stools of bamboo.

She listened for Henry. There was provisional silence, but no real stillness; hidden streams ran with a deep, secret sound in the throat of distant ravines, and the air was pierced and tremulous with birdcalls, flutings, cries, cheeps, whistles, breaks of song; response and request; somewhere away, lower than all the sounds but that of water, the single, asking, contemplative note of the mourning dove.

All at once, there was Henry. When she saw him, she realized that some portion of her had been afraid, as though, like the police on their little horses, he would melt into the greenness for good.

"Did you realize I'd forgotten my binoculars?" he asked, infuriated with his stupidity. "Of all idiotic times!"

Suddenly, she flung herself at him, winding her arms about his neck, linking their legs, covering his face with quick, light kisses. He held her off to look at her, and then folded her tightly in his arms, as though she too had come back from somewhere. "We haven't a flashlight, *either*," he said, "and, if we don't look out, we'll be plunging about in the dark, breaking everything."

On the way home, they went more rapidly. The birds were almost completely silent. Now and then one would flash in the tree crests far above them, settling to some invisible perch. We've left this island, Mary thought. There came a turning point—on a wharf, on a station platform, in the eyes of a friend—when the movement of jointure imperceptibly reversed. Now they were faced outward—to their suitcases, to their plane, to the Port of Spain airport, to Connecticut and typewriters. Mary began to worry about the dead snake, in the thick dusk; she didn't want to brush against its chill with her bare, sandaled feet. But, when they came to the spot, she saw it at once. It seemed somehow flatter and older, as though the earth were drawing it in.

As they rounded the bend to the final decline, a sound came to them, stopping them both, Mary with her hand digging into Henry's arm. They thought at first it was an animal in a trap, mistreated or dying. It was a sound of unhuman, concentrated, self-communing pain, a dull, deep crying with a curious rhythm, as though blood and breath themselves caused pain. "What *is* it?" cried Mary, terrified.

"It's a human being," said Henry.

He was right. Drawn close together, they turned the bend in the road, and saw the group from which the sound came; just up the steep slope to their left, in front of the cabin. Raw light from a kerosene lamp on the porch fell on the heads of the men and women, in an open semicircle. Around this space crawled on her hands and knees a woman. Her head was tied in a red kerchief and the light caught her gold earrings. She pounded the earth with her fist, and round and round she crept in short circles.

Dark faces turned in their direction, but the woman did not stop; on and on went the sound. Alien, shocked, embarrassed by their own presence, the Americans hesitated. Then Henry caught his wife's elbow and steered her, stumbling, down the path.

"Oh, Henry, *Henry...*" she whispered frantically to his shadowy face. "Oughtn't we to stop? Couldn't we?..."

"They don't *want* us!" he hissed back. "Whatever it is, they don't want *us.*"

She knew he was right, but an awful desolation made her stumble sharply again. The sound was fainter now; and then, in a minute or two, gone. Below them, they could see the light-bulb lashed to the trunk of the saman tree, like a dubious star.

Later, Mary was not sure why they said nothing to Mr. Soo. Neither, strangely, did they discuss it between themselves in their bedroom, showering, dressing for dinner. It was as though its significance would have to come later. It was too new, still, too strange; their suspended atmosphere of already-begun departure could not sustain it.

This sense of strangeness, and also, perhaps, the sense of its being their last evening, seemed to constrain them to be more civil to Mr. Soo. Arthur, bringing their daiquiris, told them there would be a cold supper; the cook was away. His air was apolo-

getic; this was evidently an unexpected development. On the
terrace, he set their drinks down on the thick section of a tree
bole that served as a stand, and looked through the open casement window into their room, now transforming itself again
into Mr. Soo's room: at the open, filled suitcases, the range of
empty hangers, the toilet bottles on the dresser.

"You sorry to go?" asked Arthur. "You like it here, and so?"

"Very, very much," said Henry. "We hope we can come back."

"You know, one thing," said Arthur. A gong was struck im-
periously. Arthur took his empty tray back through the room.
The door closed behind him.

Perhaps it was too late for a more cordial response; perhaps
Mr. Soo, too, felt that they were no longer there. Above his lilies
in their yellow bowl, he was unresponsive. After one or two
attempts at conversation, the Driscolls ate their cold supper,
talking to each other in tones made artificial by several kinds of
constraint. Over coffee, Henry said, "I'd better see him about
the bill now—it's all going to be so early in the morning."

Mary waited for him by the huge open window-frames, where
they had sat on their first evening, discussing with Mr. Soo their
bird-minded friends. The moon, which tonight was going to be
purely full, had lost its blemishes of misproportion; it was rising,
enormous and perfect, in a bare sky. She could hear very faintly
the sound of the tide as she stared out over the invisible bay to
the invisible sea.

Behind her, Mr. Soo and Henry approached, their footsteps
hushed by the straw, their voices by the silence. Turning, she
was confronted by Mr. Soo's face, quite close, and it struck her
that the moonlight had drawn and sharpened it, as though it
were in pain.

"I hope you and your husband have been happy here," said
Mr. Soo.

"Very," said Mary. (Now we're in for a drink, she thought.)
"The birds have been wonderful..." she began, but Mr. Soo
was not listening.

"The driver from the airport will be here at six," he said. He
turned and left them, walking slowly over the gleaming rug.

The moon hadn't reached their terrace. Arthur, arriving with the crème de cacao, had to peer at the tree bole before setting down the little cups. He did not go away, but stood and looked at them. Finally, he said, "Do you remember Vic-tor?"

"Of course," said Henry, and Mary added, "The little boy."

"He's gon," said Arthur.

Henry said with interest, "Gone?"

"Dead, gon." Arthur stood there, holding his tray, and waited for them to speak. When they still did not, he said, "He did go off those high rocks. Back down from he house, those high rocks. He did go to swim in that sea-pussy. Like he grandmother told he not to. He is gon, out to sea; no body. No body a-tall. He was screaming and fighting. Two men fishing, they tried very hard to grab he up, but couldn't never get to he. He go so fast, too fast. They will never have no body—too much current, too many fish. He grandmother told he, but that boy, he gon to swim. He won't even mind he brother, brother Daniel, brought he up," said Arthur, turning away and continuing to talk as he left, "*or* he grandmother, took he in. The cook is gon," said Arthur, faintly, from the distance. "Now Mr. Soo, Mr. Soo is all alone." The door closed.

Mary got up, uncertainly; then she went into the bedroom and began to cry very hard. She cried harder and harder, flinging herself on the bed and burrowing her head in the pillow. She felt Henry's hands on her shoulder blades and told him, "I can't think *why* I'm crying—I didn't even know the child! Yes, he showed me the crabs, but I didn't *know* him! It's not that..." She was obsessed by the mystery of her grief. Suddenly, she sat up, the tears still sliding down over her lips. "That was his grandmother," she said.

"It's a pattern," said Henry miserably. "We saw it happen all the way from the beginning, and now it's ended. It had to end this way."

She touched his face. His living body was here beside her. She slid her hand inside his shirt, feeling his flesh, the bones beneath it. The room was filled like a pool with darkness. She ran her fingers over his chin, across his lips. He kissed her softly, then more deeply. His strong, warm hand drew her dress apart and closed over her breast.

"I love you," he said.

She did not know when Henry left her bed. She did not, in fact, wake until a sound woke her. Her bed was still in darkness, but the window was a pale blaze from the moon, now high and small. It struck light from the palms' fronds, and against it she saw the figure on the ledge, in the open window. Young and dark and clear, and beautiful as shining carved wood, it looked against all that light, which caught and sparked on the machete's blade. It was gone; she heard a faint thud on the earth below the window. She raised herself on her elbow. In Mr. Soo's moonlit room she stared at Mr. Soo's bed and at what she now made out on the darkening sheet. It was Henry's dark head, fallen forward, and quite separate. His eyes were still closed, as if in an innocent and stubborn sleep.